Racing With The Tide

BILI MORROW SHELBURNE

RACING WITH THE TIDE by Bili Morrow Shelburne

First Edition, 2020

Published by Wendover Press

Copyright © 2020 Bili Morrow Shelburne

Author Services by Pedernales Publishing, LLC.
www.pedernalespublishing.com

Hilton Head map by OpenStreetMap Foundation
Attribution-ShareAlike 2.0 license (CC BY-SA 2.0)

Library of Congress Control Number: 2020922222

ISBN: 978-0-9967430-4-4 Paperback Edition
         978-0-9967430-5-1 Hardcover Edition
         978-0-9967430-6-8 Digital Edition

Printed in the United States of America

xx-v10

For Ralph: my mainstay

CHAPTER
One

You can't go home again. Ella Winter, the Australian born writer, gifted Thomas Wolfe with that phrase for his book title. I wondered how many times it would come to mind as I drove onto Hilton Head Island from the Savannah airport.

I was ten years old when I was first introduced to this island. It wasn't until then that I felt a permanence, sifting sand through my toes and breathing salty sea air.

My father had died when I was three years old. The years following that were nothing more than a blur of cold Chicago winters in a drafty old apartment and stifling heat in the summertime. I do recall that my mother kept up a brave front, working to keep food on the table and a roof over our heads.

Roy Hubbard, an insurance salesman, became our good luck charm. It seemed the minute he laid his ice blue eyes on my mama he fell in love with her. Had it not been for his persistence, I might still be in the windy city instead of on this beautiful island. But it was here in this southern paradise that I lost both my precious mother and my beloved adoptive father.

The last time I was on this stretch of highway I was a seventeen-year-old bride, leaving the island for a new life. That was nine long years ago—1974. I never regretted eloping with my wonderful husband, and I never considered our lean college years a hardship. The short time I had with Jimmy Castlebrook was the happiest of my life. Then, one rainy night in Lexington, Kentucky as I waited for my young husband to come home from work, I learned that my love was slumped over the steering wheel of his stalled car, sitting askew on the railroad tracks.

I didn't remember anything except drops of rain running off the patent leather bills of two policemen's hats. They stood at my front door grim-faced, mustering the courage to apprise me of my terrible loss. I still can't recall my husband's funeral. It wasn't by chance that I landed in a mental hospital in Louisville, Kentucky. I know who had me admitted there and footed the bill for my expensive care and treatment. Jimmy's parents had cut him off without a penny when he married me, but they had softened their hearts to take care of their son's widow. I can't prove that any more than I can prove they're the benefactors of the fifty thousand dollars I now have to live on and get settled on Hilton Head.

I couldn't wait to see my old friend, Mama Rae. I had visited her just a few weeks ago when I met my best childhood friend, Daniel, and his wife and daughter on the island for a weekend vacation. That was when I knew exactly where I wanted to start over. I wasn't sure what I would do to support myself, but I knew I would find my niche.

I turned left off Hwy 278 and drove into Palmetto Dunes Resort, stopped at a visitor center to pick up a pass, and drove slowly down a street canopied by old live oaks clasping their shiny-leafed fingers overhead, and nearly shutting out a brilliant blue sky. Then, I made my way past clay tennis courts to a traffic circle. At the first exit, I drove off the circle and up an incline to the Hyatt Hotel. It was the middle of September, and the groundskeepers had changed out geraniums, begonias, and marigolds for the more muted hues of the first chrysanthemums of fall.

I checked in at the front desk and went directly to my room with its spectacular view of the Atlantic. The ocean's surface glittered like diamonds. The sun still held the late summer's warmth, and I thought it would have felt good to go outside in shorts and flip-flops, but I hadn't taken time to shop. Pulling a pair of jeans out of my suitcase, I put them on with one of my few tee shirts and headed for my rental car to go visit Mama Rae.

I had been an adventurous ten-year-old when I first landed on the island, wandering into the dense woods close to my family's rental house. Coming upon Mama Rae, the woman who would become my friend and mentor, had been nothing less than magical serendipity.

I wondered what words of wisdom she might have for me now. Would the two of us be able to resume our friendship as though I had never left the island? Mama Rae had taken me under her wing from the time I was a child until I married. Our relationship was far from the norm, because she was so secretive and she engaged in some pretty strange rituals, but she had always had my back.

Leaving the rental car by the roadside, close to the woods' edge, I entered the dark domain of forest denizens, including my dear friend. The worn, narrow path leading to her cabin was abuzz with insects, and the trees were filled with birdsong. It all felt familiar as I picked my way along the path. Then, I reached the clearing just before Mama Rae's cabin came into view.

I tried to be careful not to disturb the chickens that were milling around in the dust, but I accidentally bumped into a camouflaged nest with the toe of my shoe. A hen ruffled her feathers and flew off the nest. All the chickens began squawking.

"Stop scarin' my settin' hen!" came a reprimand from around the side of the cabin.

"Mama Rae, it's me, Clemmie."

"I know who it is," she said, sounding cross.

She took her time getting to the patch of grass in front of her cabin. It didn't surprise me to see my old friend looking incongruous with her surroundings. The first time I had seen her in this place she called home, she was wearing a long skirt, a man's shirt, and an old slouch hat. Her wardrobe was always unusual. My seeing her now in a floppy hot pink hat and big yellow Jackie Kennedy sunglasses called to mind the bright purple sandals she used to wear.

"I'm sorry. I didn't see the nest," I said.

She gave me a nod which I assumed was meant as acceptance of my apology. I stepped up on her front porch.

"You look thin," she said. "How 'bout some blackberry cobbler?"

She turned to go into the house, and the sun found the brilliance of a diamond stud in her right earlobe. I had given Mama Rae those earrings as I was leaving the island because I wanted her to have something special to remember me by. They had been my mama's earrings, a gift from Roy the Christmas before they were married.

I followed Mama Rae into the cabin. On our way to the kitchen I scanned the living room. Everything looked the same except the mantle. Mama Rae's doll collection was still there, but her *put together* doll was missing. She had done away with it in the wood-burning stove right after Roy died, but she never told me why. Neither of us had ever brought up the subject of my adoptive father's death since then.

I took my usual seat at the wooden kitchen table while Mama Rae dished up the cobbler. She sat down across from me.

"Eat, girl. You need some meat on your bones."

"Tell me how the island has changed since I left," I said.

My old friend looked thoughtful.

"You and your young man lef' here in 1974. Not much changed here in de woods. Well, my Biscuit met his match a while back. He liked to start fights." She sighed. "Dat what done him in. I miss dat old cat."

"I remember Biscuit. He was mean to anything smaller than he was."

Mama Rae put her skinny elbows on the table and made a tiny fist with her left hand. Resting her chin on the fist, she seemed to be searching her memory.

"You might not 'member how quick tings took off when you and your family lived here," she said. "Seem like it kep' pickin' up speed. People buyin' lan' right and lef', places to rent sprung up like weeds in a garden. Seem like a new eatin' place almost ever week, but some of 'em didn't las' long."

"I looked for changes on my way here, but everything seemed pretty much the same," I said.

"Lot of new tings you don't see right off. Hilton Head got rules to keep de islan' lookin' like de Creator made it."

"I guess that's true."

Suddenly, Mama Rae's face lit up.

"Somethin' new on de islan'," she said. "A little group of singers—all men, makin' lot of noise at de Hyatt Hotel. Folks actin' like fools over 'em."

"I'm staying at the Hyatt. Maybe I'll get to see one of their shows."

"No more changes I know 'bout. If you stay long 'nuff you'll see 'em for yourself. You want to live here, do you?"

"Why, yes. I thought I told you that when I was here a few weeks ago."

"Lot to 'member here I reckon," she said, scooting her chair away from the table. She walked out of the room, and left me alone in her small kitchen.

I rinsed my dish and went outside. Mama Rae was pulling weeds in her herb garden.

"Thank you for the cobbler, Mama Rae," I said. "I'll see you soon."

Mama Rae pushed her big yellow sunglasses up on her nose and kept pulling weeds, and I headed back to the path through the woods to my rental car. My old friend had always been a woman of few words, so I was surprised by how much she had talked during our visit.

I drove to the Hyatt and went to my room to unpack. Looking through the clothes I owned, I wasn't sure I had anything suitable to wear on interviews. I wanted to begin my job search as soon as possible. The money I had wouldn't last indefinitely. The island didn't have much in the way of clothing stores. I would go to the outlet mall tomorrow, but I might not find anything appropriate there either. If I had to go to Savannah, so be it. I would take myself to lunch on Factor's Walk where Roy used to take me when I was a teenager.

It was late afternoon when I finished putting my things away, and I wasn't good at sitting idle until dinnertime. I went out on my balcony and took in the breathtaking view. The wide beach was too inviting to pass up. Slipping on my scuffed loafers, I took off for my old stomping ground.

I was glad that none of the hotel visitors would recognize me as I walked past the pool and outdoor restaurant. The way I was dressed, I looked like I might have been going most anywhere but to the beach. The steps from the pool deck to the beach were practically empty as I descended them and stepped into the sugary sand. Feeling my bare feet sink into the sand brought a smile to my face. There were several pairs of shoes and sandals hiding just behind the bottom step. I added mine to the pile, rolled up my jeans, and headed for the water's edge.

It felt wonderful to splash my feet in the warm foam. The sensation took me back to my childhood. Daniel and I spent hours on our little strip of beach on Tybee Island. That was where he was introduced to one of life's harshest realities: racism. He was only nine years old.

Then, Daniel and I were driven apart by a storm which devastated Tybee Island. My family relocated to Hilton Head, and I didn't see Daniel again until he came to Hilton Head to live with his widowed aunt. The two of us reconnected immediately. We were teenagers by then, but it was as though we had never been separated. This big, wide, beautiful beach was one of our favorite places to talk. We splashed through the surf and told one another our darkest secrets.

The beach wasn't nearly as crowded today as it was during the summer months. School had started in lots of places, so there weren't many children making sandcastles or teenagers playing volleyball. Several young parents were leaving the beach, pulling wagons piled with beach toys and grouchy toddlers ready for naps.

I had just dug up a pretty shell. It was perfect; not the tiniest chip on its scalloped rim. I would take it to Mama Rae the next time I visited her. I rinsed the shell in the surf and stood up to see a man with the most striking features I had ever seen. There was something mesmerizing about him, and I had a hard time pulling my gaze away from his face. He and a pretty young woman were swinging a little girl between them. The child giggled as they dipped her toes into the water on the downswing. I hurried out of the water to give them the right-of-way, and the man nodded and smiled. His teeth were blinding white in the afternoon sun.

I kept walking, thinking how nice it would be to be a part of such a beautiful, happy family, and for a moment I did exactly what I knew I should never do: I felt sorry for myself. The night my Jimmy had been taken from me in that fatal accident, I had been robbed of such a fantasy life. If I dwelt on that, I wouldn't be able to go forward with the life I now had. I had every reason to forge ahead and embrace life. All I had to do was stay strong and go after it with a resolve to be happy. I was very fortunate, indeed.

As I continued my stroll down the beach, I noticed that more and more people were calling it a day. I hadn't heard a weather forecast, but a few dark clouds were gathering. I looked out over the water and spotted something I hadn't seen in years: a waterspout. That might mean nothing, or it could be a signal for me to head back to the hotel. I decided to heed the omen.

I hurried back to the steps leading to the Hyatt. Nobody had taken my old loafers, not that anyone would want them. I climbed the steps to the foot showers on the landing and rinsed the sand off my feet. The pool concession had closed for the day, and there were no towels available, so I pushed my wet feet into the shoes and squished my way into the hotel to the elevator.

I took a shower and put on a big, fluffy, white robe provided by the hotel, thinking whoever made it must have thought they were dressing a giant. I rolled up the long sleeves and propped myself up on pillows, prepared to relax for a while. Flipping through the TV channels, I came across island events, and there it was: Larry Perigo's The Headliners now playing at Club Indigo in the Hyatt Hotel, 9:00 p.m. I called and made my reservation.

It was still early, and I was out of the mood to watch television or listen to music, so I decided to call Daniel. So much had changed for my friend, and I was happy for him. When we first met, Daniel was a skinny little black kid with an attitude big enough to stand up to white bullies more than twice his size. He hadn't had a very stable childhood. After he and his mother were displaced by the storm on Tybee Island, she remarried, and his uncle who lived on Hilton Head passed away, leaving his wife alone and lonely after a thirty-year marriage.

Daniel was sixteen when he came to Hilton Head to live with his aunt. Things were going well for him until he had the misfortune to meet my adoptive father's vicious secretary. Addie Jo Simmons had a tremendous dislike for any person whose skin was darker than hers. She plotted to turn Daniel's aunt against him and won that battle. It came to an end with the aunt turning Daniel out of her home to fend for himself.

In spite of all that, Daniel worked hard to make something of himself. He stayed with Mama Rae for a while and picked up any odd job he could find. Then, he struck out on his own, living like a homeless person but continuing to work. He had to work instead of finishing high school, but he took the GED test and passed it easily. After that, he moved to Savannah where there were more job opportunities, and he worked even harder. Finally he landed a job with a construction company which paid a decent salary. He met

Catherine, the girl he would marry, who was a paralegal at the law firm where he was tasked with delivering a contract.

Catherine had a degree, and her goal was to attend law school, but after meeting Daniel and getting to know him, what she wanted more than anything was to be his wife. The couple only dated for a few months before deciding they couldn't live without one another. The money they made was just enough to rent an apartment and save whatever they could each month to pursue Daniel's dream of becoming a civil engineer. If he could build bridges, he could take care of his wife in style.

When the young couple realized Catherine was pregnant, they couldn't wait to become parents. Daniel continued working for the construction company, and Catherine stayed with the law firm until almost time for the baby to arrive. Suzanne was a beautiful baby. Daniel knew how important it was for a child to have parental love and support since his had been spotty. He insisted that Catherine be an *at home* mom until they deemed Suzanne ready to be separated from her mother during the day. When they were on Hilton Head a few weeks earlier, Catherine told me that she was about ready to go back to work.

The phone rang several times before Daniel answered it.

"Hi, Daniel. Clemmie here. I'm on the island, staying at the Hyatt."

"Great. I guess that means you definitely have sand in your shoes."

I laughed. "I sure do. All I have to do now is get a job so I can afford to stay here."

"Maybe we can drive over and meet you for dinner one night soon."

"I'd like that. I hope I'll be able to tell you about my fabulous new job."

"I hope so, too. Hey, do you hear my little angel screaming bloody murder?"

"Yes. What's going on?"

"Catherine's grocery shopping, and Suzanne's teething. I'm in charge here. I'd better go."

"Okay. Good luck. We'll talk soon."

CHAPTER
Two

I hadn't felt so free since I was released from Still Waters Mental Hospital. The care I received there had been miraculous. I was in a terrible state at the time I was admitted to the hospital. The last four years of my life had been blotted from my memory. The patience and persistence of Doctor Fitzpatrick, my psychiatrist, enabled me to dig deep into my psyche and discover the naked truth which was so painful I had buried it. I had a love-hate attitude toward my doctor, because I didn't like his methodology. Between my sessions with him, he insisted that I write everything I could recall from my past in a journal and share it with him. Seeing the hurtful things I had suffered in black and white was proof that they had really happened. Dr. Fitzpatrick knew that I would have to acknowledge that proof. Each entry was a piece of the puzzle which I had finally been able to complete.

The social director at Still Waters had taken me shopping for several essentials before I was released from the hospital. I was grateful to her for initiating that trip to a mall as I slipped into one of my three dresses and a pair of flats.

I was hungry for seafood, so I drove to a restaurant that seemed like an old friend: Hudson's Seafood House on the docks. Roy and I went there often after Mama was killed in that automobile accident. Our suppers at home didn't have a lot of variety. Sometimes we ate sandwiches or shared a half bucket of shrimp. If we weren't in the mood for either of those, we would jump into the car and head to Hudson's. Each time I got to the door, I had the feeling the slanted concrete slab the restaurant sat on might slide into the sea at any minute.

I didn't need a menu; I knew exactly what I wanted. A waitress came to my table smiling and handed me a menu. She left and was back with a glass of water and an order pad.

"Made up your mind?" she asked, still wearing a smile that said she liked her job.

"I'll have the Neptune Platter and sweet tea, thanks."

It amazed me to see how fast this diner-type restaurant filled up around suppertime. It hadn't changed since I left here. Everything tasted just the way I remembered. The fried fish was flaky and light, the french fries were greaseless, and the hush puppies were mouthwatering. I was so tired of eating healthy that I completely ignored the coleslaw.

I was sated as I drove back to the hotel, and once again took note of how careful the town of Hilton Head was to keep the island's appearance as close to nature as possible. The new businesses were held to strict regulations with regard to signs and paint color choices, making them blend in with the island's natural beauty. There was nothing gaudy on this island.

I barely had time to freshen up before going to hear the group everyone was raving about. I would go to the show and catch their act.

Club Indigo was on the ground floor of the Hyatt. The room wasn't large, and it was nearly filled to capacity when I arrived. I was seated at a tiny table crammed against a wall with barely enough room to squeeze into my seat. A cocktail waitress wove through a tangle of feet and legs pushing out from under the small tables to take my drink order. Then, she picked her way back through the crowd.

A hush fell over the room just as the waitress brought my glass of chardonnay. The superstars had arrived. They poured onto the stage like a school of fish and burst into song. Applause broke out, muting the sounds emanating from The Headliners. Mama Rae had told me they were supposed to have fantastic singing voices, but that was an understatement. These guys were multi-talented. Their voices blended perfectly, and each man played an instrument.

At the close of the first number, Larry, the leader, addressed the audience. He didn't pause for breath before beginning to interact with the crowd, asking people where they were from and silly questions like asking a man if he was there with his wife.

It was easy to understand why these guys were so popular. They were consummate entertainers. They played and sang, did skits, and told jokes. Between sets they changed out of their white sport coats and donned high school letter sweaters. Then, they belted out more songs from 50's and 60's chart toppers.

Larry frequently left the stage to roam through the audience to sing. He would stop singing in the middle of a line and stick his microphone in someone's face to have them finish the phrase. My favorite of the evening was *Blue Moon*, a 1961 hit by the Marcels. Larry sang, "bom-ba-bom-bom, a-dang-a-dang-dang," and pushed the microphone toward a balding gentleman who grabbed it from the singer, stood up and sang, "a-ding-a-dong-ding, blue moon."

I thoroughly enjoyed the show. On the way back to my room, I decided I would have to tell Daniel and Catherine how entertaining The Headliners were. Maybe they would come to the island to catch a show.

As I went through the lobby, a buttery yellow sport coat caught my eye. The tall man wearing it was headed toward the front of the hotel. As he pulled the door toward himself, his profile was illuminated by the overhead light. Then, I recognized him as the man I had seen on the beach with whom I had assumed was his wife and little girl, but now he was alone. That seemed strange to me, but I dismissed all thought of the good looking man as I pressed the elevator button.

Dread washed over me as I got ready for bed. It was a feeling of loneliness I couldn't shake whenever I thought about my future. I hadn't felt it this dramatically since I was released from Still Waters. I undressed and put on a nightgown. The lingerie Jimmy had bought for me when we couldn't afford any luxuries had made me feel beautiful. Tonight I felt as plain as this cotton nightgown.

I had been forced to face the awful fact that my husband was gone. Now, I had to accept it and move on with my life. There was nobody left to turn to. I would have to do it alone.

I turned off the bedside lamp and tried to make my mind go blank. What would I do with the rest of my life? I was past my mid twenties. Dr. Fitzpatrick had told me over and over how strong I was. All I had to do was keep pushing myself. That was what made me face the truth about my painful past. I would buy a local paper first thing in the morning and learn what job opportunities were available on the island. Then, I would pump myself up for interviews. I had done it before; I could do it again.

I fell asleep, dreaming that I was in my husband's loving arms, listening to his even breathing, and thinking how lucky I was to have him.

The drapes weren't closed, and sunlight pushed its way through the sheers, introducing the morning. I showered and dressed, then headed to the coffee shop where I picked up a copy of The Island Packet.

I ordered coffee and a bowl of oatmeal, then turned to the employment opportunities section. Each ad looked duller than the last: Gal Friday, Secretary with two or more years of experience, Office manager for large insurance firm, Receptionist with good people skills. I was about to fold the paper and leave it for someone else when, at the bottom of the last column, a nondescript ad caught my eye: Looking for adventure? If so, this could be the job for you. Salary: open. The job might be anything from pyramid sales to strange odd jobs, but the open salary piqued my interest.

After breakfast, I hurried back to my room and dialed the number listed in the ad.

"Hello," came a brusque masculine voice over the line. "Are you calling about the ad in today's paper?"

"Yes, I am. Can you tell me what the job entails?"

"I'm sorry. I can't do that over the phone. Can you come for an interview this afternoon at two o'clock?"

This guy sounded like some sort of kook, but his voice and enunciation were refined.

"Yes," I said.

He gave me the address, and I scribbled it on a pad by my phone.

What would I wear? I didn't have time to go shopping, and even if I did, I wouldn't know what to buy. My meager wardrobe looked like it had been packed for an unexciting weekend trip. I decided on a navy skirt and a white blouse, thinking I looked more like a school girl than someone about to go to a job interview.

I had time to go for a walk on the beach, but I didn't want to have to get another shower and redo my hair before the interview, so I decided to drive across the road to look around Shelter Cove. There were some interesting shops and several restaurants. I hadn't tried any of the restaurants. Maybe one of them would strike my fancy for lunch.

I walked around the buildings to the cove and couldn't believe how many boats were docked there. Some were small sailboats, and there were cabin cruisers of various sizes. There were even several gorgeous large sailing vessels which could only be described as yachts. I wondered what it would be like to have enough money to own one of those.

Passing the thought off as a pipe dream, I began

window-shopping. Quite a few of the shops sold nothing but island souvenirs, but I stepped into one which sold swimwear. I needed a couple of swimsuits if I intended to live on an island, so I picked out several pretty ones to try.

I left the shop with two suits and a cover-up and began looking for a place to eat lunch. Just as I made a left turn, a little boy jerked away from his mother and ran into me full force. The shopping bag flew out of my hand, and my purchases lay scattered on the walk. I bent to retrieve them before someone stepped on them. As I reached to collect them, a tanned, muscular forearm beat me to the punch.

"These yours, ma'am?" the Good Samaritan asked, handing me a bikini bra and a cover-up.

"Thank you very much," I said, staring into the gray eyes of the striking man I had first seen on the beach.

I stuffed my belongings into the bag and walked away, deciding to skip lunch. Being in the same place at the same time more than twice with this stranger seemed like more than a coincidence to me, and it was beginning to make me feel uncomfortable.

I drove back to the Hyatt to put my new purchases away and freshen up for the interview, wondering if I could possibly be losing touch with reality. Surely, that wasn't happening after all I had been through to get a clean bill of mental health. I had lost enough already—more than most people, I thought. Getting off track again might be more than I could take.

Wondering if the upcoming interview would be a hoax of some kind, I did my best to be positive. I told myself that all I had to lose was time. At the first sign of something fishy, I would call the interview to a halt.

I sat tall behind the wheel of my rental car, trying to convince myself that I was about to walk into the perfect job—one that I was competent to do and truly enjoyed. I had taught school when Jimmy and I were in Lexington, because the position was available, I was certified, and we needed the money. I wasn't unhappy teaching, but I hadn't been passionate about it.

I was twenty minutes early when I arrived at a one-story building, sitting back from the street in the tall pines. It blended so well with its surroundings that I would have missed it if I hadn't been looking pretty hard. I looked down at the oyster shell tabby walkway. Tabby was all over the island, and I was comforted by the familiar sight. I was gearing up to feel confident regardless of what I might learn when I met the interviewer. I opened the door into a large room containing no furniture but a gray, metal desk and two chairs. A man who looked to be middle-aged was seated behind the desk. He had snow-white hair down to his shoulders and black, bushy eyebrows.

"Ahem, pardon me, sir. I'm here to interview for the position listed in the paper."

The man appeared to be studying his hands which rested on the bare desktop. It took a minute for him to acknowledge me. Clearing his throat, he stood to introduce himself.

"Max Palmer" he said. "Please take a seat."

"I'm Clemmie Castlebrook," I said, lowering myself into the chair he indicated.

"Where are you from, Clemmie Castlebrook?"

"I grew up here on the island," I said, hoping to skip my recent history.

"Are you married?"

"I'm a widow."

"How old are you?"

"I don't want to be rude, but you can't ask me that."

Max Palmer continued his questions as though I hadn't spoken.

"Do you enjoy fine dining, Clemmie?"

"Of course."

"How about black tie affairs?"

"I've never attended one."

He pulled a postcard from his back pocket.

"Read this, please," he said, handing the card across the desk.

I looked at the jumble of words and read through the list.

"Very good. You seem to have perfect diction."

"Thank you. Mister Palmer, I would really like to hear a job description."

"Do you live on the island?" he asked, ignoring my growing frustration.

"I just arrived yesterday, so no, I don't have a residence yet. I'm staying at the Hyatt until I find a job."

"Do you object to shopping and running small errands?"

"Mister Palmer, where is this going?" I asked, irked.

"When can you come to work for me?" he said.

"Excuse me?"

"I'm offering you the job. When will you be available?"

I didn't know what to make of this strange man. He couldn't possibly know what my capabilities were, and I had no idea what he might want me to do to earn my salary which he hadn't mentioned.

"I'll pay you handsomely," he said, not bothering to give an amount.

I had to find out what the job was, and the only way I knew to do that was to agree to do it. If it turned out to be anything illegal or dangerous, I would simply quit.

"All right, Mister Palmer. I've never walked into any situation blind, but I accept your offer."

I wasn't foolhardy, didn't trust myself enough to gamble on anything that mattered, so I couldn't imagine why I agreed to accept the job. For all I knew, this secretive man had just hired me to be a drug mule.

CHAPTER
Three

I drove to the woods' edge and parked in my usual spot, thinking that Mama Rae might well be upset with me when I told her what I had done. She made no secret of being averse to technology, refusing to own a telephone, television, microwave, or computer, but I trusted her judgment completely. My old friend possessed a sense that other human beings did not.

I had felt at home the first time I ventured into the woods' darkness with the redolent mixture of decaying leaves, pine straw, and sweet-smelling blossoms. The trodden path, just steps away from island traffic, was welcoming in spite of the whir of wings, buzzing insects, and the rustle of ground activity. I had subconsciously learned the sounds made by squirrels, playing up and down tree bark and the quieter sounds of swamp rats, darting through the underbrush.

Mama Rae had taught me to respect the woods.

"You respec' dat big ocean?" she had asked, looking directly at me with piercing eyes deep-set in her wrinkled, black face.

"Sure."

"Dat's good. De whole world got good and evil. Same for dees woods. Show respec'."

Remembering the numerous times this woman had given me sage advice, I began my trek into the woods. I gave the chickens a wide berth as I approached my old friend's cabin. She was sitting on her small porch, shelling peas.

"Hello, Mama Rae."

She continued her work, discarding the pods into a pan on her left and dropping the peas into a bowl on her right. I took a seat on the porch step and waited for her to acknowledge me.

"You got news," she said. It wasn't a question. She didn't look up from her task.

"Yes," I said, excitement finding its way into my voice. "How did you know?"

She motioned for me to pick up the bowl of peas and lifted the pan of discards. She was awfully quiet today. I followed her into the cabin, wondering if she had talked herself out during my last visit. She took the bowl from me and set it on the counter, nodding for me to sit.

I thought she would come to the table with a delectable berry tart or a big slab of apple or peach pie. She was a fabulous cook, and I had always relished her homemade treats. She shuffled to the table and sat down across from me, pushing a cup toward me.

The liquid in the cup looked like apple juice.

"Thank you," I said, taking a sip.

It had a mild flavor I couldn't identify, and a hint of rosewater lingered on my tongue.

"What you have to tell Mama Rae?"

"I just had a very unusual job interview. The salary is open. I know I'll be well paid, but I'm not sure how much."

What I had just said would have caused most people to knit their brows, but Mama Rae's face remained expressionless.

"Here's the part that's really strange: I don't know what I'll be doing to make the money."

My old friend got up and went to stare out the window over her sink. I thought she was about to turn around and tell me to forget it. It would be foolish to accept any position without knowing what it entailed.

"When you start?" she asked.

"Next Monday, if I actually take the job. Do you think I should take it?"

Mama Rae did something I had never seen her do: she shrugged.

"Never know 'til you try."

She turned and left the kitchen, so I knew I was being dismissed. As I passed her open bedroom door, I saw her lying on her bed. She was speaking some kind of mumbo jumbo in a singsong voice. I took that to mean that she wasn't sick, and that she wanted me to leave.

I picked my way back through the woods to my car. It was still early, so I decided to drive to the outlet mall stores. I found a parking spot in front of a shoe store. There were rows and rows of various kinds of shoes. I bought a pair of tennis shoes, all purpose flip-flops, a pair of dress pumps, and a pair of yellow sandals. These shops were overflowing with all sorts of play clothes. I bought a few pairs of shorts, tee shirts, and a couple of sun dresses, but as far as business clothes and better dresses were concerned, I was out of luck.

My clothing situation dictated that I make a trip to Savannah to shop. I went to my hotel room and dialed the Grovers' number, hoping for a lunch date.

Catherine told me Daniel would be working the next day, but that she could meet me. I was pleased to be able to spend some time alone with her, because I wanted to get to know her better. Daniel and I had vowed that nothing would ever destroy our friendship, and I wanted to become close friends with his wife. She gave me the name and address of a tearoom just down the street from their apartment and said it was small and quiet, a good place to converse over lunch. She would be able to tell me the best places to shop for business clothes.

Catherine was at the tearoom when I arrived. She looked lovely in a salmon colored crepe dress which illuminated her tawny skin and draped beautifully on her slim figure. Her greeting was genuinely warm, and I knew the two of us would become close friends. She seemed to be the perfect match for Daniel, and I hoped she was. He deserved the best life had to offer.

We engaged in the perfunctory small talk. Then, Catherine let me in on the secret that she would be going to work for a law firm located on Factor's Walk. She had arranged for Suzanne to attend a nearby day care center, and would begin her new paralegal position in two weeks.

I was too embarrassed to tell her that I had accepted a job without knowing what it was. When she inquired about my job search, I told her that I had only had one interview, but that I wanted to spruce up my wardrobe to be prepared for the perfect offer. She told me the best places to shop for business attire. When we were ready to leave the tearoom, we decided to get in touch later in the week to firm up a dinner date.

I purchased a few basics I thought would suffice until I learned what kinds of things I would be required to do. Then, I headed back to the island. It was one of my favorite drives. I deliberately drove in the right lane, so it would be easy to look out over the salt marsh at low tide to see the scatterings of Spartina grass rising out of the shiny gray pluff mud, swaying in the breeze.

Looking at such scenes called to mind the years I had lived here. I could almost hear my mama's lovely laugh, and the beautiful music she and Roy made when they harmonized, sitting outside on the porch after supper. It seemed only yesterday that I heard Roy's voice crack. It happened each time he looked at me with those pain-filled ice blue eyes, telling me how much I looked like his lost love. Then, my family was gone, and I started a new life with my Jimmy.

I had just driven back onto the island. This was my life now; I had to shake off the past. Mama Rae had told me to always look for the beauty in everything, and I knew that would be better than dwelling on the pain that would never quite go away. Maybe I should invest in a self-help book. I needed an attitude adjustment.

I went to my room and changed into play clothes. Walking on this beach caused me to forget my cares. Feeling the shifting of sand beneath my feet while looking out over the expanse of ocean meeting sky made me feel very small in nature's grand scheme, and grateful to be a part of it. I kicked off my flip-flops at the bottom of the stairs leading to the beach. There was the usual accumulation of footwear behind the bottom step, but I decided to carry mine with me in case someone thought they were too adorable to pass up.

I splashed along in the surf, looking for shells and the possibility of a jellyfish even though I knew this was the wrong season for them. It would be wonderful to live on the beach, but I had picked up a booklet of local real estate listings when I went to breakfast just for fun. Beachfront property was sky high, so I dismissed that dream in a hurry. I might never be fortunate enough to buy a house or condo anywhere on the island. Only time would tell.

I stopped to watch two dolphins following a shrimp boat. They were putting on quite a show while sating their appetites.

"Entertaining creatures, aren't they?"

I turned to see who had spoken. Max Palmer had lost his jacket and tie. His shirtsleeves were turned up to his elbows, and he had rolled up the legs of his pants to reveal ghost-white calves and feet which looked incongruous with the rest of his tanned skin. His long white hair was tied in a ponytail, and he had on mirrored sunglasses.

"Oh, Mister Palmer, I didn't expect to see you here."

"I venture here sometimes when I'm bored. So, Clemmie Castlebrook, this isn't about me. I see you enjoy watching the dolphins."

"Yes, I do. Most everything about the beach appeals to me, but I should be getting back to my hotel. I need to make some phone calls," I lied.

"Of course. Sorry to detain you. I don't suppose you're free for dinner this evening."

I thought he had a lot of nerve, asking me to dinner. Maybe he thought I would be easy, because I had accepted his strange job offer.

"No, I'm not. Thank you for the offer. I'll see you first thing Monday morning," I said, backing away.

He didn't tell me goodbye, but made some sort of silly salute in my direction and began walking down the beach.

What had I gotten myself into?

Monday morning was just around the corner, and I made up my mind to enjoy the next few days like a retired person. I never set an alarm clock, and stayed awake until the wee hours if I was watching a good movie. I rented a bicycle and rode along the paved bike paths which seemed to be everywhere. But my daily ritual of a walk on the beach was my favorite. The beach's beauty with the sun-silvered Atlantic was indescribable. It was unspoiled nature at its finest hour, before vacationers began making their way to the beach from their rental units with mugs of steaming coffee to greet the day island style.

I told myself not to clutter my mind with the *what ifs* I might be facing the next time I met with Max Palmer. It was impossible to understand the motives for his strange and secretive nature. Mama Rae had encouraged me to dip my toe into his water, so I would show up for work the first day to see what it was all about. She had never steered me wrong.

My four days of self-indulgence flew by like a flash. Monday morning had arrived. When the insistent ringing of the alarm clock wouldn't stop, I resisted the urge to hit the snooze button and go back to sleep.

I made coffee in the room while I showered. Eight o'clock was the appointed time to meet. The coffee tasted like mud, but I forced myself to drink it. I was too hyped to eat breakfast.

I chose a forest green tailored dress and pumps for my first day on the job, and I took more time than usual with my hair and makeup. No matter what this job turned out to be, I wanted to make a good first impression. I couldn't help giving myself a once-over in the floor-length mirror before leaving my room. Then, I drove to the address of the business without a title to meet with my new boss.

"Good morning, Clemmie," Max Palmer boomed.

He looked very different from the day of the interview. Today, he was dressed in casual attire—khaki pants and a golf shirt. He came toward me with an outstretched hand.

"I hope you haven't eaten," he said. "Breakfast should be here any minute."

I didn't know what to say. Why would he provide breakfast for the new hire?

"That's very nice. Thank you."

"Don't mention it. Coffee?"

"Yes, please."

He disappeared down an unlit hall and returned with a small tray bearing a pot of coffee, sugar, and cream.

"I'm afraid we'll have to sit at the desk," he said, gesturing for me to take a seat.

He filled the two mugs and slid the tray toward me to doctor my coffee as I deemed fit.

Just as he was sitting down, a young woman in shorts and a tee shirt came from the hall, carrying a large tray. She deposited it on the desk and removed metal covers from plates of eggs Benedict and asparagus.

"Thank you, Gretchen. That'll be all."

Max Palmer shook out his napkin and draped it over his lap.

"Enjoy," he said, apparently waiting for me to begin.

I retrieved my napkin, sliced a small bite of an asparagus spear, and ate it, smiling my pleasure with a nod.

My boss attacked his meal with gusto, his knife and fork working in tandem. His manner was much like that of most Europeans, except at a much faster pace. The scraping of his utensils on the stoneware plate was the only interruption of quiet in the large room. His plate was clean before I barely started. Neither of us had said a word since he began eating.

He pushed back from the desk, cradling his coffee mug, and heaved a contented sigh. I didn't know whether I should continue eating or not, but took a small bite of egg.

"Do you have medical insurance, Clemmie?" he asked, continuing his questioning from a few days ago.

I dabbed the corner of my mouth, then placed my napkin on the desk beside my plate.

"Not at the moment," I said.

"I'll take care of that, of course. Do you own an automobile?"

"No. As I said before, I just arrived here. I intend to buy one soon."

"I plan to pay you weekly if that meets with your approval. Do you need an advance now?"

"No, thank you."

"Very well. Let's take care of all the necessary paperwork this morning. Take the afternoon off. Did I tell you that I won't be needing you every day?" He smiled. "Don't worry. "You'll be paid regardless."

"I don't understand."

"My dear, you worry too much. I'll meet you in the lobby of your hotel at six o'clock to go to dinner."

I began recalling snatches of our conversation during my interview and realized that accompanying my boss to dinner was part of the bargain. I had spent the best part of a morning with my new boss and still had no idea what would be required of me, or if I should back out now before I got in over my head in Max Palmer's mysterious business.

CHAPTER
Four

I changed into a swimsuit and my new cover-up, then went down to have lunch poolside. It was rare for me to drink wine during the day, but I ordered a glass of crisp chardonnay to accompany my shrimp salad.

It had been my plan to take a walk on the beach after lunch, because I had skipped it earlier to meet with Max Palmer. A gentle breeze was blowing in off the ocean, and the sparkling water of the pool beckoned to me. When I came out of the pool dripping wet, a hotel employee offered me a towel. I stretched out on my chaise to catch a few rays and relished the sun and the soft sea air. The wine must have made me sleepy, because I drifted off and awoke about two hours later to realize I was well-done. I bought a tube of Aloe Vera gel from the gift shop and went to my room. The cooling gel gave sufficient relief for me to go back to sleep for most of the afternoon.

Max Palmer had given me what should have been an easy task to earn my first day's pay. All I was expected to do was accompany him to dinner. But making myself presentable was posing quite a problem. The shower's needles stung my skin, and dressing hurt even more.

I looked at my employer's calling card. It was nearly bereft of information, containing nothing but his name and a phone number. I traced the raised print with my index finger, thinking that if I called to cancel dinner it would be the end of my new career before it started.

Mister Palmer hadn't bothered to let me know what might be proper attire for the dinner venue, so I assumed one of my off-the-rack dresses would pass muster. I managed to get into a cream colored shift and a pair of flats. My feet were sunburned and swollen, but I would have to tough it out through dinner.

When I walked off the elevator into the lobby, I saw my boss lean into a huge flower arrangement in the center of the room. He moved slowly around the floral display, smelling the various blooms. His Hawaiian print shirt was unbuttoned midway down his chest and was accessorized with a wide gold chain which caught the light when he moved. A Rolex graced his tanned wrist.

I walked toward him on stiff, sore feet and legs. He looked up and smiled. Then, he tossed his long white mane like a teenage girl.

"Good evening, Clemmie."

"Good evening."

"I see you're something of a sun worshiper. Are you in pain?"

"I'm afraid I stayed in the sun too long, but I'm fine."

"Well, then, shall we?"

My boss guided me outside to wait for a valet to bring the car. Standing close to him in silence while waiting for the car made me feel uncomfortable, and that sparked another feeling of apprehension. How in the world would I be able to carry on an intelligent conversation with the man over dinner? I hadn't given him a resume'; I didn't even have one. What if he inquired about my past? I couldn't tell him I had spent time in a mental hospital.

A bright red Ferrari with its top down pulled up to the curb.

"This is us," Max Palmer said.

The valet held the door for me, and I slid into the seat. We made our way down the live oak shrouded street to the island's main drag, then to the Harbourtown Marina in Sea Pines Plantation.

My boss found a place to park at the end of a long line of cars, and came around to open my door. I gingerly got to my feet. It hurt to put weight on them. Sunburned, swollen flesh pushed out over the tops of my shoes. I tried to smile.

"Ever dined on a yacht?" Max Palmer asked.

"No, I haven't," I said, beginning to feel nervous. I didn't know the first thing about this man, and I didn't relish the thought of being alone with him on a yacht. He took my hand to lead me through a small group of tourists and past some shops to the marina.

He hadn't let go of my hand the entire time we had been walking, and I thought he held it a little tighter as he led me out onto the pier and to a yacht in a sure-footed manner.

Something about this strange situation heightened my senses. I heard the water lapping at the pier and the yacht's hull, and saw the glitter of water droplets catch the sunlight when a fish jumped. The salt air was strong in my nostrils. I heard the tiny squeak Max Palmer's topsiders made when he took a step.

"This must be how the other half lives," I said, taking in the size of the large craft. *Pearl* was scripted on the side of the yacht. I wondered who Pearl might be. Was Max Palmer married? He didn't wear a ring.

A couple of deck hands came out to greet us and escort us onto the yacht. They looked to be little more than teenagers, much the same as the young woman who had served our breakfast.

"There's someone I want you to meet, Clemmie," Max Palmer said, taking my hand once again to lead me into an elegant salon.

The scent of gardenias permeated the tastefully appointed room. Seated in a wheelchair in powder-blue evening attire and a triple string of unusually large pearls was an attractive elderly woman. Her short-cropped hair was thick and snow white, and her wrinkle-free face appeared never to have seen the sun. The woman sat straight as a soldier at attention as my boss steered me toward her. When we were directly in front of her, she retrieved some reading material from her lap, placed it on an occasional table to her right, and affected a tight smile.

"Clemmie, this is Pearl, the yacht's namesake," Max said.

The older woman extended a white hand, keeping the smile, which never reached her eyes, glued in place.

"I'm pleased to meet you," I said, taking her cool hand in mine.

I felt awkward, because I didn't know what to call the woman. Max should have done a better job with his introduction. I wasn't sure I could bring myself to address this older woman by her first name. She exuded so much confidence she seemed aloof.

"I'm happy to make your acquaintance as well," Pearl said.

I had a feeling she wasn't sincere.

Max stood in front of the wheelchair and beamed at Pearl, and I stood idly at his side, thinking he must be waiting for her to issue some sort of command. I couldn't seem to keep from shifting my weight from one sunburned foot to the other, and my clutch felt slippery in my sweaty palms.

"So, Clemmie, do you indulge in alcoholic beverages?" Pearl finally asked.

Her question was unexpected, and I wasn't sure how to answer. What if she turned out to be a teetotaler? Max Palmer seemed more than a little fond of her. What if she disliked me because I indulged a little bit? That might cost me my brand new job, but I decided to give an honest answer.

"I enjoy a glass of wine," I said.

"Excuse me while I see to cocktails," the woman called Pearl said.

Max steered me out of the way just before Pearl pushed a button on the arm of her wheelchair and shot forward across the room. She touched another button, and the wall beside her folded back to one side, revealing a well-stocked bar complete with a young woman to tend it.

"Gretchen, we're ready for cocktails," she said.

Pearl, Max, and I were seated in the salon, sipping cocktails. I felt that I was being scrutinized whether I spoke, or not. The view of the harbor was lovely, and I occasionally glanced out at it through what seemed an entire wall of glass. Pearl had just speared an olive from her martini and examined it as she began her interrogation.

"Tell me, Clemmie, what might bring an attractive young woman such as you to our little island?" she asked, popping the olive into her mouth.

"I grew up here," I said, hoping that explanation would suffice.

"So, you have relatives on the island?"

"No. My parents are deceased, and I don't have any siblings. I always loved Hilton Head; felt at home here."

"But I understood Max to say that you had just arrived."

"That's correct. You see, I left the island when my late husband and I married. We lived in Lexington, Kentucky."

"You said your late husband? You're a widow?"

"Yes, I am. My husband was killed in an accident."

"How terrible for you," she said, but her expression showed no sympathy.

"Mrs. ... Pearl, I'm sorry, but I can't talk about this right now," I said, feeling tears gather in my eyes.

"Why don't we go in to dinner now," Max suggested.

Pearl drank the remainder of her martini in one unladylike gulp.

"Gretchen, we're ready for dinner," she said, and pushed the button on her wheelchair to lead us into the dining room.

Tears still leaked from the corners of my eyes as Max seated me at the linen-clad table.

"Perhaps you'd like to freshen up a bit," Pearl said. "Take your time. Max and I have some catching up to do." She put on her frozen smile.

"Excuse me, please," I said, getting to my feet to escape.

Gretchen, who seemed to be a full-time employee, showed

me to a powder room where I finished my silent crying jag and freshened my makeup, wondering how I would get through the evening.

Feeling composed, I made my way back to the table. If anyone expected me to apologize for being upset when asked about the loss of my husband, they would be disappointed. I had no idea what Max might have said to Pearl in my absence, but at least her interrogation had stopped. The two of them carried on a discussion about some of the cultural events which were taking place on the island, and they barely included me in the conversation.

Every now and then, Max would slide his eyes in my direction and say, "You might enjoy that, Clemmie. We'll go."

I found the word *we* ambiguous, because I didn't know whether he meant the two of us, or if he was including Pearl.

After the meal, Pearl suggested that we return to the salon for after-dinner drinks, but Max begged off, saying he had an early morning. There were lots of questions I wanted to ask my boss on the ride to my hotel, but I couldn't summon the courage to be that straightforward.

"Your yacht is beautiful," I said.

"It's Pearl's."

"Well, it certainly is impressive."

"What's your impression of Pearl?"

Max Palmer never ceased to amaze me with his bold questions.

"She's very attractive," I said.

"Clemmie, you know very well that's not what I'm asking."

"Mister Palmer, I've barely met the woman. I don't know her well enough to form an opinion."

Max snorted out a horse laugh.

"My dear, if you don't have a vivid impression of Pearl after having spent an evening in her highness's company, you're not nearly as intelligent as you appear."

I didn't know how to respond. Max Palmer and Pearl obviously had some sort of close relationship. I wondered if she could be his mother. They looked nothing alike, and their behavior wasn't similar, except for their prying questions and outspoken remarks.

"I found her to be somewhat distant," I said.

"That she is, in addition to being highly intelligent, overbearing, sometimes condescending, and usually rude. That said, I owe her a great deal, and she will always be a part of my life."

I wished he would refrain from saying things which dumbfounded me. He certainly wasn't asking for my input.

The Ferrari rolled up to the front of my hotel. If I'd had more time to think about it, I might have told Max Palmer I had decided that this was not the job for me.

"Take the day off tomorrow, Clemmie," he said. "You've earned it."

I was exhausted when I hobbled into my room. My feet were so swollen it was a chore to get my shoes off. The thermostat was set within the comfort range, but the sunburn was causing me to have goose bumps. I adjusted the air to get warm, and traded my clothes for the big, fluffy robe.

Many times during my stint at Still Waters Mental Hospital, I had felt this kind of exhaustion. It overtook me when I pushed myself to reach back into my memory to retrieve and relive my most painful experiences—those which had blocked my memory and stolen four years from me.

I was too tired to fall asleep, so I raided the mini bar for a cognac. The alcohol burned with every sip I took, and I could feel my limbs getting heavier by the minute. Finally, I began to relax. My evening spent with Max Palmer and Pearl faded to nothingness, and I succumbed to sleep.

CHAPTER
Five

My body was stiff and sore when I awoke. Blinding sunlight invaded the room. I didn't know what time it was, but I could see that the sun had climbed fairly high in the morning sky. White cumulus clouds scudded slowly above the expanse of the Atlantic. It looked like a perfect vacation day on the island. A walk on the beach crossed my mind briefly, but my tender flesh reminded me that I didn't want any sun exposure today.

I made my way into the bathroom, and examined myself in the mirror. The color of my skin resembled that of a shrimp that was ready to be retrieved from the boiling pot. The shower looked inviting. I adjusted the water to lukewarm on the gentlest spray, and stood under it for a long time, allowing it to knead my tight muscles. Dreading the thought of clothes touching me, I smoothed on a layer of Aloe Vera gel, let it soak into my sunburned skin, then eased myself into the robe I had slept in, and ordered breakfast from room service.

Instead of having a healthy meal, I indulged in the most buttery croissants imaginable and slathered them with orange marmalade. I ate three of the flaky delights, and consumed an entire pot of coffee, thinking that I would truly enjoy being spoiled, especially by someone who loved me.

Every time I allowed myself to slip into such self-absorbed thoughts, daydreams, or whatever they were, my beloved Jimmy took over my mind. I could see his slightly crooked smile, his laughing gray eyes, and the unruly lock of hair that liked to flop over his right eye when he shook his head. The heat from his body next to mine, and his arms holding me close, felt so real that I nearly whispered his name.

A knock on the door jerked me back to reality.

"Maid service." The voice was nasal, and sounded irritated.

I went to the door in my robe, and asked that my room be cleaned later in the day. Then, I settled back into the down pillows to decide how to spend the day with nothing to do while being paid for it. Leaving my room would require my getting dressed and wearing shoes of some kind. I was beginning to feel bored when the phone rang.

"Hello, Clemmie, it's Catherine. I didn't know if I would catch you in your room before you left on your job search. I assume you haven't found the perfect position, or we would have heard from you."

"Hi, Catherine. I'm glad you called," I said, not bothering to tell her that I had accepted a job which had no description.

"Do you have interviews today? I don't want to keep you. Daniel has to be on the island to put in a bid on a job late this afternoon. He'll be finished with his business right before the dinner hour. We've hired a sitter, and I'm coming with him. I know this is a last-minute invitation, but are you free to join us for dinner?"

I would enjoy spending time with Catherine and Daniel, but I knew that one of them would ask about my job search. There was no way I could look Daniel in the eye and lie to him. Maybe I would be able to dodge answering questions about it by telling my friends that I felt certain the perfect position would come my way.

"Yes, I'd love to join you, Catherine. Where shall I meet you?"

"We have a reservation at The Harbormaster in Shelter Cove at seven o'clock."

"I'll see you there."

I watched daytime television until nearly lunchtime, wondering what kinds of people actually enjoyed such a pastime. Then, I managed to get into a loose sundress and sandals to go down for lunch. I threw a light sweater around my shoulders, because restaurant air conditioners are always set on low temperatures. I had just ordered a crab salad and handed my menu to the waiter when I happened to glance toward the hotel lobby. Max Palmer's hands were animated as he and another man, deep in conversation, both wearing suits, walked hurriedly toward the front of the hotel.

The crab was fresh and delicious, but I couldn't fully appreciate it for thinking about my mysterious new boss. He presented himself as something of a big shot on the island, except when he was in Pearl's company. Then, his pomp appeared to shrink, and he seemed subservient to the wheelchair-bound ruler of his universe.

After lunch, I decided to visit Mama Rae and tell her all about my unusual new job. Her opinion was important to me. She had no formal education, but she was the wisest person I had ever known. People on the island respected this old woman who lived in the woods.

I felt nostalgic, maneuvering through the dense foliage on the path I had known so well before I left the island for another life. Hearing the rustling of a small critter through the underbrush didn't alarm me at all. I knew what to fear and what to ignore. If I happened to spy a snake draped over a low-hanging branch of a tree, I would give it a wide berth, but small animals on the ground would be anxious to do the same for a human intruder.

A welcoming aroma wafted through the mesh of Mama

Rae's screen door as I reached her front porch. I knocked on the doorframe. There was no answer.

"Mama Rae, it's Clemmie. May I come in?"

I didn't hear footsteps, but as I turned to leave, my old friend shuffled to the door. She wore a floral print housedress and kneesocks, and she seemed to move very slowly. I wondered if she was ill.

"Did I wake you, Mama Rae?"

"I wasn't sleepin'; jes restin' a bit. Come in dis house."

I followed her into the living room. She had never moved this slowly. We went to our respective chairs—the ones Mama Rae had assigned when we first met. Her chosen chair was overstuffed and draped with hand-crocheted antimacassars. Mine was a plain wooden rocking chair.

My eyes automatically panned up to Mama Rae's doll collection above the mantle. The dolls were arranged in size from left to right: an old wooden baby doll with hairline fractures in its face, a fragile china doll, a black rubber baby pinned into its diaper with big safety pins fastened with yellow ducks' heads. They were all present except for her ugly *put together* doll. I recalled the doll vividly. It appeared to have been nothing more than a conglomeration of odds and ends glued together.

Mama Rae did away with that special doll right after Roy's death. She never told me why she reduced the doll to ashes in the woodstove, but I've always thought it had some connection to my adoptive father's demise. I'll never know for sure, because that secret will die with my old friend and mentor.

"I came to tell you about my new job, Mama Rae."

"Go ahead."

"I accepted the offer I was telling you about the other day."

"Uh huh."

"I still don't know what the job is. The first day, all I did was have breakfast with my new boss. My job for the second day was to have dinner with him and an overbearing woman on a yacht. He and the woman seem to have some sort of close relationship, but I don't know what it is."

"You tellin' me all you've done is eat?"

"That's it. My boss's name is Max Palmer, and he seems to be a bigwig here on the island. Have you heard of him?"

Mama Rae shook her head.

"He said he wouldn't be needing me today, but that I would be paid, even for the days I don't work."

"Can't beat dat with a stick."

"Maybe not, but I don't like the fact that I don't know what I'm supposed to be doing to earn my wages. I have no idea how the man makes his money. Does he run a company? Is he independently wealthy? I'm in the dark about everything. I guess I'm supposed to do whatever Max Palmer hatches each day. It might be picking up his dry cleaning, attending an elaborate dinner, or doing something illegal like delivering a package containing drugs, wearing a blindfold the entire time."

"You tellin' me you're not curious to stick with it another day or two; maybe find out more about it?"

"Of course, I'm curious, but I don't want to be involved in something that might be illegal or dangerous."

"Maybe you fret too much."

"Mama Rae, are you sure you don't know Max Palmer? You seem to be encouraging me to stay in this mysterious job situation."

"You sayin' dis old woman would lie to you? I been knowin' you since you a chile."

She got up and shuffled from the room. Then, I heard her bedroom door close.

I made my way back through the woods, thinking about the first time I met my old friend. It was as clear to me as the day I came upon her in the woods. She was gleaning from nature's abundance along the footpath not far from her cabin. I was taken with her immediately, possibly because of her strange appearance. Her gruff voice didn't frighten me; it made me want to get to know her.

"Dis here a puckerbush," she said. "De berries are good for what ails you. Go on; pick 'em. Eat one; see you likes it."

From that day forward, we became more than friends; she appointed herself my mentor.

I wasn't sure why I had questioned Mama Rae concerning Max Palmer. She had never done anything to make me distrust her. While she had always been a private person, to the point of being secretive, she had never led me astray. She had always been on my side, helping me over life's difficult hurdles.

My sunburn didn't hurt quite as much while I dressed for dinner. The Harbormaster was an upscale restaurant with a lovely view of Shelter Cove. I knew Catherine would be dressed to the nines, but I was definitely in the mood for comfort, so I put on my other sundress which was dressier than the one I was wearing, and took my cotton cardigan.

I arrived a few minutes early, and had just rounded a corner of the building. As I was almost to the stairs leading to the second-floor restaurant, I was stopped short. Max Palmer was pushing Pearl's wheelchair from the elevator close to the stairs, and Pearl was smiling broadly at none other than Mama Rae. She held my old friend's wrinkled hand in both of hers as they said their goodbyes. Max leaned down, took off the brake, and pushed the chair toward the parking lot. None of them saw me flattened against the wall of the enclosed stairs. Mama Rae walked slowly toward the cove opposite the parking lot.

I realized I had been holding my breath, and stayed where I was until I could breathe normally. What I had just seen made no sense to me, and I didn't bother trying to rationalize it. I simply wondered if Mama Rae had walked to the restaurant from her cabin, and if Pearl was so wealthy, why she didn't have a motorized wheelchair like the one she used on her yacht. Maybe it would be too cumbersome.

Just as I reached the top of the stairs, I heard a familiar voice behind me.

"It's surprising you're getting so soft at your age. Maybe you'll wear comfortable shoes the next time you challenge me to race up a set of stairs," Daniel teased.

I turned to see Catherine as she swatted at Daniel with her purse. The couple looked like models, or maybe movie stars, dressed in their finery. Catherine was gorgeous in a pale pink shift and a single string of pearls. In her stiletto heels, she was nearly as tall as her husband. I had only seen my dear friend in a coat and tie once before. It was the day Mama Rae had taken him to the police station to prove his innocence after Addie Jo Simmons, my adoptive father's secretary, had made false accusations about Daniel. Tonight, he stood tall and handsome in a dark suit, exuding a confidence I had never seen in him as he spoke to the maitre d'.

The three of us were seated at a table with a lovely view of the cove. A party boat was coming in from a sunset cruise to dock. The revelers were a rowdy bunch, laughing and waving at tourists milling around on the walkways by the shops and restaurants.

My Jimmy had brought me to dinner here a couple of times before our parents had forbidden us to see one another. We had made the mistake of telling them that we were in love and wanted to get married. After that, we were forced to see one another in secret, even after we had eloped.

I had continued to live in the house with Roy, and Jimmy had stayed with his parents. He would wait until everyone was asleep, then sneak out of his house. He would park his car two blocks from my house and come on foot to climb into my bedroom window and spend the night with his new bride. Our marriage remained a secret until after Roy's mysterious death. The coroner's report stated the cause of death: snakebite.

Jimmy's parents disowned him and cut him off financially when he told them we were married. After that, we had no reason to stay on the island.

"So, how's the job search going?" Daniel asked, interrupting my thoughts.

"I knew you would ask that," I said. "I'm sure I'll be rolling in money very soon."

"I know you will." Catherine smiled.

"Speaking of jobs, you'll be returning to the salt mines soon, won't you, Catherine?" I asked.

"Yes. I'll report to work the first of next week. I have mixed emotions about it. It'll feel good to contribute to our income, but I know I'll miss being with Suzanne every day."

"She's a sweet natured and friendly little girl. I'm sure she'll enjoy socializing with the other children," I said.

"I hope I won't be too tired to play with her when I get home."

"Why would you be tired? You'll be sitting at a desk all day instead of chasing after Suzanne," Daniel said.

"That's true, but I haven't let you in on my little secret," Catherine said.

A huge smile stretched across Daniel's face as he looked lovingly into Catherine's eyes.

"You're pregnant, and you kept it secret so you could tell Clemmie and me at the same time. I knew you two would be close friends."

He reached across the table and took Catherine's hand in his and kissed it. Catherine smiled at her husband, then made a timeout sign just as I was about to congratulate the couple.

"Daniel, I'm not pregnant. I'm sorry if that disappoints you. I might be tired when I get home, because I've decided to join a gym. There's one just down the street from the law firm where I'll be working. I thought I would need to work in some exercise since I'll be sitting all day."

"You're always a step ahead of me, my love," Daniel said. "The thought of having a little sister or brother for Suzanne does appeal to me, but I'm not really disappointed. We have plenty of time."

I felt like an intruder listening to their intimate conversation.

"I think joining a gym is a wonderful idea," I said. "Maybe I'll join one when I get settled."

"People use the excuse that they don't have time to exercise, but that isn't true," Daniel said. "I work out every morning before I go to work, because I'm now in a position that isn't physical labor. My body needs exercise to stay strong."

"But you make time to work out; you get up with the birds," Catherine said.

"Getting up early doesn't hurt me; it makes me feel good."

It seemed that I had worried about an inquisition by my friends that never came to fruition. Mama Rae was right again; I fret too much.

CHAPTER Six

*I*t would have been impossible for me to write a description of my new job. I did something different each day, unless Max Palmer decided he could get through twenty-four hours without my assistance. I never knew how to dress in the mornings, because I didn't know what I would be required to do.

This particular morning I slipped into a lightweight shift. My sunburned feet were no longer swollen, and I was able to wear heels for the first time since I was hired. I walked into the big empty room Max Palmer called his office in my grown-up attire, feeling quite professional, and greeted my boss. His hands were clasped in front of him on his desk, and he was studying them as if they held the answer to some mystery.

I tried again.

"Ahem! Good morning, Mr. Palmer."

His eyes left his hands and scrolled up to my face.

"Good morning, Clemmie. You look lovely this fine day."

"Thank you," I said, waiting for him to share the day's agenda. My boss looked like someone who had dug in a rag bag to find something to wear. His ensemble consisted of khaki cargo shorts, a tee shirt full of holes, and a pair of dirty tennis shoes. He stood and handed me a ticket.

"Please pick up these things from my dry cleaner. You can bring them when you come to work in the morning."

Then, he began patting the pockets of his cargo shorts. He located his wallet in the bottom left, extracted a twenty-dollar bill, and handed it to me. I took the money.

"Are you telling me that picking up your clothes is the only thing I'm supposed to do all day?"

"No. I want you to do that, then enjoy the rest of your day however you choose."

Max Palmer didn't wait for my reply. He turned away from me and began punching buttons on his desk phone. He was the most frustrating human being I had ever encountered. I clicked across the floor in my four-inch heels and left the building.

Thank goodness, the dry cleaner's address was stamped on the ticket, and I happened to know where it was. My boss must have had to wrack his brain to conjure up a menial chore for me to perform. He treated money as if he had a tree full of it in his back yard. It didn't cost twenty dollars to clean the two pairs of slacks I had just picked up.

What was I supposed to do with the better part of a day? I decided to drive around and familiarize myself with the island. I needed to find a safe, reasonably priced place to live, and I needed to buy a car.

I was tooling down the main drag when I suddenly began to feel overwhelmed. I felt nervous, almost panicky. This horrible feeling hadn't assailed me since I was released from Still Waters. I didn't know what to do. The rubber band I had snapped so many times to pull myself out of this hellish feeling was no longer on my wrist. I wasn't supposed to need such a crutch anymore. My palms were so sweaty that I had trouble holding the steering wheel, but I managed to maneuver the car off the road and onto the sandy shoulder beside a fruit and vegetable roadside stand. I killed the engine and closed my eyes. Then, I made myself take a few deep breaths. I tried to relax and concentrate on my breathing. After several minutes I was able to breathe normally. I felt weak, but I opened my eyes and stared at a basket of green beans for what seemed a long time.

I looked at the clock on the dashboard. It was ten o'clock. There was plenty of time to check out the island. It didn't take long for me to locate grocery stores, a movie theatre, a hospital, churches, and a post office. Specialty shops were tucked away everywhere I went.

I had seen a used car lot when I drove onto Hilton Head. It wouldn't hurt to see what the lot had to offer in my price range. Until I received my first paycheck, I didn't know what that might be. Lines of brightly colored plastic flags fluttered in the breeze above the array of used vehicles as I turned into the car lot. I had heard all of the tales about how car salesmen sometimes tried to take advantage of women who were looking for reliable used cars. Admittedly, I knew next to nothing about the workings of an automobile, and I wouldn't know a good deal if one smacked me in the face. Today's mission was to see what was available and get price ranges.

I had barely gotten out of my rental car when I looked up to see two salesmen practically racing to offer their assistance. The taller of the two stretched toward me, extending his hand, and the other guy turned and headed back to the building.

"How do you do, young lady?"

He gave me his best smile, and I allowed him to shake my hand.

"I'm fine. Thank you. Before you show me the car that's just right for me, I want you to know I'm not here to buy today. I just want to see what's available."

"Of course. Look around all you want. Take your time, and I'll be around if you have any questions. My name's Richard."

Whoever owned this lot hadn't spent much money on it. Parts of it had the remnants of blacktop, but most of the surface was nothing more than sand with a bit of gravel. There were a few puddles here and there, and I regretted having on my best footwear for this particular errand. The physical lot left a lot to be desired, but it had a huge array of vehicles. There were cars and trucks of every description, but when I started down the last row at the back of the lot, my eyes settled on a little canary yellow Jeep. It was so bright, so little, so cute, and I thought it would be the perfect transportation on an island.

I stood transfixed, smiling at the inanimate object, parked in a puddle of muddy water, and fell in love. It took no time at all for the salesman to come rushing toward me. He had a practiced smile in place as he began his spiel.

"It's you, young lady, bright and youthful."

He touched my elbow to guide me around a puddle to the driver's side of the Jeep.

"Just look at that interior. Neat as a pin. And check out the super cool stick shift. You gotta love it. Look at this ridiculous price tag: $1999; it's a steal."

The salesman pushed a hank of greasy hair away from his eye, took a breath, and continued.

"This," he said, touching the top, "is what we call a bonnet. You can take it off when the sun shines, and put it on when it rains; very versatile."

"Thank you for your time," I said, smiling. "I'll probably come back later."

"Thank you for stopping by. You'll find out we have the best deals of any lot around here."

I was picking my way to my rental car.

"My name's Richard," the salesman called.

I nodded, got into my car, and drove out of the lot.

It was past lunch time, and I was hungry. I poked down the main drag, looking for someplace to have lunch when an unobtrusive sign caught my eye: Hilton Head Diner, it read. Open twenty-four hours. I wasn't in the mood for anything fancy, so I pulled into a parking space and went inside. It was pretty crowded, but I was led to a booth by a window immediately. This establishment looked like a real diner, and the menu echoed that. It was a lot like the diner where Mama had taken me for my tenth birthday dinner.

Mama had saved barely enough out of our weekly budget to take me out for a birthday dinner instead of sitting in our small kitchen, eating the last of our leftover spaghetti. We had walked to the diner, deciding that we would rather spend our money on a decent meal than on transportation. Chicago winters were cold, but our apartment was only a few blocks from the diner.

Eating at that particular venue turned out to be a real stroke of luck for Mama and me, because that was where we met Roy Hubbard, our savior. Roy was sitting in the booth right behind Mama, and he was facing me. I remember how I couldn't keep from staring at the man with the ice blue eyes. Roy would take a bite, begin chewing, then roll those pretty eyes up toward the ceiling. He did that eye thing after each bite he took. Mama had nudged me under the table with the toe of her shoe to make me stop staring.

We lingered over dinner, because it was so cozy inside the diner. We were seated by a window, and we could see shoppers hurrying by. Big snowflakes had begun to fall, and I dreaded the trek home. I didn't say a word about the December weather, or the fact that I wished I had opted to wear my ratty old coat instead of my heaviest sweater. Instead, I put on my most radiant smile before blowing out the candle stuck in the middle of my fat slice of lemon meringue pie.

We had finished our dinner, and there was no reason to stay any longer.

"It's starting to snow in earnest," Mama said. "We'd better go, Clementine."

We were standing in line to pay the bill, and I noticed that the man with those pretty eyes was just in front of us. He put his wallet into a back pocket, then stepped to the side and smiled down at me.

"Well, Happy Birthday, you pretty girl!"

I looked around to see if he might have been talking to

somebody other than me.

"I'm talking to you, honey," he said, looking directly at me. "Which birthday is it?"

"Tenth," I said. "Thank you, sir."

Mama fastened her purse and gave me the look.

"Excuse us," she said, and ushered me out into the snow.

The streets were getting slick; so were the sidewalks. Mama and I ducked our heads and tucked our chins into our chests, attempting to keep our faces out of the wind. We hadn't gone very far when the heel of Mama's navy pump got stuck in a crack in the sidewalk. Try as she might, she couldn't pull it out, even after she stepped out of the shoe onto the freezing concrete. I was trying to loosen the shoe when a car pulled over to the curb, and the man from the restaurant rushed to our aid.

"Looks like you lovely ladies could use a little help," he said.

I was freezing, and I figured Mama's stockinged foot was probably stuck to the sidewalk. But my mama was unbudging when it came to talking to strangers.

Roy Hubbard squatted down and retrieved Mama's shoe. He handed it to her.

"I'm afraid it's ruined," he said. "I guess there's a chance a shoe shop might be able to save it. How about I drive you ladies home?"

I would have bet anything Mama was going to refuse his offer, but she looked at me and saw that I was shivering. Then, she surprised me.

"Thank you kindly, sir," she said. "We accept your offer."

We had only driven a couple of blocks when Mama told our Good Samaritan to let us out at the next corner.

"Nonsense. I'll take you to your door," he said.

Mama wouldn't argue with him.

"This is where I want you to let us out, sir," she said. "Thank you for the ride."

Our chauffeur pulled to the curb, got out, and held the door for us to go back into the cold.

"Well, it was nice meeting you," he said. "Um, I don't believe I got your name, ma'am."

Mama was in such a hurry for him to leave so we could walk the block and a half to our apartment that she gave her real name.

"Emily Martin and this is Clementine. Thank you again. Good night."

"Good night, then," he said. "By the way, I'm Roy Hubbard."

Roy must have been a pretty good detective, because he tracked us down the next day and wouldn't go away until my mama agreed to marry him.

Oh, how I missed my adoptive father. Roy and I loved one another as much as if we had been blood kin. Most of our time together as a family had been right here on this island, and I had come back, because it felt like home. This diner had brought back a flood of memories.

I reflected on my past here on Hilton Head the entire time I ate, and I was afraid that I might slip back into that horrible feeling that had stopped me cold earlier, but that didn't happen. I stuffed the last gravy soaked french fry into my mouth, and slid from the booth to pay my bill.

Was I going to bump into this guy everywhere I went? The good looking man I had first seen on the beach was holding the door. He glanced my way and said something to the pretty woman and little girl who were with him. They went outside and walked around the side of the building, and he walked boldly up to me.

"So, we meet again," he said, in a southern drawl which seemed to come naturally to him.

He was looking directly into my eyes, so I knew he was speaking to me.

"Excuse me?" I tried to sound offended.

He seemed to be looking me over as he slowly shook his head. Then, he smiled that toothpaste ad smile.

"This has to be fate," he said. "Don't you think so?"

"I don't know what you're talking about, mister," I said, and started out the door.

"What's your hurry?" he said, catching up to me. "We seem

to be at the same place at the same time, so I was thinkin' that we might just as well get together on purpose."

"What kind of man are you?" I said. "Your wife and little girl are sitting there in your car, watching you hit on a stranger."

Then, he laughed. It was the sexiest laugh I had ever heard. I didn't know why I stood there with him beside a newspaper rack instead of heading to my car, but that's what I did.

"Ma'am, I do spend a lot of time with the pretty lady and little girl who seem to be starin' at us, but she's not my wife, and that's not my little girl. That's my sister and my niece."

That revelation caught me off guard.

"Oh. Well, you still don't know me, and I don't know you, so let's just agree that this is a small island."

CHAPTER
Seven

$\mathcal{I}$ kicked off my heels as soon as I got back to my hotel room, thinking I might never be required to dress professionally for my day job.

I traded my dress for a pair of shorts and a tee shirt and headed to Mama Rae's. I parked in the same spot where I had parked ever since Roy surprised me with a Volkswagon Beetle for my sixteenth birthday.

The woods were alive with activity on this near perfect day. Insects buzzed, different species of birds seemed to be trying to outdo one another, singing their various and sundry melodies. Since I was so familiar with this route, I was enjoying nature's choir instead of paying attention, and walked directly into a spider web which spanned the width of the path.

Mama Rae's chickens appeared peaceful, pecking away at bugs and scratching in the sand as I made my way through the clearing to her cabin. I was about to call out to my old friend through the screen door when I heard someone singing. It had to be Mama Rae. To my knowledge, she didn't own a radio or anything else that played music. The voice was pretty and clear, but I couldn't make out one word of the song, and I was unfamiliar with the tune. I had never heard her sing before, and I wondered if she might be performing another of her strange rituals.

I was about to leave when the singing stopped abruptly. Should I stay, or go? I wouldn't want to upset her. She took those rituals seriously. Everything was quiet for a couple of minutes, so I decided to let her know I was there.

"Mama Rae," I called. "It's Clemmie. Are you busy?"

"Hold on a minute," came a weak voice from somewhere inside the cabin.

Her singing voice had sounded strong, but now she sounded like the old woman she was. She came to the door then, looking exhausted. Whatever she had been doing must have taken a lot out of her. She wore a white floor-length dress and a blood-red turban on her head.

"You want a cup of tea?" she asked.

"I'd love one."

I followed her through the dark living room to the kitchen and took my seat at the table.

"I have the day off," I told her. "The only thing I was asked to do today was to pick up Mister Palmer's dry cleaning."

"'spec you won't be very tired at de end of de day."

"How could I be? I don't do anything. Mama Rae, Max Palmer is the strangest person I've ever met. From what I can tell, he simply wants me to be available in case there might be something for me to do each day."

"Uh huh."

"Are you sure you've never heard of him?"

Mama Rae poured two cups of tea from a little pot and brought them to the table. She was frowning.

"Since when don't you believe what your Mama Rae tell you?"

"Of course, I believe you. I just thought since you seem to know everyone on the island that you might have forgotten who he is."

I wanted to ask why she was wearing this strange garb all alone in her home, but I didn't dare.

"You like dis tea?" she asked.

"Yes. It's delicious."

"I jes' mixed some dried leaves up together, mostly from fruit trees and mint." She smacked her lips. "Not too bad" she said.

I noticed several small jars sitting on the counter and nodded at them.

"Is some of your tea in those little jars?"

Mama Rae shook her turbaned head and laughed.

"You ask as many questions now as you did when you was jes' a tyke."

I knew she wasn't going to tell me what the jars held, so I didn't press.

"I should be getting my first pay check in a couple of days," I said, changing the subject.

"Better hope he gonna pay you to look pretty, 'cause you haven't done anyting to earn dat check 'less dar's tings you not tellin' me."

"You know I would never keep things from you, Mama Rae."

She got up and shuffled from the room. Our visit was over.

I rinsed our cups and walked out onto the small front porch where Biscuit, Mama Rae's old cat had held forth much of the time. He wasn't a sweet natured animal, and I always wondered why she had thought so much of him. I assumed it was because he was a living thing she felt responsible for. Lonely people need to be needed.

I trekked back through the woods, hoping I hadn't upset my old friend. She was very dear to me.

There was no reason to go back to my room, and I didn't want to look at places to rent until I knew what my salary was going to be. I cut through the hotel and the pool area which led to the beach and stood at the top of the steps, admiring the scene before me. What I wouldn't give to wake up each morning and look out at this magnificent beach with the great Atlantic ebbing and flowing, leaving bubbly patterns of lace on the wet sand. It was a pipe dream that had been ever present since I returned to the island.

I descended the stairs and added my flip-flops to more of the same behind the bottom step. The tide was out, and the sand was hard-packed and smooth. I walked all the way to the low rock wall that separated this private part of the beach from the public access section.

Thinking about my strange new job had become nearly all-consuming, but I felt my mind straying from that frustrating topic to the good-looking hunk who wanted to *get together* with me. He didn't just have a southern drawl; he sounded pretty much like a backwoods redneck. I couldn't imagine why that didn't turn me off, but it didn't. A hundred questions about him warred for my focus. What was he doing on the island? I was pretty sure he was single, or he wouldn't have an interest in me. Had he ever been married? Was he a widower? Did he live with his sister and niece?

I heard footsteps pounding the hard surface of the sand close behind me and the hard breathing of someone who had been running. Then, he was beside me, matching my steps.

"Well, hello again. I thought that was you."

"This can't be a coincidence," I said, attempting to sound miffed.

His smile was slow to stretch across those perfect teeth, and was followed by his sexy laugh. It sounded kind of lazy, the way Dean Martin sang on the tapes Mama used to play.

"I'll come clean," he said. "The day I saw you at Shelter Cove, I watched you get into that maroon Honda and followed you to see where you were goin'. It was pretty clear you were stayin' at the Hyatt, so I figured I would see you again if I hung around the beach close to your hotel."

"That's downright conniving."

"True, but I swear I'm harmless. You might even like me if you'd give me a chance."

I couldn't help myself; I returned his smile, and wondered where this might lead.

"Would you consider lettin' me take you to dinner tonight?"

"I don't go to dinner with strangers," I said. My smile was still in place.

"'Course you don't. I'm Clay Singleton, and you are?"

"Clemmie Castlebrook."

"So, Clemmie Castlebrook, we're not strangers anymore. How about that dinner?"

I hadn't dated anyone since I lost my beloved Jimmy. If I took Clay Singleton up on his offer, would I be betraying my late husband? I might not know how to behave on a date, especially with someone I had just met. I decided to throw caution to the wind; this was my brand new life.

"I accept your offer of a get-acquainted dinner," I said.

"Great. That's what it'll be: a get-acquainted dinner. I'll pick you up at seven o'clock."

"I'll be ready."

Then, my date-to-be did the strangest thing. He delivered a gentle cuff to my arm and trotted off down the beach. I wasn't at all sure about this guy.

I tried to feel positive about my upcoming dinner date as I walked back to the hotel. After all, it was just dinner. He hadn't mentioned a venue, but he seemed like a laid-back type, and I thought he would choose a place with a casual atmosphere.

I had just put the finishing touches on my makeup when my phone rang. I couldn't imagine who might be calling, unless it was Daniel or Catherine.

"Hello."

"Hello, Clemmie Castlebrook. Max Palmer here."

"Oh, hello, Mister Palmer."

"Clemmie, I've made dinner reservations for us at Stripes for seven this evening. I'm sorry to call so late, but I've been very busy today. Can you be ready in about a half hour?"

"Um, Mister Palmer, I didn't know you wanted me to go to dinner with you tonight. I'm afraid I have other plans."

"That's unfortunate. I'm sorry, my dear, but you'll simply have to change those plans. I need you to accompany me this evening. If you'll recall, this is something we discussed the day you were hired. I'll be at your hotel in a half hour."

I hung up the phone, feeling stunned. My boss hadn't said a word about our going to dinner tonight. What would I do about Clay Singleton? I didn't know his phone number or where he lived. There was no way for me to get in touch with him, and I would have already left the hotel when he came to pick me up. If I refused to accompany Max Palmer, he might fire me before I received my first pay check.

I didn't know anything about Stripes, but if this dinner was important, I assumed it would be upscale. I took off my sundress and sandals and changed into my best outfit and heels. Then, I went down to the lobby to wait for my overbearing boss.

I went to the front desk and left a message for Clay Singleton along with an apology. Max Palmer was entering the lobby as I turned away from the desk. He smiled as he approached me. I didn't return the smile, but tried not to scowl at him. He was wearing a dark tailored suit, a tasteful tie, and wingtips you could see your face in—power attire.

"Good evening, Clemmie."

"Good evening," I said, doing my best to keep anger out of my tone.

"You look lovely" Max said.

"Thank you."

We were headed to the front door. My boss turned away from me and began circling the floral arrangement in the center of the lobby. He took small steps and stopped to smell certain blooms as he moved around the huge vase. Then, he returned to take my elbow and escort me from the building.

We stood in silence while the valet ran to bring Max's Ferrari.

I wondered if he would tell me what was so important about this dinner during the drive to Stripes. It seemed to me that he enjoyed keeping me in the dark.

When we reached the restaurant, Max killed the engine and turned to face me.

"I hope you'll take this the way it's intended, Clemmie. I would prefer for you to refuse a cocktail before the meal. A glass of wine with dinner will be fine. Do you understand what I'm telling you?"

"I think it's pretty clear that you want to make sure I'm sober as a judge all evening," I said.

"That's correct. We're going to be dining with a very important gentleman. Please don't offer your opinion unless it's requested. And for God's sake, don't giggle like a school girl at something that amuses you. I want you to be at your best the entire evening: a beautiful, intelligent young woman with excellent manners and perfect diction—one of your most impressive assets."

I wasn't sure where my bravado hailed from, but I felt bound to tell my boss how he was making me feel.

"Mister Palmer, I realize what I'm about to say might cost me my job, but I want you to know that you're not only treating me like a stupid, naughty child; you're scaring me. If this man is so important, and you're so in awe of him, why in the world would you want him to meet me?"

My boss looked a bit dumbfounded.

"I'm sorry you find my instructions condescending or frightening, Clemmie. Perhaps I sounded rather blunt, but I needed to let you know what was expected of you. I don't have time to go into details, because we need to be punctual. The gentleman we're meeting isn't used to having to wait."

"Very well," I said, swallowing my pride.

My boss gave the hostess his name and told her we were expecting another party, so we would wait where we were.

"Oh, I can take you to your table now," she said. "Mr. Wingate is already seated."

Our important dinner guest stood as we approached the table. His suit looked rumpled, and he had loosened his tie and the top button of his shirt. He had a smile on his mustached face and a martini in his hand.

"Here you are, Max," he said. "And who is this lovely creature?"

"This is Clemmie Castlebrook, my able assistant. Clemmie, I'd like you to meet Ralph Wingate."

"How do you do?" I said.

"I'm delighted to meet you, my dear."

Mister Wingate abandoned his martini and stepped around the table, dismissing the hostess with a wave of his hand.

"Allow me," he said, pulling my chair back from the table.

I took my seat and nodded my thanks. Then, he lifted my hand and graced it with a kiss.

Max waited for Mister Wingate to return to his chair before he sat down.

Mister Wingate hailed a waiter and smiled at me.

"What would you like to drink, dear girl?" he asked. He seemed to have forgotten that my boss was in attendance.

"A perrier with lime would be nice," I said.

Max asked for Scotch on the rocks, and Mister Wingate ordered another martini.

I assumed the business conversation between my dinner companions would begin immediately, but it didn't.

The way Mister Wingate looked at me across the table made me uncomfortable. I knew I was expected to be polite to the old coot, but he was beginning to creep me out.

"So, Palmer, where did you find this wonderful girl?" he asked.

"I didn't actually find her. Ms. Castlebrook answered an ad I listed in the paper. She hasn't worked for me very long, but I must tell you, I don't know how I managed before I hired her."

After we had ordered dinner, Max asked for the wine list and ordered a bottle of chardonnay. Mister Wingate said he'd stick with martinis and ordered another. I had a feeling he might not be discussing much business this evening. He had begun to slur his speech. His inebriated state didn't affect his appetite. Max had told me to make sure my manners were impeccable, because he wanted to impress this man who ate like a starved animal.

I noticed that Max hardly touched his dinner. He tried to bring up the subject of the business venture he had apparently spent the day pitching to Mister Wingate, but his attempts didn't appear to faze the older man.

"Mister Wingate, I know that section along the east coast of the state would be perfect for what I have in mind," Max Palmer said. "It's untouched and ripe for the right buyers. I'll wager that within five years of building the development, it'll be swarming with all kinds of new businesses."

My boss was wasting his time. Ralph Wingate was busy telling me how gorgeous my hair looked when the candlelight hit it a certain way.

CHAPTER
Eight

*M*ax Palmer had ruined everything. Clay Singleton might not have turned out to be the man to make me happy, to help me ease the pain of missing my Jimmy, and relish my new life here on Hilton Head Island, but he had made me want to give it a try. I doubted that Clay would bother to speak to me the next time we bumped into one another, and I would be willing to bet he wouldn't show up at my hotel anxious to see the woman who had stood him up for a first date.

My being in a snit kept me up half the night. I couldn't stop fuming about my boss's selfish attitude. He obviously didn't care what my plans had been. The only thing that mattered to him was getting what he wanted from Ralph Wingate. Whatever that was, the old goat seemed to have no interest in dealing with my boss, and I couldn't help feeling a small amount of pleasure because of that. It somehow made me feel that Max had gotten his just desserts. I hoped I wouldn't be asked to be in Ralph Wingate's company again. I decided that as soon as I received my first paycheck, I would give Max Palmer notice that this was not the job for me. I couldn't deal with his constant spur-of-the-moment requests.

Max hadn't said anything about needing me over the weekend. Tomorrow would be Saturday, so I assumed I would be free. I should receive my paycheck on Monday since there had been no mention of it yesterday or last night. If my boss didn't surprise me with another phone call by mid-morning Saturday, I would call Daniel to see if he could come to the island and go with me to check out the little yellow Jeep. If Daniel thought it was sound, and the price was fair, I would buy it.

I hadn't set an alarm, but my eyes popped open just before eight o'clock. Bright sunlight was invading the room, and I had to squint as I got out of bed. Why couldn't I remember to pull the drapes each night? I showered and dressed, willing the phone not to ring. Then, I got on the elevator to go to breakfast. I was walking through the lobby on my way to the coffee shop when a desk clerk motioned to me. Reluctantly, I went to see why. I feared that Max Palmer had left a message, requesting my presence at his office.

"You have two messages, Ms. Castlebrook," the clerk said, handing me a slip of paper and a plain envelope with my name on it.

"Thank you very much," I said.

Whatever I was about to learn would have to wait until I was sitting at a table for one with a cup of black coffee in front of me. My boss knew how to reach me by phone, so why would he bother leaving a message at the desk?

The coffee was always fresh here, and I savored my first sip before looking at the messages. I ordered a croissant and fresh fruit, then opened the envelope, dreading what might be inside. I did a double take as I looked down at a check for $1200. Max Palmer had scrawled a note on the back of what looked like a cocktail napkin: Clemmie, I hope this remuneration will be satisfactory. I appreciate your professionalism and your willingness to perform the duties asked of you. Enjoy your weekend. Max Palmer.

$1200 was my payment for doing nothing my first week on the job. It made no sense. My mind traveled back to last night's dinner conversation when Max Palmer told Ralph Wingate what a valuable employee I am. The situation was so strange it seemed there must be something illegal or corrupt about it.

I studied the check Max had left with the desk clerk. It was a cashier's check made out to me. That didn't tell me anything. There was nothing on the check that linked it to Max Palmer or his business with no name. But there was no way I could turn down that kind of money for doing nothing. I knew I would continue to heed my boss's beck and call, and he knew it, too.

I folded the check and slipped it into my pocket, then looked at my other message. It was a short neatly printed note signed by Clay Singleton: Sorry it didn't work out. I understand.

I felt like crying. Clay was the only person I'd had the slightest interest in since Jimmy's demise. I wanted to discover who he was, what he enjoyed, and what he did for a living. He had somehow made me want to know everything about him. Now, that would probably never happen.

I left my breakfast untouched and went back to my room to call Daniel. If he wasn't busy he would come to look at the Jeep with me and check out everything about it. My dear friend would be able to see that something was troubling me simply by looking into my eyes. That's how close we were. He would come right out and ask me, and I would spill the whole thing, mysterious job and all.

"Hello."

"Daniel, it's Clemmie. I'm calling to find out whether or not you're busy today and if you and Catherine have plans."

"Hey, Clemmie. Catherine and Suzanne are going to some kind of mother-daughter thing that's supposed to last most of the day. It has something to do with play dates for little kids. But yours truly is free all day. What's up?"

"I was wondering if you'd be willing to go with me to a car

lot here on the island to check out a good used vehicle. I'll spring for lunch."

"Sure. I'd be happy to share my expert opinion with you. I wouldn't want you to get stuck with a lemon. I'm sure you've heard how car salesmen take advantage of the fairer sex." He laughed.

"I don't know about that, but I know I'm ignorant when it comes to the insides of cars. Come on over and help me, buddy."

"I'll leave Catherine a note and head right over. See you in a bit."

I knew it would take Daniel about forty minutes to get here. That gave me plenty of time to go to the bank where I had opened an account and deposit my check. I gave the check another long look, because that amount of money for one week's work was unusual for any kind of office work, or however one would describe my job, in the early eighties.

Daniel met me in the lobby of my hotel, ready to help me buy my ride.

"Let's take the car I'm driving to the lot, so I can drop it off at the rental agency if I buy one today," I said.

"You're the boss."

My mind was one big contradiction. I was upset about what Max Palmer had done to ruin my chances of a relationship with Clay, but I was also excited about the prospect of buying that cute little yellow Jeep. If not the Jeep, maybe I could find some kind of reliable transportation to call my own.

Daniel and I wheeled into the lot and I parked on a dry spot. It was beyond me how all the puddles could be holding water, since it hadn't rained in the last two days. The lot was busy today. Salesmen were all over the place, spouting their spiels to customers. I wanted to show Daniel the Jeep before one of them spotted us. But it seemed we weren't fast enough, because Richard, the salesman who had told me his name twice, was on us like bees on honey.

"Well, hello there, young lady." He put on his special smile which showcased tobacco stained teeth. "I see you've brought the mister to make sure that Jeep's in perfect condition."

"I would like to look it over," Daniel said, "and we'd like to take it for a short drive if that's okay."

"Sure it's okay." Richard gave Daniel a little slap on his shoulder. "I'll just run inside and get the keys. Be right back."

He took off at a near run.

"Don't get excited until we get away from the lot. I want to drive it and check it out," Daniel said. "And stop looking like you can't wait to buy it. I might be able to get him to come down on the price."

"You're right. Here he comes."

I took the keys and hopped into the driver's seat, and Daniel got in on the passenger side. The salesman headed back to the building and waved to us as we chugged over potholes and out of the lot.

Daniel laughed. "I wasn't sure you'd remember how to drive a stick shift," he said.

"You underestimate me, my friend," I said, shifting into second, then third gear.

The main drag was nearly free of traffic, and I pushed the speed limit, making a golf course on our right appear to be nothing but a colorful blur.

"Well, how do you think it handles?" Daniel asked.

"Just the way I thought a Jeep would. It's not a luxury car, you know. It makes me feel like a kid."

"Turn onto the next street and let me look under the hood before I drive it on the open road. Then, I want to take it by a service station where my friend, Jay, works. I'll ask him to look it over, too."

Being with Daniel was like a tonic for me. Our relationship hadn't changed since we were kids. But a lot had happened since our teenage years. I had been through what seemed a lifetime of the best and the worst life had to offer. My years at Still Waters had brought me back to life in a sense. I had been forced to face reality through reliving the happy times and the unthinkable. Now, I would make the best of my situation. I had most of my life before me. And

Daniel would always be a part of it as far as I was concerned. I was glad he had his little family. His childhood had been little more than a disconnect. He had been shifted from pillar to post. Now, it was his turn for happiness and stability.

Daniel, Jay, and I were all in agreement: the Jeep was perfect for me.

I was back at the wheel when we returned to the car lot, trying my best not to appear too anxious to become the owner of the cute yellow toy. We were getting out of the Jeep when the salesman came dashing toward us.

"Well, whadda you think?" he asked, giving us that toothy smile.

"The mileage isn't bad," Daniel said, "but you're asking more than the blue book listing."

Daniel had no idea what the blue book listing was, but Richard didn't know that.

"It's got a couple of years wear on it, but I'm sure you can tell it's in great shape. Runs like a top, don't it?"

"It missed a time or two," Daniel said, "but I don't think that's much of a concern. We'd be willing to go $1800 smooth. What do you say?"

"I'll have to run that by my boss. Why don't you two come inside and sit in the air conditioning for a few minutes. This won't take long."

Daniel winked at me as we followed the salesman into a small room where another couple sat on a ratty couch, watching a talk show on television. We took seats in folding chairs to wait for an answer.

After about ten minutes Richard returned, smiling.

"It was hard to convince my boss, but he finally agreed. Let's go over to my desk and fill out the paperwork."

After what seemed an eternity and lots of paperwork, I drove my Jeep from the used car lot, and Daniel followed in my rental car. We drove down Airport Road and parted with the rental car at the agency. Then, Daniel hopped into the passenger seat, and we cruised Route 278.

"What'll it be for lunch, Daniel?"

"Let's do burgers and fries the way we did when we were teenagers."

Minutes later we were seated in a booth at the Hilton Head Diner. Daniel flipped through the offerings on the miniature jukebox on our table. Then, he looked at me with his big brown eyes. Without saying a word, he was asking me what was going on.

I swallowed. There was so much to tell him, and I wasn't sure where to begin.

"I'm not in any kind of trouble, and I'm not sick," I said.

Daniel continued looking at me. His expression said, "Just tell me, Clemmie. You know you can trust me."

"I'm ashamed that I didn't tell you part of it sooner. I have a job, Daniel. I've had it for a week. My first paycheck in the amount of $1200 has already been deposited in my bank account."

"That's great. What's the job? Sales? It's obvious you're not teaching, because school has already started. I'm sure you're not working in an office, because those jobs don't pay that much."

"No, it's neither of those."

"Pushing dope?" he joked.

"I don't think so," I said. "All I've done is accompany my boss to dinner a couple of times and pick up his clothes at the cleaners."

"There has to be more to it than that."

"He introduced me to a businessman as his assistant, but I haven't assisted him in doing anything."

"What's his name?"

"Max Palmer. That's all I know about him. I have one of his cards. There's nothing on it but his name and phone number."

"Does Mama Rae know you have this job?"

"Yes. I told her all about it. She doesn't seem at all concerned. I asked her if she had heard of Max Palmer, and she told me that she hadn't."

"I thought she knew every person on this island," Daniel said.

"I thought so, too. Daniel, I think she's lying to me."

"She wouldn't do that."

"The night I met you and Catherine at the restaurant in Shelter Cove, I saw Mama Rae. Max Palmer was pushing a wheelchair. An old woman named Pearl was in it. She and Max have some sort of close relationship. Pearl was holding both of Mama Rae's hands, and they were saying goodbye to one another. The three of them were together. How can you explain that?"

"Obviously, I can't. Mama Rae does some odd things, and she's all wrapped up in those weird rituals, but she's never lied to either of us."

"Would you be willing to go with me to see her? She doesn't know I saw her with Max and Pearl, because they didn't see me. I don't want her to think I was spying on her. If she knows I've told you about my job and my strange boss, she might open up to us."

"I'll go with you, but if she wouldn't tell you, she won't tell me, either."

"I really appreciate this, Daniel. Now, I have something else to tell you."

Daniel raised his eyebrows.

"I've met someone. We made a date for last night, but my boss derailed it. He insisted I change my plans so I could accompany him to a business dinner with a dirty old man who gave me the creeps."

"Did your someone understand? Have you set up another date?"

"No. I really want to get to know him, but it doesn't look like that's going to happen. I don't have his phone number, so I couldn't get in touch with him. I left a message for him at the desk, because I didn't know what else to do. He left a note for me saying he understood. I'm sure he thinks I simply changed my mind and stood him up."

"Bummer."

"It sure is. He's the first person who has interested me since

Jimmy died. His name is Clay Singleton, and that's pretty much all I know about him. We kept showing up at the same place at the same time. He suggested that we get together intentionally, and I agreed."

"What's happened to your detective skills? Look him up in the phone book."

"I suppose my brain is taking a hiatus; I didn't think of doing that."

Daniel laughed. "Okay, kid, let's have lunch. Then, we'll take a walk through the woods to see our old friend and interrogate her until she comes clean. If she does know your boss, she might know why he hired you to do nothing."

"That's a good point. She seemed anxious for me to take the job when I told her about it."

Daniel had been special to Mama Rae from the moment I introduced them, so I assumed she would answer any question he might ask. I was wrong. She appeared happy to see us, but when it came to admitting she knew Max Palmer, she kept mum.

"I don't know why you keep pesterin' me 'bout dat man," she said. "I don't know dat name; never heard it."

I decided it would be cruel to question her further. She wasn't going to cave.

"What smells so good?" Daniel asked.

Mama Rae laughed. "You know dat's my gooseberry tarts. Don't preten' you don't. Come on to Mama Rae's kitchen."

The three of us had sat at the small wooden table in Mama Rae's kitchen so many times that it felt like we were reliving the past. But our visit hadn't turned up any information. So shortly after we savored the tarts, we said goodbye to our old friend and wended our way back through the woods. I drove Daniel to his car and thanked him for helping me with the Jeep.

I wasn't sure why, but I felt let down after Daniel headed home to his wife and child. I was so happy for him, and so sorry for myself. Self-pity is not an admirable trait, and it was something I truly wanted to ditch and get on with my life.

I went to my room and lifted the phone directory from the nightstand drawer, thinking I would see a listing for Clay Singleton. Scanning down the page, I ran across three Singletons—none of them Clay. Maybe he lived with his sister. It was possible that he lived in a nearby town and commuted to the island to work each day, but that didn't seem likely. I had run into him during the day and at night, so it stood to reason that he lived on the island.

I decided to go for a walk on the beach, so I changed into shorts and a tee shirt and headed for what I now considered my haven—my safe place where nature's splendor always made me glad to be alive. The beach wasn't crowded, and I felt free to stroll along the surf, letting my mind wander where it would. All thoughts of Max Palmer and his strange business disappeared. Tomorrow I would look at the listings in the Island Packet for a good place to live. I was home.

After my walk, I took a shower and stretched out on my bed to daydream about where my new digs might be. A beach house would be too much to ask for. Most of those were rentals. They were large enough to house families who were on vacation. I would have to look for a rental unit in an apartment complex, or I might luck out and find a unit for rent by owner in one of the resorts. Many of those were on golf courses or lagoons with gorgeous views. I wouldn't let thoughts of buying a home enter my mind until I had saved enough money to be comfortable. A person on her own needed to be circumspect. There was no point in wondering what might be available until I looked in the morning paper.

I'd had a busy day, and I was in the mood for comfort food. There was a quaint Italian restaurant, tucked in the trees just outside Palmetto Dunes Resort. I remembered that it was family run and the food was delicious. It was only minutes away from my hotel.

I didn't have a reservation, and the place was packed, but the owner assured me that I would be seated soon. In the meantime, I could sit at the small bar. I ordered a glass of cabernet while I waited for a table, and perused the menu. It would have been impossible to miss a conversation taking place behind me.

"Do you have a reservation, sir?"

"Yes, I do; Ralph Wingate."

CHAPTER *nine*

A rampage of scenarios raced through my mind. I wasn't supposed to let this happen. My doctor had warned me about it. He had told me that I must concentrate on one thing at a time. Jumbled thoughts could interrupt the calm he had been able to instill in me, and throw me off track. I had to be careful, or I could end up back at Still Waters or another mental hospital.

Lying on the bed in my hotel room, fully clothed, I tried to make my mind go blank. I attempted recalling the aroma of gardenias, and was unsuccessful. Then, I tried to picture a mountain stream with sunlight playing on its ripples, turning them into diamonds. Nothing worked, and my woes continued to war for my attention.

I needed to find a place to live. I couldn't stay at the Hyatt much longer; the nightly rate was eating into the money I had been given to make a new start. My chances of having a relationship with Clay Singleton were slim and none. And what about this *do nothing* job I had landed? The salary was fantastic—more than I could make doing anything else, but it kept me on pins and needles. On top of all that, I was afraid I would be asked to dine with that lecherous old Ralph Wingate again. Did he live here on the island? I prayed that he didn't; that he was only here on business for a few days.

I had been lucky enough to avoid Mister Wingate at the restaurant last night. I had sat at the bar sipping wine while the hostess led him to a table in the back of the room. Then, I was squeezed into a tiny table close to the front door. I wolfed down my dinner and left the restaurant as fast as I could, and I was sure he hadn't seen me.

I had to focus on positive things. This island was exactly where I wanted to begin my new life. My best friend lived in Savannah, less than an hour away. My old friend and mentor lived here on Hilton Head. I had a job of sorts, and as of today, I had a little yellow Jeep. I was fortunate indeed. Tomorrow I would peruse the Island Packet and look for my new home. Finally, sleep came.

The next morning I was in a positive mood, seated in the coffee shop with the rental section of the paper spread out before me. A furnished apartment or rental unit was a must, since my only possessions were my clothes and the Jeep. I circled several possibilities. The island was small enough that it didn't matter where my new home was located; it wouldn't be very far from Max Palmer's office.

There were a few listings on the beach, but they were all too large and too expensive for me. I had circled a couple of rental units located inside Palmetto Dunes. I wouldn't have to bother with stopping to pick up a pass, since I already had one. I decided to look at those first.

The first unit I looked at was pretty rundown. I knew I couldn't be too picky, but I wanted to live in surroundings that were cheerful. The unit didn't have to be on the beach, or on a golf course, but it had to be someplace I wanted to come home to.

The second unit on my list seemed familiar. I hadn't recalled the address, but as I climbed the low front porch steps, my recollection sprang to life, and I could picture every nook and cranny in the villa before the owner came to greet me. Jimmy's parents had owned it when he and I were dating. The door swung open wide.

"Hello," said a very attractive woman.

I thought she looked to be in her mid-fifties. Her blond hair was in a ponytail, and she wore a sundress and sandals.

"I'm Eleanor York," she said.

"Clemmie Castlebrook," I said. "I'm glad to meet you."

"Well, Clemmie, I do hope you can forgive the mess. Please come in, if you can make your way through the jungle of boxes. I'm packing things which haven't been used in years. We have wonderful charities here on the island, and they're always glad to receive most anything that still works."

I stepped inside to admire the foyer. The linoleum had been replaced with some kind of tile that looked like free-form stone, and the walls were painted a dove-gray.

"This is a beautiful entrance," I said.

"Thank you. My husband and I did quite a bit of redecorating when we bought the villa. It was well appointed then; just a bit dated."

"Let me give you the nickel tour," Eleanor said. "We'll start with the kitchen and laundry room. This area is small, but serviceable. All of the appliances are fairly new, and I'm not taking any of the dishes, pots and pans, or utensils. I think you'll have everything you need."

I noticed that the dining area table and chairs had been replaced with a new, more modern version than what I remembered, as had the living room furniture. Wood floors gleamed where the carpet had been.

"Do you rent the villa by the month?" I asked.

"I will if that's my only option, but I hope to rent it for longer periods. You see, my husband passed away a few months ago, and I'm staying here part of the time and at our home in Atlanta when I'm not here. Eventually, I'll probably sell one of them."

"I'm very sorry for your loss. I had no idea."

I hated that expression. It seemed that was the only thing anyone could think of to say to a person who had just lost a loved one. I thought it sounded trite.

Eleanor York patted my shoulder.

"Of course you didn't. How could you have known?"

I wanted to let her know that I could empathize with her, with the emptiness she must be feeling, but I decided to change the subject instead of prolonging the topic.

"I don't recall that the paper stated you were only interested in renting for long term periods, but that doesn't seem to be a factor now," I said.

"If you choose to rent this villa, how long would you want to stay?"

"I just came to Hilton Head. I have a job, but I'm staying at the Hyatt until I find a suitable place to rent. Renting is my only option at the present time, so I would prefer long term—at least six months."

"That sounds reasonable. Let me show you the rest of the villa."

She led me back through the living room with its sliding glass doors looking out over a large deck and the eighteenth hole of the Robert Trent Jones golf course. Then, she showed me the master bedroom and bath before we headed up the stairs. The landing at the top of the stairs looked the same except for the furnishings. So did a small bedroom over the front porch.

When we went into the last bedroom, the large one which looked out over the golf course, I felt as though my knees were going to give way. I could hear the owner talking, but I couldn't make out what she was saying. My body felt heavy, like it was about to fall. Then, I was leaning against the door frame with tears squeezing from the corners of my eyes. I could feel Jimmy's nude body next to mine as we danced in the dark with rain beating its fat drops on the roof and the deck outside the glass doors. We saw lightning flash in the summer night. We were drunk with the wine we'd had and with the passion of young love. Then, we stumbled to the floor where

74

we made clumsy love. We lay there, laughing at ourselves. We were deliriously happy.

Eleanor York turned from the lovely view of the golf course just in time to rush across the room and keep me from sliding to the floor.

"Oh, my dear, are you all right?" she asked, helping me to a bed to sit down.

Of course I wasn't all right, but how could I explain my strange behavior? I had made up my mind that I would not tell her I had ever been here. Nobody had known; not Daniel, not Mama Rae, nobody, except Roy, my adoptive father, and he had died with that knowledge.

"Please excuse my behavior. I'm not sure what came over me. I suddenly felt faint."

"Stay here a minute. I'll get you a glass of water," she said.

She went into the bathroom and came back with a paper cup of water, looking as worried as if I were a loved one.

"I'm fine now," I said. "Sometimes I forget about meals if I'm busy."

"Are you sure? You should feel steady before you go down the stairs."

"The faint feeling is completely gone. Thanks for your concern."

I stood and handed her the cup. I knew that if the rate was anywhere near reasonable, I was going to rent this villa.

"Let's go back downstairs," I said. "I'd like to take another look at the kitchen, if you don't mind."

I opened a few cabinet doors and a couple of drawers before I told the owner I would like to rent her villa.

"I'm glad you like the villa, Clemmie. I know you'll enjoy it. Restaurants are close by, and golf and tennis are just a stone's throw from here. If you're a beach lover, you're in luck, because you can have your toes in the sand in less than five minutes."

"We haven't discussed the rates," I said.

"I was using an agency, but I have started taking care of the rentals on my own for the last several months. I have written the contract agreement, and I make all the rules. You'll find that my rates are more than fair. Just let me get a contract to show you."

Eleanor York left the room, returned with the agreement, and placed it before me.

"You'll notice that the rate is left blank," she said. "You see, I set the price at a rate I believe to be fair for potential renters after I've had a chance to talk with them."

She took the agreement from me and inked in a price, handing it back to me.

"Does that figure seem reasonable to you?" she asked.

"Absolutely. How much do you need in advance?"

"The first month's rent and a security deposit will be fine," she said. "I'll need a week to get all of these boxes out of your way and pack to go to Atlanta. Then, I won't bother you. I'll leave a number where you can reach me after I've left the island should you need anything. There's a list of services on the laundry room wall."

I wrote a check in exchange for a couple of door keys and shook Eleanor York's delicate hand.

"You can call this number if you have questions before I leave," she said.

I was certain I would be calling her as I thought about all the loose ends I would have to handle. I was new at taking care of business by myself. Jimmy wasn't here to make decisions for me. I could see his darling crooked smile and laughing eyes as he did whatever needed to be done. How many times had he taken the reins to fix one of my messes? "Piece of cake, sweetie," he'd say. Then, he would perform a small miracle.

I made up my mind to tackle the hurdles of my new life one at a time. Eleanor York would have one week to pack her belongings and vacate the villa. Then, I would leave the Hyatt and move into my home. Eleanor had told me I should feel free to make any temporary changes to make the villa show my personal taste. I assumed that meant adding, or changing accessories which could be restored to the way she had decorated it in the event that I chose not to renew my lease.

The electricity and water wouldn't be turned off; just switched to my name. The phone would be in my name, and I would have a new number. I would be required to pay a monthly fee for outdoor maintenance, and I would need to take care of a mailing address. Listed one at a time, those seemed like small things.

I went to visit Mama Rae with my good news. She was sure to be excited for me. Tramping through the woods I realized that I would have her cool head to advise me whenever I felt overwhelmed. Mama Rae had always been there for me; she would be here now.

I saw my old friend as I came into the clearing. She was sitting in one of the straight backed chairs on her little front porch, and she held a cloth in front of her face as I approached.

"Mama Rae?"

She didn't answer. Instead, I heard a soft moan.

I ran to the cabin and up the steps to the porch. A dishtowel covered Mama Rae's face, and she was sobbing into it. I wasn't sure she knew I was there. Startling her was the last thing I wanted to do, but I needed to discover what was ailing her.

"Mama Rae," I said, "It's me, Clemmie."

She pulled the dishtowel away from her face just enough to speak.

"Can't talk," she said, getting up and shuffling to her front door.

"Are you sick?" I asked, feeling like a fool.

"Not sick," she answered, and went into her house.

I knew better than to follow her inside without being invited, so I went back through the dark woods, wondering what in the world might be the source of my friend's tears. I had never seen her display such emotion. How would I be able to help her if I didn't know what was going on?

Back in my room at the hotel I sat down at the desk and made a list of the things I needed to set in motion in the week ahead.

Number one on the list was taking care of Mama Rae. If she wasn't sick, something else was making her sad. Maybe she was lonely. Perhaps she didn't feel up to doing the things she had always done, and that depressed her. I would have to think of some way to guide her back to being her feisty self.

I had to share my good news with somebody, so I called the Grovers' number. Catherine answered. She didn't sound particularly pleased to hear my voice. I asked how she liked her new job, and she said that she thought she would be happy with the law firm, but it was too soon to tell. I let her know that I had found a place to live, and that I would be leaving the Hyatt in about a week.

"That's good news, Clemmie," she said.

I thought her voice sounded strained, or sad—something I couldn't put my finger on.

"I know you want to tell Daniel," she said, "but he isn't here."

She didn't bother to tell me when he would return, and abruptly excused herself to take care of something for Suzanne.

I had no sooner hung up the phone when it rang. Daniel must have just walked in the door at his home, I thought.

"It's about time," I said. "I've been dying to tell you something all afternoon while you've been out gallivanting."

"I beg your pardon?" said Max Palmer.

"Oh, I'm sorry, Mister Palmer. I was expecting a call from my friend."

"That's quite all right, Clemmie. I hope you don't have plans with your friend for this evening, because I would like for you to accompany me to dinner. I'll pick you up at your hotel at seven."

I assumed this was how it was going to be. My boss would call me at the last minute and expect me to drop everything to do his bidding. I would go to dinner with him tonight, but if I continued to be in his employ, I would have to lay down some ground rules.

"No, I don't have dinner plans. I'll be in the lobby at seven."

I wondered what exciting entertainment he had in mind for tonight. Would it be another invigorating evening with Pearl, the inquisitor, or my having to steer clear of a dirty old man's reach, while wearing a plastered-on smile?

It turned out to be the latter, but the venue almost made it worth it.

"Mister Wingate is our host this evening," Max said. "I'm sure he will have already arrived when we get to the restaurant. You're going to enjoy the food, Clemmie. Charlie's L'Etoile Verte is a favorite here on Hilton Head."

"Does Mister Wingate live on the island?" I asked.

"Oh, no. He's just here for business purposes. I was afraid I had lost his interest the other night, but I was able to convince him that I know a good thing when I see it. Tonight we celebrate."

I knew that if I asked what we were celebrating, my boss wouldn't give me a straight answer. Dreading the thought of coming face to face with Ralph Wingate, I smiled as I entered the restaurant, because it was expected. Our host was at the bar, martini in hand. He slid off his bar stool and walked toward us.

"My dear, how lovely you look," he said, giving me the once-over.

"Thank you. It's nice to see you," I said.

"Our table is ready," he said. "Shall we, my dear?"

Our host offered his arm, and I took it. Ralph Wingate brushed past the hostess, taking me with him, and Max followed, looking miffed.

Ignoring my boss's previous instruction, I ordered a glass of wine to sip while looking over the menu. I almost didn't care that I might be in for a reprimand after we left the restaurant.

The menu was extensive, and it was difficult to choose an entrée. I settled on the flounder meuniere, and hoped I had made the right choice. Max and Ralph Wingate gave the menu short shrift, ordered, and forgot I was present. They were immersed in a business conversation about some parcel of land in Florida, and nothing could have pleased me more. I ordered another glass of chardonnay, and thoroughly enjoyed my dinner.

CHAPTER *Ten*

*M*ax Palmer was sitting at his metal desk, drinking coffee when I arrived. Naturally, I hadn't known what to wear; I never did. My boss had such strange behavior that I thought it might entertain him to keep me in suspense, and maybe have me go back to the hotel to change into something more suitable for my daily tasks. Today I wore the skirt and blouse I had worn to my job interview, and hoped it would suffice.

"Good morning, Clemmie."

"Good morning."

"I believe I owe you an apology for the constant business discussion last evening. You were virtually ignored. Please forgive my rudeness."

"You don't owe me an apology, Mister Palmer. I was aware that the dinner was for business purposes."

"Thank you for being so understanding. I assure you I'm not in the habit of treating women that way."

I smiled and nodded my forgiveness, wanting this ridiculous conversation to be over.

"Take the day off, Clemmie. I won't be needing your services until tomorrow."

"Thank you," I said.

There were plenty of things I could be doing today, but my top priority was Mama Rae. I had to find out what ailed her and try to fix it. What could make her so sad? I had hardly seen her show emotion of any kind in all the years I had known her.

As I drove past a pet store I had all but ignored each time I went to the office, I thought of something that might lift my old friend's spirits. I pulled into a parking space in front of the building, wondering if what I was about to do might be a stupid move. Mama Rae had thought a lot of Biscuit, and I never understood that, because he was not a sweet-natured animal.

I walked inside and went past the adorable puppies to the glass window showcasing the kittens. They were all so cute; little balls of fur. Some of them were chasing their tails, or playing with other kittens, and some were napping. I made myself focus on my mission—to find a kitten which closely resembled Biscuit. There were a few yellow ones, but I didn't see one that would do. Then, I spied him, or her, lolling on top of a fluffy cloth-covered box. The kitten was washing its face with perfect little white socks on its front paws.

I went to the counter to inquire about the kitten, but I had to wait until a customer paid the clerk.

"There's a particular kitten I'd like to see," I said. "Will you take it out so I can see if it's a male, or female?"

"Certainly. Follow me."

The clerk gently lifted the kitten out and checked its sex.

"It's a male," she said. "Would you like to hold him? He's just begun to purr."

I took the kitten from her, and I could feel a tiny vibration from its purr. The little creature felt weightless, cupped in my hands. I lifted it to feel its downy-soft fur against my neck.

"How do I know it's healthy?" I asked.

"I can give you a certificate stating that it is in good health. There's a money-back guarantee. These kittens are between eight and ten weeks old. They have been wormed and weaned. They have been thoroughly examined, and they have had their shots. Of course, they are not old enough to be spayed, or neutered."

I hadn't considered what a kitten might cost, and I didn't know anything about caring for a young kitten.

"I feel kind of silly asking this," I said, "but are kittens expensive?"

"This one is quite reasonably priced: it's not a purebred. He should make a nice house pet. This little guy would also be a good barn cat if you live in the country. My family had barn cats when I was a kid. My favorite kitten napped in my doll buggy."

The kitten was still purring, and it had begun to knead my palm with its tiny paws.

"I'll need instructions on caring for a kitten," I said. "I've never owned a pet. And I guess I'll need some sort of carrier."

I followed through with my plan, leaving the pet store with the kitten and everything it would need, including food. Loading it all into my Jeep, I hoped that I had come up with the perfect answer to cure Mama Rae's blues.

I drove to my parking spot and went into the dark coolness of the woods with the sleeping kitten. Mama Rae was going to be overjoyed at the sight of a baby Biscuit. I just knew it.

My knock on the door didn't produce a sound. At first, I thought my old friend might have been napping. Then, I saw her shuffling through the living room toward me. She looked at me through the mesh, but didn't invite me in. I held up the carrier.

"Mama Rae, I've brought you a present," I said, pleased with myself.

I turned the carrier so she could see what was inside.

"It's a kitten, and it's marked like Biscuit."

"Take it away, chile. Seem like sometin' happen to whatever I love. Can't be gettin' close to nothin' or nobody else."

She turned and made her way back to her bedroom, and I went down the steps and back through the woods, wondering what in the world had happened to my old friend to make her feel so down. My attempt to cheer her up seemed to have made her feel worse.

Now that my plan had failed, I was faced with another problem: what would I do with a little kitten? Should I take it back to the pet store, before it had a chance to learn that there were better homes than what it had known? I thought of taking it to Savannah to the Grover's, but Daniel and Catherine both worked. Even if they didn't, Suzanne was too small to have a pet. She would have to be taught how to treat a small animal. Pets were allowed in Hickory Cove, but Eleanor York was staying in the villa the rest of the week. I couldn't ask her to take care of the kitten until I could move in, and I didn't know if the Hyatt allowed pets.

Max Palmer was constantly interrupting my plans and asking me to do things I didn't want to do. I had always complied with his wishes. Maybe he would be willing to show his appreciation by letting me keep the kitten in one of the small rooms at his office for a few days. I could stop by several times each day to do whatever was necessary for my pet. Since he seemed to find me such a valuable assistant, I would simply ask for his help.

As it turned out, I didn't have to ask. I walked into the office with the carrier and placed it in front of my boss on his desk.

"Clemmie, I didn't expect to see you today," he said. "What have we here?"

He didn't wait for my answer. Instead, he opened the carrier door, reached in, and brought out the kitten. He cupped it in his big hands and brought it to his neck, stroking its fur with his thumb.

"Is this a gift for me?" he asked, smiling.

"Not exactly. I bought it for a friend, but she's been ill, and isn't up to taking care of it right now."

"I'll take care of it. I love cats."

"That's awfully kind of you. I have all of the kitten's supplies in my Jeep. I'll be right back."

Max Palmer didn't resemble any pet lover I had ever known. Being in his company was one surprise after another.

Back in my room I changed clothes and headed to the beach. The weather was perfect—not too warm, not too cool. It was just the place to clear my head, then go back to square one in the quest for a cure for Mama Rae's depression. It would be helpful if she would simply tell me what was bothering her, but such was not her way. She didn't have family, so it stood to reason that nobody close to her had passed away. She wasn't ill, or so she said.

I was running different scenarios through my mind, looking out to sea, and not paying attention to my surroundings when I was stopped cold. I nearly bounced off the hard chest of Clay Singleton.

He looked down at me and showed me his toothpaste ad smile.

"Hello, Clemmie. Lost in thought, are you?"

"I'm so sorry. Yes, I suppose I was. Listen, Clay, I want to apologize for what I'm sure you thought was my standing you up."

"No need to apologize. I got the message."

"No, you didn't. I didn't have a phone number or address for you. You're not listed in the directory. There was an emergency, and I had no way to reach you. That's why I left a note for you at the hotel desk, but the note wasn't adequate."

Clay Singleton simply looked at me, waiting for an explanation.

"You see, I've just gotten a job here on the island, and my boss is a very strange individual. I'm sort of his personal assistant, and my duties consist of everything from picking up his dry cleaning to accompanying him to dinner with clients."

Clay kept his poker face and continued to look at me, but he tossed me a bone by acknowledging what I had said with a small nod.

"My boss called me at the last minute and pretty much demanded that I accompany him to dinner that evening. He reminded me that it was one of my duties. I was afraid that if I didn't go I might lose my job."

"I see."

"Do you?"

Clay smiled, and I could tell that he had forgiven me.

"Oh, and I've found a place to live," I said.

I knew words were spewing out of my mouth like someone who was starved for conversation. I sounded like one of those ad people who was hired to push a product on television and had to speak as fast as possible to finish the script before time ran out.

"Whoa," Clay said, still smiling. "Why don't we try that get acquainted dinner again tonight. You can tell me all about your new life on the island then."

"I'd really like that. What time should I be ready?"

"How 'bout I meet you in the lobby of your hotel at six o'clock?

"I'll be ready."

I thought Clay might walk down the beach with me, but he continued in the direction he had been going when I ran into him.

Thoughts of Mama Rae were dimmed by the possibility of a relationship with this friendly handsome man. Nobody would ever replace my Jimmy, but he wasn't here, and he was never coming back. Just thinking about him made me feel uncommonly lonely. I had loved him with all my heart, and I knew that he had loved me just as much. He would want me to jump into my new life with both feet and be happy.

I walked all the way to the rock wall that separated the public and private beaches, then made my way back to the Hyatt and the room which had been the only home I had known since my arrival on the island. All of my earthly possessions were here in this room, and they could be packed into a suitcase in less than a half hour.

I took a long shower, wondering what kind of venue Clay Singleton might choose for our dinner date. He didn't impress me as the type who would pick a place like Stripes. I put on my prettiest sundress and a pair of sandals, knowing such an outfit could pass muster with most places on the island. I wished that I had a bottle of nice perfume, but I hadn't spent a cent on anything but what I considered bare necessities.

I had been so excited about this second chance date that I had gotten ready too early, so I opened the sliding glass door to my small balcony and sat in a recliner, letting a soft breeze ruffle my hair and caress my bare skin. This was a good place to relax and ponder the *what ifs*.

How would the conversation begin? Who would break the ice? Where would be a good starting point to tell one another about our lives; our likes and dislikes, our beliefs, who we were? Would we like one another at the end of the evening? Might this be the beginning of a lasting relationship? The more I thought about it, I decided to play it by ear and see what happens. I would simply be myself. If that didn't get the result I had hoped for, the relationship wasn't to be.

Minutes before six o'clock, I headed down to the lobby. My date was just coming through the front door of the hotel. We started walking toward one another, both of us smiling. At that point, I knew that whether or not a romantic relationship bloomed, I was going to be friends with Clay Singleton. Kindness and friendliness were written all over his face.

"Hey, Clemmie," he said. "You look like a magazine ad."

I assumed his remark was meant as a compliment, so I smiled and thanked him.

"You ready to rock and roll?" Clay asked.

"Sure," I said.

We walked outside, and Clay told me to stay put while he went to get our ride. Minutes later, a red Harley roared up from the parking lot. Clay brought the bike to a stop in front of me, grinning like a Cheshire cat.

"Hop on," he said.

I wasn't sure how to go about doing that wearing a dress, but I managed to tuck my skirt between my knees and get on behind him.

"Cool ride, huh?" he said.

"You're kind of full of surprises."

"Put your arms around my waist and enjoy the scenery," he said, kicking the motorcycle into gear and taking off down the incline.

Clay parked under the overhang of a tree, and we dismounted and walked through a sandy parking lot to an Italian restaurant, nestled in the trees. It was still bright outside, and inside the restaurant was dark in contrast. We walked past a long bar with its array of bottles, and through a maze of diners on the way to our table.

We were led to the back of the restaurant to a screened veranda which backed up to a copse of trees and posed a jungle-like atmosphere. The veranda was rustic—the kind of place that seemed to suit my date. We were seated in a corner where we had a bird's-eye view of nature. It was far enough away from other tables that we could carry on an intimate conversation.

A waiter came to take drink orders and produce menus.

"So, Clemmie Castlebrook, how 'bout a drink?" Clay said.

"I'll have a glass of the house chardonnay."

"Ginger Ale for me," he said.

Yet another surprise. I wondered whether he didn't imbibe at all, or maybe didn't drink because we were riding a motorcycle.

"I've never had a bad meal here," Clay said. "Everything's made from scratch, and it's all good."

"Might you have a recommendation?"

"Nope. You can't go wrong no matter what you order. Let's have our drinks and get acquainted a little bit before we order dinner."

"Okay. You start," I said.

"Sure. I'll begin with college. We can always go back to our childhood later."

"That's fine."

"I'm from Alabama, but I got my undergrad degree from LSU. Then, I took off for New York and got a JD at Columbia. As soon as I got it, I knew I didn't want to be a lawyer, so I came back down south and got an MFA from Mercer. I'm tryin' to be a writer. Your turn."

The waiter returned with our drinks and asked if we were ready to order dinner.

"Come back a little later, if you would," Clay said.

I took a sip of my wine and sighed.

"I don't have nearly the education that you do. My BA is from the University of Kentucky in Lexington. That's it. I'm certified to be a teacher, but that isn't what I want to do. The job I have now is brand new, and I don't know how long I'll do it. I accepted the position just for the salary."

"So you don't know what you want to do yet. That's not a crime. It'll probably hit you in the face when you least expect it. In the meantime, you're makin' money."

I was afraid he was going to dig deeper into my past, and I couldn't stand the thought of talking about my dead husband with him. It wouldn't seem right.

"So, you want to be a writer," I said. "Are you working on something right now?"

"I write some articles for the paper, and I'm workin' on a novel, but it's pretty slow goin'."

"I'm impressed. What's the book about?"

"I'm not sure yet. See, I don't use an outline. I like to let my characters take me places I might never have thought of goin'. I have part of the setting, but I'm not sure of the time frame. The story is gonna take place here on Hilton Head, but maybe not in the present."

"I don't want to be forward, but how do you make your living if you don't have a job?"

"I don't need a lot of money. My life's pretty simple. I live on my boat and drive my Harley. People like to go out on a boat for the day, or fish in deeper water. I have quite a bit of business, because my prices are fair."

The waiter returned, and neither of us had looked at a menu.

"We'll be ready to order in a couple of minutes," Clay told him.

We both ordered green salads and pasta; Clay wanted linguini with clams, and I chose fettuccine Alfredo. He had been correct about the food; it was all delicious.

Twilight had fallen as we lingered over cups of espresso, tiptoeing into one another's past. Crickets and tree frogs had begun their nightly concert, and I was totally relaxed in the company of Clay Singleton after having downed two glasses of wine and sipping a cognac with my coffee.

Clay held my hand as we left the restaurant and made our way through the sandy parking lot. He didn't have to remind me to hold on tight during the ride back to the Hyatt. At the elevator, he took my face in his hands and kissed me on the forehead.

CHAPTER
Eleven

*J*had never had such a hard time getting to sleep. Clay Singleton had given me a mere peck on my forehead instead of a proper goodnight kiss. It was barely more than a polite handshake. I wondered how it would feel to have his lips on mine; to be held in his arms. I also wondered if I would compare him to my lost love. Would I feel that I was being unfaithful to my Jimmy? I know it's unreasonable to have such feelings. Jimmy's gone, and I realize that I must try to be happy in my new life. But what do I know about Clay Singleton? Not much. He is one gorgeous, highly educated hunk, but he doesn't seem to know what he wants to do when he grows up. It amazes me that after all the places he's lived and gone to school that he has hung onto that strung-out southern, backwoods accent and all of those folksy little sayings from the sticks. How had he expressed the enjoyment he gets from living on his boat? I believe he said, "It makes me happier than a mule eatin' briars."

I had certainly enjoyed the evening, but there was no reason to lie awake, thinking about a relationship which might have come to its end with that peck on the forehead. Clay hadn't mentioned anything about another date.

Having slept very little the night before, I didn't feel refreshed when my alarm signaled it was time to get ready for work. I guessed at what might be appropriate attire for the day, and chose lightweight slacks and a crisp white shirt.

Max Palmer was on the phone with both feet on his desk when I arrived. I paced around the office, waiting for him to finish his call. When he finally hung up, he heaved a sigh as though he were exasperated about something. He looked up at me without his usual early morning smile and said, "You want breakfast?"

"No, thank you. I want to see the kitten. Is he okay?"

"Of course, he's okay. He's a late sleeper; still sawing logs."

"I really appreciate your taking care of him for a few days. Is he much trouble?"

"No trouble at all. He has a healthy appetite, and loves to listen to television while kneading my chest. He's smart, too. He knows to let me know when he wants to go to his litter box. He didn't stir when I put his carrier in my car to drive here."

"You took him home with you?"

"Clemmie, I wasn't going to leave him here all alone."

"But you had to haul his things home and back here this morning?"

"My dear, you must think you're working for an idiot. I picked up a few things for the house on the way home. The only things I had to transport were the kitten and the carrier."

"Oh. What do I owe you for the things you bought for the cat?"

My boss sighed. "You don't owe me anything, but you might feel that I owe you more than a day's pay when I tell you what your assignment is."

I raised an eyebrow.

"That was Pearl on the phone a few minutes ago. It seems there are a few items she needs from a couple of shops in Savannah."

"I don't understand why you're telling me this."

"I have commitments here on the island, and I can't drive her. Since I don't have anything pressing for you to do, I thought you might find it in the goodness of your heart to take her shopping. I'm sure it won't take more than a few hours."

The idea that my boss wanted me to chauffeur Pearl around on a shopping spree didn't sit well with me.

"Mister Palmer, I had the distinct impression that Pearl didn't like me. I understand that you wanted her to meet me, but she didn't seem to be very happy about it."

"Look, Clemmie, I realize you might not be fond of this assignment, but you did sign on to handle unspecified tasks such as this. It's part of your job. Pearl depends on me to assist her now and then, and without going into detail, I will tell you that I owe her that much. As I said, I can't leave the island today. I would if I could. Just consider this an errand I'm asking you to run as a normal part of your duties."

"But I can't fit a wheelchair into my jeep."

"Not a problem. I have a van with a lift for the wheelchair. All you'll have to do is push a button."

"Who's going to tell Pearl that I'll be the one to drive her and assist with the shopping?"

"I'll call her right now and tell her the arrangements we've made."

If I hadn't just signed a contract to stay in Eleanor York's villa, and if I didn't need this great salary, I would tell Max Palmer to find someone else to honor his strange requests. But that's a lot of ifs. Once again, I couldn't imagine what strange sort of relationship he and Pearl had. What kind of power could this old woman have, and how was she connected to Mama Rae? Maybe this day wouldn't be a total loss after all. Perhaps I would be able to learn a few things by spending time with this overbearing woman who seemed to have such a tight hold on my boss.

Without being invited, I took the seat in front of Max Palmer's desk while he called Pearl.

"All right, Pearl. I'll send Gretchen with the van to pick you up. Clemmie will be ready to take you to Savannah. I'm sure you'll both have a wonderful time."

I wondered how much he paid Gretchen. It seemed that she was a chef, bartender, and now a part-time chauffeur. She looked like a teenager. How did she become so accomplished at such varied positions? And why wasn't she the person driving Pearl to Savannah?

"Are you sure you wouldn't care for a light breakfast, Clemmie? I have fresh fruit and yogurt in the mini fridge."

"I'm sure, thank you. May I see the kitten now?"

"I'll give him his breakfast and let him take a trip to his litter box. Then, you can play with him until Pearl gets here."

I didn't particularly like the way he was making all the rules about the kitten. He was simply taking care of it until I had a home for it.

When Max brought the kitten to me, it was purring loudly. He held the little ball of fur next to his neck with care.

"Here you are, Clemmie. Enjoy."

Max pulled a piece of yarn and a tiny fake mouse from his pocket and placed them on his desk.

"These are his favorite toys," he said.

I played with the kitten until Gretchen came through the front door and pranced across the room toward me, holding out the key to the van.

"Want me to show you how the lift works?" she asked.

"Sure," I said, thinking that I could no doubt figure it out without her perky help.

I turned the kitten over to Max and followed her out to the van where Pearl sat in her wheelchair, applying lipstick before a magnifying mirror which was attached to the ceiling of the vehicle.

Gretchen went about the business of showing me the ropes while Pearl studiously ignored both of us.

"That's all there is to it," Gretchen said, smiling.

"Thank you. I'm sure I'll be able to manage."

93

She turned and wiggled her way to the building, and I climbed into the driver's seat.

"Good morning, Pearl," I said, trying to sound cheerful.

"Oh, hello there," she said as if she had just taken notice of me.

"I understand you're in the mood for a shopping spree," I said.

"You understand correctly. I only wish to go to three specific shops, and I know exactly what I wish to purchase. I'll give you directions when we get into town."

I put the big behemoth into drive, and we headed for the city. Pearl didn't seem to be in a chatty mood, so we were silent until we got to the city limits where she began spouting directions. She didn't miss a beat, and I drove to the first specialty shop without a hitch.

"Let the valet take care of the van," she said. "He can push my chair into the shop, and you can take over from there if I should need help."

Inside the shop I waited for Pearl to give me instructions. Since I didn't know what she wanted to buy and I didn't know the store, she would have to direct me.

"Look around and amuse yourself while I shop. I can manage until my arms get tired," she said, motioning me away from her as if she were shooing me out of her sight.

I could have stayed in this particular shop forever. Never had I seen so many gorgeous things: jewelry, handbags, scarves, and all sorts of accessories.

It didn't take Pearl long to find what she wanted and purchase it. She held a decorative bag containing her purchase on her lap and wheeled herself to where she found me gazing wistfully at a green Hermes scarf.

"It's stunning, isn't it?" she said, startling me.

"Yes, it certainly is," I answered. "I'll bet it has an equally stunning price tag."

Pearl pulled the valet ticket from her purse and handed it to me.

"Take this out to the valet, and send him inside to get me," she said. "I want to look at one more item."

I took the ticket and left the shop, thinking this overbearing woman must be used to getting whatever she wanted whenever she wanted it. It made me wonder what her childhood had been like. She must have inherited her haughty attitude from one of her parents, or maybe she had been mistreated, or ignored as a child.

The valet brought the van, turning it over to me while he went inside to collect Pearl. He came around to the driver's side of the vehicle, opened the door, and pushed a button to lower the lift. Pearl handed him a bill after she was settled, and a huge smile expressed his gratitude. Pearl was obviously a big tipper.

Then, we were off to shop some more. Pearl's instructions were the same each place we went. She preferred to shop without my assistance, and she made her purchases quickly. She took a bit more time at the last place we stopped. It was a jewelry store, and its array of expensive merchandise sparkled through the plate glass window.

Pearl had the valet push her wheelchair into the shop, asking me to stay with the van. She held a small package on her lap when she returned.

"I'm famished, Clemmie," Pearl said. "Let's go to lunch."

"Where to?" I asked.

She gave directions to the restaurant she had in mind and told me where to park.

"You'll have to try your skills with the lift and pushing me to the restaurant," she said.

I had no trouble with the lift. Pearl sat tall in her wheelchair and pointed in the direction she wanted me to push her. We crossed a street and stopped at the end of a long line of people, waiting to enter the restaurant. I was sure I must have misunderstood Pearl. With her temperament, there was no way she would be willing to wait in any kind of line, let alone one this long. I was about to question her about it when the line began to move forward.

"Leave me here and go to the front of the line," she said. "Let the person at the door know I'm here."

Was she serious? Did everyone in the States of South Carolina and Georgia know Pearl? Did she have some sort of hold on everyone she knew? Regardless of how ridiculous the situation seemed to me, I left my spot and walked around the long line to the front.

"Excuse me," I said, "I'm here with Pearl."

I felt inordinately stupid; I didn't know her last name.

The gentleman holding the door smiled, showing every tooth in his mouth. He held up a finger, telling me to wait while he summoned someone else to hold the door. Then, he followed me to the back of the line where Pearl waited, smiling at a horse-drawn carriage. He lifted Pearl's bejeweled hand, brushing a light kiss over her diamonds.

"I'll take you to your table now, Ms. Pearl," he said.

I followed, dumbfounded.

At the door, two gentlemen helped Pearl out of her wheelchair and into a dining chair. The wheelchair was whisked away, and Pearl was borne to a private table set for two. The other tables seated at least ten people, and the food was brought to the table family style. Waiters brought individual dishes to our table and served us, coming back several times with more choices than anyone could possibly consume. Everything was delicious and homemade.

"I hope you're enjoying your lunch," Pearl said, attacking the fried chicken.

"Everything is delicious."

I had intended to pay for my lunch, but after dessert, Pearl raised a hand, and with the slightest movement, summoned our waiter.

"Put it on my account, Malcomb," she instructed.

Without asking for further assistance, her highness somehow managed to conjure the two gentlemen who had carried her to our table. They whisked her away and deposited her in the wheelchair at the door.

I had made up my mind that I was going to get some information about Pearl's relationship with Mama Rae. So during the drive back onto the island, I brooched the subject. It wasn't exactly an easy topic to bring up in casual conversation.

"I'm really enjoying being back on Hilton Head," I said.

"It is lovely, isn't it?"

I didn't know how I was going to dig into the treasure trove of Pearl's past, or how I was going to pull Mama Rae into the picture, but I was determined to ask some questions whether she chose to answer them or not.

"I've always considered this island a modern day Garden of Eden, and there are so many interesting people who have chosen to make this their home."

I had the sense that Pearl was on the verge of opening up to me about something, but I wasn't sure what it might be.

"I'll never leave the island," she said. "I came here with my late husband several years before he left me for a better place. Although I'm enjoying my life here, I'm more than ready to join him at any time."

I didn't know how to respond to that, so I didn't say anything.

"He died of a massive heart attack shortly after he decided he had made all the money he could ever want. Plus, he had tired of the money game he played."

"I see," I said, but I didn't.

She had successfully led me away from my search for the information I wanted and left me in an awkward position to ask further questions. Pearl seemed to be something of a fox, extremely crafty.

CHAPTER
Twelve

My day chauffeuring Pearl all over Savannah had been just that. I had thought I might be able to learn something about her relationship with Mama Rae from casual conversation, but she had been too shrewd for me. Obsessing over my old friend's connection to Pearl was getting me nowhere. I needed to push that to a back burner and think about getting settled in my new home. Eleanor York would be moving out of the villa in a couple of days.

I hadn't heard from Daniel, and Catherine hadn't seemed very anxious to talk with me the last time I called. Daniel was my best friend, and I had been asking him to help me with lots of small things. I had never thought twice about calling him as often as I liked, but maybe that hadn't gone over too well with Catherine. After all, he was her husband. For some reason, I felt the need to connect with someone who cared about me, but I wouldn't call the Grover residence. I would wait for one of them to call me.

I parked my Jeep on the familiar sandy patch and stepped into the cool inner sanctum. When I was a child, this dark secret place had seemed magical to me. I still felt its welcoming solitude allowing me to enter a place where few trod. As a ten-year old, I had felt very small in the midst of the tall pines and the unfamiliar sounds of the woods' strange and beautiful creatures. But now, I felt a bit jaded as I walked through the trees, and I was amazed that this property hadn't been developed.

I climbed the cabin's porch steps and knocked on the door.

"Mama Rae, it's me, Clemmie."

She had to be at home; I smelled a wonderful aroma coming from the kitchen, so I called again. There was no answer. I was about to let myself in when I heard heavy footsteps coming toward me.

"Hey, Clemmie," Daniel said, opening the door for me to enter.

"Daniel, what a surprise!" I said. "How have you been? How are Catherine and Suzanne?"

"Why do you seem so nervous, Clemmie? Everyone's fine."

"I'm not nervous. Is Mama Rae okay?"

"I think she's getting a little hard of hearing. Come on into the kitchen."

Mama Rae looked up from her fruit cobbler and swallowed.

"Been a while since you been aroun' to see your Mama Rae," she groused.

"I was here just a couple of days ago. Don't you remember? I brought a little kitten to show you."

"Oh, yes," she said.

"Where's the kitten?" Daniel asked.

"Mama Rae told me she didn't want it, so I have it," I told him.

"Dis old woman not able to take care of a pet," Mama Rae said.

That wasn't the reason she had given me, but I let it drop.

Daniel cleared his throat. "Since we're all here together, I'll tell you both at the same time," he said, changing the subject.

Mama Rae and I sent him questioning looks.

"I've been made a job offer I can't afford to turn down. It pays more than twice what I'm making at my present job. The only trouble is that it isn't in Savannah; it's in Atlanta. I won't be able to come home but about once a month, because I'll have to work some weekends."

"What about your family?" I asked.

"Catherine and I have talked this to death," he said. "Suzanne's happy in her nursery school and day care, and it's convenient for Catherine to drop her off and pick her up each day. Our apartment is only a ten minute walk to both buildings. Catherine is as excited about this opportunity as I am."

"Money not everting," Mama Ray said.

"You're right," Daniel admitted, "but it'll be a step toward engineering school for me, and Catherine's all for it."

"Well, I guess congratulations are in order," I said. "When do you report for work?"

"In a couple of weeks. I've already given my boss notice. He's a nice guy; wished me luck."

"Now, we both have something new to look forward to," I said. "I'll be moving into my new digs in a couple of days. I've signed a lease on a villa in Hickory Cove. It's nicely furnished, and the woman who owns it has given me a good rate."

Mama Rae hadn't said another word. She got up from the table and shuffled out of the kitchen and down the hall toward her bedroom, leaving Daniel and me to rinse the dishes. I knew she was upset at Daniel's news. It seemed that with all of her mysterious powers, it was impossible to keep him tethered to Hilton Head.

I had introduced Daniel to Mama Rae when he and I were teenagers, and they had bonded immediately. Then, Roy's bigoted secretary, Addie Jo Simmons, had dogged Daniel constantly until he couldn't take it anymore. He fled the island. He and Mama Rae hadn't been reunited until after I was released from Still Waters Mental Hospital in Louisville, Kentucky. Then, the two of us, along with Daniel's wife and baby girl, had trudged through the woods to Mama Rae's cabin for a homecoming. Now, he was leaving again, and I was afraid I wouldn't be enough for her. I didn't know Mama

Rae's age. She had seemed old to me when we first met. Now, she seemed awfully frail to me, and terribly sad.

Daniel told me he probably wouldn't see me again before he left for Atlanta. There were quite a few things he needed to do before he left town. Catherine was perfectly capable of holding down her job and taking care of Suzanne, but Daniel wanted to make sure all the last minute preparations were made before he left his family to fend for themselves.

Mama Rae wasn't the only one who was feeling a bit lonely. Since I had been back on the island, Daniel and I hadn't spent time together on a daily basis, but most of the time, he had been just a phone call away if I needed him. Now, that security blanket would be gone.

Clay Singleton was roaming around the lobby when I returned to my hotel. He flashed a brilliant smile at me as I came through the door.

"Clay, I wasn't expecting you," I said.

"You busy?" he asked.

"Well, no."

"Good. Let's go for a ride on my Red Devil."

"Red Devil?"

He laughed. "That's what I named my bike. Everything ought to have a name."

I had on shorts, so I was better dressed for a motorcycle ride this time.

"Where are you taking me?"

"That depends. Do you have dinner plans?"

"Not at the moment," I said, wondering if I had a message from Max Palmer.

"Want to just take off to no place in particular; let the wind ruffle our hair; get a few bugs in our teeth?"

This man was a real romantic. I wasn't sure why I was so drawn to him, but I couldn't deny that I was.

"Sure," I said. "That sounds like fun."

It was late afternoon, and I was settled on the Harley with my arms around Clay Singleton and my body squeezed close to his. Heat from his muscular back warmed my breasts and midriff as we eased into light rush hour traffic. Clay maneuvered the bike down the main drag, around part of a traffic circle, and down Pope Avenue to a point where traffic wasn't a factor. Then, he made the Red Devil fly. I never gave our safety a second thought. For some reason, I trusted this near stranger completely, not simply because he seemed so good and kind, but because he appeared awfully adept at handling a motorcycle. It never occurred to me that if the cycle skidded in gravel on the road's shoulder that I might be maimed for life.

We went to a small ice cream parlor on a side street among the live oaks and licked cones of melting double dips before they dripped onto our clothes.

"Can you stand somethin' a little touristy?" Clay asked.

"Sure. I haven't been back on the island very long. I'm sure there are new touristy things I haven't seen."

It was late afternoon when we stopped at the gate of Sea Pines Plantation. Clay paid the fee to enter Harbourtown and told the guard he didn't need a map or directions. The bike didn't take up much room, and we parked under a small tree. Clay grabbed my hand and led me to the marina to view all the wealth on the water. As we strolled around the marina, he eyed the array of yachts with admiration. I didn't have the heart to tell him that I'd had cocktails and dinner on one of them not long ago. I didn't see Pearl's yacht right away, and I couldn't remember where it was moored. But, just as we were leaving to look around to see what else Harbourtown had to offer, I spotted the blue script: *Pearl.*

We visited several souvenir shops, and Clay bought his little niece a pink tee shirt with *Sunshine* stenciled across the front. He offered to buy me any trinket I might want, but I'm not much of a trinket person. Tourists were milling around, stopping for a cold drink or snack at outdoor venues.

"I assume you've been here before," Clay said. "I mean, before you left the island."

"My adoptive father brought me here a couple of times, but that was a long time ago."

"Was there a man singing under that big tree, or do you remember?"

"I don't recall."

"Well, he plays his guitar and sings after dark. He's done it for years I understand. I've heard him; he's pretty good."

"I don't remember what time of day it was when Roy and I visited this area. It must have been during the day, because I don't remember seeing anyone serenading tourists from under that big tree."

Clay reached for my hand again.

"Time for some she crab soup and a great seafood dinner," he said. "Are you up for that?"

"Sounds wonderful. I've only tasted she crab soup once. I don't recall the restaurant, but it was here on Hilton Head."

We entered a restaurant which looked like it was filled to capacity, but we only had to wait a couple of minutes to be seated.

This was my second meal with Clay, and I noticed that he opted for a glass of sweet tea in lieu of alcohol. I wondered if he might be an alcoholic, but tried to banish that thought. Alcohol had killed Roy whom I had dearly loved, and I certainly didn't want to get involved with anyone else who might get caught in its cruel web.

Clay's tea and my glass of chardonnay arrived, and he touched his glass to mine.

"To a spectacular friendship," he said.

Ours was hardly a friendship, or a relationship of any kind. We barely knew one another. I wondered if a friendship was all he wanted from me, but refused to let myself dwell on it.

"Guess what?" I said, as though we were old friends.

"What?"

"I'll be leaving the Hyatt to move into my new place the day after tomorrow. I've leased a Hickory Cove villa in Palmetto Dunes."

"That's great. I'm happy for you. Mmm, how will I get in touch with you? Do you have a phone number at the villa?"

"As a matter of fact, I do. I'll give it to you. How about you?" I said. "Is there a number where I can reach you?"

"There's no phone on my boat, but my sister takes messages for me. I'll give you her number. I see her every day."

He and his sister must have an awfully close relationship, I thought.

The meal was delicious, and the she crab soup was so good that I thought I would come back to the restaurant just for another cup.

The southern sky had turned deep purple by the time we got on the Red Devil to go back to the Hyatt. By the time we rolled up in front of the hotel, it was full dark except for the stars sneaking through the tall pines. Clay parked past the valet stand out of the way and told the doorman he would be right back to claim it.

We went to the desk and asked for paper and pen to exchange phone numbers. Then, Clay walked me to the elevator where he looked around the lobby to make sure we were alone before pulling me close to deliver a proper goodnight kiss with plenty of heat.

I went to my room, savoring the feel of his soft lips on mine, and had a feeling that I would sleep well.

I must have failed to set an alarm, because the next morning I awoke to the boisterous ringing of the phone.

"Good morning, Clemmie," Max Palmer said.

I looked at the clock on the bedside table and saw that it was nine o'clock.

"Good morning. Oh, Mister Palmer, I'm very sorry. I've overslept."

Max Palmer laughed. "So it would seem. I've always been of the opinion that if a person oversleeps, the body needs rest."

"I can be at the office in a half hour," I said, getting out of bed.

"You don't need to rush, and don't eat breakfast at the hotel.

104

I'll have it delivered here so we can go over today's assignments. I'll see you in a bit."

I gave my morning ablutions short shrift. My shower could wait until after work, so I made myself as presentable as possible in record time and headed to the office.

Max was sitting at his desk when I arrived. Covered breakfast trays had been delivered. I didn't mind that I had missed Miss Perky prancing into the office in her short shorts. Hanging my purse on a coat tree in the corner, I hurried over to the desk. My boss didn't bother with a greeting, but lifted the lids from our trays, displaying fluffy omelets, toast, and fruit.

"Coffee?" he asked.

"Yes, please. Again, Mister Palmer, I do apologize for oversleeping. That's highly unusual for me."

"Calm down, Clemmie. Relax and enjoy your breakfast. The reason I called your hotel was to make sure you were all right. You're usually here early."

I felt relief at what he had just said. It was important that I have a steady income after signing a fairly long-term lease. I took a sip of coffee, and went to work on my omelet. Max had said this would be a breakfast meeting, but we weren't having a discussion. I had taken a couple of bites, and when I looked up, his plate was clean. He was leaning back in his chair, hugging his coffee mug. He hadn't said anything to get my attention, so I took another few bites.

"Clemmie, I have to be out of the office for most of the day. I would like for you to stay here, answer the phone, and take care of the kitten while I'm gone. Do you think you can handle that?"

"Of course, but aren't there other things you would like me to do? I can type and file."

"No, nothing like that. I'm sure there'll be quite a few phone calls. Take messages and phone numbers. Tell callers you're not sure when I'll be back. I don't think there will be any unexpected visitors, but if there are, invite them to leave a message."

Max went down the hall and returned with the kitten and its

carrier. He set the carrier on the floor beside his desk. Then, he went back to get the food and water dishes.

"I put the litter box just around the corner in the hall," he said. "I have to leave in a few minutes. Gretchen will be over to pick up the breakfast trays shortly."

I could tell this was going to be another strenuous day. I was charged with answering a few phone calls and playing with a kitten.

Gretchen came to pick up the breakfast trays just after my boss left the office.

"When you're ready to place your lunch order, just press button number three on this phone," she said. "There's a menu in the top right desk drawer."

I thanked her, and she picked up the large tray, swinging her ponytail from side to side as she exited the room.

I stared at the phone, willing it to ring. If I didn't have a more demanding assignment than this, my brain would turn to mush. I played with the kitten until it ran out of gas and curled up for a nap on my lap. I looked in the desk drawers to see if I could find something to read; there was nothing but the menu Gretchen had mentioned. Pulling out a yellow pad and a pen, I began making a list of supplies I would need to buy before moving into the villa.

The phone rang, and it nearly startled me.

"Max Palmer's office," I said, in my most professional voice.

"No, I'm afraid I'm not familiar with that transaction, but I'll be happy to have Mister Palmer call you when he returns to the office."

I was taking down the caller's name and number when Clay pushed in through the glass door. I had given him the office address the night before, but I hadn't expected him to show up unannounced. He ambled toward me, looking sort of baffled.

"This looks more like a basketball court than an office," he said. "It's huge ... and empty."

"Strange, huh?" I said.

Clay nodded, scanning the big room.

"So is my boss," I whispered.

For all I knew, Max Palmer had his office bugged so he could hear what went on when he wasn't there.

"You're probably wonderin' why I'm here," Clay said. "Well, wonder no more. I came to ask if you'd like to accompany me to my sister's house for dinner tonight. She's a great cook, and I want you to meet one another. Whadda you say?"

I knew I should tell him I already had plans, because it seemed he might be taking me for granted. He had shown up at my hotel yesterday without calling. And here he was again, coming to my place of work unannounced. This was not the way to begin a relationship.

"I'd love to, Clay."

CHAPTER
Thirteen

Clay's sister greeted us wearing a faded pair of cutoffs and a warm smile.

"Please come in," she said. "Clemmie, I'm Sarah Briggs. Grace and I have been dying to meet you."

Clay and I had barely stepped into the foyer when pint-sized Grace dashed toward us with a smile that matched her mother's. The child held her arms up to me for a hug, and I bent to oblige.

"You're Cwemmie, and I'm Gwace."

"I'm happy to meet you, Grace." I smiled.

The formalities out of the way, Grace reached for a hug from Clay. He scooped his niece off the floor with one arm, keeping the other behind him.

"Whatcha got behind you, Uncca Cway?" she asked.

"You don't miss much, do you, kiddo?" he said. "You know you have to guess."

"A wabbit?"

"Nope. Not a rabbit. I'll give you a hint. It's somethin' to wear."

"Hair wibbons," she said.

"Nope, but that was a good guess."

Clay put Grace down and handed her the bag containing the tee shirt.

"Here you go, short stuff," he said.

Grace pulled the shirt from the bag and held it up to her chest.

"I wuv it!" she said, and threw her chubby arms around his leg.

"Dinner's almost ready," Sarah said. "Would either of you care for a drink?"

I would have enjoyed a glass of wine before dinner, but I was reluctant to ask for it. I had never seen Clay consume alcohol, and for all I knew, his sister might also be a teetotaler.

"Nothing for me, thanks," I said.

"Got a pitcher of sweet tea made?" Clay asked.

"Of course. Clemmie, are you sure you wouldn't care for something?"

"I'm sure. Thanks."

Minutes later, Sarah led us into her kitchen.

"I'm afraid this is going to be very informal," she explained. "My dining room table is being refinished. I'm hoping to get it back in a few days."

"Something smells wonderful," I said.

"I hope you'll like it," Sarah said. "It's just a seafood casserole I threw together."

"I want to sit beside Cwemmie," Grace announced.

"All right, but you must remember to mind your manners," Sarah said, settling her daughter into her booster seat.

Grace's dinner consisted of a blob of macaroni and cheese along with a hot dog cut into bite size pieces. She sat quietly, holding out her small hands for Clay and me to hold.

"God is gweat; God is good, and we thank Him for this food. Amen."

Sarah brought the casserole, a green salad, and a baguette to the table. Then, she returned with a pitcher to fill our glasses with sweet tea.

Grace sat patiently, waiting for her mother to take the first bite, before she dug into her dinner. She took care, using a salad fork to spear bites of hot dog and scoop up small amounts of macaroni and cheese.

"How long have you lived on Hilton Head, Sarah?" I asked.

"I've been here for six years," she said. "Grace was born here, so she's always been an island girl."

"I wuv the beach," Grace put in.

"I do, too, Grace," I said. "I grew up here on the island, and the beach has always been one of my favorite places."

"Clemmie's about to move into a villa in Palmetto Dunes Resort," Clay said.

"Palmetto Dunes is lovely," Sarah said. "My late husband and I used to play golf at all three of the courses in that resort. The Robert Trent Jones course was my favorite."

"My villa is in Hickory Cove. It's on the eighteenth hole of the Jones course," I said.

"Scoos me," Grace said, looking directly at me. "We don't have a husband. Our husband is in heaven, so Uncca Cway is our pwetend husband. We're a fambily."

I was already in love with this little girl, and her remark reinforced it. The lump in my throat kept me from uttering something inane. I hadn't a clue what an appropriate response might have been, so I smiled.

"I'm gonna help Clemmie move into her villa," Clay said, changing the subject.

That was the first I had heard about his helping me.

"I won't need much assistance," I said. "There's no heavy lifting. I don't have anything to move except my clothes."

"If I know anything about the fairer sex, you'll have a shoppin' list longer than my arm to stock the villa. I'll be happy to give you a hand," he said.

The remainder of the meal was polite conversation peppered with a few three-year-old observations. Then, Sarah served her homemade raspberry cheesecake and coffee.

I offered to help with the dishes, but our hostess wouldn't hear of it.

"Cleanup won't take more than ten minutes," she said.

"I know it's about Grace's bedtime," Clay said. "I think we should go. Clemmie has a busy day tomorrow with the move and all."

"I understand," Sarah said, lifting her daughter out of her booster seat.

Grace had been rubbing her eyes with tiny fists for the last few minutes.

Clay and I both stood to tell her goodnight, and Sarah carried her to me first. Grace took my face in her small hands.

"Goodnight, Cwemmie. You're so pwetty."

"Thank you, Grace. You're beautiful." I smiled.

Clay grabbed his niece and delivered a very loud kiss to her cheek.

"Goodnight, short stuff. Don't let the bedbugs bite," he said.

"Night, night," said a sleepy Grace.

"Thanks for a great dinner, sis," Clay said. "We'll let ourselves out."

Clay walked me to the elevator when we got back to the Hyatt.

"Do you really want to help me move my stuff?" I asked. "You were right; I've already picked up a few things, and I have to do more shopping."

I didn't recall telling him the exact day I planned to move, but I must have, since he mentioned it to his sister.

"I sure do," he said. "Besides, I want to see your new place."

When he was sure we didn't have an audience, Clay pulled me into an embrace to die for and claimed my lips with his. He pulled back for just a second, then did a repeat that was even better. He still held my hand as he backed away from me.

"What time should I be here in the mornin'?" he asked.

"How about nine o'clock? I like to sleep in whenever the opportunity presents itself."

"See you then. I might even take you to breakfast."

I went to my room, feeling something I hadn't felt in a very long time. I couldn't seem to come up with a name for it. Clay was letting me know that I was protected and cared for. He was welcoming me into his world, his family. He made me feel safe as I began my new life. Even though I knew very little about him, I somehow knew that he was trustworthy and kind. The extent of our intimacy had been no more than a few kisses, but it was slowly filling a hole in my empty life.

This was the first time I had gone to bed without missing my Jimmy's arms around me. Maybe he was letting me know that he was at peace, and he was urging me to get on with my life. He couldn't be with me, but he wanted me to be happy again.

I didn't wake in the middle of the night with a soggy pillow, and I didn't have the horrible recurring nightmare, seeing my love when the morgue physician pulled the sheet back from his face for me to identify him. If I dreamed, I didn't remember it. I slept soundly, and I was fully rested when I awoke before the alarm sounded.

I had already packed most of my clothes, and it didn't take me long to shower and dress. My shopping bags of supplies for the villa sat by the door, and I was packing cosmetics into my overnight bag when the phone rang.

"Hello."

"Good morning, Ms. Castlebrook. You have a guest here at the front desk, a Mister Singleton. May I send him to your room?"

"Yes. Send him right up. Thank you."

Clay showed up, wearing his moving clothes: shorts, an old tee shirt, and sneakers. He favored me with that special smile and rushed into the room, crushing me in a bear hug. Then, he noticed my packed luggage and shopping bags.

"Is this all of it?" he asked.

"Yep. You're looking at all of my worldly possessions."

"I can't believe this is all you have. We don't need a bellhop. I can carry most of it. What time do you have to check out?"

"Eleven o'clock. Why?"

"I had someplace special in mind to take you for breakfast, but I don't think we could be back before eleven."

"I'm sure the hotel has some space to hold baggage. Let's take it downstairs and ask."

The Hyatt was very accommodating, and agreed to put my baggage in storage until I returned.

Clay and I hopped on his motorcycle and headed toward the Sea Pines Circle to Palmetto Bay Road. We turned right on Arrow Road, then left on Helmsman Way. The road ended at a marina. We parked the bike, and climbed the few steps to the open-air dining area of the Palmetto Bay Sunrise Café.

When we were seated, Clay asked me if it would be all right for him to order for me. I had always considered that a rather chauvinistic thing for a male to do. But Clay had asked, so I figured he had a good reason.

"That's fine," I said. "Am I to assume that you have some delectable surprise in mind?"

"Yes ma'am. I believe you'll think it's delicious, and I'd be willin' to bet you've never tasted this. Actually, this is my friend Stu's specialty. He's the owner. I had to call ahead to see if he'd make it happen this mornin'."

We were sipping coffee and juice when our food arrived. I looked down at my large oval plate and couldn't believe my eyes.

"Looks good," Clay said, smiling. "Wait'll you take a bite. Your taste buds are about to go to heaven. This is a Kentucky Hot Brown."

"It smells delicious," I said, not bothering to tell him that I had experienced this epicurean delight more than once, the most recent having been in the Still Waters Mental Hospital cafeteria.

"Dig in," Clay said.

The dish was familiar, much like my previous encounters with it, but with a hint of dry white wine.

"This is a real treat," I said, meaning every word.

If Clay and I were going to have more than a friendly relationship, I would have to think seriously about when, where, and how I would tell him the whole truth about my past. A serious relationship is built on trust, first and foremost.

After breakfast we went back to the hotel to load everything I owned into my Jeep and take it to my new home.

I unlocked the front door, and we entered the foyer to see the message light on the phone blinking. We put down our burdens, and I pressed the button to listen to the message. Eleanor York's lovely southern voice was welcoming me to my new home. She told me that she had stocked the refrigerator and pantry with a few essentials she thought I might need so I wouldn't have to hurry to the Piggly Wiggly on moving day. What a wonderful southern belle she was.

"This place is great," Clay said, as he roamed from room to room.

He took the steps two at a time to take a look at the upstairs rooms. I followed him, hoping my heart wouldn't start to race as we stepped into the bedroom overlooking the eighteenth hole of the golf course. This was the room where Jimmy and I had danced and made love. We had even made love outside the sliding glass doors on the small balcony above the deck. Clay had opened the doors and stepped outside, and I made myself join him. I had to will my mind to stay in the present.

"I just realized this villa has three bedrooms. What are you gonna do with all this space?" he asked.

"Who knows?" I said, attempting to sound nonchalant. "I just fell in love with it the minute the realtor showed it to me."

"You're in a perfect location," he said. "I'll bet it's not a five minute walk to the beach. And you're within spittin' distance from the Jones clubhouse and the tennis courts."

Clay was sounding awfully excited about my villa. He practically flew back down the stairs to check out the lower deck.

"Hey, look at this grill. It's practically new. How about I go get us some jumbo shrimp to grill for dinner tonight?"

"That sounds like fun," I said. "Let's look in the fridge to see if we might have the makings of a salad. I'll unpack while you make a grocery store run. We'll need some good crusty bread, too."

Clay shopped for our dinner while I put away my clothes and added the things I had bought to the stash Eleanor York had left. I couldn't help but wonder if this thing with him was going too fast. He had certainly been persistent in his pursuit of me. And he had even taken me to a casual dinner at his sister's home. The little niece was a definite drawing card; he had to know that. Meeting the family is the sort of thing people who are serious do before taking a much bigger step. Had I jumped into this relationship without questioning anything about it? Was I that desperate to have a man in my life? I might have to back off and mull this situation over a bit more.

Clay was whistling when he came in with the groceries. He seemed perfectly at home as he put things away in my kitchen. I wondered if he thought he would automatically become a part of my life simply because he was going to cook my dinner on my grill and serve it in my dining area.

After putting everything away, including a bottle of French chardonnay, he found a colander and a deveining tool and started cleaning the shrimp. He appeared to be very practiced at the job, and it wasn't long before he had a colander of cleaned jumbo shrimp rinsed and gleaming, just asking to be grilled. He held one up for my inspection.

"This guy meet with your approval, pretty girl?" he asked, smiling.

If he would just stop advertising those perfect teeth, it would be a lot easier for me to back up a step or two in this whirlwind relationship. But he was so handsome, and something about that smile was so compelling that it was hard to resist. It made him look like the sexiest man alive and at the same time, about twelve years old.

Clay dumped the shrimp into a bowl, covered it with foil, and refrigerated it.

"Where would you like to go for lunch?" he asked.

I hadn't given lunch a thought.

"Let's just go to the diner for a snack. Then, I can drive you to the Hyatt to get your bike."

"Good idea. I haven't checked in with my sister today. She might have a whole stack of messages for me."

We were nearly finished with lunch when the sky darkened. Seconds later, jagged white lightning split the darkness and was followed by a loud clap of thunder. Clay dashed from the diner to put the bonnet on my Jeep and returned with wet clothes glued to his body. His hair was pasted to his head, and he hurried to the men's room to try drying himself.

This man smiled at everything, I thought. He still looked like something which had been washed ashore when he returned to our booth, but it didn't seem to dampen his spirits.

"Might as well get comfortable," he said. "These early afternoon showers could take a couple of hours, or they could be gone in the next minute."

I was ready to lay my cards on the table, because I wanted to be honest with Clay Singleton. It would be very wrong to lead him on without his knowing about my past. Having had amnesia was not something to be ashamed of. And if the relationship was to go any further, he deserved to know what I had endured to cause it. If my past caused him to drop me like a pariah, our relationship wasn't meant to be.

"Clay, do you remember our first dinner—our get acquainted dinner?"

"Sure. Why?"

"You were leading the discussion, and you wanted to begin with our college years. You said that we could always backtrack. Remember?"

"I guess that's right."

"Well, we never did—backtrack, that is."

"I'm guessin' there's somethin' pretty important you want to tell me."

"Actually, there's a lot. I assume there are things you'd like to tell me as well."

"The rain's let up. Let's go get my bike. Seems like there's some straight talk comin' up for our dinner conversation tonight."

CHAPTER
Fourteen

Clay Singleton was about to become an important part of my life, unless he chose to cut me loose after hearing the whole truth about my past. I was looking forward to our evening together, but I was also apprehensive. He wasn't due back at the villa until six o'clock. I had plenty of time to visit Mama Rae, tell her that I had met someone I was beginning to care for, and admit that I hadn't had the courage to be totally honest with him. She would know how I should proceed. Mama Rae had always known the best route for me to take, and she had never been reluctant to dish out her sage advice.

I knocked on the screen door frame.

"Mama Rae, it's me, Clemmie."

"I know who it is."

"May I come in?"

"Come to de kitchen."

I found her funneling dried bits of leaves into a small jar. She didn't look up from her work when I entered the room.

"How are you, Mama Rae?"

"Like usual."

I pulled a chair from under the table and sat down, and Mama Rae screwed a top on the jar. Then, she took a seat across from me. This was the first time I had ever been in this kitchen without being offered something to eat or drink.

"What on dat mind of yours?" she asked.

"I moved into a villa in Palmetto Dunes Resort today. I'm officially back on the island, and I'm ready to put down roots. This is where I want to make my home."

I looked at my old friend, and for the first time since I came back to Hilton Head, I saw a gleam in her dark eyes. That gleam was the first thing I noticed about her when we met in the woods many years ago. I couldn't help wondering what had changed since the last time I saw her—what had put that gleam back?

"Dat good," she said. "What else?"

It always amazed me that she could look at me and know that I hadn't said what I came to tell her.

"I've met someone. He seems to care for me quite a bit, and the feeling is mutual."

"Uh huh."

"Things are going kind of fast. I don't know much about him, and I haven't told him much about my past."

"Why dat?"

"I can't seem to bring myself to tell him that I spent time in a mental hospital. It's too embarrassing. I know it shouldn't be, but it is. Nobody can fully understand the pain I went through from the time I was a child until my husband was killed. I guess I had suffered so much by then that Jimmy's death was the last straw; it broke me. I didn't get amnesia intentionally—block out four years of my life. Those years with my precious husband were the best of my entire life."

"Life not always fair, chile. Ever rose got thorns."

"I know that. It's just that sometimes I feel so alone. That's why I come to you with all of my problems. I depend on your friendship and advice. You've never steered me wrong."

"Whew! Dat soun' like a compliment."

"It is. I know you're going to advise me to tell him the truth, but I don't know how to begin, and I don't know how much detail he needs to know."

Mama Rae scooted her chair back from the table and went to her old fashioned refrigerator.

"How 'bout a glass of lemonade?" she said.

"That sounds good."

She filled two tall glasses and brought them to the table. I could see slices of lemon floating through the glass, and it reminded me of the lemonade Daniel's mother had brought to our back porch on Tybee Island when she came to introduce herself to Mama and me. I took a sip.

"This is delicious, Mama Rae."

My old friend smacked her lips.

"Not bad," she said.

"Things are moving pretty fast, Mama Rae. He helped me move my belongings into the villa this morning, and he's coming back at six o'clock to grill shrimp for our dinner. He kind of invited himself."

"Tell me what you know 'bout dis young man."

I sighed, not knowing where to begin.

"He's highly educated, has a law degree and a couple of others. He lives here on Hilton Head on a boat in Shelter Cove. I think he's probably the friendliest person I've ever met, and he's awfully persistent. He writes for The Island Packet, and he's in the process of writing a novel. His sister and her little girl live on the island, too."

"Dis young man rich? I don't 'speck writin' for de paper pay much."

"He's not rich, but he does have other income besides writing for the paper. He takes people out on his boat to fish in the deep water and charges a fee for doing it. I don't know if those are his only sources of income."

"Why he so important to you?"

"I haven't spent much time with him, but I really enjoy his company. He's kind, seems trustworthy, has a great sense of humor, and he's down-to-earth. And to top that off, he's awfully good looking and has a smile that knocks me out."

"Sound like you 'bout ready to set your trap."

"I guess I do seem kind of excited about him. He takes my mind off my past when we're together. I think he's filling a void I've felt since Jimmy died, but we certainly haven't become intimate; just a couple of kisses."

"Uh huh."

"He took me to his sister's house for dinner last night. She and her little girl were delightful. His sister is a widow. I wasn't told how, or when her husband died, but it couldn't have been very long ago, because the little girl is only three."

"He sound safe 'nuff from what you've told me, and it plain to see you innerested in him. Bes' ting to do be to begin at de beginnin' and tell it all jes' like it happen."

"If he's still interested in pursuing a relationship with me after I tell him everything, do you think you might want to meet him?"

"Never can tell," Mama Rae said.

She pushed her chair back, got up, and shuffled from the room. The gleam in her eyes might have returned, but her personality certainly hadn't changed. I rinsed our glasses and put them in the sink. My old friend had gone to her room and closed the door. I assumed she had dismissed me to ruminate on our conversation.

As I wove my way through the woods, I wondered if a person as elderly as Mama Rae could identify with the feelings and desires of someone my age. Had my old friend ever been in love? Had she ever felt the ache of wanting sexual fulfillment? Could she understand my need for more than casual friendships?

Clay rang the tinny doorbell of my villa, and I hurried to admit him. Just the sight of him gave me a little thrill each time we met. I knew he had been around and had experienced much more than I, but there was something so boyish about him that was ever so endearing. He had changed into a pair of khaki pants and a navy golf shirt which somehow made his gray eyes appear blue.

I wanted to get right to the point with Clay. He needed to know about my past if we were to be anything more than friends. It wasn't going to be easy for me to bare my soul, standing in the foyer with his arms around me and those incredible eyes looking into mine, letting me know that he was about to deliver another of those hot kisses. I was already feeling that strange sensation deep in my belly. I pulled away from his embrace and made myself smile. He dropped his arms to his sides, and looked disappointed—maybe hurt. I took his hand and led him into the living room.

"I need to talk to you," I said, sitting at one end of the couch and indicating that he should sit at the other.

"This sounds serious."

"It is. Well, I mean it was. You need to know all about my past if you're going to understand me. I want you to know where I came from and what I've been through. You need to hear what I have to say in order to decide whether or not you want to pursue a relationship with me."

I imagined all sorts of expressions on his handsome face: curiosity, disappointment, or maybe anger, but Clay showed no emotion. He let me know he was there to listen to what I had to say.

"I'm not asking for sympathy, but I would like to have your acceptance. If you can't give me that, I'll understand. I've been in some awfully dark places."

"Tell me everything."

I followed the path Mama Rae had told me to take, starting at the beginning.

"I was born in Chicago. My father died when I was three years old. My mother and I lived pretty much from hand-to-mouth until I was ten. That's when we met Roy Hubbard, an insurance salesman who fell in love with my mother, married her, and we became a family. Roy adopted me shortly after that. We moved to

Tybee Island and lived there until a huge storm devastated the small island, and we moved to Hilton Head."

"So you've been here since you were ten. Did you and your family fall in love with the island immediately?"

"Yes, but traumatic things happened after we moved here. My mother was pregnant. She and I were crossing a road, carrying produce from a fruit and vegetable stand. A car came around a curve too fast and hit my mother, killing her. I escaped unscathed. My adoptive father was beside himself. He started drinking heavily; trying to hide the fact from me. Neither my mother nor I had known he was an alcoholic. He had kept it from us, telling us that he was going to business meetings in Savannah one night each week. After Mama was killed, that one night turned into four, or five. Roy was going to alcoholics anonymous meetings."

I wiped at the tears tracking down my cheeks with the back of my hand.

"Clemmie, you don't have to tell me things that make you hurt," Clay said.

"Yes, I do. I want to get it all out in the open. I'll give you the short version, okay?"

Clay nodded.

"Roy and I stumbled through several months, trying to live one day at a time as normally as possible, but we were both acting."

Clay sat at his end of the couch, eyes looking at me expectantly, waiting for the next secret I was about to tell him.

"Some of the pain subsided, and we seemed to be getting back close to normal, but it didn't last. Roy fell off the wagon and his life began its downward spiral."

My crying had miraculously ceased.

"I lost my beloved Roy to alcoholism. He was found dead, lying on the floor of our home. The doctors said he met his demise by a snakebite wound. There were fang marks on his neck. I didn't buy that, but what difference did it make?"

"How old were you when all this happened?" Clay asked.

"I was a seventeen-year-old bride. I don't have it in me to give you all the details right now, except to tell you that Jimmy Castlebrook and I fell in love and eloped."

Clay had an expression of wonderment on his handsome face. What was there for him to say?

"Was it after Roy's demise that you and your husband left the island?" he asked.

"Yes. We lived in Atlanta for a while before moving to Lexington, Kentucky where we went to school. We were so very happy. Then, one night the bubble burst abruptly: my young husband was killed in an accident. His car stalled on the railroad tracks, and the train was unable to stop."

Clay left his seat at the end of the couch and came to embrace me.

"I'm so very sorry. It's unimaginable what you've been through," he said in a near whisper.

I could tell that he was feeling my pain by the way he held me and stroked my hair.

"I'm not finished," I said against his chest.

Clay backed away just enough to look at me. I liked that he always looked at me when I spoke, even when I was joking.

"I've never been able to remember my husband's funeral. Selective amnesia, they called it. I spent some time in a mental hospital before coming here. I had a good psychiatrist and other wonderful, caring people in that facility to help me get back on track. I'm well. Now, I'm through."

Clay pulled me to him and held me close, gently rocking me. Then, he began kissing my sticky face all over.

"Please don't ever be afraid to tell me anything. I think you're remarkable, and I admire your honesty. You didn't have to tell me about any of the pain you've endured. I don't know if I can ever be deservin' of you."

"Does that mean you're not going to dump me?"

"Not on your tintype."

"I'm afraid I've ruined our happy evening," I said.

"You haven't done any such thing, but I'll bet you could use a glass of wine about now."

"That would be nice."

I wanted to find out why he never consumed alcohol, but I assumed that if he wanted me to know, he would have told me.

Clay went to the kitchen, uncorked the wine, and brought me a goblet.

"This is a very nice wine," he said. "Try it and give me your opinion."

I took a sip. It was lovely.

"It's really nice, Clay. Thank you."

"Go ahead and ask," he said. "It's no secret."

I gave him a questioning look, raising an eyebrow.

"I never drink when I'm plannin' to drive, but if a certain miss would invite me to spend the night on her couch, I'd be more than happy to join her in a glass."

I didn't have to think about that for a second. This man was a saint.

"The couch is all yours. Pour yourself a glass of wine, and tell me some of your deep, dark secrets."

Clay went to the kitchen and returned with his wine. He lifted his glass to touch mine and made a toast.

"Here's to a beautiful new relationship. May it deepen and thrive."

"That was lovely, Clay. Now, let me in on your past. I know very little about you."

"Ahem. My childhood was devoid of any drama that I can remember. Sarah and I were always pretty close. She's a couple of years older than I am, and she never let me forget it when we were kids. We lived a sheltered life in a small Alabama town with parents who spoiled us, but made us live by a few rules. Nothin' traumatic ever happened to anyone in our family until just a few years ago."

I sipped my wine and didn't interrupt, realizing that if Clay had asked a lot of questions while I was disclosing my past, I never would have been able to tell him everything I had been keeping from him.

"Sarah went away to college, fell in love, and married Morgan Briggs, a great guy. He was a commercial pilot. I know this is gonna seem strange, but I kind of felt lost without my sister. After she left, I turned into kind of a badass almost grown kid. I got into the beer scene with some guys, drove like a bat, and dated some girls I wouldn't have wanted my parents to meet. But that phase didn't last long enough to do much damage. Thing was, after I graduated high school, I didn't know what I wanted to do. I've told you all the things I tried—all the different schools I attended. Then, finally it just hit me: I wanted to be a writer."

"You're practicing what you preach," I said. "That's what you told me to do. 'No rush,' you said. 'Stay in this well-paying job until you know what you want to do.'"

Clay nodded and smiled.

"I moved to Atlanta and landed a job writin' human interest stories for The Atlanta Journal. It didn't pay a lot, but I figured that was because I was a newbie, writin' a column a lot of people wouldn't bother readin'."

Clay took a drink of his wine, put his glass on the coffee table, and faced me with his hands clasped in his lap.

"Sarah called. She wanted me to come to Hilton Head for her birthday. She said she had a big surprise for me. I'd been missin' her tellin' me what to do and how to do it, so I drove down for the weekend. It was summertime, and the island was runnin' over with tourists. The three of us had dinner at a nice restaurant where Sarah let me in on her surprise: she was pregnant. We had just left the restaurant and were pullin' onto the main drag when a car came barrelin' toward us, smashin' into the driver's side of the car. Morgan was drivin'. He was killed instantly. Sarah was knocked unconscious, and I was just a little shook up. The driver of the other car was drunk; he didn't have a scratch."

"Oh, Clay, I'm so sorry. How horrible for Sarah."

"Sarah's a trooper, all right. She's doin' a great job with Grace. It breaks my heart that our little Gracie never got to meet her dad."

"Sarah is lovely, and Grace is adorable. Thank you for introducing me to your family."

"So, Sarah and I made a pact: neither of us would have a drop of alcohol before gettin' behind the wheel of anything that was capable of movin'."

"Do I get to ask questions?"

"Sure. I'm pretty much an open book."

"Have you been married?"

Clay smiled.

"Nope. I thought about it once, but it just didn't feel right. I'm kind of old fashioned. In my mind, people shouldn't get married unless they love one another. Lot of my friends have been married and divorced two or three times."

"I hate to ask you this, but is there anything else I should know about you?"

"Nothin' comes to mind. You want to back out on the couch thing? If you do, I'm not havin' any more wine."

"No, I'm not backing out on the offer. You can have all the wine you like."

CHAPTER
Fifteen

I awoke to the sounds of noisy birds. Sitting up and taking in my surroundings from a king-size bed, I realized that I had spent my first night in the villa I now called home. I had chosen the large upstairs bedroom overlooking the golf course—the one Jimmy and I had favored. I hadn't set an alarm, but it was early, only 6:30. The aroma of coffee wafted up the stairs. I pulled on a robe and went downstairs to find a note on the kitchen counter. There was no sign that Clay Singleton had ever been there, except a note written on a paper towel. I picked it up and read it: *Thanks for the sleepover. The couch was very comfortable. I like your new home.* Well, that was short and sweet, but it might have been what I deserved.

There was a partial bottle of cognac sitting on the counter beside the toaster, and two brandy snifters were in the sink. I remembered the two of us having dinner by candlelight and finishing a bottle of wine, and I recalled that we sat on the couch, talking after we loaded the dishwasher. But I couldn't remember what we talked about. I had no idea when, or where we obtained the cognac, and I didn't remember drinking it. I couldn't recall going up to bed, leaving Clay to sleep on the couch with no linens. I had a bad feeling I might never see him again.

I poured a cup of coffee. It was strong, just the way I liked it. My head didn't hurt, but I thought it was pretty amazing that I didn't have a hangover. I tried to jog my memory about the previous evening, but I couldn't remember anything, except sitting on the couch with Clay. What might have been an intimate evening with the most gorgeous hunk on the planet was lost. I had wasted the opportunity.

It was the weekend, and I was all alone in my new home. I tried to make myself believe the best—that Clay had left quietly so as not to wake me; that he was out on the water with a group of fishermen, making money. I had another cup of coffee while scribbling a shopping list. There were a few more things I wanted to purchase for the villa, and I needed groceries. I should cook most of my meals instead of eating out so often. Eating in was much less expensive, and I could make healthy meals at home.

I showered and dressed. Then, I went on a mini shopping spree, buying table linens, sheets, and towels. I needed a few groceries, so I stopped at the Piggly Wiggly. It was running over with shoppers. I had forgotten that Saturday was moving day for vacationers leaving the island and coming onto it. The locals never went grocery shopping after noon on Saturdays, because that was the first place vacationers stopped before heading to their rental units.

I bought a few canned items, several frozen dinners, small amounts of meats to freeze, and some fresh produce. And just in case I got down in the dumps, a quart of ice cream. Then, I drove back to the villa to put it all away, wondering if there would be a message on my phone from Clay Singleton. I unlocked the door and stepped inside, eager to see the phone's blinking light on the table in the foyer, but there was none.

I felt so alone that I almost hoped Max Palmer would call and request my presence at dinner. Daniel was already in Atlanta, and

I was hesitant to call Catherine since I hadn't felt any warmth from her the last time we talked. I didn't want to visit Mama Rae when I was feeling less than cheerful, so I did what it seemed I usually did when I was in need of a reality check—I put on shorts and flip-flops and headed for the beach.

This was the first time I had walked to the beach from my villa, but it was easy to navigate. I went out my front door and through the small parking lot. Then, I turned right and passed a bank of mailboxes. Just ahead was Mooring Buoy. I crossed it, and I was on the short path to the beach. I went to the top of the wooden footbridge and stopped to take in the awesome wonder before me—the sparkling Atlantic. I never tired of taking in its beauty and grandeur.

I breathed in a lovely dose of salty sea air and descended the steps. Then, tossing my flip-flops behind the bottom step, I began walking in the direction of the Hyatt Hotel. Doctor Fitzpatrick, my former shrink, had cautioned me not to allow myself to slip into denial about my past, or anything else. So I forced myself to admit that I was hoping to run into Clay pounding the hard-packed sand close to the Hyatt.

The water was still warm as it slid over my bare feet on this September afternoon. I loved the way it felt, like liquid silk. It was so soothing that I nearly forgot how miserable I was. I knew I was falling hard for a man I hardly knew, and it was probably all for naught. Why had I agreed to that first dinner? Why had I told a stranger my awful past? I had been sucked in.

I did an about face and hurried back to get my flip-flops. Then, I went to my villa to shower and do something proactive to get out of my slump. I had seen an electronics store on one of my cruises around the island, and I decided to visit it and buy a television. I needed to be amused. Surely, I would be able to find something entertaining to watch and take my mind off Clay Singleton.

Most of the people who worked in the store were young, and they were all men. Several of them seemed to swarm toward me as I walked through the door.

"What can I do for you today?" said the one in front.

"I want to buy a TV. Could I see what's on sale?"

"Certainly. Follow me."

He led me to the back wall where he presented an array of choices. I told him my price range before I allowed him to waste his time elaborating on the attributes of the most expensive sets. He seemed pretty honest, only showing me three which were within my range. I chose the mid-priced one.

"Before I buy the set, I need to know if you deliver and install," I said.

"That's not the store's policy, but it might be possible. What's the address?" he asked.

As it turned out, Hickory Cove was pretty convenient for him. He lived in Leamington in Palmetto Dunes. It was almost closing time, and the manager allowed him to leave early and follow me to my villa.

Eleanor York had taken the TV, but left an inexpensive stand, and there was a hookup. The young man hooked up the TV, and I was all set. But all set for what? To force down a frozen dinner, then watch something inane on my new toy? That's what I would do, but not before I hopped into my Jeep to drive to the closest liquor store for a bottle of wine.

After dining alone and downing a glass of cabernet, I retired to my living room and my TV to relax with the remainder of the wine. And there I was—the perfect couch potato. I wondered if this would be the life I had let myself in for by moving back to the island. It was a far cry from what I had envisioned.

When I awoke, the birds were at it again, and the eighteenth hole of the golf course was a verdant green, illuminated by brilliant sunshine. The Lord's day had come on strong, and it took me back to the Sunday mornings Roy had tickled my feet to awaken me, telling me to get a move on so we could go make a joyful noise. He was taking me to church. Mama would approve.

I remembered the morning I had tried to play hooky, because

I knew a lecture from Roy was imminent. He knew I had spent the night with Jimmy. He tried to soften the blow by taking me out to lunch after church. But he delivered the message he felt was his duty: If you play with fire, you'll get burned. But that hadn't happened. I had been one of the lucky few, marrying the love of my life.

I had slept in my clothes on the couch Clay Singleton had vacated that very morning. There was a half bottle of wine on the coffee table surrounded by several wadded-up Kleenex. I had forgotten that I had cried myself to sleep, looking at the test pattern on the TV.

I put on a pot of coffee. Then, I went upstairs and took a long shower. A cup of strong coffee made me feel more alive. I poured a second cup and took it upstairs to put on a bit of makeup and don my Sunday best.

The island events channel on my TV listed the churches and service times. There was a nondenominational one which looked interesting, and I had plenty of time for a quick breakfast before the service. I drank juice and ate a bowl of cereal, feeling rather pious. I was going to get my life on the right track one way or another.

I had intended to slip into a pew in the back of the sanctuary so I wouldn't be noticed. The thing I disliked about attending a new church was the fact that all of the members paid attention to a new face. Everyone wanted to greet you and shake your hand. Most churches even passed a visitor information booklet the way collection plates were passed. I didn't escape any of that, because there were no empty seats in the back.

Immediately following the morning announcements, the greeting session began. Several smiling church family members focused on me, their hands outstretched to greet me and welcome me to their worship service. Then, a collection plate was passed along with the inevitable guest booklet. I dropped a ten dollar bill into the plate just in time to receive the guest booklet from an elderly lady on my left. I filled in my name and address and handed it to a gentleman who stood in the aisle, waiting to collect it. I wondered if I would answer my door the next week to see a small church welcoming committee.

Then, it was time to stand and sing a congregational hymn. A small ensemble made up of a keyboard, guitar, and bass appeared at the front of the church. This was not the kind of religious music I was accustomed to. The musicians struck up a lively tune, and lyrics appeared on two big screens high on each side of the pulpit. I didn't know the song, but found that since the words were in plain sight and the melody was easy to follow, I was able to sing along. *This is the day the Lord hath made, let us rejoice and be glad in it.* I found it to be rather uplifting.

The sermon turned out to be the same tenor; not exactly the sort of thing some popular televangelists proclaimed, but it made me glad that I had decided to attend a house of worship on this beautiful Sunday.

At the end of the service, I made my way to the back of the church. I shook hands with the minister who stood at the open door.

He smiled and said, "We're glad to have you. Come back again."

I didn't think that called for a response, so I just smiled and nodded. Then, I headed for my Jeep. As I was opening the door, I happened to look toward the church. I wasn't imagining things. An usher was pushing Pearl's wheelchair down a ramp by the front steps. He pushed the chair across the parking lot to turn his charge over to Gretchen, the short shorts queen. Gretchen parked Pearl by the van, pushed the lift button, and stowed her highness inside and out of sight. Then, she climbed into the van and drove away.

I went home and changed into playclothes to loll around my villa, doing nothing. I ate a sandwich, then watched an old movie, wondering what had happened to my good mood. My religious high hadn't lasted very long. I had never been one to sit around and watch the grass grow, so I decided to try to appear upbeat and visit Mama Rae.

I found her strolling around her front yard with her herb basket on her arm, but it didn't contain herbs. She was scattering colorful blossoms as she walked, and she didn't seem to notice me as I stepped into the clearing.

"Hello, Mama Rae," I said.

My old friend was wearing her hot pink floppy hat and her big sunglasses. She had on a long floral skirt and a silky white blouse with flowing sleeves. She pushed the glasses up on her nose and looked up to offer a little smile.

"Those blossoms are beautiful. Where did you find them?" I asked.

"In de woods."

I could tell that this was going to be another of those short, one-sided conversations.

"I was feeling kind of lonely, so I decided to come see you," I said.

She nodded and continued scattering blossoms. I walked along beside her.

"I went to church this morning," I said.

"It hot. Les have a cold drink," she said.

I followed her up the porch steps and into her cabin where she took off her hat and glasses, leaving them and her basket on a table just inside the door. We went into the kitchen, and Mama Rae poured two tall glasses of some sort of fruit concoction. She motioned for me to sit in my usual place at her small table. I took a sip; then another.

"This is delicious, Mama Rae. I've never tasted anything like it. Is it fruit punch? Did you blend it?" I couldn't seem to stop firing questions at her.

Mama Rae stared at me for a few seconds, then smiled.

"It jes juice from whatever I had lef over after bakin' tarts."

I took another drink and swirled it around in my mouth. Then, I downed the rest of the glass.

"Could I please have a little more?"

Mama Rae shook her head and smiled.

"It pretty rich and beginnin' to ferment. Too much make you sick."

"Oh."

My senses seemed heightened. For the first time since I arrived at Mama Rae's, I noticed the gorgeous brooch at the throat of her blouse. It was shaped like a peacock and studded with vivid blue and green gemstones.

"Mama Rae, your brooch is beautiful. I've never seen you wear it before. Is it new?"

"What you do with dat cat?" she asked.

I knew she wasn't going to answer my question. This was the second time she had abruptly changed the subject since I arrived.

"My boss is taking care of it until I get settled in my villa."

"I want it."

My old friend was in a much better mood than she had been the last time I saw her. She hadn't wanted the kitten, and I had been almost dreading the responsibility of caring for it.

I was feeling downright giddy by the time I left Mama Rae. My spirits had definitely been lifted. I didn't feel like going home, so I drove to the outlet mall to window shop and ended up with several bags of things I didn't really need.

As I drove across the bridge on my way home, I looked out at the marsh and smiled. This was definitely going to be my home, man or no man. I would take one day at a time and see what fate had to offer. Taking in the sights and sounds of the low country was enough for me on this fine day.

The first thing on my agenda for tomorrow would be to tell Max Palmer I was ready to take the kitten off his hands. I wasn't sure how he would feel about parting company with his furry friend, but Mama Rae had first dibs.

The message light was blinking when I opened my front door. I dropped my packages and pushed the button to see who had left a message.

"Good afternoon, Clemmie. Max Palmer here. Please give me a call when you receive this message. Thanks."

I hoped he wasn't about to ruin my day now that Mama Rae, or her concoction, had pulled me out of the doldrums. I was once again reminded that I had no doubt my old friend had some sort of an edge on the rest of us human beings. I punched in Max Palmer's number, thinking it was strange that he would be in his office on a Sunday.

"Max Palmer," he huffed, as if he were extremely busy or in a hurry.

After I identified myself, his tone seemed to calm; to sound relieved.

"Clemmie, thank you for returning my call. I find that I'm in need of your services this evening. I hope you don't already have plans."

"I'm free, Mister Palmer. What would you like for me to do?"

"I would like for you to accompany me to dinner. I'm afraid I can't give you much time to dress for the occasion, because the reservation is for seven o'clock. It's nearly five now, and the restaurant is in Savannah."

I would not allow myself to ask what the dress code might be. If my boss didn't have the common courtesy to offer that information, he couldn't complain about what I decided to wear. There was not time to put away my purchases. I took a quick shower and shampooed my hair, then put on one of my two best dresses. If Max Palmer didn't stop issuing these last minute dinner invitations, which were actually command performances, I would have to invest more money in appropriate dinner attire. I had given him my new address, and he was familiar with the area, so I was sure he would have no trouble finding my villa. He seemed to have permanent access to everything inside Palmetto Dunes. He had told me I wouldn't need to call in a pass for him. For some reason, I felt a bit uneasy about letting him into my villa. I met him at the door as soon as he rang the bell. He smiled at me.

"This is a nice area," he said. "I think you'll like living here."

"Thank you. I like being close to the beach. It's only a five-minute walk from here."

My boss and I made small talk on the way to Savannah. That was something we rarely did. I brought up the subject of the kitten, and his reaction was close to what I had expected.

"I'll be sorry to give up the little guy," he said. "I've kind of grown attached to him."

"I want to thank you for taking such good care of the kitten, but I did get him for my friend, and she's feeling much better. She lives alone and needs a companion."

"I understand. I'll bring all of his things to the office in the morning."

Max drove up to the valet stand in front of a swanky restaurant. A tall, skinny young man opened my door to help me out of the car, and my boss came around to take my elbow to escort me inside. We were led to our table by the maitre d'.

"What a lovely room," I said, after we were seated.

Max hadn't given me any instructions concerning my alcohol consumption for this particular meal, so I assumed I would be allowed to have a glass of wine when cocktail orders were taken.

"If you'll excuse me, I'll go powder my nose," I said. "Would you please order me a glass of a dry chardonnay?"

"I can do that."

I was just coming out of a stall when I heard someone say that she was so sorry about something. The voice was familiar, but I couldn't place it. A young woman was dabbing at the front of her blouse with a towel and muttering to herself as I washed my hands. I dried my hands and gave myself a quick once-over in the mirror, then opened the restroom door to see a tall slender woman walking into a different dining room of the restaurant. From the back, she looked exactly like Catherine. She had the same gait, the same little sway, same haircut, and same figure. But it couldn't be Catherine. Daniel was in Atlanta, and Catherine wouldn't leave Suzanne with a baby sitter and go out to dinner at a ritzy restaurant. She'd had a hard time leaving Suzanne in daycare while she was at work.

I went back to join Max Palmer. He was sipping a cocktail, and a glass of wine awaited me. Max got up and pulled out my chair. I sat and took a sip of chardonnay.

"Does this wine meet with your approval?" he asked.

"I'm sorry?"

"How do you like the wine?"

"Oh, it's lovely. Thank you."

CHAPTER
Sixteen

I was thoroughly confused. Dinner in Savannah with my boss was not what I had expected. First of all, I had assumed it would be a business dinner with someone Max Palmer was courting to make some kind of deal. Ralph Wingate came to mind. But nobody else appeared to have been invited. My boss and I dined alone. He seemed overly attentive, and I found it easy to converse with him. I couldn't imagine why he would make a reservation in Savannah just to take me to dinner. He did nothing untoward the entire evening, showing himself to be a perfect gentleman.

The second thing that caught me off guard was recognizing Daniel's wife's voice after she had left the ladies' room, and knowing beyond a doubt that it was Catherine I saw walking into a different dining room at the restaurant. I'm not sure what I would have done if she and her dining companion had been seated in the same room with Max Palmer and me. I was in a quandary as to whether or not I should mention it to Daniel the next time I saw him. It could have been perfectly innocent. Maybe Catherine had found a reliable baby sitter and had finally decided to enjoy a girls' night out with a friend. I didn't want to think ill of Catherine, but the whole scenario gave me an uneasy feeling.

I went to work the next morning wondering why my boss had taken me to dine alone with him. Surely, he intended to keep our relationship strictly one of a business nature. If that turned out not to be the case, I would simply have to resign and give up my cushy job and good salary. Then, I would be pounding the pavement to land another job that would pay my rent.

"Good morning, Clemmie," Max said. "Let's have a cup of coffee while I tell you what's coming up. By the way, the kitten is asleep in his carrier and his things are in a box."

"Thank you for taking care of him."

"I think you should take him to your friend after he has breakfast and tends to his morning business. I'm not going to tell him goodbye."

"I'm sorry you became attached to him, Mister Palmer. I had no idea this would happen."

"Don't think a thing about it. I'm an adult; I'll get over it soon enough."

I heard someone singing off key from a back room. Then, Gretchen appeared with a tray containing coffee and pastries.

"Good morning, Mister Palmer," she chirped. "Clemmie."

Gretchen placed the tray on the desk, turned, and twisted out of the room.

"We have a special assignment beginning this evening, Clemmie," Max said.

"All right. I won't make any personal plans."

"This assignment will require our spending the night on the yacht with some very important people who will arrive late this afternoon to board the yacht. I'll let them in on my business proposal during the cocktail party to give them time to mull it over. No need to overdress this evening, because there won't be a dinner; just cocktails and hors d' oeuvres. Something simple, but tasteful, will be fine."

I swallowed a bite of pastry.

"We'll enjoy a day out on the water tomorrow, so you might want to bring a swimsuit for sunbathing."

"May I ask what I'll be required to do?"

My boss smiled.

"Your only requirement will be to simply be your lovely, charming self. You'll just be spending a little bit of time on a yacht while being surrounded by very rich, hopefully enjoyable people."

I didn't feel the least bit comfortable with this assignment.

"We'll return to the island late tomorrow afternoon. My guests will be staying at the Hyatt. You and I will host a dinner at Stripes tomorrow evening. I've reserved a private dining room. Oh, you'll need a cocktail dress."

I was given the day off. If I thought too much about the upcoming assignment, I might overthink it and quit my job prematurely.

I parked my Jeep and toted the kitten through the trees in his carrier. Mama Rae was sitting on her little front porch, seeming to admire her surroundings. She didn't rise when I hauled the carrier up the two porch steps, but she smiled by way of a greeting.

"Open dat cage, and let me hold my kitten," she said.

"It isn't a cage, Mama Rae. It's a carrier. It's also where he sleeps. He likes it."

"Harumph! Nothin' like to be locked up."

I opened the carrier and brought the kitten out. I was holding it in my arms very gently. Mama Rae reached out and took the kitten by the nape of its neck, pulled it to her chest, and smiled. The kitten put a small paw on each side of her neck, started purring, and began to knead her neck.

"I'll go back and get his box of toys and food," I said.

When I returned with the box, Mama Rae was sitting on the bottom porch step, watching the kitten bat at a butterfly in her patch of lawn. It stood on its hind legs.

"See how he like his freedom," she said. "Watch him run after de butterfly and jump in de air with his back arched. He havin' fun."

"How will you keep him from running away into the woods? He isn't used to being outside."

"He do jes' fine," she said, as she looked at the contents of the box. "He won't be needin' much of dis store-bought food. Mama Rae gonna cook for him and teach him how to hunt."

"I know you'll take good care of him, Mama Rae," I said, hoping my gift wouldn't end up a predator's lunch. "I can't stay to visit, because I have to go shopping for a cocktail dress. My boss is asking me to accompany him on a yacht and then to a fancy dinner with a bunch of rich strangers."

"Want to know de kitten's name?" she asked, changing the subject.

"Sure."

"Lord."

"Lord?"

"He gonna be lord of de woods."

I left my old friend, hoping the kitten would still be alive and well the next time I visited. Then, I drove to the diner to grab a quick bite, before heading to Savannah to shop.

I had just been seated when I saw Sarah and Gracie come into the diner. I waved and motioned for them to come and join me.

It was clear to me that Sarah had taught her young daughter not to run inside, because Grace was taking something akin to giant steps as she came toward my booth. She was all smiles.

"Hi, Cwemmie," she said, opening her chubby arms for a hug.

She climbed up into the booth beside me and snuggled close. Sarah and a wait person followed her to the booth, and a booster seat was put in place for Grace.

"We're happy to see you, Clemmie," Sarah said. "How have you been? Are you keeping my brother in line? I haven't heard from him for a couple of days."

"I've been fine, but I have to tell you that I'm not keeping your brother in line, because I haven't seen him either. He must be taking fishermen out on the water, making tons of money."

"I doubt that," Sarah said. "That wouldn't keep him from getting in touch with me to get his messages. Whatever he's up to must be pretty important. I can't think of anything that could keep him from seeing Grace each day."

"If he happens to show up, would you please let him know that I'll be off the island on business for a couple of days?"

"Sure, I'll tell him. I take it you and Clay are enjoying one another's company, and I'm glad. I want my brother to be happy and stop spending every minute to make sure Grace and I are okay."

I didn't know why I had requested that she deliver such a message to her brother, because I didn't know what Clay Singleton thought of me. Maybe I'd simply been a diversion in his busy life. After all, we hadn't gotten past first base in a real relationship.

After leaving the diner, I drove to Savannah to shop for cocktail attire. I had a hard time making choices, because I wanted the dress to be stylish, but classic—not something to be worn once, then relegated to my closet. I was on my own now, and I wanted to spend my money wisely. I had to make my way through quite an array before I came upon the proverbial little black dress. I knew it would pass muster for an elegant cocktail party, but I could dress it down with a scarf or costume jewelry for an occasion more casual.

I was pleased with myself for being practical when I spied a coral colored jumpsuit. It was strapless with a bolero jacket of the same material. The legs were full and flowing to lend grace and style. A wide, beaded belt added richness. I couldn't take my eyes off it. The price tag wasn't what I'd had in mind, but I knew I was going to leave the store with the jumpsuit. I chided myself all the way home while trying to rationalize the extravagant purchase. Maybe my boss would insist that I accompany him to some function where it would be appropriate.

Back in my villa, I began pulling things from my closet. I chose the best of my casual outfits for the afternoon, hoping I would fit in with the wealthy group Max Palmer had invited to this affair he had arranged. Telling myself that I shouldn't care what the upper crust thought of me, I couldn't help doing just that.

Just as I finished packing, my phone rang. I ran to answer it, hoping it would be Clay Singleton.

"Hello," I said in my most cheerful voice.

"Good afternoon, Clemmie," said Max Palmer. "Are you about ready for our little adventure?"

"I suppose so. Should I meet you at the office?"

"No need for that. I'll come to your place to pick you up in about a half hour."

I hung up the receiver, wondering what I was about to experience.

My boss was in high spirits on the drive to the yacht. He couldn't seem to stop smiling as he ticked off the names of some of the people he would introduce me to later.

"Am I dressed appropriately?" I asked.

"Your sundress is perfect for this afternoon. We'll be having a simple meet and greet session with a glass of champagne upon the guests' arrival. Then, everyone will want to unpack and freshen up before cocktails. There won't be a dinner this evening; just drinks and an abundance of hors d' oeuvres. You'll want to change into a different outfit."

I must have gulped in air, because my chest felt constricted, and I couldn't speak.

"Clemmie, are you all right?"

"Mister Palmer, I'm not sure I have enough clothes. I didn't understand that I was expected to change into another outfit today."

Max smiled. "That's my fault. I failed to tell you that was expected. I knew you wouldn't have more time to shop, so I took the liberty of obtaining something suitable for you. I hope you're not offended."

I was offended, but it seemed that I didn't have a choice in the matter.

"I suppose I should thank you, but how do you know my size?"

"I'm pretty good at guessing such things, but size won't matter so much in the outfit I bought. It's a middy dress, and I know you'll love it."

"A middy dress?"

"Yes, a loosely fitting top that comes below the waist and has a pleated skirt and a sailor collar. It'll be perfect for this evening."

"In that case, I don't suppose I'll be offended."

We arrived at the yacht in the late afternoon. Our luggage was whisked away as we boarded, and Max had a porter show me to my quarters. He told me to meet him at the entrance hall in fifteen minutes to greet his guests as they arrived.

There were three couples, and they boarded the yacht en masse, each twosome looking like new money. I could tell that I was not going to enjoy their company simply by looking at them. The women wore an inordinate amount of makeup and enough jewelry to sink a ship, and their smiles were fake. The men were all middle-aged and boisterous. I took each person's hand and smiled as pleasantly as I could.

Champagne flutes were passed, and Max Palmer made a toast: "Here's to a prosperous venture for us all."

I had no idea how well my boss knew these people. Were they wealthy folks he had just recruited, or old friends who were eager to dive into one of his quick money schemes? By the several conversations going on around me, I had no idea. Max had introduced me as his able assistant, and pulled me into conversations by bringing up familiar happenings on Hilton Head.

When it was time to change for the cocktail party, I went to my quarters to find a list of the names of guests and a physical characteristic of each. It was easy to remember Bunny with the big blond hair and her husband, Don, whose head looked, for all the world, like a hard-boiled egg. Joel was probably close to seven feet tall, and his wife, Eva, was no bigger around than a pencil. The last of the lot were Sylvia with ghost-white skin and her husband, Marv, who sported red hair and freckles.

I found the middy dress hanging in my closet. The price tag had been removed. I undressed and tried on the middy. It fit perfectly, and I thought it was adorable. Who knew Max Palmer had such good taste? He probably had someone else purchase it. There was a shoebox in the bottom of the closet. I opened it to find a pair of navy sandals which matched the collar of the dress and just happened to be my size.

I read over the list of names to make sure I could match the correct physical characteristic with each person. Then, I went to the cocktail party, feeling prepared. Max Palmer was already there as were two of the three couples. I walked toward Mister Palmer in my cute middy, doing my best to feel confident. He smiled at me.

"What would you like from the bar, Clemmie?" he asked.

"A glass of chardonnay would be nice. Thank you."

Max went to the bar for my drink and delivered it, before excusing himself to mingle. I assumed it was my assignment to join the girls to engage in small talk, or dish the dirt about someone. Bunny and Eva, each overly animated and trying to laugh louder than the other, were sipping martinis. At my approach, they let their hilarity come to a halt to greet me.

"Hi, Clemmie," Bunny said. "Where did you find that adorable dress?" It was obvious that she had practiced dropping her jaw to show off her Lumineers.

"It came from a shop in Savannah," I said, thinking it was probably true.

"Well, I just love it," she gushed.

"Do you both live on Hilton Head?" I asked the two, hoping to find a common ground for polite conversation.

"Oh, no," Eva answered. "My husband and I are from Memphis."

Bunny chimed in. "We're from Lubbock. That's in Texas."

"I grew up on Hilton Head, but left the island when I was a teenager," I said. "I just moved back a few weeks ago."

"That's interesting," Bunny said. "So Eva, tell us all about

Graceland. I'm just dying to visit. Elvis has always been my idol."

"Well, it's always overrun with tourists, country hicks mostly. The way some of them dress is enough to make you cover your eyes," said Eva, "but I think everybody ought to have Graceland on their bucket list."

Sylvia and Marv were just arriving. They were holding hands, but they didn't look happy. Sylvia pulled her hand away from her husband and replaced her frown with a brilliant smile as she came toward us.

"Get me a drink, Marv," she ordered.

"Whadda you want?" Marv asked.

"See if the bartender knows how to make a Gibson," she said.

Her sarcastic tone told me that she and Marv had definitely had a spat, and I had the feeling that she wasn't too happy to be here.

"Isn't this going to be fun, girls?" she said.

"I'm sure it will be," Eva said. "I've heard Max Palmer's little get-togethers are the best."

My boss appeared at my side.

"Ladies, may I steal Clemmie away from you for a few minutes? I need her assistance on a small matter," he said.

He steered me to a quiet corner away from the guests.

"How do you like the women?" he asked.

"I don't know that I should have an opinion about them, Mister Palmer. I just met them. So far, nothing has been discussed except my dress and Graceland."

"Just know that you're smarter than all three of them, and be pleasant no matter what. I know you can do that. Also, I hope you'll spend some time with Don. Do you remember which one he is?"

"You've told me that this is my job, so of course I'll be pleasant. And, I know that Don is the bald gentleman."

"Don and Bunny are extremely wealthy, Clemmie. I'm sure you can charm him without threatening his wife. Be sure to take note of his interests, and apprise me of what they are."

"Charm him?"

"Yes. Just be yourself. Ralph Wingate thinks you're God's gift to men."

During the evening I learned that this was a second marriage for Bunny and Don, and that he made his money in oil among other things, as he put it. I never learned what the other things were. He mentioned that he was into golf and playing the ponies. Bunny enjoyed playing tennis, shopping, and having lunch with friends. It hadn't been easy to hear everything Don was telling me, because Bunny interrupted him constantly and managed to drown him out by talking over him. I wondered if I would be assigned to charm a different man the following evening.

I could tell that this wasn't going to be anything akin to a mini vacation. I was being asked to be a cross between an actress and a spy.

CHAPTER
Seventeen

I had gotten ready for bed and was about to turn off the bedside lamp when I heard a light tap at my door. Then, I saw an envelope slide under it. I picked up the envelope and opened it to find my instructions for the next day.

I learned that a breakfast buffet would be set up in the salon where Pearl, Max, and I had cocktails the first time I had been invited on the yacht. Small tables would be set up, and I would be expected to sit at one such table with my boss. I assumed he would take that opportunity to fill me in on my duties for the remainder of the day.

These people my boss wanted me to court were all a bunch of phonies. Surely, not all wealthy people were obnoxious. I had grown up in a loving home, but there had never been any money to spare. I didn't know how to be rich, and I wasn't sure I wanted to be.

What I did want more than anything was to be happy again. I had lost my precious husband when he was so young. Losing him had been my breaking point, and it had cost me several years of my life. I had gone through something akin to torture in an effort to reconstruct those years in my mind so I would be able to get on with the business of living.

When I met Clay Singleton, I was starting to believe that he might be the person to make me feel whole once more. I had had such hope. We hadn't had physical contact, except for motorcycle rides and a couple of kisses that rocked my senses back to life. The super intelligent handsome hunk with the winning smile and backwoods speech had made me want him; then disappeared. I fell asleep wondering if I would ever hear from him again.

I hadn't asked for a wake-up call, but the phone on the bedside table made tinkling sounds until I roused myself enough to answer it.

"Good morning, Clemmie," Max Palmer said.

"Good morning."

"I trust you slept well."

"Yes, thank you."

"I'll expect you in the salon for breakfast at eight o'clock."

"And I'm supposed to dress in casual attire?"

"Yes."

I dreaded having to play nice with these people for the next couple of days, but as the man said, "This is your job."

I had been to the outlet mall a couple of times, so I had several decent casual outfits I thought would work for daytime activities on the yacht. My outfit for today was white pants with a red, white, and blue striped tee shirt. I thought it was perfect as I entered the salon to see Max Palmer standing beside a coffee urn near the buffet. He was sipping coffee.

"Good morning, Clemmie," he said, smiling. "Shall we have coffee until the others arrive?"

"Sure."

It seemed that my boss wanted to play host to me as well as his guests. He brought my coffee to our table, and I noticed that he had chosen to use bone china for this group rather than the stoneware mugs he used in his office.

"So, what's on the agenda for today?" I asked, attempting to sound as chipper as he appeared.

"We'll have a leisurely breakfast. Then the ladies will be treated to a small designer fashion show that I took the liberty of arranging. Let those in charge know which items you'd like, and I'll take care of it. The gentlemen will engage in a challenging putting contest while the ladies shop. After that, a light lunch will be served on the upper deck. I will toss out a couple of things for our guests to consider after dessert, and everyone can go their separate ways to ponder what I have offered."

"Do I have duties during that time?"

"That's your time to do as you please. Didn't I tell you to consider it a mini vacation?"

I nodded.

"Try to have fun, Clemmie. Relax and enjoy."

The guests began drifting into the salon. I had the impression that my boss's guests might have been happy to sleep a little longer. But they all attempted bright smiles. Max greeted each one, and I followed suit. The latecomers lined up at the coffee urn, waiting to receive a dose of caffeine. Then, they carefully made their way to tables. Each couple sat at a table for two. Nobody bothered to converse with his or her spouse. The silence was pronounced by china cups rattling on their saucers.

Hand-written agendas were placed on each table, stating the times and places to meet. Nobody appeared very excited to be here except Max Palmer. I would have bet my next pay check he thought he was about to make a killing from these unsuspecting nouveau riche.

As we were vacating the salon, I summoned my best fake excitement for the ladies. It was the least I could do to earn my pay and get a designer outfit in the process.

"Isn't this exciting?" I said, slipping my arm through Bunny's. I felt like such a hypocrite.

A short time later, a boatload of tall, wafer-thin models boarded the yacht along with a woman with a script to read describing each outfit in detail and lavishing praise on the designer of each. I had to admit that I had been looking forward to owning something ridiculously expensive even though I wouldn't have any place to wear it. When the first model came out, she placed one foot directly in front of the other on stiletto heels and never looked down. She stared into space with her chin jutted out just so, wearing something that resembled a potato sack which struck her well above the knee, showing off spindly legs.

"That's stunning," whispered Eva.

Bunny stifled a snicker. "I wouldn't wear that thing to a hog callin' contest," she said.

I didn't recognize but one of the designers' names, and I wondered if my boss knew anything about any of them or their clothing lines. But by the time the last model showed her wares, I knew that my dream of a designer dress was just that.

This adventure of Max's didn't seem to be working out very well as far as the women were concerned. I was pretty sure I had the women pegged: Eva was eager to get into Max's circle of friends, probably at her husband's urging. Sylvia had no interest at all, and would like to be anywhere else. Maybe her husband had promised her a nice piece of jewelry to come along. Bunny impressed me as being the most honest, albeit homegrown, of the three. She was a genuine airhead with new money, and she was damn proud of it.

It was a sparkling day; a cloudless sky and a slight breeze to quell the sun's rays. The women couldn't have come close to having average IQs, but they were smart enough to wear sunglasses for lunch on the upper deck.

A couple of finger sandwiches, a dollop of pate' on a water cracker, raw baby carrots, and tiny shrimp cocktail bowls with two shrimps composed the lunch fare. Dessert was a fruit compote dressed with some kind of liqueur.

We were seated at a long table, and it was difficult to carry on a conversation with anyone except those in close proximity. I thought

I heard a male voice mention something about a hamburger, but I wasn't sure I had heard correctly.

As usual, Max Palmer inhaled his meal in record time. Everyone else was about to start their dessert when he left the table without bothering to excuse himself. Then, he returned to the head of the table and began laying out his plan for the guests to ante up large sums of money in his get richer quick scheme. I had known that real estate was at least one of Max's interests, because I had heard parts of his conversations with Ralph Wingate. My boss had requested my presence at a dinner celebrating their joint real estate venture somewhere in Florida.

Max Palmer sounded so excited that one might think he had struck gold. He was talking about taking over a large tract of residential real estate to raze everything that existed and develop an enormous shopping center. He went on to say that after that was accomplished, he planned to wipe out even more real estate close to the mall to build mini mansions on it. I didn't know if I was supposed to understand everything he was saying since I didn't know much about real estate, but his proposal seemed more than a little predatory to me.

"The proposed return on investment for these projects is in the neighborhood of 100% from start of construction to completion, which should be no more than three or four years. Ladies and gentlemen, you can't get that at your neighborhood savings & loan. This is an opportunity to get in on the ground floor on one of the best investments I have ever come across. I invite you to give serious consideration to joining me in it. We can discuss the matter this evening after dinner and continue tomorrow. I realize I haven't given you all of the details, but if I know you're genuinely interested, I'll explain everything and answer all of your questions."

I couldn't imagine that anyone would express interest in such a thing without knowing the last detail, but it seemed to me that Max Palmer could get away with all kinds of unreasonable things.

"Meet here at poolside for an afternoon of rest and relaxation.

What could be better than a dip and lounging around the pool with a cool drink with new friends? We'll plan to be back on Hilton Head by five o'clock. Then we'll all meet at Stripes for dinner. I've arranged for a limo to transport you to the restaurant. It will be waiting for you at the Hyatt at seven o'clock."

I was on the way to my quarters when I glimpsed what looked like the back of a wheelchair entering the spa. Could that have been Pearl? I hadn't seen her even once since I boarded the yacht. If, indeed, the yacht's namesake was on board, why was she staying out of sight?

There was another surprise for me. A gorgeous swimsuit lay on my bed along with a matching cover-up. Max had told me to bring a swimsuit, and I had brought one. I didn't know what to make of this. Max Palmer probably thought I had bought my suit at a bargain basement.

Naturally, the suit he had furnished fit me perfectly. It had probably cost a bloody fortune. The more money he spent on me, the more I was beginning to feel indebted to him. It was causing me to think I would never be able to claw my way out of this arrangement if I decided to trade it for a real job and call it quits.

I looked at myself in the full-length mirror. This life I was living didn't seem real. I wasn't used to spending tons of money on frivolous things and being on yachts, hobnobbing with the super wealthy. I felt like a big phony. That was how I had painted Max's guests, because I could tell the shoe fit.

I lay down on my bed and wondered what Clay Singleton would think of this kind of life. He would no doubt see it as *the grass is greener life*, but it wouldn't be for him. He would be more at home living on a boat and riding a motorcycle, choosing to dress for comfort instead of wearing a coat and tie except for special occasions. Yes, I knew what his preference would be. And as much as I was enjoying the feel of all the largesse my boss was throwing my way, I admitted to myself that it wouldn't be for me either.

Clay Singleton. I wondered where he was and what he was

doing. Why had he simply disappeared? Would I have to start all over again in my quest to find happiness? Just the thought of it made me feel defeated.

I met the other women at the poolside bar where they were sipping mimosas.

"I thought this guy was supposed to show his guests the times of their lives," Sylvia said. "I could lie around my pool at home."

"I think our host is sending us off to soak up the sun while he drops a few more hints to the men about the fabulous business opportunity," Eva said. "I'm sure he wants to whet their appetites a little more before we leave the yacht."

"Well, I think y'all are just bein' downright mean," Bunny said. "I'll admit that was a stinker of a fashion show, but everything else has been top-notch. Don't you think so, Clemmie?"

I didn't want to be a part of this conversation. No matter what I thought of my boss's business dealings, I knew I should appear to be loyal to him. Max Palmer was paying me for doing nothing. I couldn't stab him in the back. I would simply remain neutral and dodge the questions the women asked me.

"I've never been on a business outing like this," I said, "so I'm afraid I don't have an opinion."

The men were gathered at the far end of the pool deck. They sat at a round table shaded by a large umbrella, listening to Max Palmer deliver droplets of bait to lure them in while I did my best to put on a pleasant front for their wives. It seemed that the hands on the large clock over the bar were moving inordinately slowly.

"Oh, shit fire!" Bunny cried. "Look what time it is! I've got to get a shower and get my stuff together."

We all agreed that it was time to freshen up and pack. As we were leaving, I glanced in the men's direction and saw Joel give Max a pat on the back. Then, he hurried toward us and caught up with his wife. His smile looked genuine, and his eyes sparkled with excitement like a kid on Christmas morning. I assumed that my boss had just caught a big one.

CHAPTER
Eighteen

*B*ack on the island Max's guests were taken to the Hyatt in a limo, and he drove me home. My boss carried my small suitcase to the front door.

"I'll pick you up at six forty-five, Clemmie. Wear something pretty."

I nodded and unlocked my front door. My boss smiled and waved as he drove away.

If I hadn't gone to the kitchen for a glass of water, I wouldn't have seen Clay Singleton lounging on my lower deck, watching a foursome of golfers teeing off on the eighteenth hole of the Jones course directly across from my villa. He looked right at home in shorts and a tee shirt with his bare feet resting on a small outdoor table. I walked through the living room and opened the sliding glass door, trying not to let my happiness at seeing him show.

Clay swiveled his head in the direction of the door upon hearing it slide open. He didn't get up, didn't say a word, but turned back to watch the golfers. He held up a hand, asking me to wait for a greeting, or explanation while the last guy teed off. I stepped out onto the deck and closed the door.

"What are you doing?" I asked with my hands on my hips.

"Well, I hope you don't mind. I went by your office, but it was locked up tighter than a drum. Then, I called your number, but you didn't answer. I figured you must be walkin' on the beach. I'd already jogged a few miles, so I thought I'd just wait here for you. You've got a great view of this tee box."

I stared at him in disbelief.

"What?" He looked confused.

"Don't you think you might be taking me for granted just a tiny bit? You simply disappeared for a few days after spending the night on my couch. You didn't let anyone know you were about to drop off the face of the earth before you left. Nobody knew what happened to you—not your sister, not me. For all we knew, something horrible might have happened to you. You might have drowned at sea."

"Oh, well, if that had been the case, the Coast Guard would have found me. I'd have been on the local news." He did that little-boy grin he was so good at.

"You disappeared for days, then thought it would be alright to make yourself at home on my deck. I don't suppose you considered the fact that this is a private residence, or that it might be remotely possible for me to keep company with anyone but you."

"You're right, Clemmie. I didn't think about any of those things, because I was under the impression that we had a thing." He pointed to me, then to his chest. "I reckon I was wrong."

He stepped into his topsiders and went down the three steps to the common area behind my villa.

"I apologize for all of the above," he said, and walked away.

What had I done? I hadn't given him a chance to explain. It seemed that what was most important at the time was for me to assert myself, to let him know that I would not be taken for granted by him, or anybody else. He was barely out of sight, and I already ached for him.

The last thing I wanted to do was to put on my happy face and fake smile for people I hardly knew and didn't much like. I couldn't think about anything but Clay Singleton the entire time I was getting ready for my command performance. I pulled my new black cocktail dress from its hanger and slipped into it, realizing I had no jewelry. The shops were filled with costume jewelry. I could have bought a suitable necklace, or at least a pretty pair of earrings, but I had been in a hurry and hadn't thought about it. I would simply have to wear my hair loose on my shoulders and hope I would pass muster.

Max Palmer showed up at my front door just as I came downstairs. He rang the bell, and I grabbed my clutch and opened the door. I stepped out onto the porch instead of inviting him to come inside. My boss was a master at dressing for most any occasion, I thought. He was wearing a dark suit and those shiny wingtips for this special dinner. It occurred to me that he also wore his white mane loose when he was dressed to kill.

"Clemmie, don't you look smashing," he said.

"Thank you."

I tucked my clutch under my arm, locked my door, and we were off to spend a few hours with the rich and obnoxious. My boss had already hooked one of the fish. I wondered if the others would also take the bait.

Max suggested that we wait for his guests in the bar. He had arranged to have us seated at a round table for eight. That way it would be easy to converse without having to raise our voices. I wasn't sure why he was explaining everything to me since I wouldn't be expected to speak except to make polite responses.

I assumed that Max must have thought I had learned to hold my liquor well enough to nurse a glass of wine before dinner. He ordered drinks for the two of us before the others arrived, and we sat at a small table where he could see his guests when they entered the restaurant. He didn't bother to look at me while we waited, and he made no attempt at conversation. Instead, he looked past me, watching for his prey to appear. I was certain he had planned every move down to the last detail.

It wouldn't have been necessary for him to see the six of them arrive, because they sounded much like a gaggle of geese as they came through the door. They all seemed to be talking at the same time, and a couple of the women were giggling. Joel and Eva seemed overly excited. Joel was expounding on the attributes of Max Palmer's proposal, and Eva was showing her wifely loyalty to her husband, clinging to his arm and smiling her agreement. It was clear that they were all in.

"I'm getting in on the ground floor," Joel was saying. "If you guys wait too long, you're going to be missing out on the deal of a lifetime. You'll be kicking yourselves. Take my word for it."

Eva nodded enthusiastically.

"I'm not quite convinced," Marv said. "I'd like to hear a few more details before I jump into something this big. I'm not willing to lose a fortune on some fly-by-night scheme. Who in our little group knows much about this guy anyway? I don't know about you two, but I just met the man."

I noticed that the men were carrying on the discussion as though their wives weren't present. If that pattern continued, I would be able to enjoy my dinner without having to play games.

Max rose from his seat to greet the group, pulling out my chair on his way. A waiter came to carry my drink into the dining room, and I joined my boss who was shaking the men's hands and presenting the women with little non-hugs and air kisses. I didn't think it necessary to engage in such physical greetings, so I summoned what I considered to be a cordial smile.

We weren't only seated at a round table; it was located in a small private dining room. The table linen was snowy white, the crystal tossed off brilliant shimmers of light, and the silver shone in the glow of candlelight.

We entered the room quietly as one might step into a church, or a funeral parlor. A low arrangement of gardenias graced the center of the table.

Eva broke the silence. "I think this might be the most beautiful table I've ever seen."

Sylvia began sniffing and brought a lace handkerchief to her nose. Then, she started sneezing.

"Pardon me," she said, and sneezed several more times in rapid succession. "I think I might be allergic to the flowers," she apologized.

Max Palmer summoned one of the waitstaff who stood at either side of the door.

"You'll have to remove the centerpiece," he said. "The lady is allergic."

"That's too bad," Bunny said. "They were really pretty, but all is not lost. Look at these fabuloso candlesticks. If I had a bigger purse, these suckers wouldn't be long for this room."

Don stifled a snicker. "Y'all know she was just joking, I'm sure," he said, and patted his wife's hand.

Bunny's lip trembled at her husband's little reprimand, but it didn't take long for her to return to her bubbly self. She gave her big hair a pat, flashing her ruby and diamond ring and bracelet.

Menus were brought to the table, and cocktail orders were taken. Max Palmer interrupted the menu perusal to thank everyone for coming on his outing.

"I do hope each of you enjoyed our little getaway," he said. "I also hope you've all had a chance to think about the opportunity I mentioned."

"I've got to tell you, I need to hear the plan in more detail before I commit," Marv said.

"I take it that means you are interested," Max said.

Marv nodded.

"How about you, Don?" Max asked. "You interested in making a sound investment?"

"I feel like Marv does. I'd like to have more facts before I make a decision."

"Of course. Tell you what. After the ladies retire for the evening,

I'll meet you gentlemen in a conference room I have at the Hyatt and go over every detail. How's that?"

The three potential partners nodded in unison and appeared to take comfort in returning to their drinks. All talk of the business deal was dropped, and everyone's mood became much lighter. Dinner orders were placed, more drinks and bottles of wine were ordered, and the room took on an elegant party atmosphere. I was pretty sure that Max Palmer's fake smile hid his smug feeling from everyone at the table but me. I had only known him for a short time, but I was beginning to read him fairly well. He thought he had already won.

I was almost afraid to go to work the next morning. Wondering if I was in the middle of something illegal made me nervous, but I walked into Max's office at nine o'clock on the dot. He had on khakis and a golf shirt, and his long mane was tamed into a ponytail with a rubber band. He was on the phone with someone, and he was wearing a Cheshire cat smile. I only caught the last of the conversation. My boss was telling someone that he was looking forward to the venture. He hung up the phone, looking very satisfied.

I had no idea what he had said to the men at their meeting last night, but I had a feeling it had worked. I wondered if he might go to prison for what he was doing, and I prayed that I couldn't be connected to it in any way.

"Good morning, Ms. Castlebrook," he said. "You've just been given a generous pay hike."

"Mister Palmer, I haven't done anything to deserve a pay hike. As a matter of fact, I've hardly done anything but pick up dry cleaning and accompany you to dinners."

My boss sighed. "Dear Clemmie, you don't understand what an asset you are, and you are most assuredly naïve when it comes to the business world."

"It's just that I feel a need to earn my pay. I'm not afraid of hard work."

Max Palmer smiled.

"There are those who do far less than you're doing and getting paid well for what they do, or don't do. I want you to take today off. Go home and do your laundry if you feel the need to work."

He opened his desk drawer and pulled out a check, sliding it across the metal surface to me. I caught it before it slid off the desktop to hit the floor and looked at the cashier's check for $1700.00. I couldn't believe the amount. Max Palmer was giving me a pay hike of $500.00 a week for eating. My mouth must have been hanging open in amazement, and I couldn't seem to speak, so I simply swallowed. I didn't know whether I should accept the money. What if it entangled me even more in my boss's web?

"Don't look so shocked," Max said. "This is your new weekly salary. You might want to drop by your bank and deposit it on your way home."

I stood, hoping that looking down on the man who had just handed me way too much money would bolster my courage to the point that I could make myself thank him for the gesture, but refuse to accept the check. I could feel my heartbeat quicken in an attempt to spit out the words I knew I should say. The big clock on the wall above my boss's desk was ticking loudly. I watched the second hand. It seemed an eternity for it to complete a minute. Finally, I found my tongue.

"Thank you very much for believing in me and appreciating my efforts, Mister Palmer. The pay raise is far more than generous."

I turned on my heel and left the office. Blood was pumping in my ears, and my hands were beginning to perspire. I sat in my Jeep waiting to feel something close to normal before starting it to drive with trembling hands. Deep breaths—that was a technique I had discovered sometimes worked when I found myself without a rubber band to snap on my wrist. I managed to take four of them and began to feel a bit better.

I had intended to go straight to my bank with the check, but I ended up going to see my old mentor. She would know what I should do. I don't remember her ever being wrong about important decisions.

I knocked on the frame of the screen door.

"Mama Rae, it's me, Clemmie."

"Come in dis house," she called.

I found her in the kitchen, filling more of those little bottles she refused to discuss with me. I wondered what was in them and who their recipients might be. My old friend would never tell me. That much I knew for sure. She kept her back to me while she finished her work. Then, she screwed tops on the bottles, deposited them into a basket of woven reeds, and covered them with a dishtowel. She turned to face me.

"You want one of Mama Rae's raspberry tarts?" she asked.

"Oh, yes. Those are my favorites."

My old friend shuffled to the piece of kitchen furniture she called her pie safe to retrieve the tarts. She brought them to the table, then brought two cups of room temperature tea.

"You look like you might need some advice from dis old woman."

I cut into the tart and saw the bloodred color of the raspberries, recalling the frightening dream I had while I was in Still Waters: I was standing at Mama Rae's kitchen sink—the berries shone bright and slick, mounded in the colander under the light from the window just above the sink. My knees began to feel wobbly, and it seemed that the raspberries liquefied. Then, I remembered the blood streaming down Daniel's face after Roy hit him with his Louisville Slugger. It was the same color as the liquid. I shook my head to clear it, and brought the fork to my mouth. I sighed with pleasure. Daniel was very much alive. I had seen him not long ago at Mama Rae's when he told us about his new job in Atlanta.

"These tarts are the most wonderful things I've ever tasted," I said.

Mama Rae smiled. I thought she was still beautiful. Her face was wrinkled when I first met her, but it was much more so now.

And her toothless gums seemed to have completely receded behind her thin lips. Her small eyes had dimmed, but every now and then the twinkle that was hers alone, appeared.

"Not too bad," she agreed.

My eye caught movement from the corner of the room, and the cat left his bed of rumpled towels to stretch. He ambled over to the table and began twining himself around Mama Rae's legs; then mine.

"Not now, Lord," Mama Rae chided. "'bout time for you to go outside."

It was clear to me that she had already spoiled the cat, but she must have taught him how to avoid danger in the woods. She pushed herself up from her chair, gave her pet a quick ear scratch, and he followed her to the backdoor to become an outdoor cat for a while.

"What is it, chile?" she asked.

I pulled the check out of my purse and showed it to her even though I knew she couldn't read.

"This is a cashier's check for "1,700.00. That's a lot of money for doing nothing. Don't you think?"

Mama Rae ran her veined hand over the check a couple of times.

"Don't tink I ever touched dis much money before," she said, and smiled.

"Do you think I should keep it?"

"What he say when he give it to you?"

"He said I had earned it."

Mama Rae ran her hand over the check again.

"Let me tink 'bout dis for a while. Go on and put it in a safe place, and come back to see me in two days. Nothin' say you can't give it back to de man later. Do you have one of dem bank accounts?"

"Yes, of course."

"Dat be a good place."

I left Mama Rae to do whatever she does to help with decision making. She would probably dress up in one of her weird garbs and engage in some strange ritual. I wondered why she wanted me to wait for exactly two days before checking back with her.

I drove to my bank and deposited the check, hoping I could keep the money without getting myself into trouble and without committing myself to a lifetime attachment to the man I called my boss.

CHAPTER
Nineteen

I traded my work clothes for shorts and a tee shirt, thinking I would go for a walk on the beach, but quickly changed my mind. The fact that I had pretty much told Clay Singleton to get out of my life before he had a chance to explain his absence had been a terrible mistake. I flopped down on my bed and cried for a while. Then, I wallowed in my misery thinking *woe is me* until I truly believed it. I was like a lost child, not knowing what to do or where to turn. If only I could talk to Daniel, he would be able to settle me down and get my head back on straight.

Then, I remembered seeing Catherine in the restaurant with someone other than her husband. I didn't want to believe she was being unfaithful to Daniel, but I didn't know what else to think. Calling Catherine wasn't anything I wanted to do. I couldn't tell her that I had seen her and ask her to explain, nor could I ask her for Daniel's number. She had been rather cool toward me the last time we spoke on the phone. For all I knew, she was secretly jealous of my relationship with Daniel, but I couldn't imagine why.

I thought about calling Sarah, Clay's sister, but I wouldn't want her to think I was chasing after her brother. That would make me look as needy as I felt. I had been so happy to come back to Hilton Head Island to make a new start after spending four years in limbo. Why did I feel that I was steadily losing ground?

Then, recalling the pep talks Roy used to give me when I was a teenager, I roused myself out of bed, ditched the shorts and tee shirt, and put on my new bikini and cover-up. I splashed water on my face to wash off the salt and calm my red eyes, and headed to the beach. I had always been a strong swimmer. Daniel had been my swimming instructor, and he was the best. Swimming in that great big ocean, even against the tide, made me feel that I could do anything I was of a mind to do. I was boss.

I left my flip-flops behind the bottom step with those of strangers. Then, I made a little nest of my beach towel and cover-up away from other small piles of people's towels and beach bags. Taking a deep breath, I dug my heels into the sand and ran toward the water with determination. I would swim until I barely had the energy to get myself back to shore. Such an endeavor had always made me feel like a new person. I hoped it would make me lose the blues and cause me to feel that I was the master of my fate. It had worked in the past.

The tide was coming in, and as always, it was a great force of nature. I pulled myself through the water, feeling the strain on my muscles with each stroke. Something hit my thigh. It was much larger than a school of fish. That would have felt like little taps. I was out pretty far, and I was getting tired. It was time to swim back to shore. The tide was with me, and that gave me courage. I turned and began swimming, and was hit on my right side. It was the same sensation as before, and I could feel the rhythm of my heartbeat increase. I was swimming for all I was worth, and my arms and legs felt leaden. Then, something sharp slashed my thigh. I was so terrified that I didn't take the time to spot it. Summoning every bit of strength I had left, I focused on the shore and willed my limbs to get me to safety. I was only about fifty yards from the beach.

Praying that I could make it to shore without further damage, I screamed for help. My breath was coming in little gasps. I tried to scream again, but I couldn't make a sound. It was my good fortune to be noticed by a lifeguard. He reached me just as I was about to pass out. I remembered seeing a muscular lifeguard running toward me. Then, next thing I knew, I looked up to see a small crowd being dispersed.

"How many fingers do you see?" the lifeguard asked.

"Two," I answered. My voice sounded hoarse.

My thigh felt like it was on fire, and someone was putting pressure on it with a towel or a big bandage of some kind.

"Try to relax," the lifeguard said. "Paramedics are on the way. They'll be here in just a minute."

"My leg," I whined.

"It's not so bad. You must have gotten in the way of that pesky sand shark. I saw it heading for you. They don't normally attack people. This one was about three feet long. He scraped your thigh with a tooth. You're going to be fine."

I tried not to cry. People were scattering to make way for the ambulance. Paramedics jumped from the vehicle and began taking my pulse, shining lights in my eyes, and checking out my wound. Then, they were settling me on a gurney and loading me into the ambulance. I assumed the lifeguard hadn't known what he was talking about. If I had been fine, these guys wouldn't be taking me to a hospital.

Nobody was talking to me; they were talking *about* me to one another. The bright lights in the emergency room were almost blinding, and my thigh really hurt. Then, it felt awfully cold and wet. Someone was spraying what felt like ice water on it.

"Little sting, now," said a new male voice.

It was more than a little sting. It ached like the devil, but the pain didn't last long. I didn't feel it when someone cleaned the wound and put stitches in my thigh.

An orderly wheeled me to a checkout desk. I was afraid I

wouldn't be allowed to leave the hospital, because I didn't have an insurance card or money.

"Who can we call to come get you, honey?" a nurse asked.

I was dumbfounded; I couldn't think of a single soul to call.

"There's nobody to call," I said, feeling embarrassed. "I just moved here a few weeks ago, and I don't know anyone. I walked to the beach, so I don't have a purse. I can't pay for a cab."

"I'll take you to a waiting area at the front of the hospital," she said. "I'm sure we can make some kind of arrangement to get you home." She smiled. "What's your address, sweetie?"

I told her my address, wondering what good that might do. I understood a few minutes later. Hilton Head is a small island, and even though most of the people who inhabit it are transplants, they tend to be good neighbors—people who are happy to lend a helping hand. And that was how I met Jake Tripley, a nurse who happened to be one of my Hickory Cove neighbors.

Jake looked like a male model. He was tall, slim, and muscular with dark hair and blue eyes. I thought he looked about my age, give or take a couple of years, and he sure was easy on the eyes. His five o'clock shadow somehow made him even more handsome. He was dressed in green scrubs, and he smiled as he approached me, taking long confident strides.

"Hi," he said, extending his hand. "I'm Jake. Might you be the fair damsel in distress?"

"That's me. I'm Clemmie," I said, taking his hand. I couldn't help staring at his naked ring finger. "I'm assuming you live close to Hickory Cove and you're offering me a ride home."

"Right on both counts. As a matter of fact, I live just down the street from you. Want me to wheel you out, or do you think you can walk?"

"The numbness hasn't worn off, so I can walk. I hope it lasts long enough for me to grab my purse and get back here to pay my bill."

"Don't worry about that. The hospital will send you a bill. After all, they know where you live." He laughed.

Jake took me to my front door. I thanked him and got out of his SUV.

"If I can be of further assistance, just give me a shout," he said, handing me one of his cards. "I'm just a few doors down the street."

"Thanks again. You've been a lifesaver."

I climbed the three steps to my small front porch and got all the way to the door before I realized that I didn't have a key. My thigh was still numb, and I was thankful for that as I sat down on the top step. I had a spare key inside the villa. Why hadn't I hidden it outside someplace like under the side of the porch? There was only one thing to do, and that was to walk back to the beach barefoot and find my cover-up where I had stashed the key in an inside pocket.

If I walked as fast as I could, maybe the numbness wouldn't wear off until I could get back home. I knew I would get lots of stares, walking around in public wearing nothing but a bikini and a paper gown the hospital had provided.

I gingerly went down the steps to the beach. My flip-flops were behind the bottom step where I had left them. My feet were tender from walking barefoot on asphalt, pine straw, and sand. I was thankful that I wouldn't have to punish them more on the way back home.

I knew exactly where I had put my beach towel and cover-up, but when I came to the spot, they weren't there. Someone must have stolen them. Then, I remembered that people on this island don't steal; they return things they assume that someone else lost, or misplaced. That seemed to be true of the people who vacationed on the island as well. When I was a teenager, Roy had laid his wallet down beside the cash register at the pier. He had paid for his bucket of shrimp and laid the wallet down to shake hands with an acquaintance. Later that afternoon, he received a phone call from a young man from Covington, Kentucky who was vacationing on Hilton Head. The young man had found the wallet and wanted to return it.

But my things were missing. How would I get into my villa without a key? I was ready to give up, thinking I would have to go home and break a window I would then have to replace. I took one last survey of the area. My cover-up was bright blue. I squinted in the blinding sunlight as I panned the beach, and I thought I might have spotted it close to the small dunes where sea oats were protected by short slatted fences.

I began walking in that direction. As I drew closer, I could see a man sitting beside my possessions. After a few more steps, I saw who it was. He picked up my belongings and stood, but stayed where he was. Then, we were face to face.

"I was takin' a walk, and the tide was comin' in," he said, holding my things toward me. "These were about to get soaked, so I moved 'em back here."

I swallowed, wanting to laugh and cry at the same time. Clay Singleton was looking into my eyes, and I couldn't miss the sadness in his. What he had done was no more than a kind gesture—something he would have done for a total stranger. I took my things from him.

"How did you know they were mine?"

"I saw the cover-up the day you bought it. A little kid bumped into you and caused you to drop your package. This fell out, and I picked it up to give it back to you."

I recalled the incident clearly; it was the second, or third time Clay and I happened to be in the same place at the same time.

"I'd forgotten about that," I lied. "Clay, I'm sorry for the things I said. I wasn't in a very good mood."

"No apology necessary. You were right; I was wrong. I had no right to take our relationship for granted. You hadn't done anything to make me think of us as a couple. I overstepped my bounds. Again, I apologize."

He turned to walk away.

"Wait," I said.

I just couldn't let him walk out of my life again. That feeling deep inside me—the strange delicious unbidden ache that manifested itself whenever I was near him was nearly overwhelming.

"Walk me home?"

I wouldn't beg, but I prayed that I could persuade him to spend some time with me. I wanted to give him a chance to explain why he had simply disappeared. I knew he would have a good reason.

"Sure," he said, but he hadn't given me one of his movie star smiles.

Tears gathered in my eyes, and I tried to blink them away.

"Hey, what's the matter? Come on; I'll give you a ride home on my Red Devil. Nice outfit, by the way."

I looked down at my paper gown.

"It was a gift from the hospital. I had a little mishap earlier, and I don't think I'd better go for a ride on your bike."

I lifted the gown revealing my bandaged thigh, and a look of concern came over Clay's handsome face.

"What happened?"

"I got in the way of a sand shark's tooth," I said.

"How many stitches?"

"I don't know. I kept my eyes closed."

"Does it hurt?"

"Not yet. I have a feeling it will as soon as the numbness wears off."

"Come on. I'll walk with you."

I collected my flip-flops from behind the step, and we slowly walked back to my villa. I dug my key out to let us in, and that was when the pain began. It was also the moment that Clay Singleton came back into my world.

He made me comfortable on my sofa, then hurried back to the beach to get his bike. He returned to my villa with the over-the-counter pain relievers I had requested, because I didn't want to take the strong pain killers the doctor sent home with me. Clay scrounged around in my refrigerator and pantry and managed to concoct a savory stew for our dinner.

While the stew simmered, he went to the little general store and returned with teabags to make sweet tea and a loaf of crusty bread to have with the stew. He seemed to feel the need to explain his every move and motive.

"I would have bought a bottle of wine, but you probably shouldn't have that while you're takin' pain medication," he said, placing a pitcher of tea on the counter.

"Thanks for taking care of me," I said.

Clay turned on some music, and we ate our dinner in the living room, talking very little. After he rinsed the dishes and loaded the dishwasher, he came back to sit with me, wearing a sober expression.

"I can't take playin' games with you, Clemmie," he said. "I'm not sure why you asked me to walk you home, but I hope it's because you might care a little somethin' for me. If I'm wrong, just tell me, and I'll be history."

"I do care about you, Clay. I don't know why I was so mean to you. My life hasn't felt real since I came back to Hilton Head. I love the feel of the island and its beauty. The few people I've met here are friendly. You're the most special thing that's happened to me in a very long time. My employer and my strange job are causing me to feel that I'm living some sort of fantasy. Nothing seems real. I was just given a raise for doing nothing, but I accepted it thinking I would have been a fool to turn it down."

"Have you signed some sort of bindin' contract with this guy? If you're uncomfortable in the job, can't you just give notice and quit?"

"I haven't signed a contract. My boss is paying my medical insurance and giving me an outrageous salary I don't deserve. I guess I'll go along with the foolishness for the present. I have an old friend here whom I've known since I was a child. She has never steered me wrong. I've discussed this with her, and she told me to bide my time. She knows everything about Hilton Head, and she'll help me decide what to do."

"I hope your friend can give you good advice. You can't go on bein' miserable no matter how much money this guy throws at you. You're intelligent; you can easily find another job. I have faith in you, and I can't tell you how happy you just made me. The moment I saw you, I knew there was somethin' special about you. I wasn't sure how much I wanted you to be a part of my life then, but I knew I wanted to pursue you and find out."

I started silently crying, and I wasn't sure why. Clay dropped to one knee, reached out and raised my chin with his index finger.

"Please don't cry, Clemmie. I can't give you any more pain meds for a few more hours."

"I'm not in that much pain. I'm just happy."

That brought one of those fantastic smiles to his face. He pulled a chair up close to the sofa, sat down, and took my hand.

"You feel like listenin' to a fool explain his unaccounted for absence?"

I sank back into the pillows and smiled, brushing sticky tears away with my fingertips.

"Yes, I'd love to."

"You know I'm passionate about writin' my novel, right?"

"Right."

"Well, I met someone who is a fantastic source for my book. I took so many notes my hand got tired. I ended up buyin' a cheap recorder."

"That's great. How did you meet this person?"

"Not important. What is important is that I got so wrapped up in the information I had that I couldn't wait to do somethin' with it. I stocked up on a few groceries, gassed up my boat, and lit out for deep water. I worked pretty much nonstop for two days. That's why I left in a hurry without tellin' anybody. I realize that doesn't sound like a very good excuse, but it's the truth. I've got a real good start on my very own novel."

CHAPTER
Twenty

didn't know if I would ever understand Clay Singleton. He was a puzzle I wasn't sure I could solve. The many sides of him were mind boggling. He was a small town boy from Alabama who took his homespun speech patterns and folksy adages wherever he went. And he did go far from that small town. He went all the way to the most urban city in the United States, New York City where he received a Juris Doctorate from Columbia only to discover that he had no desire to practice law. Clay Singleton, a man with three degrees sounded like a backwater hick when he spoke. He lived on a boat and drove a motorcycle. He was also in the process of writing a novel. Everything about him seemed incongruous.

Clay had gone to great lengths to get to know me. Then, it seemed that he had automatically thought of us as a couple. He even took me to meet his family. Just as I was beginning to warm to the idea of working our way into a meaningful relationship, he disappeared without a word. He had the nerve to show up unannounced on my deck and became offended when I let him know that wasn't the way to go about doing things. He walked out of my life as if it were the easiest thing in the world.

I couldn't let that happen, so I invited him back in, hoping he would accept the invitation, which he did. How could the same man who took me for granted, unbeknownst to him, take care of me with so much tender loving care? He was a natural caregiver, and kindness was written all over him.

I had let my boss know about my run-in with the sand shark, and he offered to take care of any needs I might have. I thanked him, but told him that I didn't need anything. He insisted that I take the week off, and I took him up on the offer. I was beginning to develop the wrong kind of attitude. I felt smug, knowing that I would be paid for an entire week of doing nothing, and it was strangely comforting to have that security.

Clay stayed with me at my villa for a couple of days after the incident with the sand shark. I told him it was unnecessary, but he insisted. He bought groceries and prepared our meals, did some light cleaning, and treated me like a princess. I slept in the downstairs bedroom because it was easier than climbing the stairs, and Clay slept on the couch in the living room in case I needed anything. He was like a mother hen.

I kicked him out of the villa the third day, dismissing him with a hug and a kiss. I knew he would show up late that afternoon prepared to make our dinner, and I would let him do that. He had dropped everything to help me, and I knew that I could always count on him. My stitches would come out in ten days, and I was expected to be as good as new.

Clay had explained to me about his disappearance, and I tried to make myself understand his passion for writing a novel. He had yet to tell me anything about the book, except that Hilton Head was the setting. I wondered who his secret source was. He had studiously avoided revealing who it was, brushed it off as if it didn't matter. I wanted his novel to be a success, because he was so intent on writing it. Of all the avenues laid out before this intelligent accomplished man, writing was what he had chosen for his life's work. Money didn't seem to matter.

Max Palmer had a gorgeous flower arrangement delivered to cheer me up. Then, the following day, he sent an exotic fruit basket. He called to tell me that as soon as I was up to it, he wanted to take me out for a special dinner. It was time for me to tell him that he must stop the extravagant things he was doing for me. He paid me way too much and topped it off with a huge bonus. My employer should not be buying me clothes, and I should only accompany him to business dinners. The way he was treating me almost made me feel like a kept woman.

Mama Rae had told me to check back with her in two days after I showed her the check Max Palmer had given me, but I hadn't been able to do that because of my injury. She didn't have a phone, and I had no way to get in touch with her. I couldn't imagine what she could do in order to learn whether or not I should keep the bonus I had been given. She said she didn't know Max Palmer, and it had upset her when I questioned her about it.

Clay came to check on me every day. I was getting ready to make a sandwich for lunch when he rang my doorbell.

"Hey, sunshine. Dang! You're cute as a bug's ear," he said. "You must be experiencin' a little cabin fever by now. How about I take you to lunch. We can go in your Jeep. That won't be as bumpy as my bike."

"I think I'll take you up on that offer, kind sir. I am having a twinge of cabin fever."

Since it was my first outing, I suggested that we go someplace close. We went to a little outdoor café in Shelter Cove that looked out over the water. It was a lovely day, still warm with a soft breeze. As we were leaving, I happened to glance to the left. Max Palmer was walking away from the restaurant area to a parking lot across the street. I knew his walk, even from the back. Clay and I were holding hands, and he was sort of leading me toward my Jeep.

"Just a minute, Clay."

He stopped walking, but looked puzzled.

"Somethin' the matter?" he asked.

"No. I just want to watch someone."

I looked in the direction Max had come from, close to the Harbormaster Restaurant. Pearl was parked there in the shadow of the building, and Mama Rae was handing her something. I couldn't see what it was, but my old friend held the reed basket I had seen in her kitchen—the one where she kept those little bottles of herbs. I couldn't see the women's faces, but the scene looked awfully familiar to me. This was the second time I had seen them together. Clay tried to follow my gaze.

"What are you starin' at, Clemmie?"

"Those two women," I said, nodding.

But Mama Rae had disappeared.

"I don't see any women except that lady in a wheelchair."

"Come on," I said, practically dragging Clay to the parking lot.

I looked over my shoulder to see if I could catch a glimpse of Mama Rae, but she was gone. She must have made it to the back side of the restaurant out of sight. And what would I say to her if I found her? Whatever she was doing with Pearl was none of my business, and she would let me know that in a heartbeat. I suppose I could introduce her to Clay, but that wouldn't explain her relationship with Pearl.

Clay helped me into the Jeep and got behind the wheel.

"What was that all about?" he asked.

"It's a long story, and I don't know if I can actually explain it so it will make sense."

"Want to try, or do you just want to leave me in the dark?"

"The elderly woman in the wheelchair has a close relationship with my boss. I don't know what that relationship is, but I know she has some kind of hold on him. She isn't his mother; that much I know, but his personality changes when he is around her. He's like her puppet."

Clay looked intrigued.

"Who was the other woman—the one we let get away?"

"She's a dear friend of mine. She's my go-to person for almost any problem I might have. I've known her since I was ten years old."

"She got a name?"

I summoned a lame excuse for a laugh.

"The only name she goes by is Mama Rae."

Clay's mouth fell open. Then, he smiled.

"I know Mama Rae; well, sort of."

"You do?"

"She's my source. I met her at that little mom and pop store just down the road from the Palmetto Dunes entrance. She was doin' a real number on a Nehi Grape. The woman's comfortable in her own skin; that's for sure. Wonder what makes her dress in those crazy gitups?"

"I don't know. She's always done that. The first time I met her, I wouldn't have known she was a woman if she hadn't been wearing a long skirt. Is she really your source?"

"Yes, she is. I liked her right off. She guzzled the last drop of that soft drink, swiped the back of her hand across her mouth, and smacked her lips. Then, she walked up to me and gave me a little pat on the back."

"That doesn't sound like something Mama Rae would do. I mean the part about her patting a stranger on the back."

"Well, that's what she did. Then, she asked me what my name was, and I told her."

"Wonder why she wanted to know who you were?"

Clay shrugged.

"When I told her my name, she said, 'uh huh.' like that explained a lot to her. She told me to call her Mama Rae."

"Maybe she was just in a friendly frame of mind that day."

"I think it was more than that. She motioned for me to follow her out of the store and sat down on a wooden bench, pointin' to the seat beside her. So I sat down, and she started tellin' me all kinds of things about the island—back when it was bein' developed."

"I don't understand any of this. She didn't know you. She wouldn't have known you were writing a book and wanted information about the island."

"Did you mention me to her?"

"I'm sure I didn't tell her your name. I did tell her that I had met someone and asked if she might want to meet him. If I remember correctly, she was noncommittal."

"I had the feelin' she already knew who I was."

"I don't see how she could have, but knowing Mama Rae, maybe she did. She seems to know just about everything that goes on here on Hilton Head. She's my old friend, but sometimes she can be kind of scary."

"How so?"

"One time I went to see her, and I found her in her yard with a big snake wrapped around one of her arms. She was petting the thing. When she saw me, she unwrapped it from her arm and turned it loose into the woods. That's where she lives, you know."

"No. I didn't know that. I've only seen her at the mom and pop store. We've met there a couple of times."

"She also engages in some strange rituals. It's like she's in another world. She speaks some sort of mumbo jumbo, and I know this will be hard to believe, but she has powers that other people don't possess."

Clay looked at me with an indulgent expression that said he didn't believe me, but that he was willing to let me tell my tall tale.

"It's clear that you think I'm inventing things about her, but I'm telling the truth. You'll find out soon enough if you spend more time with her. I'm not saying she's a bad person. She's done many favors for me. I think of her as something of a guardian angel, because I have seen evidence that she has caused things to happen—things that have benefitted me."

"Yeah?"

"I'll give you one example that happened when I was a teenager: I dated a boy who got rough with me; tried to rape me. Then, I guess he repented, because he apologized, sent me flowers, and began shadowing me everywhere I went. I complained to Mama Rae about his behavior. Shortly after that, he and his family moved off the island."

"Well, Clemmie, that could have been coincidental."

"I told you, that was only one example. I know it sounds silly, but I think she practices voodoo."

Clay shook his head and allowed a small chuckle to escape.

"I'll pay close attention to the old girl and be careful not to do anything to make her dislike me. If she puts a hex on me, I'll know you weren't imaginin' things."

"Fine. Make jokes, but I wouldn't do anything to rub her the wrong way if I were you."

Clay drove me home and handed me the keys to the Jeep.

"I have to check my messages. Will it be okay if I pick up a couple of steaks to grill and come back to make our dinner?"

I was half miffed at him for not believing what I had said about Mama Rae, but I told him that having dinner together would be nice. Regardless of the little things he did that aggravated me, I had to admit to myself that I had fallen for Clay Singleton in a big way. It seemed that he was on my mind constantly. I was happy when we were together, and empty and at loose ends when we weren't. I had only felt that way about one other person, and that was my husband. For some reason I felt that I now had my husband's permission to become involved with another man.

Clay rang my doorbell at six o'clock on the dot. I opened the door, and he rushed inside whistling a tune I didn't recognize. He deposited a large grocery sack on the counter, then turned to pull me into his arms for one of those kisses that melted me. Drawing back to deliver a sexy smile, he lifted my chin with an index finger.

"You are so beautiful," he said, sounding so sincere that I had to believe he meant it.

Then, all business, he began unpacking the groceries. He held up each item for my approval. "We have strip steaks, salad fixin's, mushrooms and a baguette. Last, but not least, a fine cabernet to accompany our dinner."

"It looks wonderful. I'll be your sous chef. Just tell me what to do," I said.

"I don't want you to do a thing. Have a seat on this bar stool while I do the prep work."

He opened the wine and poured a glass for me to sip while he worked. I wondered if he made nutritious meals for himself when he was alone on his boat, or if he lived on fast food and frozen dinners. He certainly looked fit and healthy. Maybe he ate dinner with Sarah and Grace a couple of times each week. I was starved to know everything about him.

When the coals were ready, the salad made, and the mushrooms simmering on the stove, Clay carried the steaks out to the grill. I noticed that he hadn't poured himself a glass of wine, so I poured one and took it out to him.

"Thanks. I hope you don't think I was takin' you for granted by bringin' wine. I figured you trusted me enough to let me crash on your couch again. You gonna tell me I'm right, or not? It's okay either way, but if I have wine I don't want to drive."

"I know that, Clay. And no, I don't think you're taking me for granted. You've been the best nursemaid imaginable, and I no longer need anyone to take care of me. I want you to stay."

Clay took a sip of wine, flashed that gorgeous smile, and put the steaks on the grill. I sat on the wide railing of the deck and watched him. He seemed to be in his element. Soon, the meat began to sizzle and fat dripped onto the hot coals. Just being here with Clay, watching him turn the steaks gave me a feeling of well-being and heightened my senses. I watched the way he moved, his mannerisms as he tended the steaks. His back was to me, and I could see every flex of the muscles under his tee shirt.

"Dinner's almost ready," he said. "These guys are just about perfect, and it's a good thing. Look at that sky."

I hadn't paid any attention to the weather, because I was so focused on Clay. It had gotten cloudy, and it felt like the barometer was dropping. A strong breeze had kicked up, blowing wood chips and pine straw up off the common area behind the villa.

No sooner had we gotten inside than fat drops of rain began to splat on the deck.

"Perfect timing," I said, laughing.

There was a bright flash of lightning followed by booming thunder.

"That was close," Clay said.

"I've been afraid of storms since I was a child," I said. "I know this is probably silly, but let's close the drapes. I don't want to see the lightning."

Clay closed the drapes, and I put our dinner on the table.

"How's that?" he said, pulling out my chair.

"Much better."

Then, the lights went out.

I sighed. "I forgot to buy a flashlight."

"Stay put," Clay said.

He got up and felt his way into the kitchen.

"There must be some candles around here somewhere," he said as he began opening cabinet doors and drawers.

"Check in the small cabinet over the stove," I said.

"Good guess."

He had found a couple of partially burned tapers and lit them with the grill lighter.

"Someone must have been either romantic, or used to havin' power outages."

I was experiencing déjà vu. On another night in this kitchen, Jimmy Castlebrook had cooked steaks on the grill, seated me in this dining area, and found candles in the cabinet over the stove for a romantic dinner. He had given me wine—the first I had ever tasted.

My heart began to beat wildly. It felt as if it might explode. Blood pounded in my ears.

"Jimmy," I whispered.

Clay brought the candles to the table.

"I'm sorry, Clemmie. What did you say?"

His voice brought me back to the present. I could feel my heartbeat begin to calm.

"Nothing. I was just clearing my throat. This looks lovely, Clay."

CHAPTER
Twenty-One

I couldn't help wondering how long I would keep having flashbacks of my late husband. Every time it happened, I felt guilt that was nearly overwhelming. My doctor had told me to squelch that feeling as soon as it assailed me. I realized it was ridiculous to feel that I was cheating on someone who was no longer living, but when a vivid picture of Jimmy presented itself, it was too powerful to ignore.

I looked across the table at Clay. The candles flickered from the air vents. I was trying to stay in the present; to make the image of Jimmy go away. Clay seemed to be searching my face for a clue as to why I looked uncomfortable. Neither of us had touched our food.

"Want to let me in on what the problem is?" he asked.

The thunder was still booming, loud cracks every few minutes, and I latched onto that lifeline.

"I'm sorry. It's just what I told you a while ago. I'm terribly afraid of storms."

I didn't know whether he thought I was lying or not, but that was the only response I could come up with.

"Think about this logically, Clemmie. We're inside a grounded buildin'. The storm can't hurt you. I can't keep you from hearin' the thunder, but the drapes are closed. You don't have to look at the lightnin'. You're safe. I promise."

I hated lying to this man I truly cared for, but I couldn't bring myself to tell him that so many things reminded me of my late husband. Maybe I shouldn't have leased this villa. I had recognized it as the one that had belonged to Jimmy's parents as soon as Eleanor York opened the door to take me on a tour of it.

"I know I'm being silly, Clay. I had a terrifying experience during a storm when I was a child, and the fear has stayed with me ever since. My family and I left Tybee Island when the storm was raging. Roads were washed out, and we weren't sure we could make it to Savannah. We were all shaken by the time we got there. The entire island was devastated. We lost everything. There was nothing left to salvage by the time we were able to return to the island."

"I'm sorry you had to live through somethin' that awful," Clay said, reaching across the table to take my hand in his.

What I had told him about my fear of storms was the truth, but that wasn't the thing that took my breath away—the thing that felt so real as if Jimmy were watching me having an intimate dinner with another man.

"I'm fine now. Forgive my cowardice. I don't want to let this fabulous dinner go to waste."

I took a bite of salad and smiled. Clay followed suit, and I felt the tension seep from my shoulders. We ate our dinner engaged in light conversation, and the storm had passed over by the time we cleared the table.

We took our wine to the living room and Clay found a nice music channel. He didn't sit at the opposite end of the couch from me the way he usually did. Instead, he sat close enough to lightly stroke my arm and shoulder while he told me about one of Grace's antics.

"The kid's not scared of anything," he said. "She found a little garter snake and took it in the house to ask Sarah if she would buy a cage for it. She wanted to keep it as a pet." He laughed.

"How did that go over with Sarah?"

"I'm sure you can guess. Sarah's not much of a tomboy. She had to take Grace to the store to buy a toy to make up for makin' her turn the snake loose."

I could tell Clay was stalling, making conversation about anything but the two of us. I wanted him to spend the night, but not on the couch. We had been playing cat and mouse for too long. It wasn't normal for two adults to behave in such a restrained fashion. The feelings I had when I was with Clay would have propelled me not only into his bed, but into his life. Vivid thoughts of my late husband proved to be an enormous obstacle. They had a way of ruining what might have been a magic moment.

"Clay, stop."

I set my wine on the coffee table, and laid my open palm on his cheek. I could feel the slight prickle of his five o'clock shadow with my fingertips, and it awakened all of the dormant sensations I wanted to welcome. I had forgotten how much I missed touching another person in an intimate situation. It seemed eons ago. The heat from Clay's face made me long to be closer to him; to feel his muscular arms and shoulders; to press my breasts into his oh, so masculine chest, and to anticipate more.

"What's the matter?" he said. "What did I do?"

He set his wine aside and searched my face for a clue.

"You didn't do anything. You're tiptoeing around the conversation you want to have with me because you don't want to push me. I adore Grace, but I'm not interested in her choice of pets at the moment."

"I'm not tiptoein' around anything."

"Of course you are. You don't believe I'm ready for any kind of commitment. You think I'm touchy because I blew up at you once. You didn't deserve that. I just wanted to let you know that you didn't have a right to think you owned me; that you were always welcome no matter what might have been going on with me."

"You had a right to be mad."

"No, I didn't. You weren't the only one who had begun to think of us as a couple. I did, too. But when you dropped out of sight for three days, I didn't know what to think. For some reason, I felt the need to get back at you."

"Let's not beat that old dead horse anymore. Whadda ya say?"

I twisted my body around so that both of my hands were free, then took his handsome face in them and delivered a tender kiss. It wasn't what I wanted to do; I wanted to devour him.

Clay reached up and took my hands in his big ones. He looked into my eyes, and it made me feel that he could see into my very soul. I thought he was about to utter something profound. Then, he smiled.

"Would you mind if I wanted to give you a full-body hug?" he asked.

There was that little boy expression on his face again, but it was packing heat. His gray eyes shone expectantly.

"I think I'd like that a lot."

He lifted me up from the couch. We were standing, facing one another. The heat from his body was like a furnace. Then, he pulled me against him, running his hands down my shoulders, my back, and stopping to rest on my hips. He pressed gently, and I could feel my glutes tense under his hands. Our bodies were pressed together from the knees up. Clay slid his hands back up to my shoulders and started all over again.

"Clay."

"So, sweet cheeks, we through, or just gettin' warmed up?"

How could this hotter than hot hunk make me want him more than my next breath, then say something that made him sound like a high school dropout?

"I'll be careful of your thigh," he whispered.

"My thigh is practically well. The stitches are almost ready to come out."

"Oh, I forgot."

"Let's go upstairs," I said.

Clay took my hand and led me to the stairs. We reached the top step, and he stopped.

"Just take a seat on this top step, you sweet thing. Hold on just a minute."

I sat down on the carpeted step. Clay was digging in all of his pockets, looking frustrated.

"Don't move," he said. "I'll be right back."

He flew down the stairs like the villa was on fire and ran out the front door. Minutes later he was back.

"A little protection never hurts," he said, sounding breathless.

He dropped down beside me and embraced me. We rocked backward onto the carpeted landing. Clay covered my mouth with his and began kissing me. The first kiss was sweet and gentle, and lasted so long that I grew unbearably hungry for him. Then, he drew back and looked into my eyes.

"Oh, Clemmie, I can't wait to make love to you," he whispered.

I was going to show Clay Singleton that I was more than ready to give myself to him. He started kissing me again, sweetly at first. Then, he deepened the kiss, probing my mouth with his tongue, and I felt that familiar anticipatory ache. He caressed me with his big hands, gently, then urgently. I was so ready to make love with him. I wanted him to learn every inch of my body, and I knew that it would feel right. Not a single thought from my past entered my mind. Clay nipped my lower lip in a tantalizing gesture. His mouth left my face, and his teeth grazed my neck, then my shoulder.

"Now," I said. I could hardly breathe, let alone tell him how much I needed him.

Clay fished in his pocket and brought out a little foil packet. He waved it in front of me, smiling.

" I can't wait another minute."

He ripped open the packet, and the condom flew out of his hand, landing at the foot of the stairs.

"Damnation!" he hissed.

He was already out of one pant leg, but he attempted to get to the bottom of the stairs, dragging the other one. I sat on the top step half dressed, and watched him search for the condom. He held it up, looking like he wanted to cry.

"It's ripped," he said.

"Ripped? How could it be ripped? All you did was open the packet."

"It must have happened when I opened it, or I guess I might have stepped on it before I saw it on the floor. I'm sorry, Clemmie. I don't have another one with me."

I wanted him so badly I was aching. He stood at the foot of the stairs looking helpless. I watched the front of his boxers seem to shrink as he got into his pants. I started putting my clothes back on. Maybe this was an omen. Clay Singleton might not be the man for me after all.

Clay climbed the stairs and took me in his arms. I knew he was trying to comfort me, but it just made me more miserable.

"I'll go to the drugstore up the street," he said. "I can be back in just a few minutes."

His hands were a little trembly, and he had drunk some wine. I knew how he felt about driving after having alcohol.

"It's all right, Clay. You shouldn't drive tonight. You can't break your pact with Sarah; I don't want you to."

"I'm fine. I'll be right back."

He started down the stairs and was about to open the door when the doorbell rang.

"You expectin' company?" he asked, frustrated.

"No," I said, hurrying down the stairs.

I opened the door, and there stood Daniel, wearing a big grin. Clay was standing to my right behind the door.

"Surprise!" Daniel said.

He leaned in and pulled me into a bear-hug. I glanced over my shoulder at Clay who stood open-mouthed with his hands at his sides. His eyes looked larger than normal like someone who was frightened.

"Daniel! What are you doing here? How did you know where to find me?"

"You going to invite me in, or what?"

"Sure. I'm just surprised to see you. That's all."

Daniel stepped into the foyer, and I closed the door after him. That was when he saw my house guest who simply stared at him.

"Oh, Daniel, this is Clay Singleton. Clay, meet Daniel Grover, my best friend."

The men shook hands. I was sure Daniel felt that he had interrupted something, and Clay probably wanted to hit Daniel in the mouth for further ruining our intimate evening.

"Mama Rae told me where you live. I went to see her this afternoon. She fed me dinner. The old girl's still the best cook I know."

"Where are Catherine and the baby?"

"They're at home. Suzanne has the sniffles."

"I'm sorry. I'd love to see them."

"You don't want to be around my baby girl when she's not on top of her game. She can be a handful."

I took Daniel's hand and led him into the living room. Clay followed, wearing a hangdog expression.

"Were you two on your way out?" Daniel asked.

"Uh, Clay was just going to run up to the store, but it can wait. Sit down and tell me all about the new job."

"I seem to be covered up with paperwork. My muscles are turning to mush. I miss physical labor. It made me feel good, but this cushy job pays more. End of story."

"I'm sure Catherine and Suzanne miss you, but you said Catherine was on board with the decision. Right?"

Daniel nodded.

"She's the best. Oh, and she's already been told that she'll be getting a promotion after she has worked there for three months."

I wondered if that promotion was being provided by whoever had taken her to dinner at that swanky restaurant.

Daniel looked at Clay and raised his chin.

"That your bad ride just outside, Clay?" he asked.

Clay nodded.

"That it is. It's my only transportation unless I'm on the water. I have a boat over in Shelter Cove."

"How did you two meet?" Daniel asked.

"It was quite by accident," I said. "A little kid knocked a shopping bag out of my hands. I stooped down to retrieve my purchases and came face to face with this guy. He was down on the pavement, holding the bikini top I had just bought."

Daniel grinned.

"Actually, Clay, I've already heard a little bit about you. Clemmie was just a tad upset when her boss caused her to stand you up on your first date."

Clay swiveled his head toward me.

"I told you he was my best friend. We discuss pretty much everything."

"Sounds like," Clay said.

Daniel and Clay seemed to hit it off after the initial shock of my old friend's surprise appearance. The three of us talked for more than two hours. Then, Daniel said that he needed to head back to Savannah. He wanted to spend some quality time with his wife.

If Daniel and Catherine had marital problems, I had the feeling that he didn't know anything about them. He was radiating happiness just as he had been the last time we were together.

Clay and I walked Daniel to the door. After we had said our goodbyes, Clay embraced me and heaved a sigh.

"It's late, and the stores are all closed," Clay said. "I don't think I can be close to you and just go to sleep. What if I sleep on the couch again?"

I felt like crying. I had finally been ready to give Clay Singleton all my love, and it hadn't worked out. I went to the downstairs bedroom and found bedding for the couch. Then, I turned to go upstairs. Clay pulled me to him much the same as a brother might and planted a light kiss on my forehead.

"There's always tomorrow. Goodnight, Clemmie."

CHAPTER
Twenty-Two

Why was I having such rotten luck? What had I done to deserve all of the snags that kept cropping up to keep me from having a meaningful relationship with Clay Singleton? I knew beyond a shadow of doubt that Clay was a good man. He had a kind heart. He was intelligent and witty. He loved his family, and he looked like an Adonis.

I hated the fact that Clay was sleeping on my couch. He should be here in my bed making mad, passionate love to me, telling me that I was on his mind day and night. I imagined him telling Sarah and Grace that he was hopelessly in love with me, and that we were going to get married. I listened for the third stair to squeak and realize that he was on his way up to my bedroom, but there was only silence. The wishful thinking had to stop. Clay was so responsible that he would never consider having sex without protection. He would not put me in a compromising position. What if one of us decided that we were not a good match after all, and that I had accidentally gotten pregnant?

I lay on my back determined to banish thoughts of Clay from

my mind. Finally, I was able to put Daniel front and center. His timing was perfect to put a halt to what might have been a blissful experience for Clay and me. I couldn't help but wonder if his showing up unannounced was an omen.

Daniel had looked so happy, and he had spoken lovingly about his wife. If it turned out that Catherine was having an affair, it would destroy Daniel. He hadn't had an easy childhood, and I knew that marrying Catherine had made him feel complete—he was happy now. Why hadn't I called her name to get her attention and say hello instead of spying on her at the restaurant? And why hadn't I followed her to her table so she could introduce me to her dining companion? Her evening out was probably innocent, so why did I have the feeling that she was being unfaithful to my best friend?

Clay was gone the next morning. He had left another note on the counter telling me how sorry he was about our ruined evening, and he promised to make it up to me. The villa felt so empty when I awoke to find that he had left. It made me realize what a presence he had become. I had to banish this lonely feeling. Maybe Mama Rae could help.

She was sitting in a chair on her front porch denuding a stem of its leaves. Lord sat on the bottom porch step washing his face with a white-stockinged paw.

"Look who's come to see us, Lord," Mama Rae said. "Hadn't been for her, you wouldn't be here."

"Good morning, Mama Rae. I see you and Lord are taking good care of one another. He looks like he needs to go on a diet. What have you been feeding him?"

"He partial to organ meat, but sometimes I give him fish and chicken. He a good hunter; jes gobbled down two field mice."

"Mama Rae, I have a problem."

My old friend nodded toward a mesh basket too far for her to reach from her chair. I knew she meant for me to hand it to her.

"Mama Rae listnin'."

"I don't think I told you the name of the man I've met here on the island. He and I have spent quite a bit of time together, and I've grown awfully fond of him. I think he can be the person who can help me bury my painful past and be happy again. His name is Clay Singleton; I understand the two of you have met."

Mama Rae nodded.

"I know him. Nice young man, smart man, asks more questions dan you. He want to know everting 'bout dis islan'.'"

"He needs as much information as he can get. It's research for the book he is writing."

"He tol' me."

"I'm glad you like him. And since you do, is there anything you can do to make my relationship with him more intimate. We're friends, but I want a lot more than that. You've helped me lots of times in the past, so I know you can do something."

Mama Rae chuckled.

"Girl, you got some big 'magination."

"That's not the only thing I wanted to discuss with you. I don't know if this means anything or not. I was in a restaurant in Savannah with my boss not long ago. It was one of those dinners that's supposed to be part of my job. I was in the ladies' room when I heard a familiar voice. As I left to return to my table, I saw the woman the voice belonged to. It was Daniel's wife, Catherine."

"Why dat bother you?"

"I didn't see who she was there with, but it wasn't Daniel; he was in Atlanta. That's what bothers me. What if she's having an affair?"

Mama Rae dumped her lapful of leaves into the basket and rose from the chair. She shuffled to the door with the basket of leaves, and Lord was quick to follow. I didn't know if she was going to invite me inside, so I stayed where I was. She and her cat went into the cabin, and the screen door slapped to. Our conversation was over.

I went back through the woods feeling unsettled. There was no possible way for me to prove that my old friend had the ability to make things happen or to affect people's actions, but it certainly seemed that she did. She hadn't given me an inkling as to what she thought about my fears regarding Catherine. One thing I knew for certain: she loved Daniel like a son, and she would do whatever it took to make sure his bubble didn't burst.

I could see the message light on my phone blinking through the narrow window by my front door as I slid the key into the lock. I wondered what new task Max Palmer had conjured for me to do. Pressing the button, I waited to hear his latest idea.

"Hey, Clemmie," Clay said in his sexy southern drawl. "Do you happen to like picnics?"

"Sure. Would you like to take me on one?"

"Yes ma'am. I certainly would."

"When do you have in mind?"

"How about early this evenin' before the sun's about to go down?"

"That sounds like fun, Clay. I've never been on a picnic except in broad daylight. What should I bring?"

"I'll bring everything we need. You just bring you."

Clay hadn't said where this picnic was to take place, but I assumed shorts and a tee shirt would be suitable attire. I grabbed a blanket from the downstairs closet assuming men might not think of such things.

I heard the Red Devil as it pulled into Hickory Cove. Clay bounded up my porch steps and rang the bell.

"Ready?" he asked as I opened the door.

I nodded and joined him on the porch with the blanket folded over my arm.

"Good thinkin', pretty girl. The saddlebags are loaded, but I didn't think to bring a blanket."

"Where are we going?"

"One of your favorite places, the beach. I know the perfect spot."

And indeed he did. We took his bike to a place I had never

been, and Clay locked it and chained it to a tree close to the steps leading to the beach.

"People on this island are pretty stand-up, but this bike might be a little too temptin' to a visitor," he said, unfastening the saddlebags.

The sky was streaked with crimson. It was one of the most gorgeous sunsets I had ever seen. A gentle breeze barely made its presence known as Clay led the way to what was going to be our perfect spot.

"How about right here?" he asked.

"It's made to order. We'll have a clear view of that spectacular sunset, and we're practically hidden. Is there a word for *outdoor cozy*?"

"Not sure about that, but I spotted this when I was walkin' the beach and knew you'd like it."

We spread the blanket under the fronds of a short palm tree. Our nest was surrounded on three sides by sea oats doing their dance in the light breeze.

Clay began unloading our feast of cold chicken, a baguette, fruit, and cheese. Then, he produced a corkscrew and a bottle of wine.

"How did you fit all of this into those bags?" I asked as he brought out plastic cups and utensils.

"Magic. Now, hold your cup."

"Clay, we came here on your bike. You're not going to have wine, are you?"

"I thought I'd have a little. We'll be here for a while. The buzz'll wear off, and we'll hardly be on the road at all on our way back to your place. That okay with you? Goin' back to your place?"

"Sure. That'll be great."

Clay poured the wine and proposed a toast: "Here's to us and our special night."

He touched his cup to mine, and we drank to the toast. I wanted this to be an evening to remember. Not a single thought from my past entered my mind. We sipped our wine and watched people gather their things and leave the beach to go their respective ways.

We finished our picnic long before the red ball disappeared. Our trash was cleaned up and everything was put away except for the wine which we continued to sip.

"You were right about this picnic spot, Clay. It couldn't be more perfect."

Clay's smile was somehow different, and his gray eyes looked at me with an expression he had never shown me. He reached for my wine cup.

"Let's take a break from the wine for a little while," he said.

"Sure."

I assumed he wanted to pace himself because we would be taking the bike back to Hickory Cove, but I quickly understood that wasn't his reason for the break when he pulled me close and kissed me. We lay back on the blanket, and I began to ache in anticipation of his next move. I could feel my pulse quicken when he pressed his body to mine. His hands caressed my arms, my shoulders, and my back. I so wanted to experience that satisfied feeling that had been lost for so long.

"Clemmie, I want you," he whispered.

I could feel blood pounding in my ears. My entire body tingled. I took Clay's face in my hands and brought his lips down to mine, waiting for him to kiss me senseless, until I begged him to make love to me. His kiss was so passionate, so greedy that I almost couldn't breathe. I could feel his erection press against me, and it was driving me mad. He unhooked my bra, then cupped my breast. His hand was fiery hot, and it felt so good. Then, I wasn't sure what happened. I swallowed hard and pushed away from him.

"What's the matter?" he said. He was breathing as though he had been running.

"I'm so sorry, Clay. I don't know. I want you. I do, but making love with you here on this beach doesn't feel right. I don't know how to explain it."

Clay sat up and heaved a sigh, then took a gulp of his wine.

"It's all right, Clemmie. I was afraid this might not be the easiest thing for you to do. You're probably still grievin' for your husband. That's not somethin' you can just turn off."

How could he be so understanding? He had feelings and emotions too. I felt so selfish.

"You're the best man I think I've ever known. I can't believe how unselfish you are; how strong."

"Let's finish our wine and head back," he said.

We walked back hand in hand to the place where we had left the bike without talking, and made it back to my villa without incident.

"Okay for me to bunk on your couch again?" he asked.

"Of course."

I couldn't stand to let our special evening end this way. Clay thought I wasn't ready for a meaningful relationship. How could he think otherwise? I felt so guilty; not because of grief, but because I hadn't been totally honest with him. He didn't know that Jimmy and I had made love on that same beach and that thoughts of my late husband had crashed this party at just the right time to end it. He also didn't know that Jimmy's parents had owned this villa long before I decided to rent it, that we had made love for the first time in the bedroom I now claimed for my own. I needed to fill in all the blanks instead of lying to him through omission.

Tension gripped me as we entered the villa. I could tell that Clay was uncomfortable, but that he was trying not to show it.

"I can walk to my boat if it'll make you feel better," he offered.

"No. That's ridiculous."

"Okay. Thanks. You won't even know I'm here. Goodnight, Clemmie."

I didn't know what I was going to say to this man I was falling in love with, but I had to try to explain my behavior.

"We have to talk, Clay. I'm sorry I ruined our evening. Are you willing to let me try to explain?"

Clay nodded and sat on one end of the couch. The happiness had left his handsome face; there was no desire in his eyes. He looked inordinately sad, but he sat up straight, ready to hear whatever I had to say. I sat down on the coffee table, facing him and took his big hands in mine. He had to understand that I wanted him, but I didn't know how to express it after what I had done.

"There are things I need to tell you which I thought were unimportant. That's not true. I don't know why I was reluctant to tell you, but now I know I must."

"Just tell me, Clemmie. I wouldn't hurt you for anything in the world, but I don't think I can go on like this. Don't beat around the bush; just tell it like it is."

"When the woman who owned this villa was showing it to me, I realized that I had been here before. I remembered every room, how the furnishings had changed, but the view of the golf course was the same. Jimmy's parents owned this villa when he and I were dating. They didn't live here, but they did use it when they didn't have it rented to vacationers. They had another house and only used this place for a change of scenery every now and then."

"I don't understand why that's important. It's a great villa, and you love it."

"Yes, I do, but it holds lots of memories of the times Jimmy and I spent here. His parents had no idea that their son and I were using their property for afternoon delights and playing house lots of nights."

"I see."

"We also made love on that beautiful beach you and I just left. It's true that we never had a picnic at sunset, but we did have sex on the beach quite often. When you and I were about to dive into making love on the sand, my late husband pushed his way into my mind. It was forceful, and it was unfair to you. I wanted to think only of you when I gave myself to you."

Clay summoned a little smile.

"Got any more secrets?" he asked.

"None that I can think of at the moment. I just had to explain my actions. I want you to be a part of my life, Clay. Nothing should enter my mind except my feelings for you. If I need to seek help to erase my past, I'll do it. Maybe I shouldn't have been released from Still Waters. For all I know, I could still be kind of wacko."

Clay pulled me to a standing position and embraced me. His muscled arms seemed to shelter me from all harm, and I felt relaxed and safe.

"You're not wacko, Clemmie. You're just not there yet," he said as he sort of swayed with me much like one would to comfort an infant.

Hot tears leaked from my eyes. I didn't know why I was crying.

"Hey, you're gettin' my shirt all wet."

"I'm sorry," I said, pushing away from him.

"Clemmie, I'm just tryin' to make you smile," he said, drawing me back into his arms.

"I feel like an idiot."

Clay put a knuckle under my chin and lifted my face. A more tender kiss had never touched my lips. There was nothing urgent about it. I put my palm on his cheek. Clay moved it to his lips and kissed it.

"I think I love you, Clay Singleton."

"Is that right?"

"It is."

"That's convenient, because I'm pretty sure I'm fallin' in love with you. What do you think we ought to do about it?"

"I'll show you," I said, taking him by the hand and leading him into the downstairs bedroom.

"Clemmie, let's not do anything to get your head all out of kilter tonight. You explained things, and I'm good with that. I can be patient."

"I don't want to be patient. I want to let you know how I feel about you and stop letting myself live in the past. That's holding me hostage; it's ruining our relationship before it's barely started."

Clay stood in the doorway, looking like he didn't know what he should do. I turned the lamp on low and pulled him into an embrace of my own, kicking off my shoes.

"Raise your arms," I said. "I'm about to strip this wet tee shirt off you, then get you naked."

That special light came back into Clay's eyes, and he gave me one of his movie star smiles. Then, his lips were on mine, and I knew he was the man I wanted to be my life partner. I could feel Mama Rae's approval and wondered if her special powers had been at work.

CHAPTER
Twenty-Three

The aroma of coffee pulled me out of a deep sleep. I
was on the left side of one of two double beds in the
master bedroom downstairs. There was an indentation
in the pillow to my right. I felt amazingly rested. Then, I smiled to
myself, recalling flashbacks of making love with Clay, and how it
had felt like a whole new experience. Thoughts of my late husband
hadn't interfered even once. All I could think about was how much
I loved Clay, and how right it felt to be with him. I wondered if
he had made coffee, left another note on the kitchen counter, then
disappeared. My clothes were in a heap on the floor, and I felt
deliciously free.

I grabbed a towel from the bathroom and wrapped it around
me, then headed for the kitchen. The sizzle of bacon frying was
unmistakable. As I came into the dining area, I witnessed my man
breaking eggs into a bowl. He was shirtless and barefoot. And he
was whistling as he attacked the eggs with a whisk.

He must have felt my presence, because he looked up from his
task and smiled.

"Mornin', sunshine," he said, leaving his work to come and envelop me in loving arms.

"Good morning."

"I thought I'd make us a little grub after all that hard work we did last night."

I looked up into his smiling face.

"Last night was wonderful, Clay. I'm so glad you're still here."

Clay delivered a kiss to my forehead and broke our embrace. He poured coffee and handed me a cup.

"I'm gonna feed you breakfast and tell you about my plans for the next few days, because I don't ever want us to have another misunderstandin' about where I am or what I'm doin'."

"Okay. Exactly what's on your agenda?"

Clay poured eggs into a skillet and scrambled them while he laid out his plan.

"I'll be takin' people out on my boat. You might not believe it, but I make good money every time I go out into the deep water."

"Of course, I believe it. I believe everything you tell me."

"I'm glad, because we need to trust one another."

"Will I see you in the evenings?"

"I doubt it. It'll be after dark when I bring the boat back. I'll have to clean it before mornin', and I'll be dirty and pretty tired. Besides, you'll have to get up and go to work each mornin'. Things'll be back to normal in four days. Think we can handle that?"

"Sure."

We ate like we were starved. Then, we cleaned up our mess and Clay left to get his messages from Sarah and ready his boat to make money.

I didn't feel lonely like I had in the past when Clay had left the villa after scribbling a note on a paper towel. This time I knew he would be coming back to me.

I showered and dressed, then took off for the woods. Mama Rae shielded her eyes from the sun with her hand. She was looking up into a tree and threatening to climb up after Lord if he didn't come down on his own.

"You'd better leave dat bird alone or I'll put you in dat cage," she said.

As if the cat understood what she had said, he began climbing down from the tree. When he was about four feet from the ground, he leaped and landed on all four feet.

"See how smart you are," she said. "You know better dan to go after a baby bird don't know how to fly yet."

I was standing practically in front of Mama Rae, but she hadn't acknowledged me.

"Hello, Mama Rae."

"Les go in de house so I can give Lord a treat for doin' de right ting."

I followed her inside with the cat dashing in front of me. Lord sat looking up at Mama Rae, waiting for her to dole out goodies. She reached into the fridge and brought out a bowl of what looked like raw meat, pulled off a small piece and offered it to her pet. He made short work of it. Then, he strolled off to his bed in the corner to wash his face.

Mama Rae motioned for me to sit. I took my usual seat and waited to see what she might have to say.

"You keep on takin' dem big paychecks. You not in any trouble."

"How do you know?"

"Don't you trust your Mama Rae, chile?"

"Of course, I do. It's just that you never explain how you know things. I know you don't have a crystal ball."

My old friend smiled and shook her head.

"Jes take my word and believe what I tell you. Mama Rae not goin' send you down de wrong path."

"That's true. You've always somehow known what was best for me."

"What else you want to know?"

"I want to know what Catherine was doing in that restaurant. Daniel wasn't there; he was in Atlanta working. Who was she with?"

"Sometimes you let dat 'magination run away with you. Why you always tink de worst?"

"I don't. It just shocked me to realize that Catherine was out on the town with someone else while Daniel was working to make a better life for them."

"Dat girl been awful busy lately and goin' be busier dan ever."

"How do you know?"

"Mama Rae jes know."

"I want to know that Daniel is happy and that his wife is being faithful to him. He deserves a wonderful life. You know he has had to work awfully hard just to have a normal life. I met him when he was just nine years old. His mother was the only parent he had then. After Tybee Island was devastated, he and his mother moved somewhere else and I didn't see him again until he was sixteen. That was when he came to Hilton Head to live with his aunt. Roy's bigoted secretary tried her best to destroy him. You know the rest."

"Daniel be jes fine. He got a nice, happy little family."

"I hope you're right."

Mama Rae chuckled.

"Mama Rae always right."

She got up from the table and left the room.

I went back to my villa. Today it felt more like home than it had since I moved into it. I walked back into the downstairs bedroom and lay down on the unmade bed. I closed my eyes and pulled Clay's pillow close to my face. His scent still lingered. I wasn't the least bit lonely.

The unsure feeling about Catherine niggled at my mind and stayed there. Mama Rae had assured me that I didn't need to worry. If she thought Daniel's marriage was on solid ground, I should let it rest. My old mentor did always seem to know what was happening; sometimes, even before the fact. I needed to put my trust in her intuition, or whatever she possessed that I didn't.

Tomorrow would be my first day back at work, and I wondered what surprise task Max Palmer would have for me to do. Mama Rae's advice regarding the money I was raking in for doing nothing made me a bit less apprehensive about my job, but I still had no idea why Max Palmer considered me an assistant.

As I dressed for work the next morning, I couldn't stop thinking about Clay. I wondered how early he had gotten up to go out on the water. I had never thought about his safety before, but I said a silent prayer for his safe return.

Max Palmer was seated at his desk. He smiled as I came through the glass door.

"Good morning, Clemmie. I must say you look especially bright and beautiful today."

"Thank you," I said, recalling that my shrink paid me a similar compliment every time I wore blue.

"Clemmie, how are you feeling?"

"I'm fine. The stitches have been removed and my thigh isn't the least bit sore."

"That's wonderful because I'll need you to hold down the fort today. I'll be leaving right after breakfast. Just mind the phone and take messages."

As if Miss Prissy Pants had heard her boss mention the word, she appeared with a large tray bearing our breakfast. Today it was scrambled eggs, bacon, toast and juice. I had the feeling that Max Palmer thought he needed to feed me in addition to paying me way too much.

He had just inhaled his food and then glanced at me with what had the look of a plea before he spoke.

"Are you free for dinner this evening?" he asked.

That was only the second time he had actually asked if I was free. He usually told me that I would be expected to dine with him and with whomever else he had plans.

"Yes. I'm free this evening."

"Good. Pearl has requested our presence for dinner on the yacht. Casual attire will be fine."

I couldn't imagine why Pearl would request my presence; she didn't like me.

"She would like us to be there for cocktails at six o'clock. I'll come by your place around 5:30."

My boss told me to shut down the office at four o'clock, and I was happy to do that. Being in that big empty room all alone was awfully boring.

The message light on my phone was blinking when I walked into my villa. Maybe Clay had gotten back to Shelter Cove a lot sooner than he had thought he would. If that happened to be the case, I would hate to tell him that I couldn't see him tonight because I had another command performance.

I listened to the message: "Hey, Clemmie. Daniel here. I don't know what your schedule is like, but I'm still in Savannah for a couple of more days. Any chance I could tear you away from your new squeeze for a lunch or dinner? Give me a call."

Daniel hadn't said anything about Catherine. I wondered if that meant she wouldn't be coming with him. Clay wouldn't be available in the evenings because of his work commitment, so I could see Daniel any evening, or I could probably meet him for lunch unless my boss actually had some work for me to do. I punched in the Grovers' number.

"Daniel Grover here."

"Daniel, I just got your message. I have a dinner engagement with my boss tonight, but I'm free tomorrow evening. Does that work for you?"

"It does. What time do you get home from work?"

"I'll be home a little after five o'clock."

"Great. I'll come to your place if that's okay."

"Fine. Daniel, is everything alright?"

"Everything's cool. See you tomorrow night."

Why did I have a feeling that my best friend was lying through his teeth? Mama Rae had assured me that I was worrying over nothing. Why couldn't I believe her? I needed to clear my head. Shrugging out of my clothes, I threw on shorts and a tee shirt, then started to the beach.

There was a delightful breeze, but the Atlantic looked as smooth as glass. I never got my fill of this natural work of art. I shed my flip-flops, not bothering to toss them behind the step, and walked to the water's edge. I splashed through the still warm foam, walking in the direction of the spot where Clay had brought me for our sunset picnic. Then, I left the water to go to the place we had made our nest and settled down on the sand, hidden from the world by swaying sea oats.

I stared out at the ocean, willing my mind to go blank. I told myself not to think about Daniel, Clay, Max Palmer, or even Mama Rae. Meditation: that was what I needed at the moment. Maybe I was becoming a master of this simple cure. The tension in my shoulders relaxed, and I felt that nothing mattered. Everything was simply calm and peaceful. I had sat down cross-legged, but my body felt weightless as though I were lying on a cloud.

I didn't know how long I stayed in my meditative state, but I became instantly alert when I felt my face being washed by a very rough tongue. Blinking my eyes open, I was staring a big golden retriever in the face. The dog was beating sea oats with its wagging tail, and it was wiggling all over with what appeared to be happiness.

"Scrubs!"

A young man was running toward me. He reached down to grab the dog's collar and pull him away. The dog got in one last sloppy lick.

"Ma'am, I'm really sorry. He didn't hurt you, did he?"

"No," I said, laughing. He must have thought I was either very sad or in need of a bath."

Recognition dawned on the young man's face.

"Hey, I remember you. I'm Jake, your neighbor. I drove you home from the hospital."

"That's right. Thanks again. Your dog is very sweet natured."

"Yeah. He'd never bite anybody, but he might love you to death."

I got up and brushed myself off.

"I was about to go home. If you and Scrubs are going that way, I'll walk with you."

"As a matter of fact, we are. I'm glad we ran into you. I don't know many of my neighbors since I sometimes work strange hours. I apologize; I forgot your name."

"I'm Clemmie Castlebrook."

"Cwemmie!"

I looked up to see Sarah and Grace heading toward us. Grace ran to meet me. She wrapped her chubby arms around my knees just before her mother caught up to her.

"Well, hello," I said. "Are you two out for a little exercise?"

"We are," said Sarah.

Since I hadn't expected to see Clay's sister and niece, I was caught off guard. Sarah might get the wrong impression, seeing me with a great looking young man and his dog.

"Uh, Sarah and Grace, this is my friend Jake and his dog Scrubs."

Grace released my knees and put both arms around the dog's neck. He began kissing her face, and she giggled and kissed him back.

"Scwubs, you're so cute," she said, kissing him again.

"Jake lives down the street from me. He works at the hospital and drove me home from there the day I got stitches since we're neighbors."

"We're glad to meet you Jake," Sarah said. "And you, too, Scrubs. We need to be getting home now. We'll see you soon, Clemmie."

Did I imagine it, or did Sarah sound cool? She had seemed genuinely warm each time I had been around her. I wondered if she would mention our meeting on the beach to Clay.

Jake and I parted ways at his villa because I lived a little farther down, closer to the mailboxes. I let myself in, and hurried up the stairs to get ready for dinner with Pearl, the puppeteer. I wracked my brain trying to think of a reason she might request my presence.

My boss had told me that casual attire would be fine, so I dressed in white slacks, a short-sleeved silk shirt, and sandals. Then,

I went downstairs to wait for Max Palmer. The man was never a minute late. Just as I grabbed my keys and purse, the tinny doorbell rang. Max stood at my front door wearing a bright smile.

"Well, Clemmie, you certainly look cool and comfortable."

I wasn't sure it was a compliment.

"You did say this dinner is to be casual, didn't you?"

"I did, indeed. You look terrific."

We found Pearl in the salon where I had first met her. Upon our entrance, she donned her practiced smile. Her eyes were bright as if she had just thought of a fantastic idea.

"Good evening, Clemmie, Max. Come in; come in. Let's get comfortable and have a drink before dinner."

Gretchen served cocktails, and Max and I took our seats.

"I'm sure you're both wondering why I invited you here tonight. There are things I need to share with you."

I had assumed Max had known the reason for our dinner invitation, but it seemed that he, too, was in for a surprise.

CHAPTER
Twenty-Four

Pearl stabbed an olive from her martini glass and popped it into her mouth. She chewed it for what seemed an inordinately long time. Finally, she swallowed and turned her steely eyes on me.

"I don't intimidate you in the least, do I, Clemmie?" she said.

Her red lips raised at the corners in a half-smile, and I realized that she was waiting for my answer. I didn't know what an appropriate response might be. It was obvious to me that she was the head of Max Palmer's business. He was always at her service. If I said the wrong thing, I might be out of a job before dinner was served. Pearl and Max were both looking at me expectantly.

"That's a rather unusual question," I said. "I'm not sure why you would ask it."

"You are a spunky little thing," she said. "I think that's why I see potential in you."

"I don't want to be rude, but I'm not sure what you mean. Potential for what?"

"I'm not a spring chicken, and I'm not in the best of health. As a matter of fact, I'm not sure how much longer I'll be here."

Max looked horrified.

"Pearl, you can't mean that. Why, you're hale and hearty except for needing the wheelchair."

"No, Max. I'm not hale and hearty as you put it. My body is failing me. I fear that the only fire I have left is in my attitude. That will never change. People will remember me because of my somewhat abrasive disposition."

"But you don't seem sick. Whatever your ailment is, we'll make sure you see the best doctors," Max said.

Pearl held up a hand to let him know he was wasting his breath.

"Doctors can't be of assistance for dealing with this malady. It's a progressive thing, and it's on the down slope. Only God could produce such a miracle, and I don't think He's very happy with me."

Max cleared his throat and tried to compose himself.

"Exactly what is this malady?"

"I choose not to dignify the damnable thing with a name. Just know that I have done everything possible to stave it off, or at least slow its progression. I have been helped by an unnamed source to cripple this killer for the past two years, but the magic has now failed to help. The discussion of my illness has now ended."

I had never felt so uncomfortable. There was nothing for me to say to this mysterious woman. She was obviously not asking for advice from either of her dinner guests.

Max Palmer fidgeted in his chair, taking small sips of his drink.

Pearl donned her brightest smile. She took a deep breath, then spoke.

"Gretchen, bring us another round. I feel like getting drunk."

By the time we went in to dinner, I was feeling a little tipsy, and Max had begun to slur his speech. It was after eight o'clock, and I had downed three glasses of wine. Max had been drinking scotch neat, and Pearl had polished off several martinis. She appeared to be in very good spirits and couldn't seem to complete sentences.

Gretchen served what I'm sure was a delicious dinner, but I didn't recall eating it, and have no idea what it might have been. I had intended to bring up the subject of my potential from our earlier conversation, but I doubted that our hostess would be any more forthcoming than she had been when she was sober.

My boss was in no condition to drive, so I got behind the wheel of his very cool car and drove us to my villa. I had intended to invite him to sleep on my couch, but I couldn't rouse him enough to get him out of the car and up the steps to the door. I was afraid that if he awoke and attempted to drive himself home that he might have a wreck, so I left him half-sitting, half-lying in the passenger seat, took the keys inside with me and fell into bed.

I awoke the next morning to the loud chirping of birds in the tree just outside my bedroom. I hadn't set an alarm, and it was almost nine o'clock. Still groggy from sleep, I went downstairs to make coffee. I had just filled the tank of the coffeepot when I remembered that I had left my boss outside all night. It was impossible to see his car from the foyer, so I ran upstairs to grab my robe. I hurried outside in bare feet and saw the red Ferrari sitting in the space beside my Jeep. There was nobody in it.

I couldn't imagine what had become of my boss. Why hadn't he rung my doorbell when he awoke and realized where he was? I took a quick shower while the coffee perked. The phone rang as I finished dressing.

"Good morning, Clemmie."

I felt relief at hearing Max Palmer's voice.

"Mister Palmer, where are you? Are you all right?"

"Yes, I'm all right. I think I might have imbibed a bit too much last evening. You must have been more than a little put out with me since you absconded with my keys and relegated me to the great outdoors with the tree frogs and humidity." He attempted a small chuckle.

I had the impression he was trying to put me on the defensive.

"I couldn't wake you, Mister Palmer."

"You needn't explain further, Clemmie. Meet me in the coffee shop in the Hyatt as soon as you can."

"I'll be there in fifteen minutes."

My employer was slumped over his coffee cup when I arrived. He looked up at me with bloodshot eyes. His usual morning smile was missing, and his clothes were a rumpled mess. Several strands of his disheveled white mane clung to patches of his scruff of beard. He failed to issue any form of greeting. I saw that he had ordered coffee for two, so I reached for the pot and poured myself a cup, refusing to be the first to speak.

"Are you hungry?" he asked.

I nodded.

"Did we have dinner last night?"

I looked at my boss and stifled a giggle. I knew his question shouldn't have struck me funny, but it had.

"I can't say that I recall," I said.

That prompted both of us to start laughing, and Max massaged his temples.

"I'm afraid our hostess served us a liquid diet," he said. "My head is killing me, and I've no doubt you're embarrassed to be seen in public with me. I must look frightful."

"How did you get to the hotel from my place?"

"Walked. It wasn't that far. I woke up on one of the couches in the lobby a little while ago."

"Again, I'm sorry. I didn't know what to do since I couldn't wake you. You were in no condition to drive."

"Let's have a good breakfast. Then, we need to talk."

I recalled the morning my boss told me we were going to have a breakfast meeting. We ate in silence. Then, Max gave me the day off. That was the extent of the meeting.

I didn't think Max had gained any more insight into Pearl's revelation concerning her terrible illness than I had. He seemed to be as shocked as I at hearing about that and about whatever she had in mind for me.

Whatever my boss had wanted to discuss with me would remain a secret until after breakfast. Max Palmer never let conversation get in the way of a meal. His plate was clean before I had eaten a couple of bites, but I was so hungry that I continued eating while he stared at me over the rim of his cup.

"Let's get my car, then go to the office," he said.

I wondered what was about to become of my nothing job with the fabulous salary.

Max unlocked the door to the office building and turned on lights. Then, I followed him to his desk and sat across from him. He wore a perplexed expression.

"Pearl threw me for a loop last night," he said. "I had no idea she was ill. She doesn't look sick, and as far as I know, she hasn't exhibited any signs of being ill."

"Mister Palmer, I don't understand why I am being told personal things about Pearl. Your relationship with her is none of my concern, and I don't see why she has the slightest interest in me. I assume the two of you are business partners of some sort, but how do I fit into the business? I don't even know what it is."

Max Palmer sighed.

"I've always made it a practice to keep my personal business private, but since you are my assistant, I'll explain a few things to you."

I was eager to hear any tidbit my boss was willing to tell me.

"My parents were killed in an automobile accident when I was a young child. Pearl's husband and my father were partners in the business. Pearl and her husband didn't adopt me, but they raised me. I don't know how they managed to do that legally. Pearl's husband always seemed to accomplish whatever he wanted whether or not it was within the law."

I wanted to ask questions, but I was afraid to interrupt.

"I never met any of my relatives. When I was older, Pearl told me that I had no living family. I was never coddled as a child, but I never lacked for anything. Art exhibits, the symphony, and several trips to Europe were all part of my formative years. I attended the best schools. Equestrian training and sailing were two of my favorite activities. I would no doubt have been a spoiled brat had I been exposed to affection."

Learning a bit about my employer's past was fascinating to me.

"I appreciate your taking me into your confidence," I said.

"You're quite welcome."

"Would you mind answering one more question?"

Max Palmer nodded.

"Is Pearl's surname Palmer, or was that your parents' name"

"Pearl's last name is Burke. The name carries some unpleasant connotations. Pearl chooses not to use it. Everyone knows Pearl; her last name would be somewhat superfluous."

I couldn't help wondering how Pearl might have become so well-known and revered.

"Pearl does a lot of good; not just here on Hilton Head, but all over the southeast. She has always favored the downtrodden and given them her support."

"I wasn't aware of that."

"As I've told you, I'm very much indebted to Pearl."

I knew I had little hope of getting an answer, but I forged ahead.

"Just one last question, if I may. Are you acquainted with a woman called Mama Rae?"

Max smiled, looking amused.

"No, I'm afraid I'm not."

How could my dear friend and my boss both blatantly lie to me? I had seen them together more than once.

"I'm afraid I must call a halt to the Q and A, Clemmie. We'll pick it up at another time. I'm tired and in need of making myself look and feel human."

"Of course."

"I don't know what's going on with Pearl, Clemmie. I'm at a loss as to her choosing to bring a newcomer into her inner circle. You seem to be one of the chosen."

I didn't like the sound of that. My boss might have been describing some sort of cult.

"Take the day off, dear girl. I owe you. Go to the beach; go shopping. Do whatever makes you happy. Meet me here for breakfast in the morning."

"Thank you."

I left the office in a quandary. If Mama Rae would tell me the truth about her relationship with Pearl and Max Palmer, I would be on my way to seek her counsel right now.

I decided to go to the beach. Maybe if I let my mind drift while feeling sand shift under my feet and my eyes taking in the natural beauty of this big wide beach, I would stumble upon something that would help me figure out the mystery.

I went to my villa to change into something beachworthy. The message light on my phone was blinking when I stepped into the foyer. I pushed the button wondering if my boss had changed his mind about giving me the day off.

"Clemmie, change of plans." Clay had left me a message. "I'll be back on the island late today. I hope you don't have a dinner engagement."

I was thrilled that he was coming back earlier than expected, but I wondered what had cut the fishing trip short. It was supposed to have been a big money maker. Just knowing that I would soon be seeing Clay had a calming effect on me. I would still go to the beach, but it wouldn't be out of desperation.

There were fewer people enjoying the beach now that fall was approaching. Soon the beachgoers would dwindle to a few, and the golfers would swarm the island to take advantage of the perfectly groomed courses and the lovely weather.

I strolled along the edge of the surf, letting my cares drift out to sea and wondering where Clay had found a phone to call me. I knew he didn't have one on his boat. But I didn't want to clutter my mind with such things. All that mattered was that he sounded happy and would soon be home. I cut my walk short so I would have time to spiffy up the villa and make myself pretty to wait for my man.

The place was shining by four o'clock. I had showered and put on my prettiest sundress. I went out on the deck with a glass of iced tea to wait for Clay, making sure to leave the sliding glass door open a crack so I could hear the doorbell.

I watched two foursomes smack their golf balls down the fairway from the tee box across from my villa. Then, I heard the tinny chime of my doorbell. I hurried inside and rushed to the front door, yanking it open wide. Who knew it was possible to actually feel a smile leave one's face? I had completely forgotten about our previous dinner plans.

"Hi, Daniel."

CHAPTER
Twenty-Five

I was always happy to see Daniel whenever he decided to show up at my door, but lately his timing had been a bit inconvenient. Clay and I had been on the verge of intimacy the first time Daniel appeared out of the blue, but this was my fault. I had completely spaced my dinner date with Daniel, and Clay would be here any minute. Clay knew that Daniel was my best friend since childhood, and he was broadminded, but it would be understandable if he might think Daniel was spending a little too much time alone with me. Daniel was a married man.

My old friend made himself at home. He went to the kitchen and grabbed a beer out of the fridge, fell back onto the living room couch and propped his feet on the coffee table. I sat down beside him.

"Daniel, I have a confession. I forgot about our dinner date, and Clay is on his way here. Forgive me?"

"Sure. Tell me the latest about your mystery job real fast," he said, taking a pull on the longneck.

"It gets more mysterious by the day. It seems that my boss

and Pearl, the elderly woman I told you about, are partners in the business, whatever that is. I'm sure she must hold the purse strings as well as being Max Palmer's puppeteer. And this is the strangest part: she wants me involved. I can't imagine why. I had assumed that Max knew everything about the company and that Pearl apprised him of her every intention, but he seemed stymied to learn that she wanted to bring a newbie into her inner circle."

"Wow! Sounds like you could get rich overnight. On the other hand, you might wind up behind bars. What do you plan to do?"

I didn't like the sound of Daniel's flippant remark.

"I don't have a plan, Daniel. I have to find out what kind of business I'm about to be caught up in before I decide what to do. As far as I know, my employer hasn't done anything illegal, but I don't have enough information to form an opinion. I'm totally ignorant concerning the business. I know it involves real estate, but I know very little about the law."

Daniel and I had never been in the habit of sniping at one another. We had been best pals from the moment we met. It was unlike him to show so little concern about my dilemma. He looked sort of hurt after hearing my agitated tone of voice.

"I didn't mean to sound snippy, Daniel. It's just that I could be in this thing over my head. Pearl let Max and me in on the fact that she has some strange illness. She doesn't think she's long for this world. I had the impression that she wants me to assist Max in whatever the business is. If I agree to do that, I could be in real trouble."

Daniel rubbed a hand across his face. That was what he did when he realized a situation wasn't frivolous. He swallowed.

"Clemmie, I'll do my best to help you learn what's going on with Max Palmer. I don't have a clue as to what the first step will be, but I'll think of something. I'll give you a number where you can reach me in Atlanta, and I'll call you with anything I dig up."

"I know you will. I'm just afraid I'm running out of time."

"Try not to worry. I'll find out what's going on."

Daniel took a sip of his beer and looked at his watch.

"I'm not in a good place right now, Clemmie. I hope I'm imagining things, but I think my marriage might be in trouble."

I just looked at him. After he told me why he thought such a thing, I would decide whether or not to tell him about seeing Catherine at the restaurant.

"I've called home a couple of times at night, and Catherine didn't answer the phone. I asked her about it the first time it happened, and she gave me some sort of lame excuse: she had gone to an evening board meeting, and she had left Suzanne with the amazing baby sitter she had hired."

"Daniel, that sounds perfectly reasonable to me. What about the other time you called?"

"She didn't bother to explain it. And she should have been home this afternoon when I got there. She only works half days on Fridays."

"Maybe she forgot about the second time you called, and she might have had errands to run this afternoon."

"I have this feeling, Clemmie. It isn't something I can describe. I feel uneasy inside. I know that sounds crazy. Maybe I should check it out with Doctor Phil, huh?"

"Why did you come here instead of sticking around at your apartment until Catherine came home? She probably has a logical explanation."

"I don't know. Maybe I don't want to know the truth. You and I always hash out our problems together, so here I am. I just needed a sounding board."

"Don't jump to conclusions right now, Daniel. Go home and talk with Catherine."

"I'll think about it."

"Clay should be here any minute. The three of us can go to dinner together."

"I'm going to pass this time, but thanks. I think I'll go pay Mama Rae a visit."

"Give her my best."

"I wish I could be more help, but I think we're both in the same boat. Neither of us has enough information to make an informed opinion."

Daniel hugged me and was leaving my front porch when Clay rode up on his bike. He parked and toed down the kickstand, then walked toward Daniel with an outstretched hand.

"Hey, Daniel, you been takin' good care of my woman?" He smiled.

"Not exactly. I just stopped by to say hello. Good to see you, man."

Then, Daniel was on his way to see the one who knows all.

I smiled at Clay as he came toward me. His long legs took the porch steps two at a time. Then, his arms were around me. He backed me into the foyer through the open door, kicked it to with his foot, and kissed me until I was breathless. Then, he held me away from him and looked at me as though he were trying to memorize my features.

"I missed you," he said.

"I missed you as well. Why was the fishing expedition cut short? I was under the impression that it was pretty important to you."

"It was. I expected to make a tidy piece of change. It was the owner of the company who hired me. He was taking a few prospective clients on a fishin' trip to seal a deal. When we'd been out on the water for a couple of days, he got seasick big-time. He told me there was no way he could stay out on the water any longer. He apologized to the guys and told them he'd make it up to them."

"What a shame."

"Yeah, it was for them, but not for me. The man was a real standup kind of guy. I was ready to refund a hunk of his money, but he wouldn't hear of it. He paid me for the whole shebang."

"How wonderful!"

"So, since I'm flush, I'm gonna take you to dinner at Charlie's. That man flat knows what to do with a flounder."

"That sounds great. Do we have a reservation?"

"No, but I'll call and see if I can get one."

We had plenty of time to relax before we went to dinner, so I filled Clay in on my discussion with Max Palmer. I also told him about the strange evening spent with Pearl and Max on Pearl's yacht. Clay listened without interrupting, and I could tell that he was trying to piece together the disjointed things I was telling him.

"It kind of sounds like the old girl might be gettin' ready to pass the torch, but can't trust the guy who's next in line. Is that how it sounds to you?"

"Yes, but why would she want to involve me? She hardly knows me."

"Go figure."

"Daniel said he'd do some digging. He's a pretty good detective."

"I like Daniel. He seems like a real nice guy, and it's kinda cool that you two have been friends since you were little kids."

"I'm glad you think so. Jimmy was kind of jealous of Daniel even though he had no reason to be."

Clay didn't comment.

"I'm sorry, Clay. I didn't mean to bring up my late husband."

"Not to worry, sweetheart. I'm not the jealous type. Besides, the past is the past."

Clay placed a chaste kiss on my forehead and stood.

"I'd better make our dinner reservation," he said, and went into the foyer to make the call.

We had a lovely dinner, then went back to the villa. Clay took my hand and led me up the stairs to my bedroom. He took my face in both hands and kissed me so tenderly I thought I would cry. Then, we took our time undressing one another. We fell backward onto the bed, laughing. Seconds later, his hands seemed to be all over my body. They felt burning hot as he dropped tiny kisses from my head to my toes. Then, we made mad passionate love until we were spent. At some point, I fell asleep in Clay Singleton's arms feeling safe and secure. After Jimmy died, I thought I could never love and be loved again, but I was wrong.

The bed was still warm from Clay's body when I awoke the next morning. The aroma of coffee wafted up the stairs to my bedroom, and I could hear Clay whistling and rattling things around in the kitchen. I went downstairs to kiss him good morning.

"Hey, sunshine." Clay flashed that toothpaste ad smile.

He had set the table, and grabbed my plate to deliver a fluffy omelet.

"I don't think I have time to eat breakfast. I'm due at work in about a half hour."

Clay gave me a peck on the cheek and set the plate in front of me.

"I don't think the guy is gonna fire you for eatin' breakfast, sugar. Sounds to me like he enjoys havin' you around."

I made myself eat a few bites.

"Who taught you to cook?" I asked.

"Nobody. I guess when you're on your own you just learn when you get hungry."

I took my plate into the kitchen.

"This is really good, and I wish I had time to finish it, but I have to make myself presentable to go to the office."

"As you wish, my love," Clay said, handing me a mug of coffee.

I dashed up the stairs and took a shower in record time. Grabbing Clay's pillow off the bed to give it a quick hug on my way to the closet, I inhaled his scent. He had told me that he would be here when I came home from work, and I willed the day to hurry by.

The kitchen was clean when I came downstairs. Breakfast dishes had disappeared, and Clay had left a note telling me that he had gone to pick up his messages and get more clothes to add to my closet.

Max Palmer was on the phone when I reached the office. His voice had a strange quality; almost desperate.

"Let me worry about that," he said into the phone.

"No. I'll handle the zoning board. I know the right people to approach."

I took my time putting my purse away and going to the break room for coffee, because I wanted my boss to continue the conversation. Maybe I would be able to glean a bit of information about the business.

"Yes. There's new money coming in this week. I already told you that."

I mouthed a greeting as I approached Max's desk.

He motioned for me to take my seat.

"I understand. Yes, I'll let you know. Goodbye."

My boss smiled at me.

"I must say you look fetching this morning, Clemmie. You must have had a restful night's sleep. Your eyes are absolutely sparkling."

"Thank you. I did sleep well last night, but I didn't realize it made my eyes sparkle." I huffed out a small giggle.

"You're such an asset, my dear."

"Thank you."

"I'm sure you remember the three couples who joined us on the yacht for our little get acquainted outing."

"Yes, I remember all of them."

"Don and Bunny will be here on the island next weekend, and I've invited them to join us for dinner Saturday evening. We'll be in a private dining room at the Hyatt. Please mark that on your calendar."

"All right."

"I have to go out for a while. Be a good assistant and take messages for me. Ralph Wingate should be calling in about an hour. Don't take a message from him. Tell him I'll get in touch with him this afternoon."

It seemed that every crumb my boss dropped for me only confused me more. Why was only one of the three couples coming here for a dinner meeting? And what message might Ralph Wingate want to leave that Max didn't want me to hear? Who was Max talking with on the phone when I arrived at the office, and what did a zoning board have to do with any of it?

My workday was duller than dirt. I took a few messages for which I would be paid handsomely, and that was it.

Clay was on the back deck when I got home. He was sipping a beer and crunching pretzels while watching golfers tee off on the eighteenth hole. I slid the heavy glass door open and slipped my arms around his shoulders from behind. He squeezed my hand, then kissed my palm.

"What difficult task did you perform today to make your big bucks?" he asked.

"I eavesdropped on my boss's phone conversation and took his phone messages. What did you do?"

"I gambled."

"What are you talking about? We don't have any casinos in South Carolina."

"I introduced Grace to Mama Rae."

"You're kidding. Did you take Grace to the mom and pop store to make the introduction?"

"Nope. Don't you remember showing me where you park your Jeep when you go visit her?"

I nodded, confused.

"I hired a cab to drive us there. It was easy to follow that path to her cabin."

"I can't believe she invited you to her house, especially with your little niece."

"She didn't invite me. I just decided to go. She was sittin' on the porch playin' with her cat. Didn't seem a bit surprised to see Grace and me."

I found it awfully surprising that Mama Rae would allow a fairly new acquaintance to invade her privacy without an invitation.

"Grace tried to pet one of the chickens and got pecked on her hand. She didn't cry, but she was quick to jerk that hand back."

"Was Mama Rae upset that you and Grace showed up at her home without being invited?"

"No ma'am. She laughed when the hen pecked Grace. Then,

she told us to come on up to the porch. I said I hoped it was okay that we had come. She never said that it was, but I could tell she took a real likin' to Gracie. Grace and the cat had a good time."

CHAPTER
Twenty-Six

I beat my boss to the office the next morning. Lights had been turned on, and the door wasn't locked. I entered the building calling out a cheery good morning, but there was no response. The phone on my boss's desk rang, and I picked up the receiver.

"Max Palmer's office," I said in my most businesslike voice. "No. I'm afraid Mister Palmer isn't here at the moment. May I take a message?"

I wrote the message on a memo pad verbatim: Tell him Roy Hayes with the zoning board called about the parcel we discussed, and tell him to return my call ASAP.

"Yes, I'll give him the message as soon as he comes into the office"

Max didn't get to the office until late afternoon. He didn't offer an explanation for his late arrival, but he thanked me for taking messages and minding the office in his absence. Then, he told me that my work was finished for the day.

Clay's bike was parked in front of my villa, but he wasn't there when I went inside. There was a package with my name on it on the hall table. I kicked off my shoes, went to the kitchen for a box cutter, and opened the package. Inside the box was a beautifully wrapped smaller package. I couldn't imagine what it held.

Hating to tear the expensive-looking paper, I took a breath and ripped it open. There was a card with a one word script: *Welcome.* I folded back the tissue paper to see the gorgeous Hermes scarf I had coveted at the boutique in Savannah the day I took Pearl shopping.

I was sliding the silky scarf through my fingers, wondering whether or not to keep it. Pearl had obviously bought it for me since she had seen me admiring it. If I kept it, would I be beholden to her? I would not have purchased such an expensive scarf for myself. I usually wore costume jewelry if I wore any at all. I had a single string of pearls, and that was the only nice jewelry I owned except for my wedding ring which I had worn until lately. I relegated it to my small jewelry box after I met Clay Singleton and began to have feelings for him.

I heard Clay's feet hit the front porch. Then, his key rattled in the lock. I padded barefoot to the foyer holding the scarf.

"So that's what was in the surprise package," he said, grinning. "It's really pretty."

"It's a gift from Pearl, the elderly woman I told you about."

Clay took me by the shoulders, held me at arm's length, then gave me a chaste kiss while holding me away from his body.

"I'm kinda a sweaty mess," he said. "I got in a real good run. Shower time."

He took off up the stairs and left me holding the expensive gift from her loftiness.

I was about to change into shorts and a tee shirt when the phone rang. It was Daniel.

"Daniel, I'm so glad you called. I don't know if this will mean anything to you, but I took a phone message for my boss this morning. It was from someone connected to the zoning board by the name of Roy Hayes. I don't know if the zoning board he mentioned is here, or somewhere else. Hayes told me to have Max Palmer return his call as soon as possible. He said it had something to do with a parcel of property that he and my boss had discussed."

"Hmmm. It might well make sense. Did he happen to say anything about another partner, or partners?"

"No. I've just told you all I know."

"That might give me a place to start poking around."

"Oh, and my boss also told me that one of the three couples who were with us on the yacht for what he called a get acquainted getaway will be here next weekend. He instructed me to keep Saturday evening open to accompany him to a dinner meeting with them. I don't know if any of this is connected, but I'd bet it is."

"I'll keep digging and let you know what I find out."

"What did you call to tell me?"

"I just wanted to let you know that I must have been imagining things about Catherine. She was her usual sweet, loving self all weekend. She had gone to have her hair and nails done to look pretty for me Friday afternoon. I feel like pond scum for doubting her."

"That's great, Daniel."

"I just called to tell you that everything's fine. I knew you'd want to know."

"I want only the very best for you. You know that. You'll always be my best friend."

"Back at you. Let me know if you pick up on anything interesting at the dinner meeting."

"Will do. Later."

Clay came down the stairs just as Daniel and I hung up. His face held that ten-year-old boy look that I loved, as he reached to pull me up from the chair by the phone table and into his arms for a kiss.

"Let's stay home tonight," he said. "I'll go buy somethin' to grill and a nice bottle of wine. Sound good?"

"It does, indeed. I'll enjoy running this silky extravagance through my fingers and try to decide whether or not to keep it while you're gone."

Why had Pearl bought the scarf for me? She didn't like me. Surely, it wasn't payback for taking her shopping. But the thing which really had me stumped was why she would want me involved in the business. The only positive feeling I had gotten from her was that she seemed to think I was fairly intelligent and she appreciated my moxie.

By the time Clay returned with the groceries, I had worked myself into a frenzy of *what ifs*. I was sitting cross-legged on the couch, staring at the gorgeous Hermes scarf. What if I simply decided to keep the gift and feign ignorance concerning the reason behind Pearl's benevolence?

Clay took the groceries to the kitchen and came into the living room looking concerned.

"Why the glum expression, babe? You look like you're about to cry."

"I don't know what to do, Clay. Should I keep the scarf? It's awfully expensive."

"Your hands are tremblin'. Stop thinkin' about the stupid scarf. I'm gonna get you a glass of wine to calm you down."

Clay returned to the living room with two glasses of wine. He handed me one and sat down beside me, placing a caring hand on my knee.

"Listen, Clemmie, I know you like gettin' that big paycheck every week, and I know you're already in love with this little scrap of material you're holdin' in your hand, but I want you to know that you don't have to stay in a situation that makes you the least bit uncomfortable."

"If I resign from this job, I'll have to find another one. I'll never find one that pays nearly as much as I'm making. I really like this villa, and I need a good-paying job to keep living here. There's nobody to pay my bills except yours truly."

"Wrong. It's true that I'm a down-to-earth kinda guy. I live on a boat and don't have a car, but I'm not without funds. I rake in a fairly good livin' with my boat, and I've got a little part-timer with the paper. I can take care of us."

"Clay, that's ridiculous. I certainly wasn't asking you to take care of me. Of course, I'll work to pay my own way."

Clay smiled.

"All I'm sayin' is that you don't have to stay with Palmer and the old woman. Both of them keep you on edge half the time. Besides, I can get lots of real good-payin' jobs whenever I decide I want to change my lifestyle. Headhunters are knockin' on my door all the time."

"I didn't know that, not that it matters. I'm still determined to take care of myself."

"Well, now you know it. It oughta feel good to know you've got options. It's also possible that I might have somethin' else up my sleeve. You ought to know better than to trust a guy with a law degree to tell you all there is to know. Guys like us keep you guessin'."

I wasn't sure what he meant by that last statement. I had assumed he was being up front with me about everything. He had to know that I had fallen in love with him, and I thought he felt the same way about me. We were practically living together.

"What say we drop this depressin' conversation. I'll grill the shrimp and veggies and we can have a nice relaxin' evenin'. Then, I'll do my best to put you on top of the world. How's that sound?"

I heaved a huge cleansing sigh.

"It sounds wonderful, Clay."

I took the scarf upstairs and put it on my dresser, determined to forget it for the time being. Clay deserved more than listening to me whine, and I wanted to relax and enjoy our evening together.

Just as Clay was bringing our dinner in from the deck, a blinding flash of lightning split the sky. I ran to slide the glass door open because Clay's hands were full, and fat drops of rain were pelting the deck. The lights flickered, then the room went dark.

Clay made his way to the cabinet above the stove for candles. He didn't mention the thunder storm, or my fear of them. He lit the candles and placed them on the table, then went into the living room and closed the drapes.

I recalled another time shortly after Clay and I met that a storm had chased us into the villa. My heart had hammered, and I had seen spots before my eyes, but it wasn't because of my fear of storms. It was because my late husband still held sway in my mind. It was triggered by my remembering where Jimmy had found candles when the power went out. I hadn't been able to tell Clay the truth until later, because I wanted him to believe that I had buried my past along with my husband. I had wanted to believe that, too.

Clay seated me, then brought our plated dinners to the table. He raised his wineglass in a toast: "Here's to you, Clemmie Castlebrook, and to a beautiful evenin'."

I touched my glass to his and smiled.

After dinner, we left the dirty dishes in the sink and went upstairs with candles and another bottle of wine. The scarf and the storm were forgotten as I looked into Clay's gray eyes. They seemed to give off sparks in the candlelight. Clothes fell to the floor, and my breath caught at the touch of Clay's big warm hands on my body. He was whispering endearments I could only guess at because of the raging storm outside. Our lovemaking was so sweet, so all-consuming that I felt as if I were in another world.

Sometime during the night, the storm ceased, and the candles were reduced to waxy drippings on the candlesticks. I rubbed by eyes and saw sunshine crawling across the floor. The bedside clock registered eight o'clock.

I grabbed a robe and made it to the top of the stairs when I heard off-key singing:

"Life ain't nothin' but a funny, funny riddle. Thank God, I'm a country boy."

Clay was definitely a morning person. He was at the stove dressed in nothing but a pair of boxers, flipping pancakes. I didn't understand how he could be so happy this early in the morning. He had cleaned up our mess from the night before, made coffee, and now he was cooking breakfast.

"Good mornin', love," he said. "Watch this." He grinned and flipped a pancake high into the air to see it come down with a splat on the counter.

I couldn't help but laugh. That was another thing I loved about this man: he made me laugh a lot.

The grin had left his face. He stopped playing chef to clean the counter.

"It worked a minute ago," he fumed.

I kissed him good morning and smiled my most indulgent smile.

"I can't stay for breakfast. You know I'm supposed to be at the office at nine o'clock."

"I know, but you were sleepin' so peaceful like, I didn't have the heart to wake you. By the way, you had a big smile on that pretty face of yours."

He handed me a cup of coffee, and I rushed upstairs to get ready for work. I was having a deja' vu moment.

Dressed, with purse and keys in hand, I traded Clay my empty cup for a kiss and left the villa. Traffic was light, and I pulled into a parking spot in front of the office early, wondering what exciting task Max Palmer might have lined up for me to do.

The front door wasn't locked. I was just entering the room when my boss came hurrying from the break room with two mugs of coffee. He was smiling.

"Good morning, Clemmie. You look lovely this fine morning," he said, handing me a mug.

"Thank you."

"Sit," said my boss, sounding as though he were commanding a dog.

I obeyed and waited to learn what was on the agenda for the day.

"Clemmie, you have a luncheon invitation. It's from Pearl. If you like, Gretchen will drive you to the yacht."

"That won't be necessary. I'll drive myself."

I wondered why Pearl wanted to meet with me. Why wasn't Max Palmer invited to accompany me? The idea of being alone with Pearl, the formidable, was unsettling. What in the world could she possibly want to discuss with me alone?

"Do you happen to know why Pearl wants to see me?"

"She didn't impart that information to me. I assume it will be some sort of mentoring session. You know, grooming you for business meetings, the way to dress to impress, that sort of thing."

"Mister Palmer, I will go to the luncheon, but I'm not sure I want to be involved in your and Pearl's important business dealings. I don't know anything about it. As a matter of fact, I don't have working experience in anything but teaching school."

"Pearl is impressed with you, Clelmmie. She knows a good thing when she sees it. If she didn't think you were capable, she wouldn't give you the time of day."

"As I said, I'll go, but I'm not making any promises."

"Take the rest of the morning off and do something fun and relaxing. Pearl will be expecting you at one o'clock. Please be prompt."

I left the office feeling apprehensive. I needed guidance and some semblance of assurance before I came face-to-face with Pearl. I turned the key in the ignition and headed toward Mama Rae's. She would calm my nerves and share words of wisdom to help me think clearly.

I knocked and called out to my old friend. She didn't answer.

"Mama Rae," I called again.

"Come in, chile," she said. Her voice was barely audible.

I stepped into the dark living room, then walked toward the kitchen. That was where Mama Rae spent the majority of her time.

"Bedroom," she said. Her voice was a harsh whisper.

I hurried to her bedroom. The door was open, and she lay

on her bed with Lord wrapped around her head. Neither of them moved when I entered the room.

"Mama Rae, are you sick?"

"Your Mama Rae not feelin' so good today," she said.

"Can I get you something? Maybe a cup of tea?"

"No. I jes' need to res' for a while. You go to de kitchen and have yourself a raspberry tart. I know dat's your favorite."

I felt helpless. I had always depended on Mama Rae. Now, she looked fragile, and I was helpless to do anything to assist her.

"I'm going to stay here for a while until you feel better," I said, giving her hand a gentle squeeze.

I went to the kitchen. A platter of tarts sat on the counter. They smelled delicious, and I knew she had just baked them, because they were still warm. I bit into one, and my taste buds came alive with the rich flavor of the dessert. It was so good that I gobbled it quickly and reached for another, making short work of it.

To the right of the platter sat Mama Rae's basket of herbs. I knew I had no right to do it, but I lifted the cloth to look inside. There was only one bottle left in the basket. I picked up the bottle to examine it. The contents looked like nothing more than dried pieces of leaves. I unscrewed the lid and was about to see if I could tell what the bottle contained by sniffing it when I felt a presence in the room.

"Dat don't have your name on it. Why you pokin' aroun' in Mama Rae's kitchen?"

"Oh, you scared me! I didn't hear you come into the kitchen."

"I can see dat."

"I meant no harm. I'm just curious by nature, and I wondered what was in the basket."

"Um hum."

"I'm sorry, Mama Rae. I had no right. I apologize."

"No harm done. Dat's jes some dried herbs. Good for what ails you. You sick?"

I realized that I had been holding my breath. I tried to smile as I took air into my lungs. Then, I noticed that Mama Rae was wearing the peacock gem-studded brooch that I knew Pearl must have given her.

"No. I just came to see if you could give me some advice, but if you're not feeling well, it can wait. Thank you for the tart. Tarts. I ate two."

Mama Rae's thin lips curved into a little smile.

"Go on," she said. "She waitin' for you. Don' be late."

CHAPTER
Twenty-Seven

"*Clemmie,* come in and have a seat."

The young man who escorted me onto the yacht and into the salon quietly disappeared, and I walked toward Pearl. She indicated the chair beside a table close to her wheelchair containing a silver tea service. I sat facing her.

"I'm afraid you'll have to pour, Clemmie. I've asked Gretchen to leave us alone, and my hands have begun to tremble so badly that I don't trust myself to do it. Do you mind?"

"Of course not."

I hadn't expected my hostess to offer tea rather than a glass of wine. The last time I was on her yacht, she had gotten Max Palmer and me smashed, and she was definitely in her cups.

I filled Pearl's bone china cup and asked how she preferred her tea. After adding lemon, I placed her cup and saucer on the table beside her.

"Thank you, Clemmie. I'm afraid I'll have to let it rest on the table instead of my knee. This disease has managed to get a firm grip on me. I do apologize."

"Please don't apologize for something you have no control over," I said.

Pearl smiled, but her expression exhibited sadness. I could almost feel compassion for this powerful woman who seemed well aware that her days were numbered.

She lifted her saucer, then bravely grasped the fragile cup handle and took a sip of tea. I didn't dare offer assistance. When the cup and saucer were safely back on the table, Pearl turned her piercing blue eyes on me.

"I'll get right to the point, Clemmie. Let's get our business out of the way before we have a bite, shall we?"

"Of course."

"I won't mince words. Everything that is discussed here will remain between the two of us. Is that understood?"

"Yes, but…"

"No buts, my dear. This is a very private meeting, and I am about to trust you to be a loyal recipient of everything I am about to tell you."

I didn't comment, but something made me nod my agreement.

"As I've mentioned before, I'm dying. I don't know how much longer I have, but I want to make sure the business is in good hands and that everything is in order while I'm still of sound mind. It's possible that I could be on heavy medication for pain toward the end."

For the lack of an appropriate comment, I sat looking into the old woman's eyes, waiting to try to digest the plan she was about to lay out before me.

"I know you're curious about our business, so I'll explain it to you in layman's terms. We're in the real estate business; developers, if you will. We buy and sell property. We are in a position to make a great deal of money, and to assist others who are interested in investing in our ventures to become wealthy as well. We operate through limited partnerships. We are the general partner, and the investors are the limited partners. We must bring in new investors

241

if we are to provide revenue to the previous investors if they are not making money. Some of the new investors are the three couples you met here on the yacht not long ago. Do you understand?"

"If the money from new investors is being used to pay the older investors, isn't that simply a Ponzi scheme?"

Pearl donned her usual sardonic smile.

"We prefer to think of it as nothing more than an easy way to get rich. The ball keeps rolling, and everyone's happy."

"I really don't want to get involved in something that could be considered illegal."

"Clemmie, my dear departed husband started this business with Max's father. I have continued to do the work my husband started. He did very well for us, and I couldn't bear to see all the hard work and planning go down the drain with my demise."

I must have been staring at Pearl, because she looked at me as if waiting for me to let her remarks sink in before continuing.

"This will probably shock you, but I must enlighten you regardless. Max puts on a good show. He appears more intelligent than he actually is, and his business sense is somewhat lacking. I realize that he seems to be in command of the workings of this business machine, but that isn't true. I push the buttons. As for you, my dear, it would give me much comfort to think that you might transition into my role."

I couldn't believe what this woman was saying. She didn't know me, and she was scaring me to death.

"Of course, I will arrange all the details, and Max must never learn that he hasn't been handed the torch. He must be well taken care of for the remainder of his life, and he must think he's the head of the firm. You will naturally be rewarded handsomely, and you will never lack for anything."

"I'll have to think about this. I'm not sure I'm the person for the job."

"You do that. Let's go to the dining room. We have wonderful fresh crab salads waiting for us."

I had never felt so miserable. I didn't want to have lunch with this power wielding woman who was attempting to take over my life.

Pearl talked about everything but the business and her offer for me to run it during the lunch. If something she said called for a response from me, I offered only short comments. I couldn't wait to get off the yacht.

Max Palmer was no doubt awaiting my return to the office. I felt sure he would want me to fill him in on the meeting with Pearl, and I would simply have to tell him that he had been correct: Pearl wanted to groom me.

I smiled as I entered the office. If I showed my true feelings, I might cry.

"Well, Clemmie, how was lunch?"

"It was very good. Thank you."

"I imagine Pearl mentored you so well that you'll be able to do all of your own shopping. I'm sure she also schooled you regarding how to put a wonderful face on our business when meeting new clients."

"Yes. Pearl certainly knows how to accomplish her goals."

"That's true, but I know she can be a bit exhausting. Take the afternoon off and do something you enjoy."

"Thank you. I will."

I hoped my quick stride didn't betray me as I left the office. If my boss had expected me to carry on a more lengthy conversation with him, I might have had to feign a sudden illness.

My Jeep's gas gauge registered nearly empty. I pulled up to the pumps at the mom-and-pop store for a fill-up. When I went inside to pay for the gas, I came face-to-face with none other than Mama Rae. She was gulping down the last of a grape soft drink. Her herb basket hung from her left arm.

"Mama Rae, I was just on my way to see you."

"I'd like to visit with you, chile, but I don't have time right now. You come see your Mama Rae later today."

She turned and walked out the door. I thought about following her, but I didn't. I had already made her suspicious by snooping around in her kitchen.

The villa was empty when I got home. The message light on my phone was blinking. I listened to the message: "Clemmie, Clay here. I'm callin' from a pay phone at the hospital. Sarah had to be taken to the emergency room. I'll call you later."

Clay hadn't given me any details, and I wasn't sure what I should do. Had Sarah been taken to the hospital here on the island, or possibly to one in Savannah? I wondered if she had been involved in an accident, or what had made her suddenly ill. Who was taking care of Grace while her mother was in the emergency room? I was almost afraid to leave the villa in case Clay might call, but I couldn't just sit and wonder. I ran outside, jumped into my Jeep, and took off for the local hospital.

I had made the right choice. Clay got up from his seat in the crowded waiting area and came toward me, leading a frightened looking Grace by the hand. He wore a worried expression.

"Clemmie, I'm so glad you were able to come so soon. I thought you would probably still be at work."

"What happened?"

"Let's go over to that corner of the room where we can talk," he said.

I stooped to give Grace a hug.

"Cwemmie, Mommie's tummy hurts weal bad," she said, her lips quivering.

"Come on, Gracie," Clay said. "Let's sit over here. We can tell Clemmie all about it."

I could tell that Clay was shaken.

"I went to Sarah's to get my messages," he said. "The door was locked, so I rang the bell. I could see Grace standin' in the foyer. She was wringin' her hands and cryin', but she wouldn't open the door. Sarah has taught her to never answer the door unless they are expectin' someone, usually me, and she could see who it was. I had to raise my voice for Grace to hear me over her cryin', and she finally unlocked the door for me."

"Oh, my goodness."

Clay took a deep breath and continued, "Grace grabbed my hand, and pulled me into to Sarah's bedroom. Sarah was curled in a fetal position on the floor, moanin' and thrashin'. When she was able to lie still for a minute, she was barely able to speak."

"Stomach. Unbearable pain. Emergency room. Quick."

"I called 911. An ambulance came within five minutes, but it seemed like an hour."

"Have the doctors told you what the problem is?"

"No. We've only been here a few minutes."

Grace climbed into Clay's lap and put a chubby arm around his neck. Then, she did what many small children do when they are frightened: she stuck a thumb into her mouth while tears slid down her cheeks.

Clay made circles on his niece's back with his thumb and told her he loved her. He assured her that her mommy was in a safe place where doctors were going to find out why her tummy hurt and try to fix the problem. The fact that he didn't tell her everything was okay and that her mommy would be as good as new real soon wasn't wasted on me. He was the kind of person who would never lie to a child, or get her hopes up when he didn't know that to be factual.

As in most hospital waiting areas, there wasn't much conversation. Every now and then, a doctor would appear to give a report on a patient to family members. There was some movement around a coffee machine on the far wall, and a couple of small children let it be known that they were tired and wanted to be somewhere else.

Clay and I said very little to one another. There would have been no point. All we could do was wait for Sarah's doctor to come through the double doors and inform us of her condition and what would be done to help her.

Grace had fallen asleep and awoke, rubbing her eyes and

whining for her mother. Clay was doing his best to comfort her when a doctor appeared and called his name. He handed Grace off to me and went to hear what the doctor had to say. Grace snuggled close to me, but she didn't cry. I watched as Clay nodded a couple of times. Then, he came back to our corner and took his seat beside me.

"Sarah is gonna have emergency surgery. The doctors can't tell what the problem is until they open her up. It'll be exploratory surgery." He swallowed.

"Does that mean they'll operate as soon as possible?" I asked.

Clay nodded.

I knew how close he and his sister were, and it broke my heart to see him so distraught.

"I'm gonna stay here," he said. "Do you mind takin' Grace home with you? She's dead tired, and I know she must be hungry."

"Of course, I'll take care of her. How did you get here, Clay? How will you get home?"

"The EMTs let us ride in the ambulance. I had to leave my bike at Sarah's house, because I couldn't leave Grace alone. I can get a cab. I'll call you as soon as I know what's goin' on."

He reached over and lifted Grace off my lap and into his arms.

"Hey, sleepyhead," he said, kissing her forehead, "Clemmie's gonna take you home with her for a sleepover, and I'm gonna stay here with your mommy and the doctors. Mommy will be asleep while the doctors try to help her get well. I'll call you later. I love you, short stuff."

I didn't know what I might have at home that would appeal to a three-year-old, so I took Grace to the diner. I ticked off items on the children's menu until I got to the grilled cheese sandwich. Grace told me that was what she wanted. She proved to be quite hungry, consuming the entire sandwich and leaving room for a fruit cup and a cookie.

Grace looked very solemn even with a milk moustache, and asked a few questions about her mother; questions I didn't know how to answer: Why did she have to stay at the hospital? Was her mommy still crying and acting funny? How come her Unca Cway didn't come to the diner with us? I had to play it by ear. I had never been around many small children and didn't know how to be truthful without alarming them.

I did my best to give her answers which would satisfy her to some degree without being specific. I had a lot of questions of my own.

Clay had given me a key to Sarah's house, but I was afraid that if I took Grace there to get her toothbrush and pajamas, she might get overly upset. That was the last place she had seen her mother except for the ambulance ride. I took a chance on my instinct and drove us to my villa.

"This will be fun, Grace. I used to love sleepovers when I was a little girl. You can have a real bubble bath and sleep in a big-girl tee shirt instead of pajamas. I'll put the TV on the cartoon channel and we can watch television until we get sleepy. You can even sleep in the big bed with me."

The little girl appeared happy and excited one minute, and melancholy the next. My heart ached for her, and I didn't know how to help her. I knew she was wiped out from the trauma we had all been through. She fell asleep on the living room couch.

The phone rang just as I was about to carry Grace upstairs to bed. It was Clay.

"Clemmie...."

"What is it, Clay? How did the operation go?"

I knew something had gone terribly wrong, because Clay couldn't speak. I waited.

"Clemmie, Sarah...."

I heard him make a strangled sound.

"She died on the table." An anguished sob escaped his throat.

"Oh, Clay."

I didn't know what to say. I wanted to sound strong for him, but I could feel my heart begin to pound. I sat down in the chair beside the phone table and tried not to cry.

"Are there things you need to do at the hospital before you come home?"

"I've already done everything I need to do."

"I can't leave Grace alone to come to get you. Can you get a cab and come here?"

"Yes. I'll take a cab to get my bike, then come to your place."

"Oh, Clay, I'm…"

"I know. There's nothin' to say. Is Grace asleep?"

"Yes. Please be careful."

I had wanted to ask him details. Why had she died? What had been so terribly wrong that the surgeon couldn't save Sarah's life? She was so young, and she had a wonderful little girl. Life was so unfair.

I carried Grace upstairs and tucked her in. She looked so innocent, and she had no idea that her sweet mother would never come home. Oh, how I dreaded tomorrow. The sun's rays would make the live oak leaves glitter like diamonds, the Atlantic would sparkle, and nothing would be right here in Paradise.

CHAPTER
Twenty-Eight

I had counted the minutes until I heard Clay's key turn in the lock. I didn't know what to say to him, but I would hold him and let him know how much I cared. He wouldn't have to wonder if I would be by his side throughout this hellish ordeal.

He stumbled into the foyer looking dazed. I ran to him with open arms, and he put his arms around me. We stood that way without talking for several minutes while his tears dropped onto my shoulder. Then, I gently broke the embrace and led him into the living room.

"Let's sit on the couch, Clay. You can tell me about it, or you don't have to talk at all."

"Why?" he asked. "Why my brave Sarah? She soldiered on after her husband was killed. She brought her baby into the world without a father, and there was never a better mother than my sister."

"Life is so unfair sometimes," I said, knowing it was a lame response.

Clay leaned forward with his elbows on his knees and his face in his hands. His broad shoulders shook as he choked out strangled sobs. I was so glad that he was able to let it all out in my presence. It told me that he trusted me completely. He could do anything, say anything, and I would be supportive and loyal.

When he finally gained control of his emotions, he leaned back, exhausted. I handed him the box of tissues I had been using before he got home.

"I've got to get a grip," he said, taking a deep breath.

"You needed that release, Clay. Can I get you something to drink?"

"We got any of that cognac left?"

"Yes."

I went to the cabinet and poured each of us a drink, then brought them to the living room. Clay's hand trembled as he took the glass from me.

"Can you talk about it?" I asked.

"I already told you the surgeon had to do exploratory surgery. Well, it turned out that the awful pain was caused by a twisted bowel. The doc couldn't explain it all to my satisfaction, but he told me that somehow the bowel's contents had leaked into Sarah's bloodstream and poisoned her system. The procedure was complicated. It took longer than it should have. He said they did their best. It just wasn't good enough."

"Oh, Clay. What a tragedy. I'm so very sorry."

"I'm the only family little Gracie has left. I love that child so much."

"I know you do."

I was afraid to ask what might become of Grace.

"Just so you know, nobody's gonna take Grace away from me. See, I know what's in Sarah's will. She and I had our wills made out together by the same lawyer. I'll inherit her estate. That way, Grace will be able to live in the house she's lived in her whole life. The will also states that I'll be the executor of Sarah's will. The judge will appoint me as my niece's guardian as soon as the will is admitted to probate."

I hated to ask, but I couldn't stop myself.

"What happens to Grace in the meantime?"

Clay took a long pull on his cognac, then stared into the amber liquid, garnering strength to continue.

"A Social Services Representative at the hospital told me that she can give consent for me to act as Grace's guardian since I'm Sarah's closest adult relative. God give me the words to explain these things to my precious little niece. How do you tell a three-year-old her mother's not ever gonna come home?"

"Grace adores you, Clay. I know you'll be up to the task."

"I'll have to be."

Clay drained the contents of his glass and leaned his head back. I could tell he was whipped. I took the glass from his hand and kissed his forehead. Then I maneuvered his body into a prone position, placed a cushion under his head, and removed his shoes. I didn't think he was aware of anything I did.

I turned off the lights and went upstairs to curl up with Grace. She didn't rouse when I slipped into bed, and I was grateful for that. I stared into space unable to sleep and dreading the dawn.

I hadn't fallen to sleep when daylight crept into the room. I felt exhausted. The clock on the bedside table read seven o'clock. Grace was lying on her back, snoring softly like a kitten. I couldn't imagine how Clay was going to explain what had happened to her mother; that her mother was gone forever.

I was only ten when my pregnant mother was killed. I remembered it like it was yesterday because I was there when it happened, and I knew it would always haunt me.

Mama, Roy, and I had been out for a drive. Mama interrupted one of Roy's stupid jokes to ask him to stop at a roadside fruit and vegetable stand. She was craving a homegrown tomato. Roy stayed in the car while Mama and I went across the road to buy the produce.

I laughed at Mama because she rubbed a tomato on the side of her stomach to clean off the garden dirt and bit into it, squirting juice. We started back across the road. Mama was eating the tomato, and I was carrying the paper sack. Out of nowhere came a little red sports car. It was going so fast when it rounded a curve that there was no way it could have stopped. I was just a few steps ahead of Mama when the car hit her, throwing her into the air and into a ditch. I dropped the sack and stood in the middle of the road unable to move.

I watched as Roy jumped out of the car and ran to his wife. His hoarse pleas for her to be alive hurt nearly as much as seeing my mother crumpled in a ditch by the side of the road. It took Roy and me months to wade through our grief enough to live something close to normal lives. I wondered how long it would take Clay and Grace.

There was no aroma of coffee, so I knew Clay wasn't up yet. I was careful not to wake Grace as I slipped out of bed. I had left the small lamp on the dresser turned on the night before in case she was afraid of the dark.

Clay lay on the couch just as I had left him. I couldn't tell whether he was asleep or not. I walked past him into the kitchen to make coffee.

"Mornin'," he said, pulling himself into a sitting position. "Thanks for tuckin' me in last night."

"You were beat."

"Yeah, but I've got to pull it all together and put on my big boy pants this mornin'. I've gotta be strong for Grace."

"I know. Do you want to be alone with Grace when you talk to her, or do you want me with you?"

The coffeepot began making its familiar sputtering noise.

"I don't know," he admitted.

I was on my way into the living room to sit beside Clay when I glimpsed movement in the foyer. Then, Grace came through the door rubbing her eyes. She ran straight to her Unca Cway. He opened his arms, and she climbed up into his lap. He kissed the top of her head.

"Mornin', short stuff," he managed.

"I had a sweepover with Cwemmie. I got to wear this big girl tee shirt and sweep in the big bed. It was fun. Where's my mommy?"

"I had a sleepover all by myself here on Clemmie's couch," Clay said.

"That's silly. You can't have a sweepover by yourself. Where's Mommy?"

"Tell you what," Clay said. "You go upstairs with Clemmie and get dressed, and I'll take you out for breakfast. We can have an uncle-niece conversation and I'll tell you about your mommy. Okay?"

"Okay. Can I have a pancake with a chocolate chip smiley face?"

"You bet."

Grace slid off Clay's lap and grabbed my hand.

"Come on, Cwemmie. Will you help me get dwessed?"

"Sure."

The two of us climbed the stairs together, and Grace chattered the entire time I helped her dress for breakfast.

Clay hadn't invited me to tag along, so I realized that he thought his task might be easier without me. He asked to borrow my Jeep. He certainly wouldn't let a three-year-old ride on his bike.

After Clay and Grace left, the villa seemed so empty. I wondered if I would see a lot less of Clay now that he would be responsible for Grace. If she was going to be living in the home she had always known, he would have to move in with her. He could send her to a day care facility most days, and I was sure he would take her to visit Mama Rae. I had let him know that I would take care of Grace as much as I could, but selfishly, I wondered if I would ever have him all to myself. I was ashamed of those feelings, but I couldn't deny that I had them.

I thought about calling a cab to get to work. Then, I thought better of that. I wanted to be here when Clay and Grace returned to the villa. Surely, there would be some way for me to help them through their devastation.

I had never refused to show up for work, but today I felt the need to play hooky. I waited until I thought Max Palmer would be in the office to make the phone call.

"Max Palmer." His tone was brisk.

"Mister Palmer, I hate to call at the last minute, but I need to stay at home today. I'm not feeling well."

"I'm sorry to hear that, Clemmie. Is there anything I can do for you?"

"No, thank you. I just need to rest. I'll drink hot tea with honey. I'm sure I'll be fine in a couple of days, and I'll be fine to go to the dinner with you Saturday evening."

My boss didn't question me further. He told me to rest and to take care of myself and that he would pick me up at six o'clock tomorrow evening.

I made myself choke down a bowl of cold cereal, then showered and dressed. Clay and Grace would be back soon, and I was afraid that Grace would be inconsolable.

I was on the back deck when Clay slid open the glass door from the living room. He squatted down in front of me, took my hands in his, and turned them over to kiss my palms. His eyes were bloodshot.

"Clay, where's Grace?"

"I left her with Mama Rae and the cat. Clemmie, Mama Rae is one amazin' old woman. She's got the magic charm or somethin'."

"I don't understand."

"I managed to put Grace off until I got some food into her. When we left the diner, she started whinin' for her mother. I didn't know what I was gonna say to her, and it was too noisy to explain things to her while we were in the Jeep, so I drove to the edge of the woods and parked."

"Oh, Clay."

"I've always been a pretty straight shooter with Grace, so I just told her the truth in terms she might understand. I told her that her mommy went to sleep on the operatin' table and didn't wake up."

"Did she understand what you were saying?"

"She did when I explained that her mommy had gone to heaven to be with her daddy, and that she was happy to be with him 'cause she missed him a lot."

"Was she heartbroken?"

"Of course. She cried some, and I held her and kissed her for a little while. Then I told her I was gonna take her to see Mama Rae. She likes Mama Rae. She wanted to know if she could pet the cat, and I told her she could. Mama Rae seemed to know we were comin' for a visit."

"She seems to know everything before it happens."

"She was sittin' on the porch when we got there. Grace climbed up the steps and held out her arms for Mama Rae. They hugged one another, then Mama Rae led Grace into her house and told me to come back later."

"You can rest assured that Mama Rae won't let any harm come to Grace. She's had my back from the day we met."

"I know that. Not sure how I know it, but I do. If I'd had any doubts, I wouldn't have left Grace with her."

I didn't know how to help Clay. He would have to make some sort of funeral or memorial arrangements. It wasn't the kind of thing I could bring up without seeming like I was telling him what to do and how he should do it. It was as if Clay had just read my mind.

"The day Sarah and I had the attorney draw up our wills, she told me that she wanted to be cremated. She had always thought wakes and funerals where people stood around talkin' like they were at a cocktail party and lookin' at the corpse was creepy. She said she didn't want people who knew her starin' at her when she was dead."

"I understand."

"We'll have a memorial service at that nondenominational church. We went there quite a bit as a family, and that's where Grace goes to Sunday School."

"I've been to that church. I liked the minister."

"I arranged for the cremation after I left Mama Rae's. Now,

I'll have to meet with the minister and make arrangements for the memorial service. It's all I can do to make myself do these things. I feel like I'm just doin' whatever needs to be done to get rid of my sister."

"Please don't feel that way, Clay. You're doing what Sarah requested. I'll be happy to go with you to meet with the minister if you want me there for support."

Clay nodded.

"I'll take you up on that. Let's go and see if the preacher'll see us now. I'd like to get this done before I pick up Grace."

We were quiet on the drive to the church. Clay turned off the ignition and stared at nothing. Then he pounded the steering wheel with his fists, took a deep breath, and got out of the Jeep.

It didn't take long to make the arrangements. The minister was very helpful. He was familiar with the family, so Clay didn't have to tell him very much about Sarah. He said he would get in touch with the crematorium and have the ashes brought to the church ahead of the service. He was also going to speak with the organist and have her choose appropriate music.

The only thing left to do was to write an obit for The Island Packet. Clay would have to do that without anyone's assistance.

I thought Clay would probably drop me off at the villa before he went to Mama Rae's, but he drove straight to my sandy parking spot by the woods. He took my hand as we stepped into the woods. Our feet sank into pine straw and dried leaves as we started down the path. Birdsong was so sweet and sounded lighthearted and carefree. It was nothing akin to the funeral dirge that I knew was playing in Clay's mind.

I wondered what my old mentor had cooked up to cause Grace's face to light up with her pretty little smile. She was turning around and around in Mama Rae's patch of grass. The cat was batting at a butterfly. Then, Grace plopped down on the grass on her bottom, giggling. Lord abandoned his game and went to lie on his back for Grace to tickle his tummy. She was quick to oblige.

"Word, you're so funny," she said.

"Hey, short stuff, you havin' fun?" Clay asked.

"Uh huh."

Mama Rae sat in a chair on the porch. She seemed to ignore Clay's and my presence.

"Thanks for entertainin' Grace, Mama Rae," Clay said.

"Grace no trouble at all," Mama Rae said. "She been havin' a good time with Lord."

"We were about to go have some lunch," I said. "I'll bet you're hungry, Grace."

The little girl shook her head.

"I'm not. Mama Wae gave me some squirrel soup. It was good."

"Squirrel soup?" Clay asked.

"Stew," my old friend corrected.

"And we had some kind of pie with bewies in it and some gweat juice," Grace added.

I wondered what Mama Rae had put into the *gweat* juice to make Grace so happy, but I kept quiet.

"We need to leave now anyway, Grace," Clay said. "We'll stop by your house and get you some more clothes. You and Clemmie can have another sleepover tonight. Okay?"

Grace nodded, making her blond curls bounce in the sunshine.

"Can Word come too?"

"No. He lives here with Mama Rae. She'd be lonely if we took him away."

"The way Mommy missed my daddy?"

I had a lump in my throat, and I wasn't sure I would have known how to answer if I had been able to speak.

"Kinda like that. Yeah," Clay said.

Mama Rae opened her skinny arms, and Grace ran to hug her goodbye.

"One day Lord might get to go home with you. We'll see," Mama Rae said.

I wondered if she was giving us a hint of things to come.

CHAPTER
Twenty-Nine

I thought Grace would cry when we went into her empty house, but she didn't. She wanted Clay and me to help her choose clothes to take to my villa. When we got to her room she began pulling play clothes out of her closet, and it was clear that she didn't need our help. She was able to choose socks to match every outfit and called out the name of each color as she put ensembles together.

"Grace, you're doing a great job of matching colors," I said.

"Thanks, Cwemmie. I know my shapes, too."

"You're a very smart girl," I said.

Clay was standing on the other side of the room looking out the window. I knew it was awfully hard for him to be here while trying to act as if his and Grace's lives hadn't changed.

"Do you want me to take a dwess?" Grace asked.

"Yes. I think it would be a good idea to take one pretty dress and a pair of dress-up shoes and socks," I answered, not knowing if Clay would want her to attend her mother's memorial service.

The service was to be on Saturday, and I was supposed to

accompany my boss to a business dinner with big-haired Bunny and her husband from Lubbock, Texas. I wasn't sure I would be able to pull that off. How could I be cordial, let alone upbeat.

Clay managed to put on his brave face as we packed Grace's clothes and locked up Sarah's house. We stopped by the Piggly Wiggly for items we would need to grill hamburgers for dinner. Then, Clay and I did our best to keep things light for his orphaned niece.

After dinner I took Grace upstairs to play dress-up while Clay worked on his sister's obituary. I even offered her my one pair of heels to wear over her shoes. After a little while she began rubbing her eyes with her tiny fists. It was her bedtime. She and I brushed our teeth together and I let her sleep in one of my big-girl tee shirts. It didn't take long for the little girl to conk out.

Clay read me what he had written, and it was beautiful. We went into the downstairs bedroom, lay down on the bed, and held one another for a long time without talking. I could feel Clay's tears on his face and the pillow where my cheek rested. Finally, I felt his body relax as he fell asleep from grief and exhaustion. I stared at the ceiling wondering what our lives would be like after we bade Sarah goodbye. Would Clay move into his sister's house with Grace and invite me to join them whenever it was convenient? Would our relationship be so compromised that we would completely lose what we'd had? I couldn't bear the thought of losing the love I had thought I would never find after Jimmy's death, but only time would tell.

Clay's eyes were red-rimmed the next morning, but he offered a half-hearted smile as I came into the kitchen where he was mixing batter for pancakes. He opened his arms, and I fell into them. I could feel his love by the way he held me, and it nearly brought tears to my eyes.

"Darlin', can you do me a big favor today?"

"Anything."

"Grace will be wakin' up in a few minutes. We'll have pancakes together. Then I have to take care of some business before the service. Would you mind entertainin' her until I can take her to Mama Rae's? She's too young to see her mother sittin' at the front of a church in an urn. I wouldn't know how to explain that to her."

"Of course I will. You don't have to take her to Mama Rae's. I'll be happy to take her, and I'll be back in plenty of time to get dressed for the service. What else can I do?"

"Just keep me from makin' a fool of myself at the service. Sarah would want me to stand up like a man instead of bein' a wimp because I'd lost my sister. She'd want me to be strong."

"I'll never leave your side."

"That's my girl. Now, go get Grace and come down to breakfast."

Clay already had Grace set up when we came downstairs. He had stacked two cushions on the seat of her chair since I didn't have a booster seat and the Hilton Head phonebook was only about as thick as a comic book. Her place was set with a glass of milk, orange juice, and a large pancake with a chocolate chip smiley face.

Grace ran straight to her uncle, and he scooped her up into his arms for a kiss.

"Look what I made for you, short stuff," he said.

Grace giggled. "I can eat the whole thing," she told him. And she did.

Clay rode away on his bike to take care of business, and I took Grace for a walk on the beach. We waded in the surf and gathered some shells, and the little girl behaved as if nothing had happened to interrupt her happy young life and turn her world upside down. We had peanut butter and jelly sandwiches for lunch. Then, I took her to play with Mama Rae and Lord.

I hadn't known that Sarah had so many friends on the island. The church was filled to capacity, but I didn't recognize anyone in attendance. The service was lovely, and Clay was able to maintain a stiff upper lip as he listened to the minister's kind words and when thanking each person who shook his hand, or patted his shoulder when expressing their condolences. The sight of him standing tall in that dark suit nearly took my breath away.

When the church was empty, Clay shook the minister's hand, handed him an envelope, and lifted the urn containing his sister's ashes. Then, we drove my Jeep to the island's small airport to board the prop engine plane that Clay had chartered. Clay instructed the pilot to fly out a good distance from the beach and make a wide circle while he emptied the urn into the Atlantic.

"Goodbye, my sweet Sarah," he said as the little plane dipped down low over the water. "I'll raise Grace the best way I know how."

We went back to the villa to change our clothes and go to the woods to collect Grace, but it occurred to us that we were alone for the first time in three days. The realization of that must have hit us both at the same time, because we rushed into one another's arms and began fumbling with buttons and zippers between kisses and caresses. We were like animals in our haste, getting out of our clothes to feel skin on skin, for each of us to feel the other's heartbeat, and to get as close as humanly possible; to become one.

Our lovemaking was passionate and uninhibited. We were on fire, and it was a most exquisite feeling. After a shuddering climax, before my breathing slowed to something resembling normal, I mustered courage I hadn't known I possessed.

"Clay Singleton, you're going to ask me to marry you," I blurted.

"Yes, I am," he said, looking stunned, "but I've just inherited a huge responsibility. Grace is my blood, and I can only offer you the whole package. I don't pretend to know how you feel about that. I'm sure you haven't had a chance to consider what this might mean to our relationship."

His last sentence struck me dumb. I stared at him, unbelieving.

"I'll certainly understand if you don't want to sign on for a ready-made family."

"Clay, don't you know that I love that little girl? I think she's wonderful."

"That doesn't mean you want to be tied down with a child as soon as we're married."

"I haven't heard a proposal."

Clay sat up, raked a hand through his hair, and got out of bed. I watched his gorgeous backside disappear into the bathroom. Then, I heard the spray of the shower.

What had I done? I had dredged up the nerve to tell him that he was going to propose to me, and then I sniped at him because he didn't do it fast enough.

I was curled into a fetal position when Clay came out of the bathroom. He sat down on the side of the bed and pulled the sheet back from my face.

"Would you please sit up, Clemmie?" he said in a near whisper.

I tamped down the lump in my throat and pushed myself into a sitting position beside him. He stood beside the bed with a towel wrapped around his waist and lifted my chin with a finger so that I was looking up at him. Then, he dropped to one knee and took my hand to kiss my palm.

"Clemmie Castlebrook, will you do me the great honor of becomin' my wife? If the answer is yes, you'll make this old Alabama boy the richest guy in the world."

I took his face in my hands and attempted to express my most heartfelt feelings with a kiss.

"Yes, Clay Singleton, I can hardly wait to become your wife and a substitute mother to Grace."

Clay stood and pulled me up from the bed and into his arms.

"Now I think I can go on livin'," he said. "You've just taken away some of my hurt. I have somethin' to look forward to instead of wantin' to die."

"Let's go get Grace and take her to get ice cream," I said. "We don't know if Mama Rae has been able to work her happy magic today."

There was nobody in sight when we walked into the clearing at the edge of Mama Rae's grass patch. We went up on the porch and knocked on the wooden frame of the screen door.

"Come in dis house."

We went into the dim living room where my old friend was seated in her floral print chair and Grace sat in the rocking chair cradling Lord like a baby. Mama Rae was using the toe of her shoe to rock Grace and the cat.

"We jes havin' a little res," Mama Rae said. "We been playin' hard."

Clay smiled. "Thank you for lookin' after Grace, Mama Rae. Are you ready to go, short stuff?" he asked his niece.

"Okay. Word's through with his nap."

Mama Rae leaned over and took the cat, and Grace scooted to the edge of the rocker and hopped to the floor.

"I had a gweat time, Mama Way. I wuv you so much."

Mama Rae smiled her toothless smile, and Grace stood on tiptoes to kiss her new best friend's weathered cheek.

"Grace makes the sun shine in dis old heart," said Mama Rae. "You bring her back to see me real soon."

I wanted to hug my old friend, but she and I hadn't had that kind of closeness. She was always there for both Daniel and me, but there was never any physical affection. I supposed that only a small child would be so bold as to engage in the unsolicited behavior Grace had just exhibited.

Mama Rae must have worked her magic once more on this the saddest of days for Grace's family, because the little girl seemed very happy. One would never have guessed that she had just lost her mother.

We took Grace to get ice cream, then for a ride in Clay's boat. She giggled while he let her pretend to steer the craft. We stayed out on the water until late afternoon, then went to the villa. Clay made sandwiches for Grace and himself while I showered and dressed to accompany my boss to dinner.

Max Palmer arrived at six o'clock to pick me up. I didn't give him a chance to ring the bell because I didn't want to introduce him to my house guests. All I really wanted to do was get through the evening and be done with it.

"You look lovely, Clemmie," Max said. "I do believe island life agrees with you."

"Thank you."

We met Bunny and Don at Charlie's. They were in the bar drinking martinis. Bunny spotted us coming into the restaurant.

"Hey, Clemmie, Max," she said around an olive. "Clemmie, you look positively divine. Where on earth did you find that adorable little dress?"

I wanted to say, "This old thing," but I didn't. I simply greeted her and Don and smiled.

"I'm sure our table is ready," Max said. "Shall we?"

"But I'm not through with my drink," Bunny said.

"Yes, you are," Don said, taking her drink and placing it on the bar.

I did my best to make small talk with Bunny while keeping an ear open to catch snatches of the men's conversation. I had the impression that Bunny wasn't paying attention to anything I was saying; she was too busy pouting because her husband had embarrassed her in public.

I managed to get through the evening with the decorum pleasing to my boss, and he complimented me on the fine job I was doing on the drive back to my villa. I hopped out of the car as fast as I could and said a hurried good night, then headed for the villa before he had a chance to get out and walk me to my door. I breathed a sigh of relief when I heard Max's Ferrari leave.

"We need to start makin' some weddin' plans, sweetheart," Clay said, handing me a glass of wine.

Neither of us had given such plans any consideration since we hadn't discussed getting married until that afternoon.

"I'd like to get married in a church," I said.

"Glad you said that, 'cause I would too."

"I know you're feeling overwhelmed," I said. "The last couple of days have been awfully tough. You've not only been shocked by Sarah's death, but you haven't had a chance to grieve properly because of your added responsibilities. We don't have to pile more weight to your shoulders right this minute by planning a wedding."

"I want to marry you, Clemmie. I almost feel like I'm already married to you. That might not make much sense, but I don't think I could feel any closer to you if we'd been married for years. I want to wake up every mornin' with you beside me. I want to wake in the middle of the night and watch you sleep with the moon shinin' through the window on your beautiful face. And now that I know you're okay with Grace bein' a part of our family, I'm ready to do this thing. I think I started fallin' in love with you right after we met."

"I feel the same way, Clay, but you need a breather to grieve and get your bearings. We don't need to rush. I want to enjoy the moment, and right now I know you need to give yourself a little time. Then, you might need to crash and burn before you make any huge decisions like how we will manage finances, where we will live, how we will take care of Grace."

Clay rubbed a hand over the back of his neck.

"I know you're right. I still can't believe Sarah's gone, even after I scattered her ashes over the Atlantic. Do you think I'm in shock?"

"No. I just think you need time to sort everything out. I'm not going anywhere, Clay. I'll be right here when you've healed a bit and we both have our heads on straight to make our plans. I love you."

"When do you think Grace will wake up and realize her life has changed?"

"I don't know, but you and I will do everything within our power to make this as easy for her as possible."

The next day was Sunday. Clay and I whispered about the possibility of taking Grace to church, but we decided against it. Someone might look at her with pity, or say something that brought Sarah's memory and the realization that she was indeed gone and never coming back to the forefront of Grace's mind. So far, Grace appeared to have accepted that her mother was in heaven with her father and that her parents were happy to be together. It seemed that she hadn't felt the overwhelming sadness that one would expect. I attributed that to Clay's explanation and to Mama Rae's unique ability to affect behavior.

We decided to take Grace for a picnic on the beach and build a big sandcastle. Grace thought that was a fantastic idea, and we stayed there for most of the afternoon until it was obvious that the little girl was getting tired. Back at the villa we washed off the sand and the three of us took a nap.

That evening we drove my little yellow Jeep to Hudson's for a fish supper. Grace was thrilled to ride in the Jeep with the top off. She had played hard at the beach and had worked up quite an appetite. She cleaned her plate and allowed that her fried fish was super yummy. I didn't know how long we would be able to keep her floating on a cloud, but today had been a winner.

CHAPTER *Thirty*

Grace would go for hours without mentioning her mother. Then, out of the blue, she might begin to cry. When that happened, the child was inconsolable, but the tears would eventually stop on their own. At other times, she might say something cheerful about her mother.

"My mommy was happy all the time, and she tickled me to make me giggle. We had fun. Mommy's with my daddy now. She's happy."

"That's right, short stuff," Clay said. "Hey, do you think it would be fun if you and I had lunch at your house? We could stop at the store and get whatever you like to make sandwiches."

"Okay," said Grace, but she didn't sound excited. "Why can't Cwemmie go with us?"

"Clemmie went to work this morning. Remember?"

"Will she be gone all day?"

"I think so, but we'll see her later this afternoon. You like Clemmie, don't you?"

"I do. She's pwetty, too."

"Do you want to do that? Have lunch at your house?"

"If you do."

"Grace, we could spend the whole day at your house. We could even stay there tonight. You could sleep in your own bed. Would you like that?"

"No. I don't want to do that. Mommy's not there. I want to have another sweepover with Cwemmie."

As it turned out, Grace didn't want to return to her house at all. Clay wasn't sure what to make of it, but I thought Grace feared that she would be sad that her mother wasn't there. She knew her mother would never come back to that house.

I left work early and took Grace to see Mama Rae and Lord. My old mentor seemed to be able to always put Grace in the best of moods. We were treated to tarts still warm from Mama Rae's oven, and Grace was gifted with another glass of what Mama Rae called happy juice.

Grace was sleepy when we got back to my villa, so she and I took naps while Clay borrowed my Jeep to collect most of his niece's clothes and toys to bring to my place. We planned to give Grace the small bedroom upstairs.

Clay had planned to keep Sarah's house and move into it with Grace, but when the estate was settled, he was now thinking of selling it.

I wasn't sure how I felt. Everything seemed to be in limbo. Clay, Grace, and I went through the motions of living day-to-day. None of us appeared to be extraordinarily sad, nor were we brimming with happiness.

Little Grace had stolen my heart. She was so sweet-natured and loving. Clay adored his niece, but he made sure not to spoil her to the point of turning her into a brat.

Sometimes Clay would have nightmares. He would make unintelligible noises, tossing and turning in bed beside me, wringing wet with perspiration. And sometimes he cried, but only in the privacy of our bedroom in the dark of night.

I was roused from sleep in Clay's embrace. He was peppering my neck with tiny kisses. I turned my head to look into his eyes. He had something he wanted to discuss with me.

"Good morning." I smiled for him.

"Oh, did I wake you?" He feigned innocence.

"Yes, and in a very nice way."

"Clemmie, it's time we let Grace in on our plans to get married. I think she's ready to hear it."

"You don't think it's too soon? She's had an awfully big shock."

"That's true, but she's used to the three of us being together most of the time, and she seems fine with it. I want to tell her so we can begin our new life together as a family."

"I love you, Clay, and I love Grace. We don't want to do anything to make her think I'm trying to take her mother's place. That would be horrible."

"I don't think Grace would ever think that, Clemmie. She knew you and Sarah had become friends. She trusts you, and I don't want to put our marriage on hold."

"When and how do you think we should break the news to her?"

"How about we give her the good news this afternoon when you get home from work? I don't have plans today, so I can spend the whole day with my little cuddle bug."

"I'm sure this is all I'll be able to think about all day, but if you don't think the big announcement will damage our relationship, I'm with you. You know I can't wait to become your wife."

"I'm more anxious than you are, hot stuff. I'm more than ready to be your lord and master."

He laughed. "You know that was a joke, right?"

"Absolutely."

Max Palmer was at his desk when I arrived at the office.

"Good morning, Clemmie. I'm glad you're here. I just received a call from Pearl. She said that she needs to see you right away."

"Did she tell you why she needs to see me? I just had lunch with her the other day."

"No, she didn't. It seems that she has decided to take you under her wing, so to speak. Regardless of her reason, I told her that I was sure you would be happy to accommodate her. I don't have anything pressing for you to do today."

I was getting tired of Pearl's demands and equally tired of Max Palmer sending me to the yacht to please the old girl. I had a lot on my mind, and having to deal with a spoiled narcissistic old woman who was used to getting her way at her slightest whim was just too much.

"I suppose you consider this another of my duties like taking her shopping in Savannah."

"As a matter of fact, I do. While it's clear that Pearl isn't trying out for Ms. Congeniality, she is an important member of this company. I assumed you were aware of that."

"Of course I'm aware of that."

Max smiled.

"Should I come back here after I leave the yacht?"

"No, that won't be necessary. Take yourself on a shopping spree, or get a massage. I'll see you in the morning."

I didn't know what to expect when I was escorted onto the yacht. I entered the salon to see Pearl in her wheelchair waiting for me. The tea service sat on the table beside her highness, ready for me to pour.

"Good morning, Pearl."

"Good morning, Clemmie. Thank you for coming. Please have a seat."

I did as I was told and waited for further instructions. Pearl was staring at me, or through me. I couldn't tell which.

"Shall I pour?" I asked.

Pearl heaved a sigh, and her body seemed to slump. Her head fell forward, and her chin rested on her chest.

"Pearl! Pearl!"

"Gretchen! Help!"

Was I alone in the room with Pearl? I didn't know what to do.

She didn't look like she was breathing. I made myself check to see if she had a pulse. I was so nervous that I had to start over a couple of times. My heart was racing, and I was trying to decide what to do next when one of the young men who had escorted me onto the yacht came running into the salon.

"I heard yelling." He was panting. "What's the matter?"

I looked at his sincere expression and wasn't sure how to tell him that the yacht's owner had suddenly stopped breathing.

"Do you know CPR?"

The young man collected himself.

"I do, but let me check for a pulse first."

I had begun to perspire while the deck hand went about his business with what appeared to be a cool head.

"Ma'am, I'm afraid it's too late for CPR."

"Call 911," I said.

"Of course. I'll get right on it."

The young man turned to leave the room, and new panic assailed me.

"I'm going with you. You can't leave me here alone in the room with a dead person."

I sounded like a blithering idiot. Pearl had told Max Palmer and me that she was suffering from a progressive disease that was in the process of killing her. Her fate had simply come to fruition. But, as I moved away from Pearl, I glanced down at the tea service. There was a trace of tea in the bottom of the cup closest to Pearl's wheelchair. Maybe she had already had a cup of tea. Could the tea have been poisoned? If so, who could have prepared it? Gretchen? My imagination was running away with me. Why would Gretchen want to get rid of her bread and butter?

The deck hand stood staring at me, waiting for me to follow him. My feet didn't seem to want to move.

"Ma'am, I think you're in shock. Just stay where you are. I can use the phone by the salon door."

My breathing became labored as I watched the young man

hurry to the wall phone. He lifted the receiver and began speaking into it, but I couldn't hear what he was saying for the blood pumping in my ears. I stared at the deck hand's back, then down at Pearl's delicate teacup.

"Someone will be here in just a few minutes," said the deck hand. "Let me take you out on the sun deck and make you comfortable in a chaise lounge. I'm sure you don't want to stay here."

I allowed him to escort me out of the salon. Time crawled by while I waited for someone to come to the yacht, pronounce Pearl dead, and take her away.

"We have to call Mister Palmer," I told the young man. "He and Pearl were very close."

"I'll do that right away," he said, and left me staring out at the glittering water.

I was sure Max Palmer would be beside himself. If Pearl had been correct, he would no doubt fall to pieces without her to guide him. How dare she check out and pass the buck to me. I didn't want to take her place in nebulous moneymaking schemes. I knew absolutely nothing about her business. I could be sent to prison before my new wonderful life got started.

I heard a siren and saw the flashing lights as an ambulance parked. Two white-clad men rushed onto the yacht with a gurney. They were accompanied by whom I assumed were a couple of police detectives and a man in a dark suit, probably a coroner. They rushed into the salon en masse and went directly to Pearl. The coroner did a quick examination and pronounced her dead. I heard him say something about rigor mortis and time of death.

Max Palmer raced into the salon out of breath. His face was red. He pushed his way past the men who were raising the gurney to remove the body.

"Pearl! Pearl! This can't be happening," he said. He was on his knees in front of the wheelchair, combing the fingers of both hands through his hair.

"Sir, you need to let these men do their jobs," said one of the detectives. He and the other detective helped Max to his feet and led him across the room to a wing chair.

"Oh, Mister Palmer," I said, "I'm so very sorry."

I didn't know whether he had heard me, or if he was too stunned to answer.

"Is Gretchen here?" I asked one of the deck hands.

"She was here earlier. I heard her talking to Pearl when she brought in the tea."

"I think Mister Palmer could use something a little stronger than tea. Do you think you might accommodate him?"

"Certainly. Would you like something as well?"

"No, thank you."

I took a seat on the loveseat close to where my boss was sitting.

Max Palmer was crying and wringing his hands. He hadn't said a word to anyone except the dead woman. I wasn't sure he even knew I was in the room. He accepted a snifter of cognac and took a sip. Then, he swirled the amber liquid around and around, staring into the glass as if searching for the truth regarding his mentor's demise.

One of the detectives leaned down and spoke quietly to Max, then nodded. He turned his attention to us while Pearl was being whisked from the salon.

"Which one of you called us?" he asked.

"I did," answered the young man who had been alone with Pearl and me.

"Has anyone touched anything at the scene?"

"No, sir. The only person who was in the room at the time of death was this young woman," he said, pointing to me.

The detective came and stood before me with a pad and pen. I couldn't have been thinking straight, because his stance made me feel like laughing. It reminded me of an old Charlie Chan movie. I made myself don a sober expression and look up at the man.

"Ma'am, you were here with the deceased when she expired. Is that correct?"

"Yes, I was."

"Can you explain the circumstances? Tell me in your own words what happened?"

"I had just arrived and had come into the salon. Pearl had summoned me to come here about some sort of business matter. I didn't know why she wanted to see me; just that she did."

"Did she appear alright upon your arrival?"

"I didn't really have time to make an assessment. I walked into the room, and we greeted one another. She invited me to take a seat. Then, she simply stared at me. I didn't think too much about that until just now when you asked me how she appeared."

"Is staring at people a habit of hers?"

I couldn't imagine why he was questioning me.

"I never noticed her doing it before today."

"How long would you say she stared at you?"

"I don't know. I think I asked her if she would like for me to pour the tea, but she didn't answer."

"I don't know much about etiquette, but I thought the hostess always poured."

"That's true, but Pearl asked me to pour the last time I was here because her hands had begun to tremble."

"She didn't answer you—about pouring the tea, I mean."

"No. She heaved a sigh, and her head fell forward on her chest."

"I see," he said, closing his small notebook. "Well, it appears the decedent died of natural causes. You're all free to go. Please don't leave the island until we get an all clear from the morgue."

I started walking toward the door.

"Ma'am, one more thing," the detective said.

"Yes."

"What made you think this Gretchen person was on the yacht?"

"She's usually here when Pearl has visitors. She serves drinks and meals. She's like a personal assistant to Pearl, doing whatever is asked of her. She also does that sort of thing for Mister Palmer at his office."

"But you didn't see her this morning."

"No, but one of the deck hands told me he heard her talking with Pearl when she brought in the tea."

"Thank you, ma'am. You have a nice day."

Max Palmer must have somehow pulled himself together because I felt him take my elbow.

"I'll walk you out, Clemmie. I know you're as shocked as I am. Take the rest of the day off. I have important arrangements to handle this afternoon. I'll see you in the morning."

I didn't know what to say to my boss, so I just nodded and headed to my Jeep.

I turned the key in the ignition and looked back at the *Pearl*. Max Palmer was pacing back and forth on the deck finger-combing his hair, looking like a lost soul.

CHAPTER
Thirty-One

*I*t seemed that every time I felt panicked, I made a beeline to Mama Rae. Why hadn't I run to Clay? I asked myself this every step I took on the narrow path through the woods.

I knocked on the frame of the screen door.

"Mama Rae, it's me, Clemmie."

There was no answer. I didn't hear a sound, nor did I smell the aroma of anything mouthwatering coming from Mama Rae's kitchen. I tried the door. It wasn't hooked from inside, so I opened it and let myself into the cabin. I called out to my old friend as I walked through the living room to the kitchen. Then, I made my way to the bedroom. Mama Rae was lying on her back with her arms stretched out horizontally. Lord was curled around her turbaned head.

"Mama Rae," I said softly.

She didn't move. I touched her outstretched hand and gave it a gentle squeeze. That produced a fluttering of my old friend's eyelids. Then, she blinked and looked up at me.

"I been 'spectin' you," she said, and stretched. "Your Mama Rae tired, and dis spoilt cat won't leave me alone."

She reached up and extracted Lord from around her head to cradle him like a baby.

"He a pretty good cat," she allowed, stroking him until he began to purr.

"Why were you expecting me?"

"You upset 'cause Pearl passed. Les go to de kitchen."

I wasn't surprised that she knew. I started to help her get out of bed, then thought better of it. Any unsolicited assistance would have rubbed her the wrong way, so I stood aside, then followed her to the kitchen. The first thing she did was give Lord a nasty-looking treat which he obviously expected.

"I have some of dat fruit juice you favored de other day. You want some?"

"Yes, please. It was very good."

Mama Rae poured the concoction into a tall glass and handed it to me.

"Aren't you having any?"

"Not thirsty."

As I was pulling out my chair, I noticed my friend's basket sitting on the counter. The towel that usually covered it was missing, and the basket was empty.

Mama Rae sat down, tucked her small fists under her chin, and looked at me.

"It possible for a person to live too long," she said. "Pearl did a lot of good here on de island. She a natural leader: strong, on a mission, in control, never let people tink she had a weak spot. Tings happen sometimes. Pearl got knocked down by dat sickness. She tried to fight it, but it was winnin'. She was tired of bein' here de way she was. It best dis way."

I wasn't sure what she was telling me.

"Were you and Pearl friends?"

"No, not friends. When doctors couldn't help her, she asked me to try. Everbody knows Mama Rae helps folks with herbs."

"Did the herbs help her?"

"Helped her leave dis island like she wanted to leave–quiet like."

I had finished the glass of juice and felt calm and peaceful. Mama Rae had just told me in so many words that she had helped Pearl commit suicide. I assumed it had been a slow, but painless process. Her mission accomplished, she stood, took my glass to the sink, and left the room.

I went back through the woods taking in nature's beauty without a care. Blossoms perfumed the close air, and birds chirped their lovely melodies. What a beautiful place this was.

Clay and Grace were sitting on the front porch steps, licking dripping ice cream cones when I pulled into my parking spot.

"Well, it looks like you two are having a party," I said, smiling.

"It's not a party," Grace explained. "It's a tweat."

She held her cone toward me to offer a taste.

"No, thanks, Grace, but it was nice of you to offer."

"How was work?" Clay asked.

"I didn't have much to do. That's why I'm home so early. I want to get out of these clothes, change into something comfortable, and maybe go for a walk on the beach," I said, hurrying into the villa.

I would have to let Clay know what had happened, but Grace would be with us until bedtime. I couldn't go into detail about Pearl's demise in the presence of a three-year-old who had recently lost her mother. Hearing something of that nature could damage the little girl for life. Clay and I were about to let her know that we were getting married, and she would be a part of our family. Who knew how she would take that? Clay could be wrong, and Grace might think that I was going to try taking her mother's place. All of this new information might be overload for a small vulnerable child.

As I was changing into shorts, I came up with a plan. I would invite Clay and Grace to accompany me on my walk and take a couple of beach toys along. Grace would be content to shovel sand into her pail, and that would give me an opportunity to give Clay the bare bones of what had transpired on the yacht.

Clay and Grace were washing the ice cream off their hands when I came downstairs.

"Let's all go to the beach," I said, swinging Grace's pail and shovel, hoping to entice her.

I must have donned a telling expression by the look Clay gave me. He knew I had something important to tell him.

"Good idea," he said.

Grace knew the rules: she was not to wander far away from us, and she was not to go near the water unless one of us was with her. She went to work with the shovel immediately, telling us that she would start working on a sandcastle by herself. We could help later.

"What's going on, Clemmie?" Clay asked in a near whisper.

"I'll give you the short version and fill in details after Grace is in bed."

"This sounds important."

"It is. Pearl had told Max Palmer that she wanted me to meet her at the yacht to discuss a business matter. When I got there, she was in the salon. We exchanged greetings. Then, she simply stared at me. I thought that was strange, but she had been unpredictable in the past. I volunteered to pour the tea, because her hands had been shaky lately. She continued to stare, took a deep breath, then stopped breathing altogether."

Clay seemed to be at a loss for words.

"Don't be so stunned. She was an elderly woman who had been in ill health for a long time."

"I understand, but I'm sure you were shocked when she died before your very eyes."

"Yes, I was, but I'm okay now. I went to see Mama Rae. She always calms me down."

"I don't like the things this job puts you through."

"I'm fine."

Grace had been filling her little pail, then dumping the sand to build her castle wall, all the while singing the alphabet song. She appeared to be in a very happy state of mind. I wondered how she would feel after learning that Clay and I were planning to marry and that the three of us would comprise her new family. I hoped her uncle would be able to deliver this news in a way that Grace could accept it as a good thing. She had been dealt a terrible blow at an early age. Clay had told me that she would be turning four in another month, but that was still awfully young to be bombarded with an information overload.

We had chicken pot pies and Twinkies for dinner. It was during dessert that Clay chose to bring up our plans for marriage.

"Grace, you and I both like Clemmie a lot, don't we?"

Grace licked some cream filling from her index finger and nodded enthusiastically.

"You know when grownups like one another a whole lot, they fall in love and get married."

The little girl nodded again.

"What would you think if I told you that Clemmie and I love each other and we want to get married? Would that be okay with you?"

Grace took the last bite of her Twinkie. Then she smiled and nodded.

When Grace was tucked into bed, I sat on the living room couch with Clay and we toasted his success at explaining our situation to his little niece. Then, I told him all the details of my day. He listened without interrupting until I finished as he always did.

"Max Palmer expects me to show up at the office tomorrow morning," I said. "Clay, I don't know whether to stay in this job or not. I believe that the business dealings are barely within the law, if they are at all. As far as I know, neither Pearl nor Max has ever had charges of any kind brought against them, but I feel uncomfortable."

"I've told you that you don't have to stay in the job, Clemmie. I meant it; I can take care of us. You can find a different job, or you don't have to work at all. I'm Sarah's beneficiary. She was pretty well fixed. She named me as her beneficiary instead of Grace because she knew I would take care of her child. I'm gonna sell Sarah's house, and I have other resources. We're gonna have to make plans to get settled as a family, and that'll take some time. We'll need to get Grace enrolled in a good preschool program and work around that schedule."

"I'm sure Max will let me know the particulars about the arrangements for Pearl's funeral in the morning. I have to admit I feel sorry for him. He seemed to think the world of Pearl, and she led me to believe that he wouldn't be capable of running the company without her to guide him."

"So why was she tellin' you all of that?"

"... She wanted me to take her place."

"You can't be serious. Everything you've told me about those two and their company sounds like somethin' out of a bad movie. My advice is to get out of that mess as fast as you can."

"I know you're right. Daniel did his best to dig into Max's past and find out if the company was doing anything illegal, but he hasn't been able to find any useful information."

I should have let my worries drift away and sleep peacefully with my love's arm draped across my side, but I slept fitfully. Clay's breathing was even, and I envied his ability to let his cares go and relax.

Hearing my breakfast chef rattle around in the kitchen told me it was morning. I sat up and put my feet on the floor. I felt like I had a hangover, but that was impossible since I had only sipped one cognac the night before. I stumbled to the bathroom and brushed my teeth, then went downstairs.

Clay met me with a mug of coffee and a kiss. I buried my face in his neck and breathed in his scent. This man would love me and take care of me, and I would do my best to be the kind of wife he deserved. I would love Grace as much as I might love my own child, the way Roy had loved me.

"Don't tell me you don't have time for breakfast," Clay said, leading me to the table.

He went into the small kitchen and returned with omelets and juice, then sat down across from me.

"Eat up, sweetheart. I don't want you to meet that guy you call a boss on an empty stomach."

I made myself take a few bites. Clay spoiled me in every conceivable way, and he didn't know how much I appreciated it.

"I'll have to attend the service, you know," I said.

"Of course."

I didn't know what to expect as I drove to the office. Max Palmer would probably be a wreck, and I didn't look forward to seeing him in pain, especially if he expected me to take any part in helping with Pearl's sendoff.

My boss was pacing the large room when I got there. He was dressed in a dark suit and wore a somber expression.

"Good morning, Mister Palmer."

"Clemmie."

I wasn't sure what to say, or do next, so I stood by the door waiting for his instruction.

"The service will be tomorrow afternoon at two o'clock at that little nondenominational church Pearl attended. There'll be an obit in the paper today although that wouldn't be necessary. I've decided not to have a viewing. I don't think Pearl would want such a thing. She never told me how she wanted things handled, but I'm sure she wouldn't want the island's populous staring at her after she departed this world. I couldn't bring myself to have her cremated, but her casket will be closed from prying eyes. Everyone on this island knew Pearl, and word travels fast. I'm sure it will be standing room only and the parking lot will be running over all the way out to the roadsides."

I wondered why he was rambling on and on, but I dared not interrupt him.

"You'll want to take the morning off and shop for suitable attire for the service. Of course, you'll be sitting with me and a few of Pearl's closest associates in the front of the church."

He pulled a money clip from his pocket, peeled off a wad of hundred dollar bills, and handed them to me.

"Mister Palmer, I can't accept this," I said, holding the money toward him.

"Of course, you can. Buy something nice. I'll meet you at the church."

I took the money, walked to his desk, and laid the wad of bills on the blotter. Max Palmer didn't say another word as I walked past him and left the building.

I parked my Jeep at the woods' edge and started down the path wondering what words of wisdom Mama Rae would have for me. She knew every detail regarding Pearl's death. She also seemed to know a lot about Pearl in general. When I had gone to see her the first day Pearl had requested my presence on the yacht, Mama Rae had admonished me to cut our visit short, telling me that she, meaning Pearl, would be waiting for me. I wondered if she would still think it was a good idea for me to continue working in this mysterious job. She had never admitted knowing Max Palmer even though I had seen the two in one another's company on more than one occasion.

When I came into the clearing, I saw her sitting on the front porch. She seemed to be looking directly at me.

"Hello, Mama Rae," I said, as I came close to the porch.

My old friend nodded, then motioned for me to come and sit on the steps. I did as I was told and waited for her to say something else. She still hadn't uttered a word. The two of us sat in silence until I couldn't take it any longer.

"Mama Rae, Max Palmer was Pearl's good friend. The two of them were in business together. He's the man who pushes her wheelchair when she leaves the yacht. You've told me several times that you don't know him, but I've seen you talking with Pearl when he was with her."

I hadn't meant to let her know that I had spied on her. She would probably never forgive me for having done that, but I had blurted it out and couldn't retrieve it. I could see the hurt in my old friend's rheumy eyes when she looked into mine.

Bili Morrow Shelburne

"You don't believe your Mama Rae, and you been sneakin' around followin' me. I don't know dat man; never met him. You tellin' me de man pushes Pearl's wheelchair is your boss?"

"Yes. That's exactly what I'm telling you."

I was afraid Mama Rae was going to get up, go into her house, and leave me sitting on the steps. If that happened, my visit would have been in vain.

"Lot of strange tings," she mused, "but it'll all be okay."

"I hope you're right. Mama Rae, I think maybe I should tell Max Palmer that I don't think I'm the right person for this job. He pays me way too much, and I would hate to give up the salary, but I think he's into some shady dealings. I don't want to get into trouble with the law."

"You askin' dis old woman to tell you what to do?"

"I'd like your opinion. Clay thinks I should quit."

"Uh huh."

"All I ever heard about Pearl was de good tings she did for folks, and if dis man was in business with her, he prob'ly alright."

I hadn't learned anything except that Mama Rae had been telling me the truth all along when she had denied knowing Max Palmer. She had been adamant about it. It had been hard for me to believe that she would deliberately lie to me about anything, but I had thought she had lied to me about that. There had been many instances when she had been evasive, and times when she had simply refused to answer by changing the subject. I supposed that could be considered being untruthful by omission, but she had never told me a bald-faced lie.

284

CHAPTER
Thirty-Two

$\mathcal{I}$ arrived at the church early, but the parking lot was already full. I had to park on the side of the road and walk through loose gravel in my only pair of good heels. Max Palmer was solemnly holding forth in the vestibule and accepting condolences as mourners formed a long line to shake his hand. I wasn't sure where I was supposed to be in the crowd, so I waited at the end of the line.

It seemed an eternity before I inched my way up to the visitor register. I wrote my name, then extended my hand to Max Palmer.

"I'm so sorry, Mister Palmer."

Max took my hand in his and nodded before turning me over to an usher.

"Take Ms. Castlebrook to my pew," he said.

I allowed the young man to escort me to the front of the church and took my seat. The organist began playing *In The Garden*, then followed that with similar fare as the mourners trickled into the sanctuary. Max brought up the rear and took a seat beside me. I had assumed that miss sexy pants would have been considered one

285

of Pearl's close acquaintances and that she would have been seated with us, but that wasn't the case. The mayor of Hilton Head and his wife sat with us.

I felt conspicuous sitting with Max Palmer. I certainly wasn't well-known on the island, and I thought I could feel people staring at the back of my head. The minister came forward and gripped the pulpit with both hands.

"We have gathered here today to celebrate the phenomenal life and legacy of Pearl who has done so much for our small community."

Didn't anybody use the woman's last name?

"When you look around our little island, you can see Pearl's footprint in nearly every bit of progress from medical facilities, the library, and small businesses. The list goes on and on. She was so selfless, so giving. Her generosity was almost overwhelming. The building fund of this church would have been nothing without her contributions."

My mind strayed to the Pearl I had known for the short time I had been here, and I wondered if anyone in this group of mourners knew that the dearly departed swilled martinis like Kool-Aid, had a hateful and overbearing personality, and was what I strongly suspected to be a common crook.

The minister droned on, extolling Pearl's virtues, and I noticed Max Palmer swipe a hand across his eyes. I straightened my posture and brought my attention back to the fervent remarks of the minister's prepared send-off, making an effort to temper my judgment.

After the benediction, the minister announced that there would be no gathering of any kind following the service. That was fine with me. I had done what I considered my duty to my boss and I wanted to go back to my villa to those I loved.

I was picking my way through the parking lot and had gotten almost to my Jeep when something in my peripheral vision caught my attention: Gretchen was helping Mama Rae into Pearl's van. I hadn't seen my old friend inside the church, but I was certain I wasn't mistaken. She had on her navy crepe dress and big-brimmed hat to match.

I drove straight home to change my clothes. Clay and Grace weren't there, and I assumed that he had taken her somewhere within walking distance to entertain her. I changed into shorts, then took off for Mama Rae's.

I tapped on the door and called her name. She didn't answer, but I knew she was home. I tried the screen door. It wasn't hooked, so I opened it and stepped inside.

"Mama Rae, it's Clemmie."

"In de bedroom."

My friend still had on her navy dress. She was lying on her back with her hands folded on her abdomen like a corpse.

"Mama Rae, are you alright?"

"I'm wrung out, chile. Got to rest."

"Can I get you anything? Water? Tea?"

"Just want to rest."

She was telling me to leave. I would have been more than glad to drive her to Pearl's funeral if I had known she wanted to go. That hadn't occurred to me because she had told me that their relationship was only business.

"You rest, Mama Rae. I'll check on you later," I said, and left the cabin.

I had just parked and started up the porch steps when I saw Daniel's little blue pickup turn into Hickory Cove. He pulled up beside my Jeep and cut the engine, and out jumped Clay from the passenger side of the truck. He counted to three, and Grace leapt from the truck into his arms. Daniel got out, and Clay lowered Grace to the ground. She ran around the truck, giggling and grabbed Daniel's hand.

"That was fun," she said. "Thank you. I wuved my Happy Meal."

"We'll do it again soon, Grace. Maybe I'll bring my daughter along. I'll bet you two are going to be good friends."

"I see Grace has a new friend," I said.

Grace nodded enthusiastically, and we trooped into the villa.

"I take it you're here by yourself, Daniel," I said.

"Yes, I am. I had to be on the island for a little business and just wanted to stop by to say hello and see how things are going. I also plan to visit Mama Rae while I'm here."

"I just came from her cabin. She didn't seem to be in the mood for company."

"Oh?"

"I don't suppose Clay told you the latest, but there was a special service for Max Palmer's old friend, Pearl, today. That's where I've been. Mama Rae was there, too. I went to see her just now, but she was too tired to visit, so I left so she could rest."

"Hey, Clemmie, why don't you and Daniel go for a walk to catch up," Clay said. "Grace and I had him all to ourselves this afternoon. We're both stuffed, and a nap sounds kinda good to me. How about you, short stuff?"

"Okay," Grace said, taking Clay's hand to go inside.

Daniel and I headed down the narrow street on foot, and I began telling him everything that had happened in the last few days. We didn't go to the beach since Daniel wasn't dressed for it. Instead, we took a bike path. Every now and then, we had to step off the path to give bikers the right-of-way.

"So the old girl bit the dust before she had a chance to tell you why she had summoned you."

"Yes. It was awful. Then, I was questioned by a detective as though I had known what killed her, or possibly that I'd had something to do with her death. I had never seen a person die before. Well, I thought I watched Roy kill you with his baseball bat."

"I'm kind of glad you were wrong about that." Daniel grinned.

"Daniel, what am I going to do? Max Palmer's real estate business is nothing more than a Ponzi scheme, and you and I both know it. We haven't found any evidence that he has ever been caught, but maybe he's just been lucky. Pearl knew she was dying. She told me that she wanted me to get more involved in the business since she didn't think Max was smart enough to handle it alone."

"I say get out while the getting's good. You can get another job—one that doesn't keep you on edge."

"That's what Clay says."

"Speaking of Clay, what's up with the two of you? I get the impression things are getting serious."

"Your impression is correct. We're getting married."

"Congratulations! You know I'm happy for you. Girl, you've had more than your share of hard knocks."

"It'll be a very small wedding. Neither of us has family, and we don't know that many people."

"But I'll be giving you away, right?"

"Who else?" I laughed. "After you walk me down the aisle, you can be Clay's best man."

"Have you set a date?"

"No. We just told Grace last night. I'm not sure she's had time to digest it. She's still just a baby."

"Let's go back to your villa. I want to congratulate Clay, then go to Mama Rae's to see if she's up to a visit."

We had a low-key evening and went to bed early. Clay and I talked about initial plans we were about to make: our wedding, settling Grace in a day care facility, and finally, about my resignation from Max Palmer's company with no name.

Grace hardly ever had a nightmare, and when she did, Clay was able to calm her down in no time. We always left the bedroom doors ajar so we could hear her if she was having trouble sleeping. I was already developing a maternal instinct, and I knew that I could be someone Grace could depend on for love and comfort without trying to replace the mother she had lost.

Max Palmer was sitting at his desk when I arrived at the office the following morning. He wore a somber expression instead of his usual early-morning smile. He didn't offer coffee or breakfast.

"Good morning, Clemmie."

"Good morning, Mister Palmer."

"Clemmie, I'm going to be out of the office all day. I'd like for you to take phone messages. You can close up early, around three o'clock."

"Mister Palmer, I need to talk to you. Are you in a hurry to leave the office?"

"Yes, I am. Whatever it is will have to wait. I apologize for the inconvenience."

I had rehearsed my resignation speech on the drive from my villa. I was ready to give my boss two weeks' notice and hoped I wouldn't have to spend very much time with him until I left the office for good.

"It's important that I speak with you today," I said.

"I'm sorry, my dear," he said, brushing past me to walk out the front door.

Gretchen didn't bother to show her face, so I went down the hall to the kitchenette to make coffee. I wondered what to do about lunch if she didn't show up. I could skip it all together, or lock the place up and go get a sandwich to bring back to the office.

The phone rang just as I returned to my desk.

"Max Palmer's office."

"Ms. Castlebrook?"

The voice sounded vaguely familiar, but I couldn't place it.

"Yes. How may I help you?"

"This is Don Garrison. Remember me?"

"I'm sorry, Mister Garrison. I assume we've met. I've met quite a few people since I've been on the island. Would you mind refreshing my memory?"

"We met on the yacht. I'm Bunny's better half." He laughed at his tired joke.

"Oh, yes. Of course, I remember you. How may I help you?"

"I need to talk to the man."

"I'm afraid Mister Palmer is out of the office today. May I take a message?"

There was a long pause; then a sigh.

"Just tell him that I'm the designated caller for the little group you met at that boating party. We want a meeting with him ASAP."

I hung up the phone wondering if something had gone wrong with the deal my boss had put together for that group. Max might have gotten in over his head this time. I had a feeling the scheme wasn't working the way it was supposed to, and this little trio of nouveau riche were no longer envisioning the profitable returns Max had promised them. For his sake, I hoped they weren't dangerous.

The phone didn't ring but that one time all day, and I had decided to skip lunch. There was nothing for me to do but pace the office, drink coffee, and count the minutes until three o'clock. I turned off the lights and locked up at three on the dot.

Clay was disappointed when I told him that I hadn't had a chance to let Max Palmer know I was giving notice.

"There was nothing I could do about it, Clay. He was leaving the office for the day when I got there. He was in a big hurry and said that whatever I wanted to discuss would have to wait."

"Well, try not to worry about it. You can tell him in the morning. It's only one more day, then you can breathe easy."

Grace was a little whiny. This was the first time I had seen her this way. Clay had taken her to the beach where they splashed in the surf and played in the sand. Then, they ate lunch at Possum Point, but those things weren't at the top of Grace's priority list. She wanted to go see Mama Rae and play with Lord. Clay explained that it was too far to walk, and he couldn't take her on his bike, but she wasn't interested in his explanation.

"We could drive over to see Mama Rae since I'm home with the Jeep," I said.

Clay shook his head.

"Sorry, but we're not gonna do that. Grace has to learn that she can't have everything she wants. I explained why we couldn't go. She needs to accept what we tell her 'cause we're adults and know what's best for her. I love her, but I'm not gonna spoil her rotten."

I just stared at him. He was talking about Grace as if she weren't listening to the conversation. I probably shouldn't have suggested caving in to a small child. After all, she was his niece.

"Maybe we can go see Mama Rae and Lord tomorrow, short stuff," Clay said, ruffling her hair. "But right now I think you could use a nap."

"Okay," Grace said around a sniffle. She reached for her uncle's hand.

Clay came downstairs after Grace was tucked into bed.

"I'm sorry, Clay. I shouldn't have interfered with your disciplining. That won't happen again."

"Sweetheart, I have to do what's best for Grace. If we let her make up the rules, she'll turn out to be a spoiled brat. Little kids don't know what's best for 'em. Sarah always made sure Grace knew who was boss. That's why the kid's such a joy most of the time."

"I know. I'm probably not thinking straight. I was so ready to cut my ties with Max Palmer. Then, when he wouldn't take time to listen to me, I was frustrated. I guess I felt vulnerable and weak, and that's how Grace seemed to me. I hated to see her unhappy."

Clay wrapped his arms around me.

"She'll be smilin' when she wakes up. You'll see. She's a forgivin' little thing."

I knew he was right. He would do his best to rear Grace the way Sarah would have wanted him to do it. We both would.

"Clay," I said against his chest, "Daniel wants to give me away at our wedding."

"That right?"

"Yes. I love Daniel like a brother. I'd be honored for him to walk me down the aisle."

"I think he's a great choice. He's a real good guy."

"I'm glad you approve. Now, when and where do you think we should tie the knot?"

Clay laughed. "You're beginnin' to sound like me. Are my speech patterns rubbin' off on you?"

"Come on, Clay, nobody talks like you." I gave him my best smile.

"We don't know enough people to have a big weddin', but I guess we could probably talk the preacher we've been spendin' time with into makin' us legal."

"That sounds perfect. Of course, Catherine will be there, and I'll ask Mama Rae to be my maid of honor."

"That sweet old woman is a wealth of information," Clay said. "I'll bet she knows more about this island than anybody else who lives here. Matter of fact, she knows a lot about most everything."

When Grace awoke from her nap, she was all smiles, and I decided that Clay knew his little niece pretty well. We told her our plans for the wedding, and she was excited at the prospect of being the flower girl although she wasn't sure what that entailed.

Clay planned to get in touch with the minister first thing in the morning while I was at work. When all of the arrangements were final, we would call Daniel and Catherine to give them the details. I couldn't wait to tell Mama Rae.

The office was dark when I arrived. Max Palmer's Ferrari wasn't parked outside the front door where he always left it. I dug out my key, unlocked the door and went inside. I flipped on the lights. The room was stuffy as though the air conditioner had been turned off. There was a plain white envelope propped up by the phone on my desk. It had my name on it.

CHAPTER
Thirty-Three

*E*verything felt surreal to me. Max Palmer had left a
cashier's check made out to me in the amount of ten
thousand dollars. I had found it in a plain white envelope
on my desk with my name on it. He hadn't bothered to leave a note
of explanation. My boss was nowhere in sight, and the office was so
hot and stuffy that the stale air felt heavy, making it hard to breathe.
Why would he turn off the air conditioner?

I stuffed the envelope into my purse, turned off the lights,
locked the door, and got into my Jeep. What to do next? I closed
my eyes and tried to recall details of the past two days; anything that
might give me a clue as to the present situation. Max Palmer was a
strange one. That wasn't a revelation to me.

I couldn't imagine where he might be or why he had left me a
check for that large amount. Maybe he had decided to fire me but
didn't want to face me because he was so grief-stricken over Pearl's
demise. It occurred to me that he might have gone back to the place
he had last seen his mentor, so I drove to the pier. The *Pearl* wasn't
in her slip, but I glimpsed a familiar figure hurrying from the pier

toward the parking lot. Don Garrison walked purposefully with his head down.

I turned on the ignition of my Jeep and hoped I could drive out of Don Garrison's field of vision before he spotted me. He must have been planning to make a surprise visit to Max. I had left his phone message on Max's desk, but that didn't mean he had returned Garrison's call. If my boss had put his investors in a position to lose their money, and they had gotten wise to it, Max could be in danger. They might be the kind of people who would do him physical harm.

My heart was hammering in my chest, and I was afraid that I was on the verge of a panic attack. I had made it out of Sea Pines Plantation to the main drag to a casual seafood restaurant which was nearly always crowded with tourists dressed in shorts and tennis shoes. Even though the summer season had ended, there were families with lots of little kids outside the restaurant waiting for the next available table. I found an empty spot to park at the very back of the sandy lot as far from the highway as possible. Then, I let my head loll back with my eyes closed and began my deep breathing exercises. I must have ignored the noisy children running among parked cars and allowed myself to fall asleep, because when I opened my eyes, the pounding in my chest had stopped and I was able to breathe normally.

I had to think, but I also felt the need to tell someone about this strange situation. Instead of heading to my old friend and mentor, I drove home. I was about to become Clay's wife; I should be sharing my information with him.

Clay and Grace were on the back deck playing with a Nerf ball. I slid the glass door open and stepped out on the deck. Clay looked at me with a concerned expression.

"Did you tell him?" he asked.

"No. I didn't. He wasn't at the office when I got there. The building was locked, and the air conditioning had been turned off."

I pulled the envelope out of my purse and handed it to him.

"This was on my desk."

Clay opened the envelope and looked at the check. His eyes showed a look of disbelief.

"There wasn't a note," I said. "What should I do?"

Clay rubbed a hand over the back of his neck and continued to stare at the check.

"My first inclination would be for you to cash the check, then elope with Grace and me, but since we don't know what Max Palmer has up his sleeve, how would you feel about my puttin' it in my safe deposit box for the time bein'?"

"Okay, but why?"

"I don't have a reason—just a feelin'. We don't need the money right now, and it can't do any harm to wait until we know what's goin' on with Max Palmer."

"That's fine with me. I'm not sure how I should react to his extravagant gesture. Should I go to the office in the morning as usual? If Max was firing me, and the money was intended as a huge severance package, what should I do with the key to the building?"

"I think we can assume the man was firin' you. He might have felt kinda bad about doin' it, so he left you a big check. Just to be on the safe side, we can take Grace to Mama Rae's in the mornin'. I'll go with you to the office. I don't much like the idea of you goin' back there alone."

"You don't think I could be in any kind of danger, do you?"

"No, but I'll just feel better if I'm with you. I'll stay in the Jeep if the lights are on. You can go in, give him your resignation speech, and leave the key with him. End of story."

"What if he isn't there?"

"We leave and don't look back. He's put you through enough."

I had to agree to go through with Clay's plan because I didn't have a better one. He was looking out for my best interest. He wanted to take care of me, and I was grateful to have his guidance. Without it, I didn't know which way to turn.

I was tired the next morning from tossing and turning all night.

Clay was a bit bleary-eyed, too, but I could tell he wanted to keep any anxiety he had been having to himself. I knew he would be my rock for the rest of our lives.

Grace was still asleep when Clay carried her from the villa to my Jeep. He held her, and I drove us to Mama Rae's. The little girl stirred, but managed to stay in a state of half-sleep all the way there. Mama Rae was rubbing her eyes when she shuffled to open the door. She signaled for Clay to follow her to the bedroom and deposit Grace on her bed. Then, she climbed in beside her. We were being dismissed.

I was nervous as I drove to the office.

"I can tell you're gettin' all worked up, Clemmie," Clay said. "Please don't worry; I'll be ready to run inside at the first sign of trouble."

As we pulled into the small parking area in front of the building, we saw that the office was dark. A big black Cadillac was parked in the spot where Max Palmer always parked his Ferrari. I recognized the car and the man sitting behind the wheel immediately and drove back onto the street as fast as I could.

"Was that Palmer's car parked in front of the building?" Clay asked.

"No. It belongs to a creepy old man Max talked into investing in a large parcel of real estate on the coast of Florida. I've had the misfortune of dining in his company a couple of times. I told you that attending business dinners with Max was part of my duties although I was never given a written job description."

"You sure got away from the office fast. Were you afraid of that guy for some reason?"

"I didn't want to face him, because I have a feeling he has a bone to pick with Max. I'd bet almost anything he lost a lot of money on that deal and he wants answers, and maybe retribution. And there's something I failed to tell you yesterday. It completely slipped my mind."

I could feel Clay staring at me, waiting for an explanation.

"When my boss wasn't at the office, I took the envelope containing the check and drove to the yacht. I thought Max might have gone there. I didn't see his car, but that didn't mean anything. I could have simply overlooked it. The parking lot was crowded. But the yacht wasn't in its slip. Nobody but Max could have moved it."

"So are you sayin' you think the old guy in the Caddy had come to break your boss's knees or somethin'?"

"Not just him. As I was driving through the parking lot at the pier, I saw Don Garrison hurrying from the yacht's empty slip toward the parking lot. He looked like a man on a mission. I'll bet he was out to get Max, too. My boss was a real hustler, but it looks like he might have just gotten caught."

"Who's Don Garrison?"

"I told you about the three couples who went on that little outing on the yacht a couple of weeks ago. Garrison and his wife were one of the couples. Max told me that another part of my job was to charm those people. They were a bunch of rich phonies, and I was miserable the entire time."

"Why would any of those people want to harm you? You didn't swindle them."

"They probably think I'm involved in Max's shenanigans. He introduced me to them as his able assistant. I'm sure they think I know everything about the business. They probably think I do more to help my boss than attending dinners and cocktail parties with him. When Max introduced me to Ralph Wingate, the guy in the Cadillac, he told Wingate that he didn't know how he got along without me before I took the job."

Clay scrubbed a hand across his face and sighed.

"I think you're probably overthinkin' this. I understand that both of those men seem to be interested in meetin' with Palmer. It's possible that they might want to work him over, but they probably just want their money back. So, let's say he's a crook who simply hasn't been caught. Just because you work for the man doesn't mean you know what a low-life he is, or that you're involved in his unscrupulous business practices."

"I hope I'm overthinking it. But I think it's more than a coincidence that they would both show up here on the island in the last two days."

"I agree that it does look that way, but if they're here to see him for whatever reason, they're lookin' for him, not you. The office is locked up tight, the yacht's gone, and it looks like Palmer's gone with it."

"I hope you're right."

Clay looked at me in a way that could cause me to follow him anywhere. Then, he showed me that million-dollar smile.

"Please try to forget about the crazy job and the anxiety and fear you're feelin'. You can't let it run your life. Let's go see that nice preacher and see how soon we can get married," he said.

"Whatever you say, lord and master." I felt myself grin.

The Reverend Williams was in his office when we arrived at the church. Clay had called him earlier, and was told that we could drop in anytime; we didn't need an appointment. The young minister had impressed me the Sunday I'd attended one of his services. What I hadn't known was that he had a wicked sense of humor.

Clay tapped on the open office door, and the minister looked up, his handsome face creasing into a big smile.

"Hi, there, you two. Come on in."

We went inside and stood in front of a battered wooden desk covered with stacks of paper.

"Ready to make it all respectable?" the minister asked with a wink.

I felt the unease of embarrassment begin to creep up inside me, but Clay shook the preacher's hand and nodded, accompanied by something close to a belly laugh.

"Yes, sir, we are," he said.

"Well, sit, sit. Make yourselves comfortable."

We took our seats in front of the desk.

"So, how long have you two known one another?"

"Not long at all," Clay admitted, "but we've been through a lot together since we first met."

The minister didn't say anything; just waited for more information.

"We met by accident," I said. "Then, we seemed to be at the same place at the same time a lot. Clay suggested that since fate kept throwing us together, maybe we should plan such a meeting. We've grown very close."

"Clemmie was real supportive when Sarah died," Clay said. "She's been wonderful with my little orphaned niece."

"Young Grace is quite a presence. She blew me a kiss during one of my sermons." He smiled. "How is she?"

"She's much better than I thought she would be. I credit Clemmie for helpin' with this painful time in Grace's life. She does things like a mother would do, like playin' dress-up. I think it helps."

"You know I'm a certified counselor, and I'd be happy to help if any of you should feel it would be helpful."

"I think we're okay, but thanks."

The minister acknowledged that with a nod and a smile.

"I won't ask how either of you grew up; what denomination your parents were, because it doesn't matter. This church is nondenominational, and since you're asking me to perform the marriage ceremony, denomination must not matter to you. By the way, it doesn't matter to The Big Guy either."

"Neither of us has family, and we don't know many folks here on Hilton Head, so we'd just like a simple service. We'd like to get married as soon as it fits your schedule," Clay explained.

"I'm pretty open. I assume there's no particular reason for the rush."

"No, of course not," Clay answered. "We love one another, and we want to start our new life together. Grace will be included in our family."

"In that case, how about next Saturday afternoon? Say two o'clock? Will that give you time to let those you want to attend know about it and to get your license? You know it'll take twenty-four hours to get the license after you make an application for it at the probate judge's office. There's a satellite office here on the island, so you won't have to go to the main office in Beaufort."

I didn't know the answer, so I looked at Clay.

"Saturday's perfect," he said.

When we were on our way to Mama Rae's to pick up Grace, it hit me that everything seemed to be moving at warp speed. Our wedding was about to happen. First, we would have to get a marriage license. We needed to make sure the date worked for Daniel and Catherine. I couldn't wait to let them know our plan. We also needed to introduce Grace to a preschool, get her enrolled, and make sure she was comfortable with it. We couldn't just take her to Mama Rae's and drop her off whenever we needed a sitter.

I parked at the woods' edge and killed the engine. Clay started to climb out of the Jeep, but I stayed behind the wheel. I must have looked as anxious as I felt. With one foot on the sand and the other still in the Jeep, Clay looked at me with raised eyebrows.

"What's the matter, sweetheart? You're not overthinkin' things again, are you?"

"There are just so many things we need to do before the wedding and not enough time to do all of them. Also, those men who have it in for Max Palmer might come looking for me since they can't find him."

Clay put his hands on my shoulders and made me face him.

"Forget about them. We've gone over all of this. They have no reason to think you're involved with your boss's underhanded practices. Besides, there's no way I'd let anybody hurt you."

I wanted to believe him. My vivid imagination might be working overtime because I actually did understand Max's plan. I didn't know the details, but I had a vague understanding of how it was probably supposed to work. I knew that people had gone to prison for engaging in Ponzi schemes. Even if Max were caught, these people might not recover their money.

"I'll try not to worry so much," I said. "Let's go get Grace."

We started into the cool woods, and Clay grabbed my hand. Just having my hand in his big protective one made me feel safe.

We climbed up the porch steps, and Clay knocked on the doorframe.

"In de kitchen," Mama Rae called.

The aroma of apples and cinnamon permeated the small cabin. It reminded me of all the times I came to my mentor's kitchen for a special treat as a child.

"Somethin' smells great," Clay said.

Grace stood beside Mama Rae with hands on her hips, looking like she owned the place. She had a dishtowel tied around her neck like an apron.

"We've got a tweat for you," she said. "You can sit at the table."

After we were seated, Mama Rae set a platter of fried apple pies in the center of the table. Then, she brought small plates and forks and instructed Grace to distribute napkins.

"These look wonderful," I said.

"We have to wait for Mama Wae to take the first bite," Grace said, remembering her mother's lesson for table manners.

Mama Rae patted Grace's shoulder.

"She a lot of help in de kitchen. Gonna be a real good cook," she said.

I tried to push all thoughts of Max Palmer and the men who were obviously pursuing him out of my mind on the way back to my villa. There were much better things to occupy my mind. The remainder of the week was going to be filled with preparations for our wedding and becoming a brand new family.

Clay volunteered to do our laundry and settle Grace for a nap while I made a quick trip to the Piggly Wiggly to pick up supplies for our dinner.

The parking lot was crowded, and the only place to park was all the way at the end of the lot close to the highway. I was familiar with the store by now, so it didn't take long to grab the items I needed and get in a checkout line. I was putting my purchases into the Jeep on the passenger side when a blue sedan pulled up beside me and stopped, making it impossible for me to go around to the driver's side. Before I could turn around, someone threw a hood over my head and hauled me into the sedan. I banged my head as I was pulled into the car. I felt my hands being tied together and tried to call for help as the car took off.

CHAPTER
Thirty-Four

I hadn't recognized the blue sedan. I'd barely had a glimpse of it, and I hadn't seen my captor because he had grabbed me from behind. This couldn't be happening. I was being kidnapped within a five-minute drive from my villa. I felt the car moving, but I couldn't hear any traffic. The radio was blasting country music with the volume turned up to the max. I was so disoriented that I didn't have a feel for how far we had traveled.

I fell over on my side and slid for what felt like several inches. My head bumped into something hard, maybe an armrest or a door handle. Pressure on my head persisted for a short time, and I reasoned that we were probably going around a traffic circle. I tried to maneuver myself into a sitting position, but I couldn't do it with my hands tied behind my back.

The car stopped for a few seconds, then slowly began moving. After several minutes, it stopped and the driver got out. He opened the back door and pulled me into a sitting position.

"Get out," he said. "Don't make a sound."

He must have been holding something over his mouth to disguise his voice, because I didn't recognize it. I was afraid I was about to be killed. Tears stung my eyes, and it was hard to breathe under the hood. My captor didn't wait for me to try getting out of the car. He reached in and grabbed my arm, pulling me out. Then, he started walking and dragging me along with him. It felt like we were stepping on sand and gravel. I kept stumbling, and he uttered several oaths. He was wearing a sickeningly sweet smelling aftershave lotion. It had to have been awfully strong for me to be able to smell it from under the hood.

I felt heat from the afternoon sun on my arms. My captor knocked on a door, and someone opened it. He pulled me inside. I had no idea where I was. Inside, it was fairly cool, but not air conditioned. He led me several feet and pushed me down onto a metal chair. The man and his partner walked away from me. I couldn't hear anything they were saying, only murmurs. I had been warned not to make a sound, but that seemed to be my only chance of survival.

I filled my lungs with air as best I could and screamed for all I was worth. It didn't take but a second to realize my mistake. Something smashed into the side of my head, knocking me out of the chair. I landed on a concrete floor with ringing in my ear and my head throbbing. It felt like all the skin on my right elbow had been scraped off when I hit the floor.

Minutes later, I was lifted back into the chair. Someone held my head still, and the hood was removed. I didn't have a chance to see my surroundings because a blindfold covered my eyes immediately. All I saw was a glimpse of a Hawaiian-print garment before the blindfold was in place. Following that was excruciating pain from someone pressing on my jawbones to force my mouth open to accommodate some sort of gag.

My head hurt, and I was afraid they might have burst my eardrum. My dress felt wet from my bleeding elbow. They certainly weren't going to take a chance of my escaping. One of them tied me into the chair with a heavy, rough-feeling rope. Then, they left the building. I heard car doors slam, and an engine roared to life.

I had no doubt that these people were going to kill me, but I didn't know why. I could only assume it had something to do with Max Palmer and the fact that I worked for him. I tried to make myself pay attention to every little thing if, by some miracle, I were to have a chance of escaping.

The blindfold was tied tight. It felt like giant thumbs were pressing on my eyeballs. I could barely see glimmers of light, but that was all. I could tell that I was close to water, because I could hear a fish jump every now and then. I could also hear water lapping against something—a building, or a maybe a boat. This wasn't the ocean. My nose and skin were very familiar with that salty air. This had to be a lagoon, or a creek.

It was mid-afternoon when I left the villa. I didn't know how long I had been gone, but I was certain that it was long enough that Clay would be concerned. He would be wondering what was taking me so long. He knew that I was only going to pick up a few things for our dinner. It shouldn't have even taken a half-hour.

The gag was cutting into the corners of my mouth, and I was thirsty. I tried to swallow, but it felt like I had a mouthful of cotton. There was no point in thinking about my discomfort. I had to do something to try to get away.

The rope was around my midriff and my arms, and my hands were secured behind my back. But my feet were free. My only hope was to scoot myself and the chair from this spot and hope for the best. If I went forward or backward, I might turn over, hit my head, and give myself a concussion. I didn't know which way to go, so I chose the path of least resistance. That meant walking my feet sideways to the right, hoping to bump into some means to escape.

I heard men's voices. They sounded like they were outside the building. Then, I heard a squeaking, or scraping noise, maybe a rusty hinge, and a door swung open. The men entered the building and continued their conversation. They weren't my kidnappers. I didn't recognize either of their voices, but they weren't attempting to disguise them.

"It's in good shape," one of them said.

"I'm gonna want to see it in daylight," said the other man.

Why were they ignoring the fact that a blindfolded and gagged woman was tied to a metal chair? Couldn't they see me?

I tried to call for help, but nothing emanated from my throat but a tiny muffled sound.

Then, the men were leaving the building, and I was alone again. I went back to my plan of escape and began inching myself and the cumbersome chair to the right in hopes of coming in contact with something—anything that might help free me.

I realized that my attempt had been futile when I was stopped short by a rough-hewn wall. I could feel a slight breeze coming through a wide space between two planks, making me think I was in a building like a barn or shed.

The men who had been here must have left the door open. If they had closed it, I would have heard the raspy sound it made when they entered the building. I could hear the murmur of their conversation as they came back within earshot.

Once inside the building, they began doing something that sounded like they were moving things around.

"Back it up about another couple of feet," one of them said.

A few seconds passed.

"That's good. I'll back my truck up to the door, and we can hook it up and pull it outside."

Whatever they were planning to pull outside must be what blocked their view of me. I had to get their attention; I rocked the chair back and forth, banging it into the wall.

"What was that?" one of them said.

"I didn't hear anything. Let's do this."

I heard the guy start his truck. He must have been just outside the building when he killed the engine. Then, there was some movement followed by a metallic sound. I tried to bang the chair

307

against the wall again, but it was no use. They didn't hear the dull noise it made.

As soon as the truck pulled away, the door screeched shut. I was alone again and had no idea where I was. It was hard to believe that anyone would consider me, a nobody, important enough to kidnap. That only happened to someone worth a lot of money. While it was true that Max Palmer no doubt had quite a bit of money, it should be clear that he wouldn't be willing to pay ransom money for my release. If he had cared a fig about my wellbeing, he wouldn't have hightailed it away from the island, leaving me to fend for myself.

I could hear the crunching of gravel again. It was only a couple of minutes before I knew who was opening the door to my prison. The one guy wearing the strong after-shave lotion was again disguising his voice, and the other one had yet to speak.

"Well ain't you the ambitious little thing," he said. "How'd you plan to get outta here?"

My mind had gone from planning a getaway to fear of being murdered as the door closed. I was at the mercy of my kidnappers. I began feeling dizzy, and I knew where this was going. A huge panic attack was beginning. It was hard to breathe, and I felt like I was about to pass out.

There was a loud knock on the door.

"Go see if that's our guy," said the talker.

The door opened; then closed.

"Sold it to the sucker."

I recognized his voice from a little while ago. He was the guy who seemed to be telling the other one how they were going to hook something up to his truck.

"Good for you. Now, go help him get it into the water. By the way, I know you're not real smart, but tell me you weren't stupid enough to bring him in here."

The guy didn't answer.

"Get outta my sight and keep your mouth shut. You didn't see nthin'. You got that?"

My heart was pounding, and even though the blindfold was pressing down on my eyes, I thought I saw colors dancing.

"Now, girlie, I'm gonna ask you a question. Then, I'm gonna take the gag outta your mouth so you can answer it."

I was dizzy, and my entire body hurt.

"Just so you understand, I know who you are, and I need to talk to your boss. I've got a feelin' you can tell me where to find him. My boss is gonna be awful disappointed if you don't come up with the right answer. Oh, and my boss ain't so nice when he's disappointed."

I heard the man speaking, but his words sounded garbled. I caught a few words followed by static. Then, I heard a few more words. The panic attack had seized my mind and body.

"All you have to do is just tell me where Max Palmer is. That's all. Static. Be a good girl and tell me. Static......back to your yellow Jeep right where you left it. I'm ..... remove the gag now. Don't do somethin' stupid like scream."

I felt the gag being loosened, but I couldn't feel my mouth or my cheeks. I didn't understand that. Nothing made sense at the moment. I sat slumped in the chair, saying nothing.

"Tell me where he is!"

I felt something cold against my neck, and then something like a sting. The man was yelling at me. I felt myself start to tremble. I tried to make my mind go blank for long enough to understand everything he was saying.

"Spit it out, or I'll cut your pretty throat," he said.

I couldn't speak. I tried to take a deep breath, and that caused me to begin hyperventilating.

"Hey, man, you've screwed up. She's gonna die on us before we find out where Palmer is."

I was so out of it that I didn't know who said those words. My lungs felt like they were about to explode, and the hyperventilating accelerated.

"Come on. We've got to get her into the car and take her to the hospital. We'll dump her at the emergency room door. Then, we get to start this little operation all over again, tough guy."

One of them was getting rid of the rope, and the other one was pulling me to a standing position. My knees buckled, and the trembling got worse. The guy who was holding me up began shaking me. I felt like a ragdoll, unable to speak or control anything that was happening to me. I was still hyperventilating.

"We've got to hurry up and get her into the car before she croaks. Come on. Help me pick her up. Don't look like she weighs much."

I didn't feel anything after that.

All I could see was a white ceiling. It had tiny little dots on it. I hurt all over, but I was so thrilled to be alive that the pain didn't matter. I said a silent prayer of thanks, then attempted moving different parts of my body. It really hurt when I opened my mouth more than a fraction.

I saw that my arm was bandaged, and an IV needle was taped into my wrist. I was in a hospital, but who had rescued me and brought me here? I might never know who had saved my life.

A middle-aged woman wearing a white coat with a stethoscope around her neck strode into the room.

"Well, you're awake," she said.

"You're a doctor," I said, feeling foolish for having made such an astute observation.

"I am, indeed. How are you feeling?"

"I think I'm pretty bunged up, but I'm happy to be alive."

"Do you feel up to answering a few questions? I'll fill out the form for you."

"Certainly, if I can."

The doctor took a clipboard from the foot of the bed, pulled a pen from her pocket, and smiled at me.

"Name, please."

"Clemmie."

"I need your full name."

For the life of me, I couldn't come up with my last name. Maybe I had suffered a concussion after all. Then, it came to me.

"Hubbard," I said, so happy to have recalled my last name.

"Do you live here on Hilton Head, Clemmie?"

"Yes, of course."

"Your address, please."

"I'm sorry. I can't remember my address. It's next to the last cottage on Folly Field."

Why was I feeling so addlepated?

"I'm feeling awfully confused," I said. "Could we finish this later?"

"Of course. One more question: can you tell me the name of your insurance company? You didn't have any identification with you when you were admitted.

"I'm sorry. Maybe I'll be better at answering your questions after I sleep for a while."

"That sounds like a good idea. I'll give you a little something to help you rest."

I thanked her and watched her leave the room. A few minutes later, a nurse came into the room. She undid the cap on the IV and inserted a hypodermic into it. Then, she emptied its contents into the IV and recapped it.

"Sweet dreams," she said, and left the room.

When I awoke, I was lethargic. I was so tired that I could hardly lift my hand. I looked around the room, taking in my surroundings. Then, I remembered; I was in a hospital. I was cold, and I had to go to the bathroom. Surely, there was a button for me to push for assistance. I couldn't go to the bathroom while I was hooked up to the IV. I couldn't find the button. Maybe I wasn't all the way awake.

"Help!"

I could see that the door was open. Why didn't someone come to help me?

"Help!"

An aide sauntered into the room.

"You need somethin'?"

"Yes, I need help getting to the bathroom."

She walked to the foot of my bed and looked at the chart. Then, she helped me out of bed. She held onto my arm with one hand and pulled the IV caddy with the other. She refused to close the bathroom door to give me a bit of privacy. Instead she stood in the doorway watching me relieve myself.

When she had me back in bed, she grabbed the chart and began asking me about any medications I was taking.

"I'm not taking any medications. I'm healthy," I told her.

"Well, you're just one lucky girl. You have insurance of some kind?"

Max Palmer had taken care of my insurance, but I didn't know the company name, and I hadn't received a copy of the policy.

"I don't know."

CHAPTER
Thirty-Five

I lay on my back watching the slow drip of the IV make its way down the clear plastic tube. The nurse had told me that I had been dehydrated, so I was getting a saline drip. The cocktail to help me sleep was wearing off, but my mind was still muddled.

Someone had kidnapped me thinking that I was in Max Palmer's inner circle. Pearl was no longer here to direct Max, and he had obviously fled the island in fear of the people he had swindled because he couldn't come up with a better plan. Pearl had been correct when she told me that Max couldn't think for himself; he needed someone to steer him toward viable solutions. She had wanted that person to be me, but I had never agreed to accept the position.

I became a little more alert as the minutes ticked by, but I was still confused as to who had arranged for my kidnapping. It had to have been arranged, because I didn't recognize any of the men's voices. Max Palmer's only victims that I knew were the three couples from the yacht and Ralph Wingate. If there had been others before

I came to work for him, I had no way of knowing who they were. It only made sense that there had been others since Pearl had run the business until her demise.

I tried to remember how I got to the hospital. Somebody had to have brought me, but who? And how did my savior rescue me? Nobody had known where I was, or even that I had been kidnapped. I had no idea how any of it had happened. I did know that I had barely escaped losing my life, and for that, I was truly grateful.

I pushed the call button for assistance, and a nurse came into the room.

"I need to make a phone call. You can put it on my bill. How do I get an outside line?"

"Dial nine."

"Thank you."

"Hello."

"Daniel, thank goodness you're home."

"Clemmie?"

"Yes. Daniel, I'm in the Hilton Head hospital, and I need your help."

"What's happened? Are you okay?"

"Yes. I'm okay, but can you come to the hospital right now? I'll explain everything when you get here."

"On my way."

I kept my eyes on the open door, waiting for Daniel to come into my room. Something kept me from feeling safe until I knew my best friend was here to protect me. What if those men showed up intending to do me harm, or maybe even spirit me out of the hospital with nobody's knowledge? I wanted to close my eyes, but I was afraid to. It had been about forty minutes since I had talked to Daniel. I could feel panic begin to build again, but just as I was about to push the call button, he came through the door wearing a worried expression. He hurried across the room and reached for my hand.

"What's going on, Clemmie? Why are you hooked up to an IV, and what happened to your arm?"

"You won't believe what happened. I was kidnapped this afternoon."

"What?"

"I had gone to the Piggly Wiggly to get supplies for dinner. When I was putting the groceries into my Jeep, someone grabbed me from behind, put a hood over my head, threw me into a car, and took off with me. I don't know where he took me."

"This sounds like a bad dream."

"He pulled me out of the car and dragged me through some sand and gravel. It must have been a parking lot. Then, he knocked on a door. Whoever opened the door didn't say anything."

"So he took you to some sort of building. Do you think it was here on the island?"

"I think so. We weren't in the car very long."

"Then, what happened?"

"They gagged me, blindfolded me, and tied me into a chair. My hands were tied behind my back. They left me there alone in the building for a while. I could hear water, but I could tell it wasn't close to the ocean."

"Did they hurt you? Is that what happened to your arm?"

"One of them hit me and hurt my head. It knocked me to the concrete floor. That's what happened to my arm. They tell me it isn't broken, and the doctor told me that I don't have a concussion. My mouth is sore from the gag; otherwise, I think I'm okay."

"You don't have any idea who did this?"

"I do, but I have no proof. Max Palmer has left Hilton Head on Pearl's yacht. The people who kidnapped me think I know his whereabouts, but I don't. They threatened to kill me if I didn't tell them; one of them even held a knife to my throat and left a little cut."

"You poor baby. No wonder you're afraid. Have you called Clay?"

"No. I know he must be beside himself. He might be furious with me for calling you instead of him, but…."

I looked past Daniel to see Clay coming through the door. He practically ran across the room and didn't bother to acknowledge Daniel.

"Clemmie, I've been out of my mind wonderin' what happened to you. Are you hurt bad?"

"No. I'm just scruffed up and upset. How did you find me?"

"After a couple of hours I started to get worried. I kept thinkin' you might come home and tell me you'd had a flat tire or somethin'. After a while, I couldn't stand it any longer, so I called a cab to take Grace and me to Mama Rae's. I couldn't leave Grace alone, and I couldn't take her on the bike."

"That's why I called Daniel instead of calling you," I said, wondering if I were telling him the truth.

It seemed that Daniel and I had depended on one another for most of our lives, and Clay didn't appear the least bit upset at hearing my explanation.

"Mama Rae didn't seem surprised to see us," he said. "She took Grace's hand to lead her into the house. Then, she looked at me and said, 'Try the hospital.' That old woman's scary sometimes."

Daniel and I exchanged looks, then nodded our agreement.

"The Piggly Wiggly was on my way to the hospital," Clay continued, "so I stopped there first. I could see your Jeep from the highway. I rode into the parkin' lot to check it out. A sack of groceries had turned over and spilled across the passenger seat. That was when I was pretty sure somethin' bad had happened to you. I'm thinkin' this has somethin' to do with that no-account Palmer."

I looked up at the saline bag; it was empty.

"Please spring me from this place. The doctor said I could leave as soon as I was hydrated and someone was here to take me home."

"I'll go check you out and take care of the damage," Clay said. "Daniel, would you drive Clemmie home? I'm on my bike."

"You bet."

Daniel and I had just climbed the porch steps when Clay pulled into the space next to Daniel's car. I started to reach for my key and realized I didn't have my purse. My billfold was in it. I could be a victim of identity theft.

"We have to go to the Piggly Wiggly to see if anyone turned in my purse," I said.

"Okay," Clay said. "We can stop by there on our way to the police station. Clemmie, I know you're tired and frustrated, but we have to report this to the police."

"Oh, Clay, don't you understand that we can't do that? They'll think I'm somehow involved in Max's business, and I can't let that happen. A police investigation can drag on forever. I can't be tied to Max Palmer until this all comes to a head. I don't have any information to give the police, but I can't prove it. So far, nobody knows anything about what happened today except you, Daniel, and me."

"Maybe she's right, Clay," Daniel said. "It could blow over in a few days since the bad guys' attempt to get info failed."

Clay sighed. "Okay, I'm willin' to mull it over for a little while. You two sure do know how to gang up on a guy. Let's go to the store and find out if they have your purse."

I knew getting my purse back was a long shot, but it was worth a try. We went straight to the manager's office, and it was then that I decided miracles do happen. A young woman had seen my purse lying on the ground beside my Jeep. She took it into the store and gave it to the manager. He told us that he figured the owner would hurry back to the store as soon as she realized it was missing. He hadn't looked inside it to check for identification. I opened the purse and looked inside. Nothing was missing.

Daniel stayed with me while Clay went to pick up Grace. I went to sleep on the couch, and Daniel called his wife, then went out to the deck to watch the golfers on the eighteenth hole.

Daniel was spending as much time as he could in Savannah with Catherine and Suzanne. His boss had been understanding about the young man's family situation and was putting Daniel in charge of most of the jobs in the Savannah area. Because of that, Daniel was showing up on Hilton Head fairly often. It was fortunate that he had been so close to the island today.

Clay had stopped to pick up pizza on the way home from Mama Rae's. He, Daniel, and I sat around the dinner table after Grace was tucked into bed, trying to decide what our next move should be. I knew we were all thinking the same thing: someone would be watching me, waiting to grab me to get information about Max Palmer.

"I think we need to leave the island for a while," Clay said. "It seems like those goons have the scent of blood. They're not gonna have a chance to get close to you as long as yours truly has a breath left in him."

"We're supposed to get married in three days," I reminded him.

"I know, honey, but in my heart we're already married. We can wait a little longer for a piece of paper. For that matter, we can go to a Justice of the Peace in Savannah or Atlanta."

"There's an empty apartment for rent in our building in Savannah," Daniel said. "Catherine would love it if you were in the same building."

I felt emotional, and tears squeezed from my eyes. It embarrassed me to behave this way. I was closer to these two men than anyone else in the world. Each of them loved me in his own way. I should be grateful to have them want to protect me in this dangerous situation.

"I won't feel like I'm married unless we have the ceremony in a church. We already made plans with the minister."

"I'm sure he'll understand when we give him a reasonable explanation."

"Clay, we can't tell the police, the minister, or anybody else. Nobody knows about the kidnapping but the three of us. The hospital staff doesn't know what happened to me. I told them that I couldn't remember anything."

"How about I call the minister and tell him we need to postpone the wedding? I'll tell him we'll get back in touch with him when we're ready."

"That'll be fine. I know you want to do whatever it takes to keep us safe. I've been acting like a spoiled child, and I apologize. It's just that this is a big step we're about to take. Marriage is sacred to me. I hope you can understand how I feel."

"I do, babe. Got to admit I was just thinkin' about gettin' off the island as fast as we could. Daniel, can you recommend a decent hotel in Savannah?"

"Sure, but I'll bet you can rent that apartment I mentioned. The landlord's been known to rent by the week."

"Could you call and find out if we can do that?" Clay said.

"On it," Daniel said, and headed to the foyer to make the call.

He was smiling when he returned.

"You're all set. I called Catherine, and she took care of the deposit. I told her I'd spend the night here on the island and drive back to Savannah in the morning. Okay if I crash in your spare room?"

"Of course," I said.

Clay was the first one up the next morning. The aromas of coffee and bacon mingled and found their way upstairs. I jumped out of bed and threw on shorts and a tee shirt and was on my way downstairs when I saw Daniel dragging himself through the living room. His clothes were a rumpled mess.

"It looks like someone slept in his clothes," I said.

He ignored me and headed straight for the coffee pot, nodded at Clay, and helped himself to a cup.

"I have plenty of room in my car for whatever you guys want to take to Savannah," he said. "There's not much room in the Jeep."

"That's a good idea," I said. "We'll need to take a few toys for Grace. We can't expect her to sit quietly while we hide out in an apartment."

"Hey, Daniel, how would you like to take Grace to tell Mama Rae and Lord goodbye while Clemmie and I go over our check list?"

"That's a great idea," Daniel said. "Don't you think so, Grace?"

Grace nodded enthusiastically. "I wuv Mama Wae and Word. I'll hug 'em."

Daniel and Grace went to the woods to visit with Mama Rae to reassure her that I was all right and fill her in on what had happened. He told her that we were going to be in Savannah for several days and that we would get in touch with her as soon as we returned to the island

We spread heavy-duty trash bags on the foyer floor and parked Clay's bike there. Then, with both vehicles packed, we took off for Savannah. Clay drove my Jeep, and Grace and I rode with Daniel. Clay was afraid that if the people who kidnapped me were still on Hilton Head, they might spot the Jeep and try to ambush it. He was confident that he would be able to handle any situation which might arise. He was a big guy, and a tire iron lay on the seat close to his right hand.

With Daniel in the lead, we caravanned to the city, careful to drive within the speed limit. We got to the Grovers' apartment building just before noon. I took Grace to the small playground beside the complex while Daniel and Clay went to the manager's office to get keys. Then, we unloaded our things in the small two bedroom apartment that would be our home for at least a week.

"Our apartment's just down the hall," Daniel said. "Catherine and Suzanne won't be home for a while. Come join me at our place for lunch."

"You sure are takin' good care of us, my man," Clay said.

"Hey, that's what friends are for," Daniel said. "Somebody grab paper plates out of that cupboard. Soft drinks are in the fridge. I'll make some sandwiches."

We passed a little time sitting around the kitchen table when Grace began rubbing her eyes.

"Grace needs a nap, and we need to unpack and put things away," I said. "Thanks for everything, Daniel. If Catherine and Suzanne aren't too tired to go out, we'd like to take you all to dinner. I'm sure you know lots of good kid-friendly restaurants."

"Sounds great. Come to our place for drinks at around six o'clock."

It didn't take Clay and me long to get things squared away, and Grace fell asleep as fast as if she had been in her own bed.

"I know you're worried and still scared, Clemmie, but I swear I'll keep you safe. I let you down by allowin' you to venture out alone yesterday, but I've learned my lesson. We'll stay here until we know those goons are long gone."

We were on the sofa and Clay had his arm around me. He always made me feel so safe. My head rested against his chest, and I felt tension leaving my body. Then, I slept.

It was after five o'clock when I awoke. I was stretched out on the sofa with my head on a cushion and a lightweight blanket covering me. Grace was lightly smoothing my hair away from my face. I looked up into her pretty little face and smiled.

"It's time to get weady for the party, Cwemmie."

"So it is. I guess I'd better hurry," I said, remembering another thing on our *to do* list: speech therapy for Grace.

Clay came into the living room dressed in Dockers and a golf shirt.

"We must be going to a pretty casual restaurant," I said.

"Yeah. Daniel came by a few minutes ago and said not to get too dressed up. We're goin' to a place with an indoor playground for the girls."

We walked down the hall to the Grovers' apartment. Catherine met us at the door. Suzanne sat in the middle of the floor playing with a fuzzy elephant. We had barely gotten inside and exchanged greetings.

"Daniel, turn off the TV," Catherine said, embracing Clemmie.

The local news was on, and when Clay reached to shake Daniel's hand before he picked up the remote, he turned to look at the TV screen.

"Wait, Daniel," he said. "Don't turn it off. Clemmie, look!"

CHAPTER
Thirty-Six

"*Turn* it up," Clay said.

The Grovers, Clay, and I stood in the middle of the room with our eyes glued to the TV.

"That's the *Pearl!*" I said.

".... thought it strange that the yacht floated sideways, blocking other crafts from coming in to dock at the Charleston Harbor Resort," said the reporter. "Authorities later discovered that the yacht had no captain or crew. The body of Maxwell Palmer, a well-known Hilton Head Island businessman was found dead on the floor of the wheelhouse. A nine millimeter handgun lay by his right hand. There has been no mention of foul play. An investigation is ongoing."

Another news item followed immediately, and Daniel killed the remote.

"Looks like there's no need to wonder about Mister Palmer's whereabouts anymore," Clay said.

"Let's let this information sink in and have that drink I promised," Daniel said, going to a small bar in the corner of the room. "Anyone have an objection to something stronger than wine?"

322

Nobody did since we would be going to a child-friendly restaurant within walking distance of the apartment building, so my best friend made a couple of shakers of martinis for the adults while the little girls worked on becoming friends. Grace, the elder, took it upon herself to instruct Suzanne in the art of burping a baby doll.

We walked down the street to the restaurant and were back at our apartments before dark. Since the children were tired, we decided to call it an early night. Grace went to sleep as soon as she got into her pajamas, but I knew that Clay and I would stay awake trying to decide what to do next.

"If any of the people Palmer swindled watched the news tonight, they know he's dead," Clay said. "If they were comin' to the island to shake him down, they're just out of luck."

"But if they think I'm connected to his business, they might assume I have access to the money and come after me again."

"What about the old guy who was parked in front of the office in the Cadillac? Is he connected to the couples who were on the yacht?"

"I don't know. I don't think so, but I guess he could be. Max Palmer introduced me to him before I met the others. I got the impression that he was a pretty powerful man. Max had to work really hard to suck him into that Florida real estate deal. I'm not sure, but I think he was the only person who financed that project. He's probably the one who lost the most money. Regardless, I feel sure they all lost their money, and they want to get it back."

"Well, try not to worry about what might happen. We're not goin' back to the island 'til we know the coast is clear. If any of those guys stick around for a couple of days tryin' to find you and can't, they'll think they've scared you off. There's no way they can find out where you are."

"Clay, I knew exactly where I wanted to spend the rest of my life as soon as I was released from that mental hospital in Kentucky. I can't tell you how much I was looking forward to coming back to Hilton Head. The island felt like home the minute I crossed the bridge. I had the feeling that everything was going to be just what the doctor ordered, even with the mysterious job offer I was about to accept."

"I'm sure you were lookin' for a sense of belongin'. You prob'ly felt like you could kinda step back in time and see the island like it was before you lost Roy and your world fell apart."

"That's true, but things felt off-kilter the first day I walked into Max Palmer's office. I knew something wasn't right. No legitimate company would pay an employee for doing nothing. All I did was dine in fine restaurants, smile at a cocktail party, and pick up Max's dry cleaning."

"I gotta admit that was strange. On the other hand, it would be pretty hard to turn down a sweet paycheck for doin' practically nothin'."

"Max gave me that huge pay hike right after he sucked old Mister Wingate into his web. I wanted it, but I knew I shouldn't accept it. I even took that big check to show Mama Rae. Her advice was to put it into the bank, which I did."

"You told me she denied knowin' Palmer, but she encouraged you to take the job."

"That's right. If she had told me to turn down his offer, I would have. I've always trusted her, and she had never steered me wrong. She denied being acquainted with him every time I asked her, and it made her angry that I questioned her about it. She admitted knowing Pearl and that she tried to help her by furnishing her with special herbs for her medical problems. I also know she attended Pearl's funeral. I saw her there."

I couldn't bring myself to tell Clay that Mama Rae had all but admitted assisting Pearl in committing suicide.

"That old girl sure knows a lot about the island. I'll give her that."

"I've known her since I was ten, and I can tell you that she knows a lot period. Mama Rae appears to be able to read people's minds, and she seems to be able to make things happen. I know that sounds crazy, but I honestly believe she has some sort of edge on the rest of us human beings."

"Back to our next move," Clay said, "Daniel told me that he'll be here for a couple of more days before he has to be back in Atlanta. I think I'll ask him to swap vehicles with us tomorrow. I'll drive his car back to Hilton Head and look around. If any of those guys are still there, they would recognize your Jeep. I don't know what the other guys look like, but I saw your old man Wingate. I know what his car looks like, but he doesn't know me. I'll drive by the office and by your villa; just look around. Since you believe our old friend who lives in the woods is somethin' of a seer, or maybe practices voodoo, I'll pay her a visit. Maybe she's privy to somethin' we're not. If that's true, she might be able to point us in the right direction to get past all of this craziness."

"It all seems surreal; it's like a bad dream, and I never imagined that I could be caught in the middle of something so bizarre. I'm a nobody. It's unbelievable that anyone would want to kidnap me and threaten my life."

"This nightmare's gonna be over before you know it; promise," Clay said, taking my hand and pulling me up from the couch.

This man had a way of making me feel safe just by the touch of his hand.

"Come with me, my little flower," he said. "I will take you to pleasurable heights you never thought possible."

I loved it when he lapsed into one of his silly fake accents to make me laugh.

"Your little flower will be more than happy to accompany you," I said, as he backed me into our temporary bedroom and kicked the door closed.

Making love with Clay Singleton never failed to make everything right with the world, and this was to be no exception. I let myself get lost in the passion of our lovemaking and blocked out all thoughts of what tomorrow might bring. I wanted to be in my happy place, safe in Clay's arms, and sleep like a baby.

The magic had worked again, because Clay had to wake me the next morning. He had already showered and dressed before he called me to breakfast. He met me with a kiss and a cup of coffee.

"Let's let Grace sleep until she wakes up on her own," he said. "She acts all happy-go-lucky, but she's just a little kid, and we've been haulin' her around like she was a sack of potatoes. She prob'ly needs some extra rest."

"I agree, and since you're going to trade cars with Daniel, Grace and I will have to entertain one another all day. Catherine and Daniel will be at work, so I thought I might volunteer to take care of Suzanne. She and Grace seemed to get along real well."

"Good idea. I'll go down the hall and see if our plans work for them."

Clay was back in minutes, dangling Daniel's keys on a key ring.

"Daniel and I made our switch, and Catherine'll drop Suzanne off here on her way to work. She'll come back to take you and the girls to lunch around the corner at noon."

It seemed that my day was easily planned, but I was anxious to hear what Clay found out when he came back from the island.

Catherine brought Suzanne to my apartment in her pajamas and handed me her playclothes. I gave the little girls their breakfast, then dressed them to go to the playground beside the apartment building. Grace, the adventurer, tried everything in sight. The slide was her favorite. Suzanne was happy to just play in the sandbox. As they played, I sat on a wooden bench under a live oak tree, keeping an eye on them while wondering how Clay was faring on the island.

We walked to the diner style restaurant for lunch. Both little girls were busy with their chicken nuggets, and Catherine smiled at me across the table.

"I have a secret to tell you," she said.

I raised my brow waiting to hear it.

"I'm going to law school part time. My boss strongly encouraged me to apply, and I was accepted. She took me to a very upscale restaurant one night to expound on the virtues of becoming an attorney instead of spending time working for one. She told me that she was impressed with me and was confident that I would make a good lawyer."

"Wow! I'm impressed, too. I didn't know Savannah had a law school."

"I didn't either until my boss handed me the brochure from John Marshall Law School. It's on Hodgson Memorial Drive; not far from my office. I've been going to classes three nights each week. I know getting a JD will take a long time, but I hope to be able to attend classes full time at some point."

"That's wonderful, Catherine."

"I'm my great aunt's only heir. She's in her late nineties and quite well off. She's in an assisted living facility, and hasn't been well for some time. I love her dearly, but I know she isn't long for this world. The last time I visited her, she told me that she was tired of just taking up space. Her words. She wants to go to sleep and not wake up."

"I can understand that thinking. I can't imagine that anyone would want to simply exist."

Catherine nodded in agreement as a tear slid down her cheek.

"The inheritance will enable me to go to school full time, and that will hopefully make her proud of me one day."

Catherine's secret had just set me straight about her night out in the fancy restaurant. She had been perfectly innocent of infidelity. I felt ashamed that I had thought otherwise.

"Is Daniel excited that you're taking the classes?"

Catherine laughed. "He is now that he knows all about it. I wanted it to be a surprise. Now I know that was silly. Daniel would come home unexpectedly or call the apartment from Atlanta, and I wouldn't be home. I'm sure he thought I was having an affair, but he never accused me of it."

I wanted us to become close friends, but I wouldn't burden Catherine with the fact that Daniel had come to me thinking there was a possibility that his wife was being unfaithful. And I wouldn't tell her that I had seen her in the restaurant and thought the same thing.

After lunch, the girls and I went to the playground for a few minutes. Then, we went to my apartment for a nap. I closed my eyes but couldn't fall asleep for thinking about what Clay might be doing and why he hadn't returned to Savannah. Clay could take care of himself, but I couldn't help feeling apprehensive. He wasn't the kind of man to back away from a confrontation. I hoped he hadn't seen or heard anything about any of the men I feared.

After the girls' naps, I gave them snacks. Then, they played with Grace's toys we had brought from the villa. They played happily while I fumed so much that I thought I felt my blood pressure spike.

Relief washed over me when Clay walked through the door. He had an Island Packet under his arm, and without saying a word, he tossed it on the coffee table. Then, he turned on that special smile.

I snatched the newspaper off the table and fastened my eyes on the front page story. The story of Max Palmer's suicide was tastefully reported, failing to label it as such, but stating that there had been no foul play. It was succinct—bare bones with very little detail about the man or his demise.

I turned to the obituary page and found even less information: Maxwell Palmer, 58, passed away on his yacht October 22. He was a successful businessman in the Hilton Head area. There were no survivors.

"Oh, Clay, do you think this nightmare is over? Do you think it's safe to go back to the island?"

"Sweetheart, I searched that island with a fine tooth comb, and I didn't see hide nor hair of old Mister Wingate. I went to see Mama Rae in hopes that she might know somethin' about the others, but she claimed she didn't have any knowledge of any of 'em. I think they've all given up on gettin' their money back. The man's dead, and you've disappeared. Those guys are long gone."

"What if they're not?"

"I'm virtually sure they are, but we'll stay here for a few more days if it'll make you feel better. We can tour Savannah. It's a great little city."

"That would definitely make me feel better."

"Daniel's gonna have to go back to Atlanta in a day or two, but we can spend some time with Catherine and Suzanne. We'll do a little baby sittin' for Catherine; take the kids to do some fun things together. It'll be real good socialization for Gracie to get her used to bein' with somebody other than adults before we put her into preschool."

Just minutes earlier, one could have bounced quarters off my shoulders, but I could literally feel the tension seeping from them.

Clay opened his arms. The laugh lines around his eyes crinkled, and his easy smile lit up his entire face.

"Come here, you. I want to feel your heartbeat. You've been wound tighter than the old Big Ben clock I had in college."

CHAPTER
Thirty-Seven

The next few days we spent in Savannah had an air of normalcy. We went about the business of immersing ourselves in the city's southern charm and hospitality. Tours of the city with its historic mansions and glittering leaves of old live oaks were glamorous. The restaurants' cuisine boasted outrageously delicious fare. But the thing I held most dear was the feeling of being free from danger. It made my spirits soar.

Clay made two more trips to Hilton Head: one, to once again case the island for any sign of predators. The second trip was to transport most of the toys and clothes we had brought to Savannah since there wasn't enough room in the Jeep for the three of us and our belongings.

Grace cried as she hugged Suzanne goodbye. Then, we climbed into my little yellow Jeep and headed for home. I drove, and Clay buckled Grace and himself into the back, packing the front seat with our belongings. The wind whipped our hair this way and that, making it tickle our faces as we cruised across the bridge to the island. The tide was out, and the Spartina grass danced in the breeze, urging the pungent odor of pluff mud up above its decaying inhabitants and into our nostrils.

It seemed like an eternity since I had felt so light hearted. I was with the people I loved, and we were on our way to the place I wanted to spend the rest of my life. I hadn't realized just how much Pearl and Max Palmer had been weighing me down, making me feel trapped and afraid to break off my relationship with them and their company.

The first thing we did after unloading the Jeep was accept the preacher's invitation to drop in for a visit to his office unannounced.

"Well," said the smiling padre, "does this mean you're ready to make it legal, as they say?"

"We most certainly are," Clay said.

The minister addressed Grace. "Am I to assume that you approve of this union, Miss Grace?"

"What's a union?"

"Remember when I asked you if you would like for Clemmie and me to get married?" Clay asked his niece.

Grace nodded. "And we'll all be a fambily." She grinned.

"Do you have a date in mind?" asked the preacher.

"We do," I said. "Can you fit us into your schedule this coming Saturday?"

The young man walked behind his battered desk to check his calendar. Then, he looked up and smiled again, showing a crooked tooth.

"Saturday is wide open," he said. "Pick a time."

We decided on 5:00 p.m. Mama Rae and Daniel's family could accompany us to an early dinner following the ceremony. I could hardly wait to become Clay's wife.

The next couple of days were a blur. We went back to Savannah to shop for our wedding attire. Clay chose a cream-colored summer suit, and I found an off-the-rack wedding dress that I thought was perfect for our tiny ceremony. Grace was not to be left out. She picked a gauzy pink affair that made her look like a little princess. She was so excited about the wedding that she had trouble sleeping.

I was in a state of euphoria, and I found nature's beauty all around me to be nothing less than magical. I looked out at the emerald carpet of the golf course which would remain vivid until fall; it put me in awe of the Creator's magnificent paintbrush. And when the three of us went for a walk on the wide beach, I once again felt humbled by the expanse of that big body of water.

Clay and I flanked Grace. We swung her into the air, then dipped her toes into the surf on her descent. She shrieked and giggled all the way down the beach, and I was reminded of my first encounter with Clay and Sarah delivering that identical happiness to the little girl. Only now Sarah was absent, and I was in the picture instead of watching the scene.

The hours and minutes seemed to tick by ever so slowly, and I thought I could almost hear each one until my wedding day finally arrived. The villa was a melange of hustle and bustle all morning, and I had a hard time concentrating on the small tasks which needed handling before we headed to the church. When I was virtually certain that my checklist was complete, I took time for a short walk on the beach all alone. I wanted to clear my head of any trace of unhappiness or confusion to make room for my brand new life.

As I splashed through the surf, stopping occasionally to dig my toes into the soft sand, my eyes were drawn to the shore and rested on a small stretch of undeveloped beachfront thick with tall pines.

My mind traveled back to my childhood days when I first came upon an old woman gleaning herbs in the woods. She was dressed in a long skirt and a man's shirt, and an old slouch hat shaded her wrinkled face. I learned right away that she was by no means shy, but that she was a woman of few words. I perceived her as being quite rude because of her abrupt departure after educating me about a berry I was about to pick. That encounter lingered in my ten-year-old mind constantly, and I knew that I wanted to know more about the old woman who lived in the woods.

Mama Rae was a walking encyclopedia concerning the island.

She taught me volumes about the flora and fauna of the woods, and she was well acquainted with the beach inhabitants and marine life. She was also a pharmacist of sorts, having the ability to mix herbs and potions not only for medicinal purposes, but also to somehow affect the mind. It would be impossible to prove that she possessed special powers that other human beings lacked, but I knew beyond a shadow of doubt that she did. I had witnessed her magic.

My wedding day was a far cry from my perception of most others. I didn't have appointments to get a manicure and pedicure, and I didn't go to a beauty salon to have my hair braided into a glamorous up-do. I showered and dressed in my inexpensive wedding dress. Then, I made sure Grace was put together for the occasion.

My groom was waiting for me at the foot of the stairs in his new suit, looking, for all the world, like a movie star. I could see the love in his eyes as I descended the stairs.

"You take my breath away," he said, pulling me into his arms.

The romantic moment was cut short when Grace appeared on the landing. She was so excited that she couldn't seem to contain herself.

"I'm weady! Wets go get mawied now!"

She flew down the stairs and leaped into her uncle's arms.

Daniel had volunteered to pick up Mama Rae and drive her to the church. We all met in the vestibule. Mama Rae was clad in the only dress-up apparel I had ever seen her wear. It consisted of a navy crepe dress with a matching straw hat. She wore it whenever she wanted to impress an authority figure. Roy would have dubbed it her Sunday-go-to-meetin' outfit.

The minister came to greet us. Then, after seating Mama Rae, he and Clay made their way to the altar. Catherine handed each of the little flower girls a small basket of rose petals to scatter down the aisle. Then, she and the children took their seats on the front pew while Clay helped Mama Rae to the respected place of maid-of-honor. The preacher nodded to his wife who sat in the choir loft with a boom box. She pushed a button, and suddenly the small church was filled with the familiar strains of *The Wedding March*.

Daniel placed a chaste kiss on my forehead. Then he escorted me down the aisle to become Clay's bride. Both little girls wiggled like puppies as Clay and I said our vows. Catherine wore a delighted smile, Daniel grinned like a hyena, and a tear slid down Mama Rae's beautiful, wrinkled face. My old mentor looked up into my eyes, and Mama's diamond studs flashed their brilliant colors proudly from under a blue straw hat. I had never been happier.

We were all in high spirits by the time we arrived at Charlie's L'Etoile Verte. We emptied a bottle of champagne during toasts and well wishes. Dinner at Charlie's was never a disappointment, and this was no exception. But both little girls began rubbing their sleepy eyes, and Mama Rae slumped a little lower in her chair by the end of the meal.

Daniel and Catherine drove Mama Rae home and Daniel made sure she was safely inside her house before leaving to drive back to Savannah.

Grace was asleep before I got her out of her dress-up clothes and into her pajamas. I left her door open a crack the way I always did in case she had a nightmare. Clay met me on the upstairs landing and led me into our bedroom. He took my face in his big hands and kissed me tenderly.

We took our time undressing one another. Then, instead of tossing our clothes on the floor like rags, we hung them on hangers. After all, they were our wedding attire.

For some reason I expected our lovemaking to be different this special night, and it was. We weren't in a rush, afraid that our passion might fade, afraid that something could suddenly happen to derail the closeness two strangers had stumbled upon on a small island. Now, we were one.

When I awoke, the clock registered 9:00 a.m. The aroma of coffee wafted up the stairs to greet me, and I knew that my new husband was cooking breakfast. As I walked into the living room I heard him whistling. He dropped what he was doing to pull me into a bear-hug and deliver a sloppy kiss.

I laughed. "You're acting like a caveman."

"I feel like a caveman. Watch your step, or I'll throw you over my shoulder and take you to my cave to have my way with you."

"You already did that, and Grace will be up any minute. What's for breakfast?"

"Pancakes and crispy bacon."

Grace was singing to herself as she trotted into the dining area.

"We have to go see Mama Wae today," she said. "I want to give her and Word a hug."

"We sure can do that, short stuff," Clay said. "Our Mama Rae looked a little tired last night. We need to make sure we didn't wear her out. She's helpin' me with my novel."

Clay and I certainly weren't engaged in what one thinks of as a honeymoon. We were going about our business just as we had been before we became man and wife with the exception of danger at every turn.

After breakfast we drove the Jeep to the edge of the woods and tramped down the path to Mama Rae's cabin. I tapped on the door. No sound emanated from inside.

"Maybe her hearin's not as good as it used to be," Clay said, giving the wood a firm rap.

"Mama Rae, may we come in?" I called.

"In de bedroom."

The door wasn't hooked, so we went into the dark cabin and down a short hallway to the bedroom. My old friend was lying supine on her bed. She was dressed in white from head to toe. Lord was curled into a ball beside her. He was purring and kneading her shoulder. Her turban headdress was secured in the front with the peacock gemstone brooch Pearl had given her, and her diamond studs peeked from just under the headdress.

"Mama Rae, are you feeling all right?" I asked.

The old woman issued a slight nod. Then, she motioned for

me to help Grace up on the bed to snuggle beside her. She patted Grace's chubby knee, and Grace put her cheek next to Mama Rae's.

"I was happy to see Daniel and his little family," Mama Rae said. It was hardly more than a whisper. "Both of Mama Rae's chilren be all right now—two sweet little families."

She took my hand and gave it a little squeeze. "You home now, my precious. I knew you'd come back to de islan'."

I felt my old friend's forehead. It was clammy, but there was a peaceful light in her rheumy eyes. Clay moved to the other side of her bed and took her other hand. He lifted it to his lips and kissed it. Mama Rae smiled, showing her toothless gums, and I thought my heart would break. I knew she was telling us goodbye, and I would have given anything if we hadn't had Grace with us.

"Clay, you know dat paper you made fer me?"

He nodded.

"It in dat top drawer," she said, nodding at a chest. "You take it; do Mama Rae proud."

She pulled her hand out of Clay's and stroked Lord.

"Grace, you always wantin' to take Lord home with you. Do you still love dis cat?"

"Yes, I wuv Word a bunch."

"You take him today. Make sure you spoil him."

"Thank you, Mama Wae. I wuv you so much."

Grace was so excited and happy that she missed the deep sigh breathed by her old friend. She gathered the cat in her arms and scooted to the side of the bed. She didn't see the looks that passed between Clay and me. I helped her down, and she allowed me to carry Lord as we turned to leave.

Clay closed our good friend's eyes, then slipped a hand into the top drawer of the chest and retrieved Mama Rae's last will and testament which he had drafted for the old woman who lived in the woods.

Grace was practically dancing with happiness.

"Bye-bye, Mama Wae."

I had a terrible time keeping my tears at bay on the way home. I had to drive because I wasn't strong enough to hold a scared cat. I had brought him to the woods in a carrier. Clay put Lord in the villa with Grace and me while he went to the hospital. He went with the EMTs and led them into the woods to Mama Rae's cabin to transport her to the hospital. The hospital staff made arrangements with the mortician to follow through with our old friend's wishes for cremation.

Clay told me how hard it was for him to switch roles so he could come home with a smile on his face. He drove to a pet store and bought supplies and a harness for the cat. When he came home, he brought his purchases inside, including a big fuzzy-covered box with a round hole in the front and a bed for a floor. The cat had done nothing but pace and meow, but when Clay set the box in a corner of the living room, Lord went to it, sniffed, and climbed into the hole.

I supervised Grace as she gave Lord his supper. Then, Clay introduced him to a litter box. He seemed to adapt quickly to his new surroundings, and I hoped that being a pet owner would help little Grace over yet another rough spot in her short bumpy road. She had been through an awful lot for one so young.

"I want to sing Word to sweep."

"All right. Then, we need to have a family meetin'," Clay said.

Grace sat down beside the big box and began to sing.

"*Cwose your sweepy eyes, my widdle buckawoo, while the stars in western skies are shinin' down on you. Cwose your sweepy eyes, another day is thwoo, so go to sweep, my widdle* buckawoo.*"

Grace had to be the smartest child I had ever encountered. Her mother had sung that song to her and she had memorized it. She had a memory like an elephant.

"He's gone night-night now. Don't make noise, okay?" she said.

I nodded.

"Mama Wae knew I wanted Word to spend the night," Grace said.

Clay pulled his niece up onto his lap.

"Mama Rae likes you so much that she gave Lord to you. You get to take care of him and play with him every day."

"We can take him to bisit her."

Then, once again, I witnessed my husband's wonderful way with children. He always managed to tell the truth, even when it hurt, but he softened the blow by the way he told it.

"No. We won't be able to do that, short stuff. You see, Mama Rae was real tired. She went to sleep today, and she just wants to rest. She doesn't want to wake up. She wanted to go to sleep and wake up in heaven with your mommy."

"Oh, okay. But we'll miss her, won't we?"

"We sure will."

I stood just inside the sliding glass doors and looked up into the branches of the ancient hickory trees canopying the back deck. How many times had I looked into that dense foliage wondering what my life would be like? Years had passed, and so many things had happened. My thoughts meandered back to the year 1966 when I was first introduced to this verdant paradise. My life had been filled with tragedies, but there were a few triumphs along the way. It seemed to have been in a constant state of flux. The entire time, I had been racing with the tide to get back to the place where I belong.

Epilogue

Clay followed Mama Rae's instructions to the letter. Although she considered her relationship with the woods her religion and the place that gave her wisdom and strength, she had asked Clay to make arrangements with our young minister to preach her funeral. She knew nearly every person on Hilton Head, and she felt she owed them a farewell of sorts.

The church secretary had graciously agreed to stay at our villa with Grace and Suzanne while we adults went to say our last goodbyes to Mama Rae. The children played with dolls and the cat while Daniel and Catherine joined us at the church.

A rough-hewn box containing my old mentor's ashes sat on a table at the altar. It was flanked by candles on either side. There was no other adornment.

The crowd overflowed from the church and out into the gravel parking lot. The minister rattled off a long list of good deeds Mama Rae had seen fit to bestow on residents of the island. Such a large number of folks wanted to add to the list, the preacher found it necessary to cut them off.

As soon as the church emptied, Daniel and Catherine went to the woods with Clay and me. Clay carried our old friend's ashes.

Each of us scooped handfuls of ashes from the wooden container until it was empty, and scattered them along the path we had often trod on our way to the cabin in the woods.

The moon bathed our bedroom in its soft light. We liked to leave the glass doors open so we could hear sketches of the ocean waves as they lapped the sand and leaked into the sea oats.

"Clay, do you think you'll be able to finish your novel?"

My husband propped his head up on an elbow.

"Sure I will. You wouldn't believe the amount of information Mama Rae gave me. All I have to do is put it all together in a way I think she would approve."

"Have you actually written part of it?"

"Yep. The prologue goes like this: *Once on a very small island there was a wise and knowledgeable old woman who lived deep in the woods. She was kind enough to share a bit of that knowledge with me.*

Acknowledgments

Reading naturalist Todd Ballantine's descriptions of Hilton Head Island is a step in the right direction, but living on the island for a time brings it to life. Breathing the air, listening to the sounds, and taking in the natural beauty of such a place is something one never forgets.

I want to thank the residents of the island for keeping that beauty intact.

I thank my husband, Ralph Shelburne, for his constant love and support and for being my most diligent critic and loudest cheerleader.

I also want to thank the very talented Jose Ramirez for his ability and hard work in making this novel a reality.

Finally, I sincerely thank my patient readers: Joan Hill, Pat French, and the ever faithful Rennie Langman.

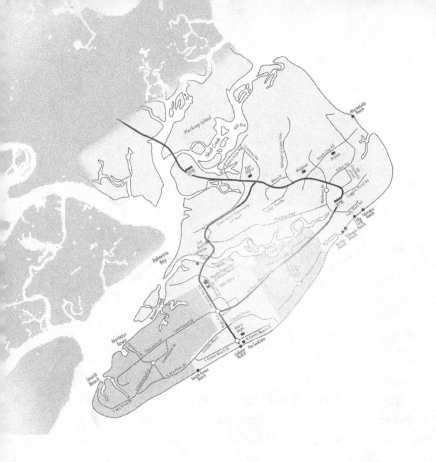